Amelia Cole
and the
UnknownWorld

WRITERS
ADAM P. KNAVE & D.J. KIRKBRIDE

ARTIST
NICK BROKENSHIRE

LETTERER & DESIGNER
RACHEL DEERING

COLOR ASSISTANT
RUIZ MORENO

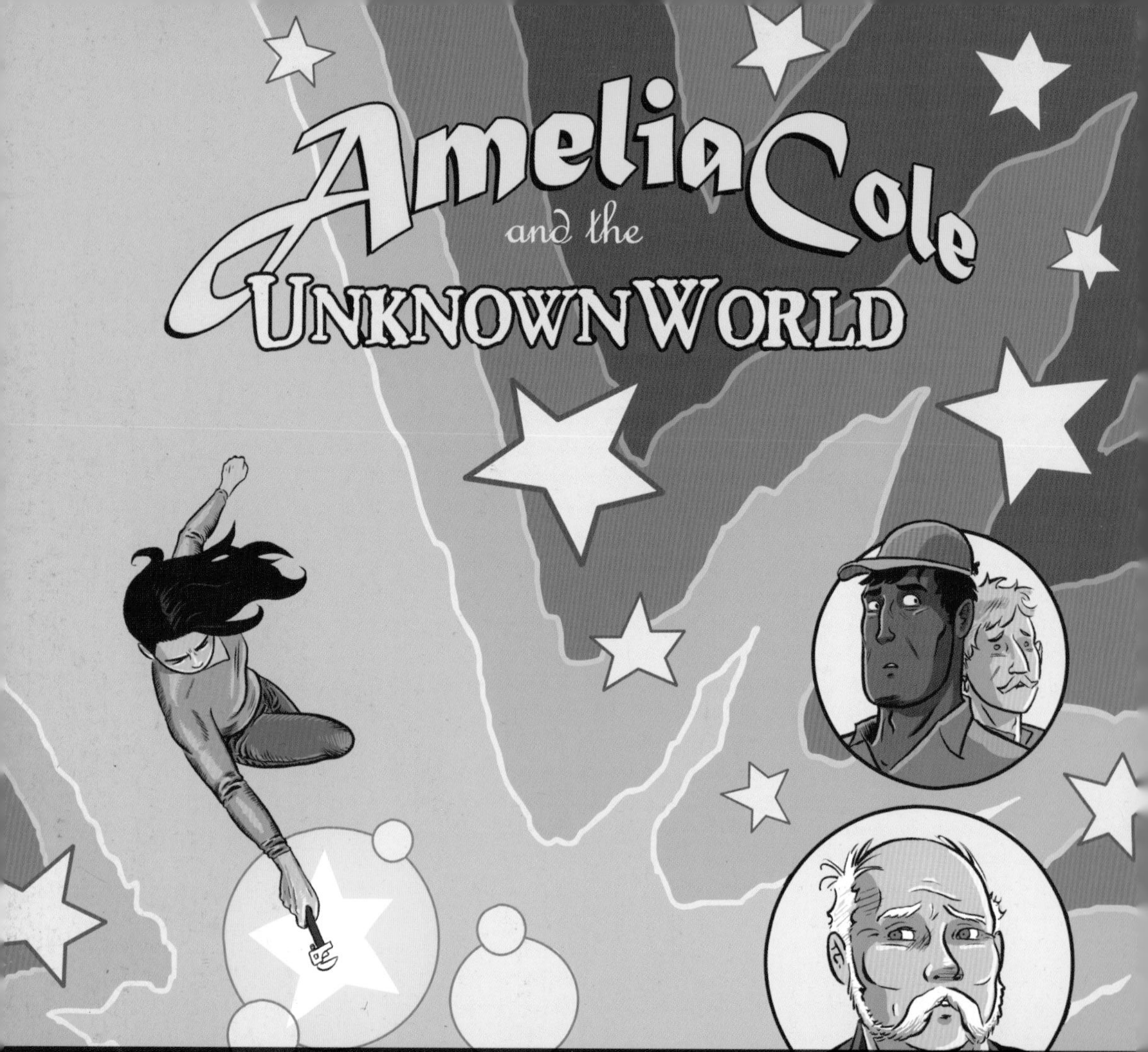
Amelia Cole
and the
Unknown World

SPECIAL THANKS TO

ALLISON BAKER, VICTORIA BROKENSHIRE, DEBBIE CHATTIN, GREG CHATTIN, FRANK CVETKOVIC, LAURA DARBY, JESSICA DEERING, THE LYTHS, BRITTANY MORENO, EMMA MORENO, CHRIS ROBERSON, & RACHEL ROVERE

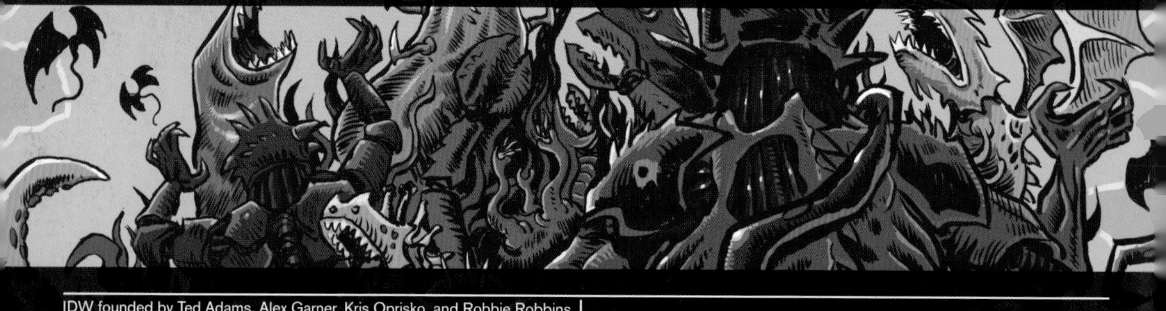

IDW founded by Ted Adams, Alex Garner, Kris Oprisko, and Robbie Robbins

ISBN: 978-1-61377-700-8

16 15 14 13 1 2 3 4

IDW®

Ted Adams, CEO & Publisher
Greg Goldstein, President & COO
Robbie Robbins, EVP/Sr. Graphic Artist
Chris Ryall, Chief Creative Officer/Editor-in-Chief
Matthew Ruzicka, CPA, Chief Financial Officer
Alan Payne, VP of Sales
Dirk Wood, VP of Marketing
Lorelei Bunjes, VP of Digital Services

Become our fan on Facebook **facebook.com/idwpublishing**
Follow us on Twitter **@idwpublishing**
Check us out on YouTube **youtube.com/idwpublishing**
www.IDWPUBLISHING.com

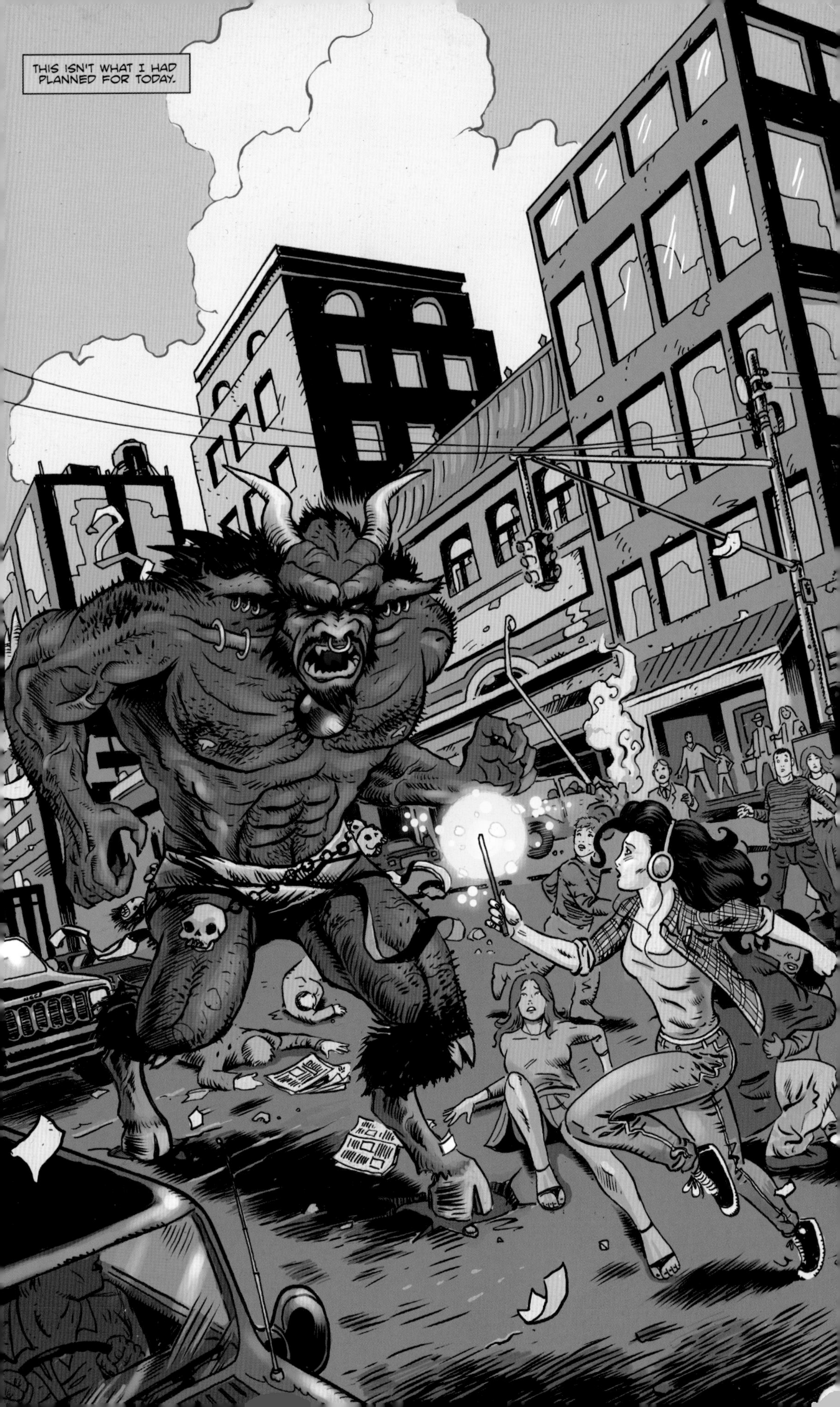
THIS ISN'T WHAT I HAD PLANNED FOR TODAY.

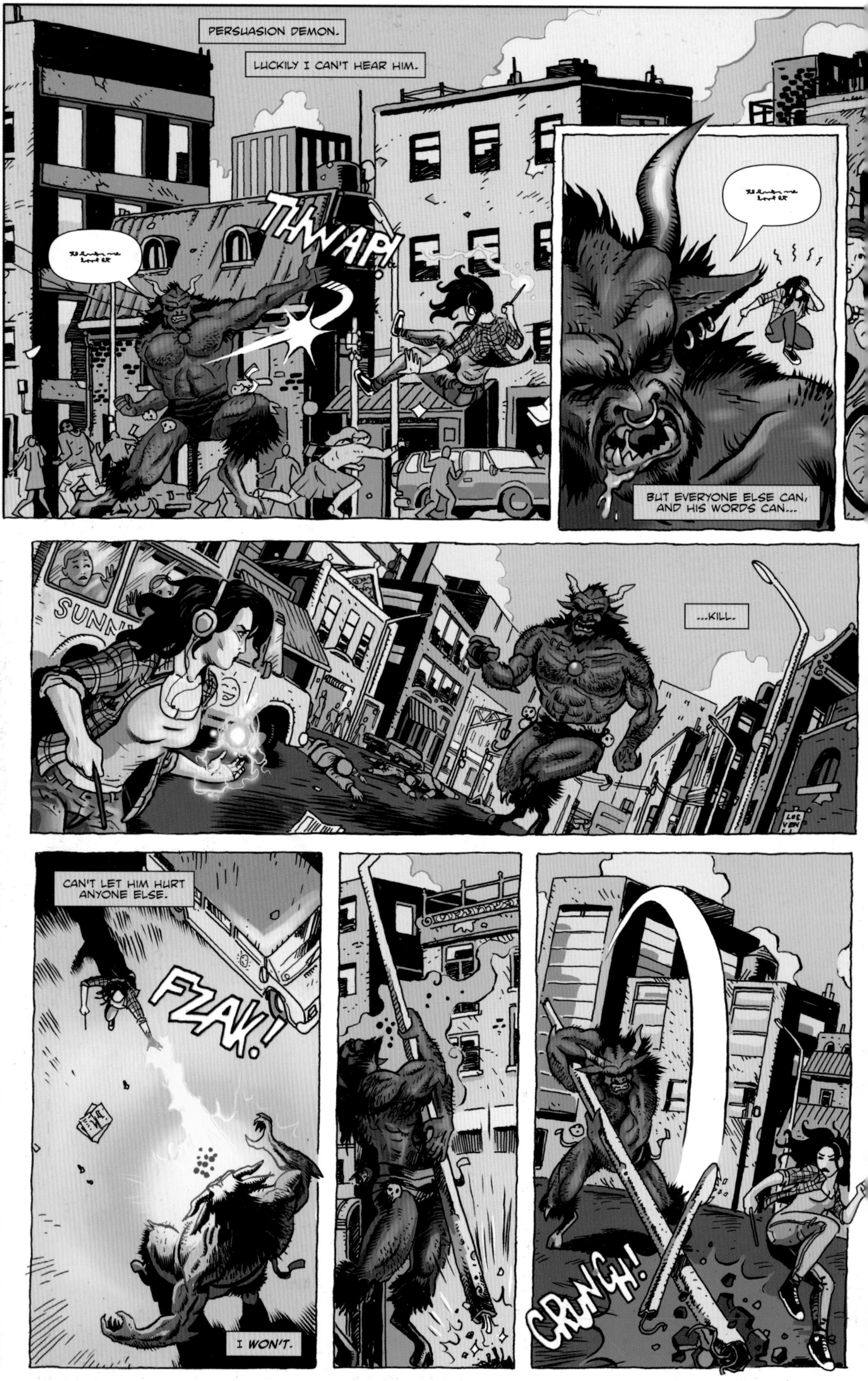
PERSUASION DEMON.
LUCKILY I CAN'T HEAR HIM.
THWAP!
BUT EVERYONE ELSE CAN, AND HIS WORDS CAN...
...KILL.
CAN'T LET HIM HURT ANYONE ELSE.
FZAK!
I WON'T.
CRUNCH!

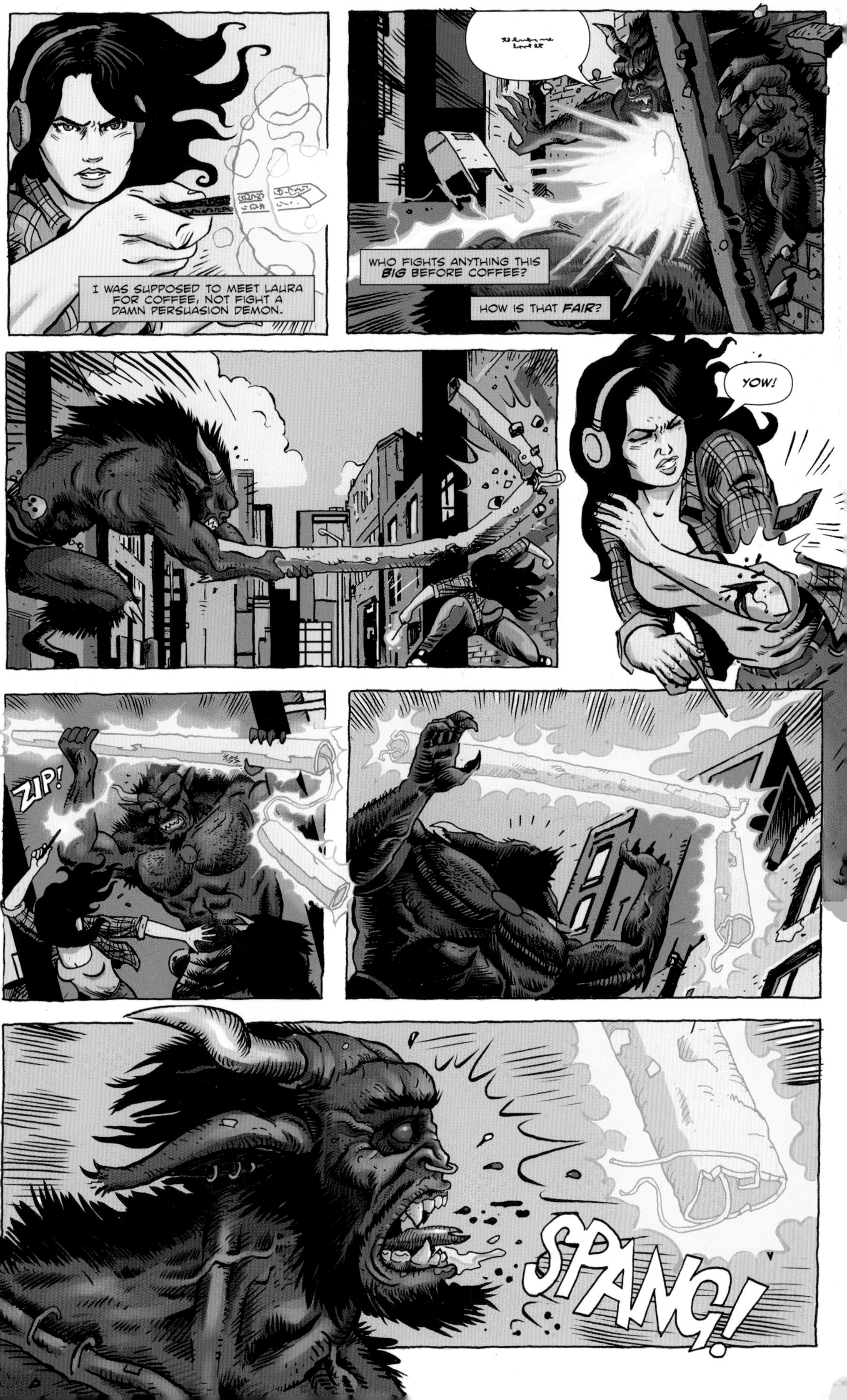
I WAS SUPPOSED TO MEET LAURA FOR COFFEE, NOT FIGHT A DAMN PERSUASION DEMON.
WHO FIGHTS ANYTHING THIS BIG BEFORE COFFEE?
HOW IS THAT FAIR?
YOW!
ZIP!
SPANG!

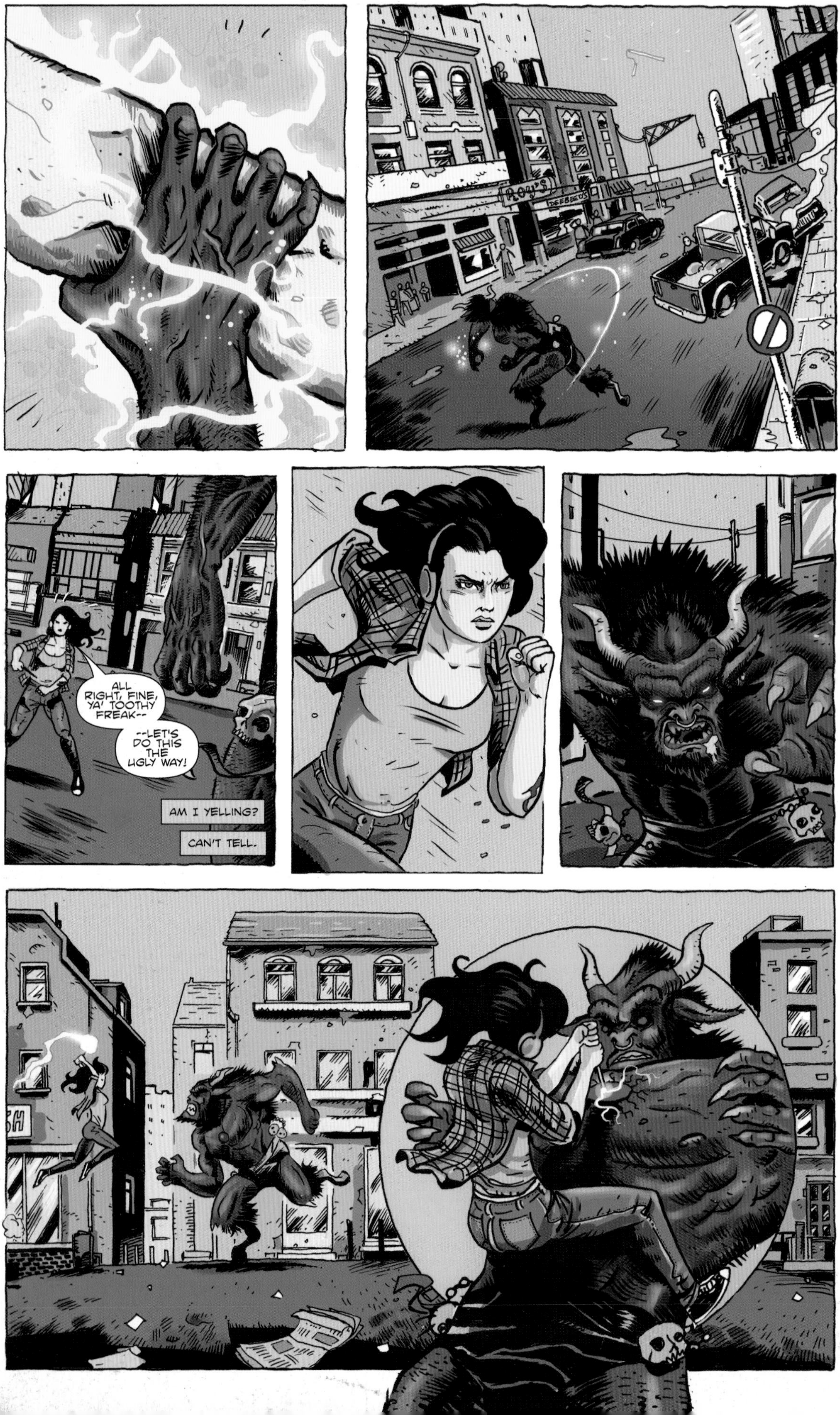
ROY'S
ALL RIGHT, FINE, YA' TOOTHY FREAK--
--LET'S DO THIS THE UGLY WAY!
AM I YELLING?
CAN'T TELL.

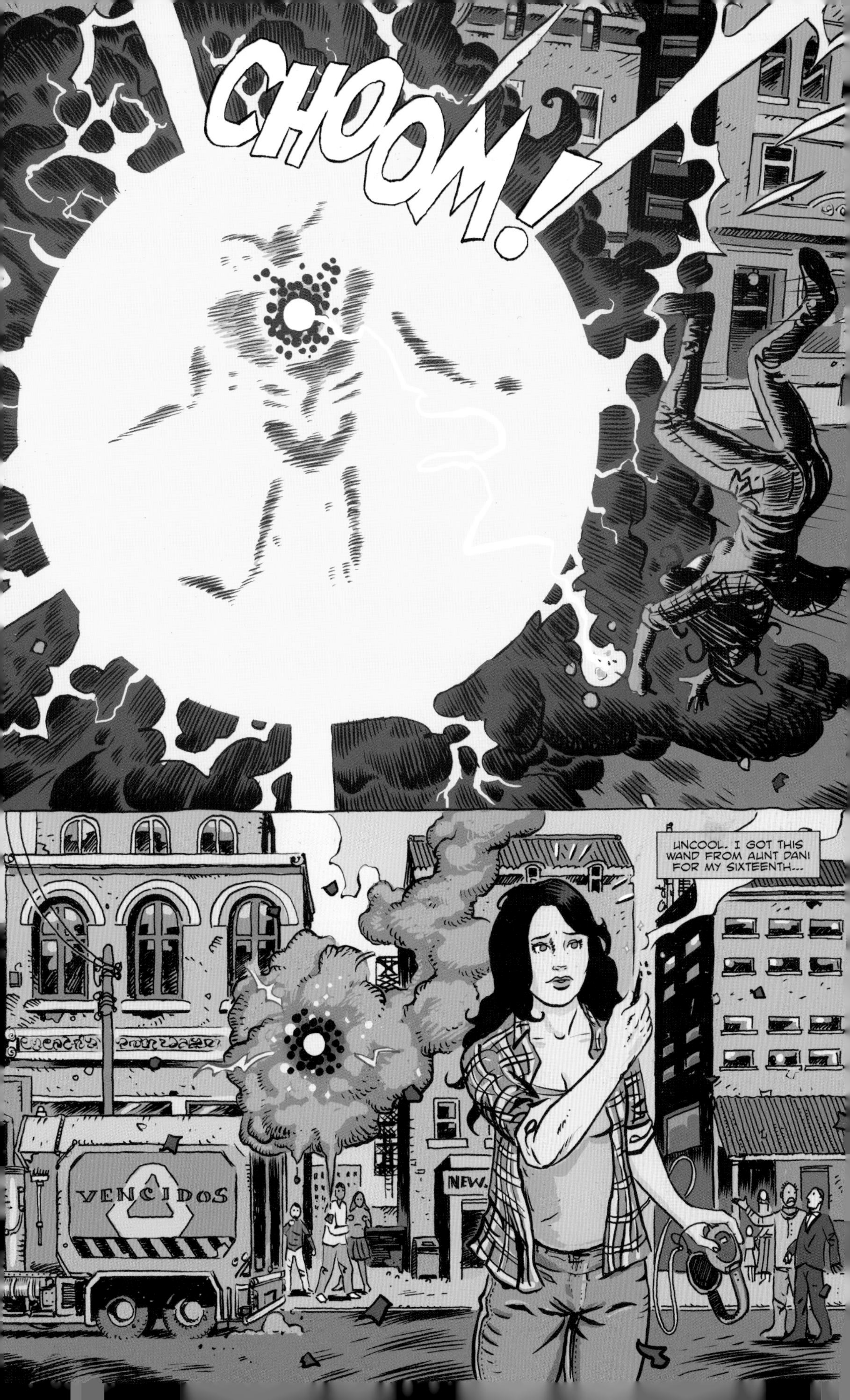
CHOOM!
UNCOOL. I GOT THIS WAND FROM AUNT DANI FOR MY SIXTEENTH...
VENCIDOS
NEW.

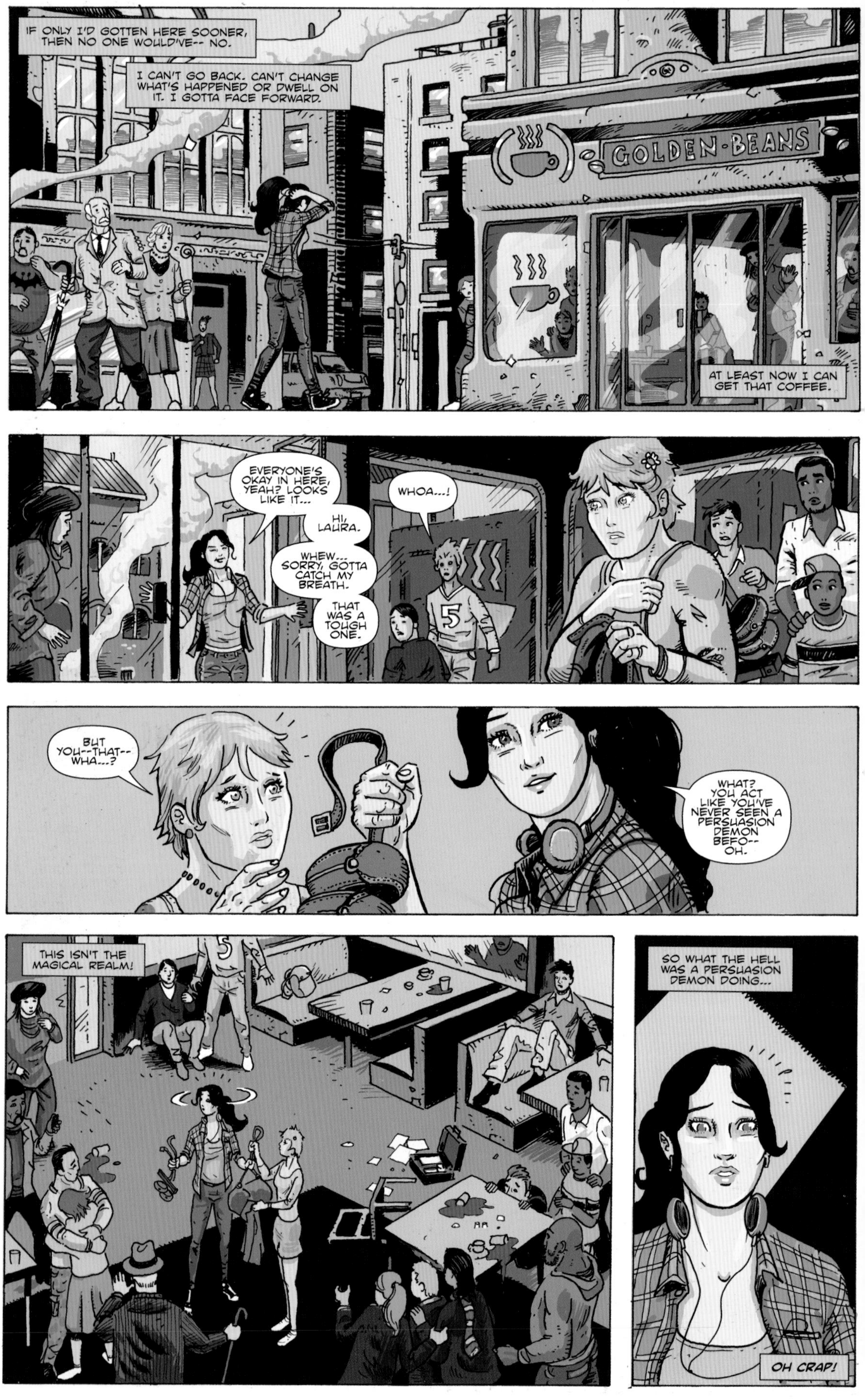
IF ONLY I'D GOTTEN HERE SOONER, THEN NO ONE WOULD'VE-- NO.
I CAN'T GO BACK. CAN'T CHANGE WHAT'S HAPPENED OR DWELL ON IT. I GOTTA FACE FORWARD.
GOLDEN-BEANS
AT LEAST NOW I CAN GET THAT COFFEE.
EVERYONE'S OKAY IN HERE, YEAH? LOOKS LIKE IT...
HI, LAURA.
WHEW... SORRY, GOTTA CATCH MY BREATH.
THAT WAS A TOUGH ONE.
WHOA...!
BUT YOU--THAT-- WHA...?
WHAT? YOU ACT LIKE YOU'VE NEVER SEEN A PERSUASION DEMON BEFO-- OH.
THIS ISN'T THE MAGICAL REALM!
SO WHAT THE HELL WAS A PERSUASION DEMON DOING...
OH CRAP!

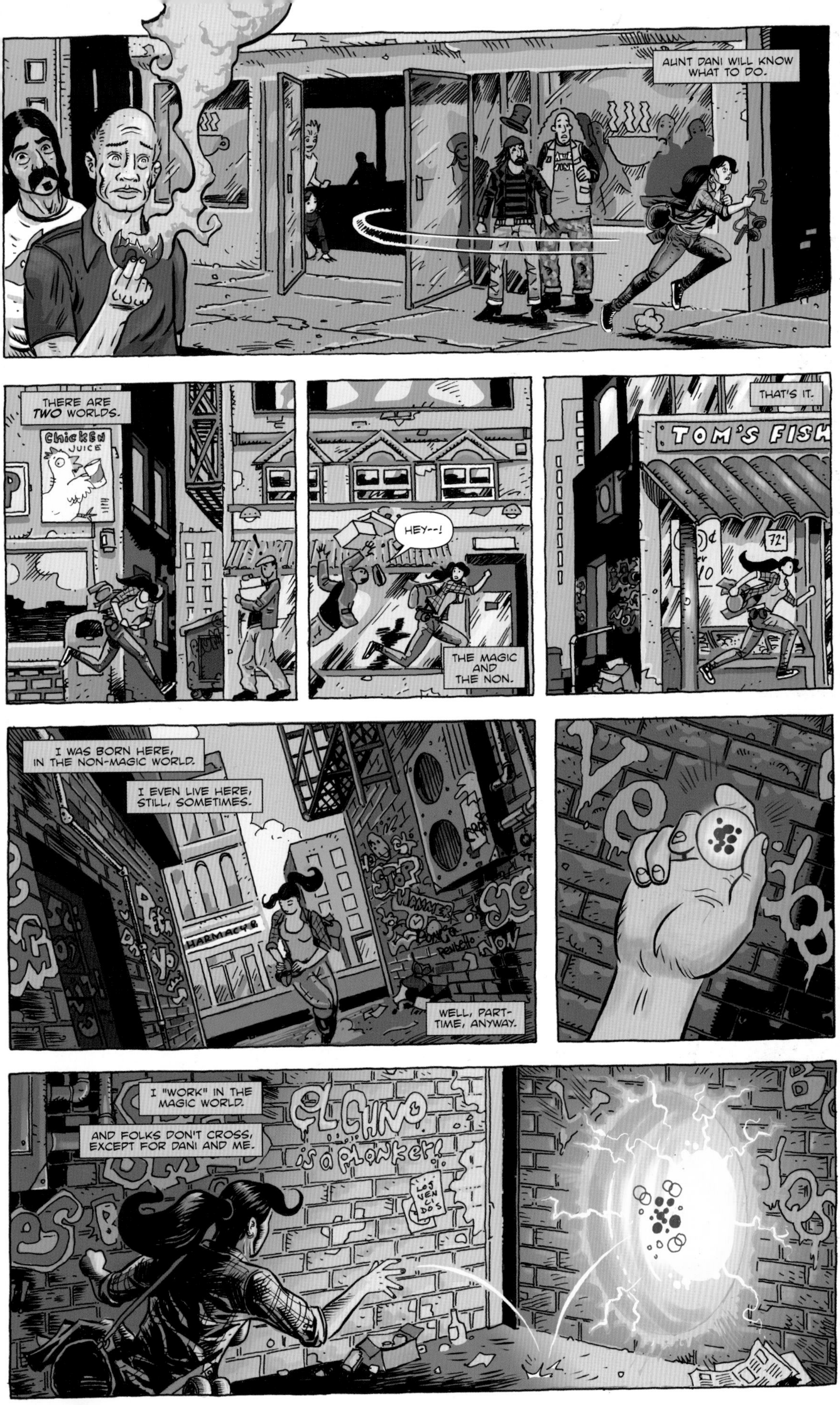
AUNT DANI WILL KNOW WHAT TO DO.
THERE ARE TWO WORLDS.
CHICKEN JUICE
HEY--!
THE MAGIC AND THE NON.
THAT'S IT.
TOM'S FISH
I WAS BORN HERE, IN THE NON-MAGIC WORLD.
I EVEN LIVE HERE, STILL, SOMETIMES.
WELL, PART-TIME, ANYWAY.
I "WORK" IN THE MAGIC WORLD.
AND FOLKS DON'T CROSS, EXCEPT FOR DANI AND ME.
EL CHINO is a plonker!

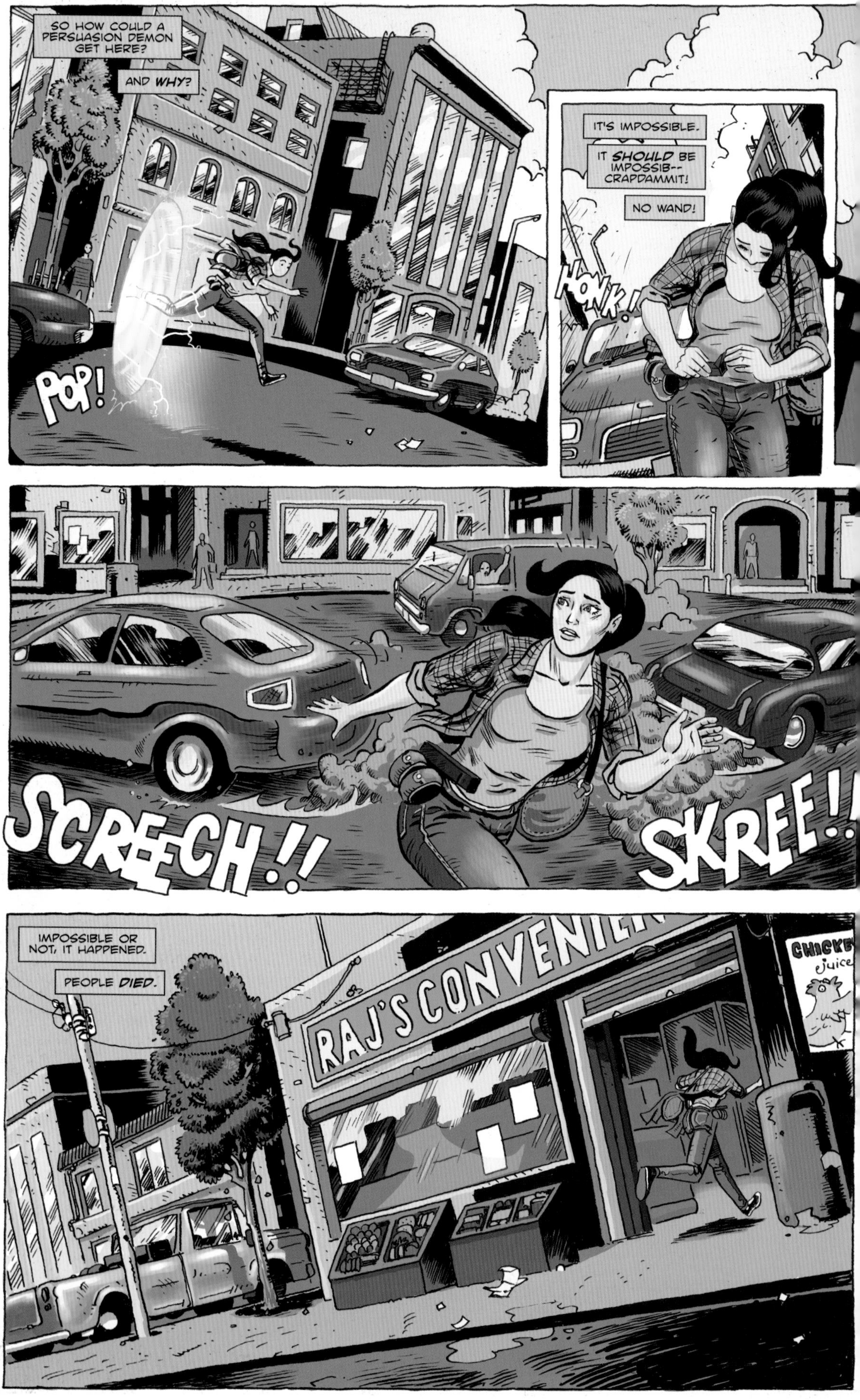

SO HOW COULD A PERSUASION DEMON GET HERE?
AND WHY?
POP!
IT'S IMPOSSIBLE.
IT SHOULD BE IMPOSSIB-- CRAPDAMMIT!
NO WAND!
HONK!
SCREECH!!
SKREE!!
IMPOSSIBLE OR NOT, IT HAPPENED.
PEOPLE DIED.
RAJ'S CONVENIEN
CHICKE
juice

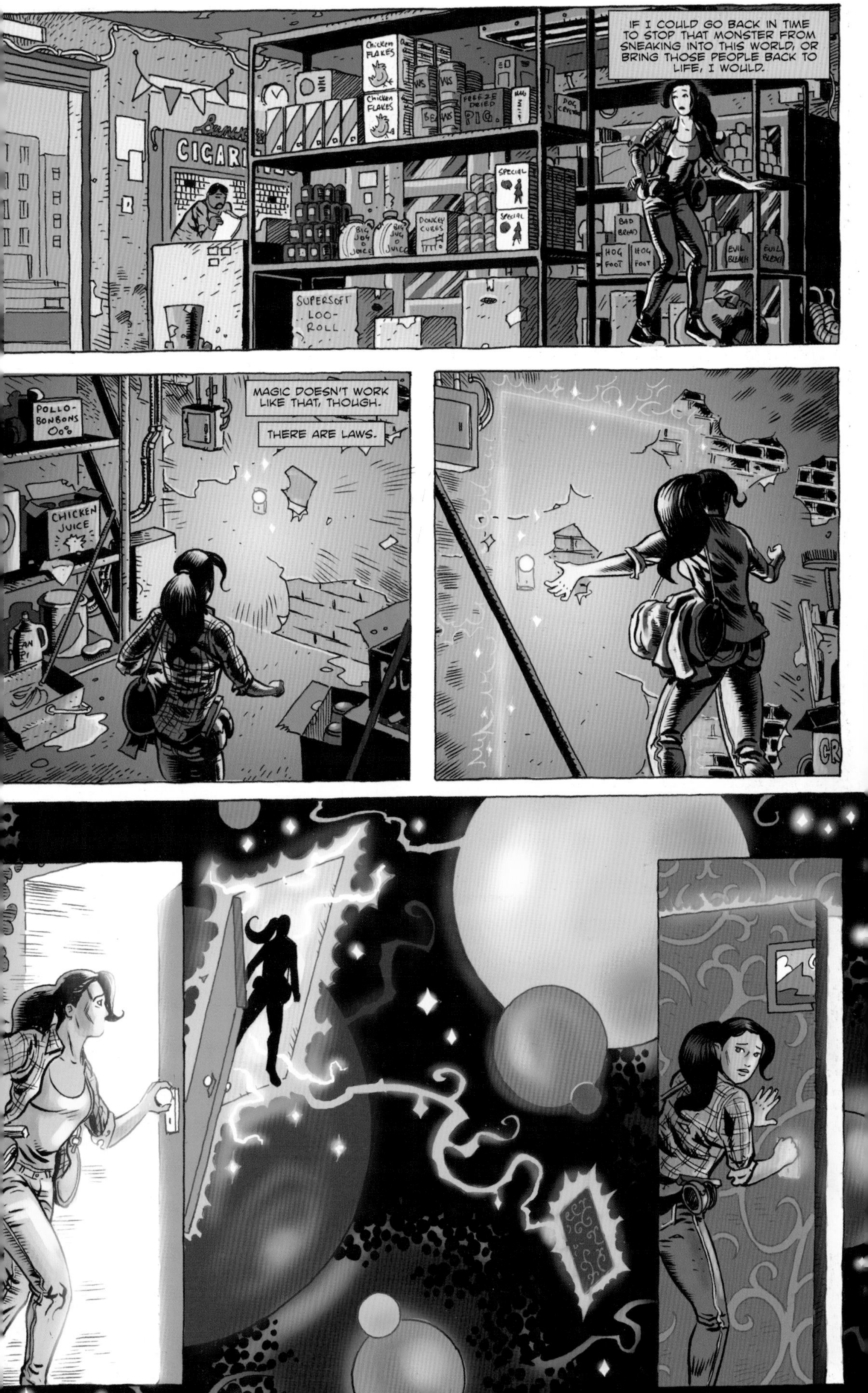
IF I COULD GO BACK IN TIME TO STOP THAT MONSTER FROM SNEAKING INTO THIS WORLD, OR BRING THOSE PEOPLE BACK TO LIFE, I WOULD.
CIGAR
Chicken FLAKES
Chicken FLAKES
FREEZE DRIED PIG
SPECIAL
SPECIAL
BIG JUG O JUICE
BIG JUG O JUICE
DONKEY CUBES
BAD BREAD
HOG FOOT
HOG FOOT
EVIL BLEACH
EVIL BLEACH
SUPERSOFT LOO-ROLL
POLLO-BONBONS
CHICKEN JUICE
MAGIC DOESN'T WORK LIKE THAT, THOUGH.
THERE ARE LAWS.

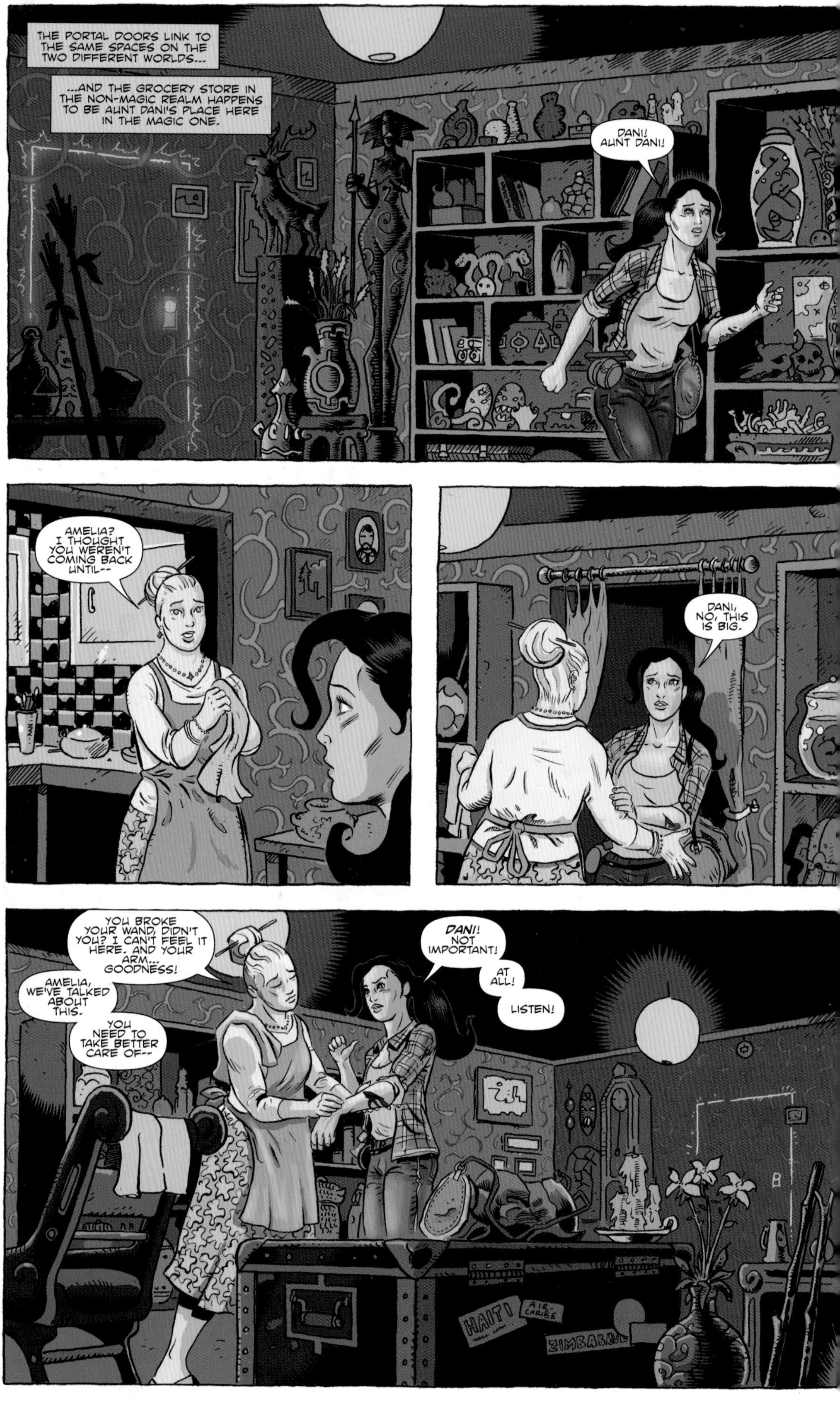
THE PORTAL DOORS LINK TO THE SAME SPACES ON THE TWO DIFFERENT WORLDS...
...AND THE GROCERY STORE IN THE NON-MAGIC REALM HAPPENS TO BE AUNT DANI'S PLACE HERE IN THE MAGIC ONE.
DANI! AUNT DANI!
AMELIA? I THOUGHT YOU WEREN'T COMING BACK UNTIL--
DANI, NO, THIS IS BIG.
YOU BROKE YOUR WAND, DIDN'T YOU? I CAN'T FEEL IT HERE. AND YOUR ARM... GOODNESS!
AMELIA, WE'VE TALKED ABOUT THIS.
YOU NEED TO TAKE BETTER CARE OF--
DANI! NOT IMPORTANT!
AT ALL!
LISTEN!
HAITI
AIR-CARIBE
ZIMBABWE

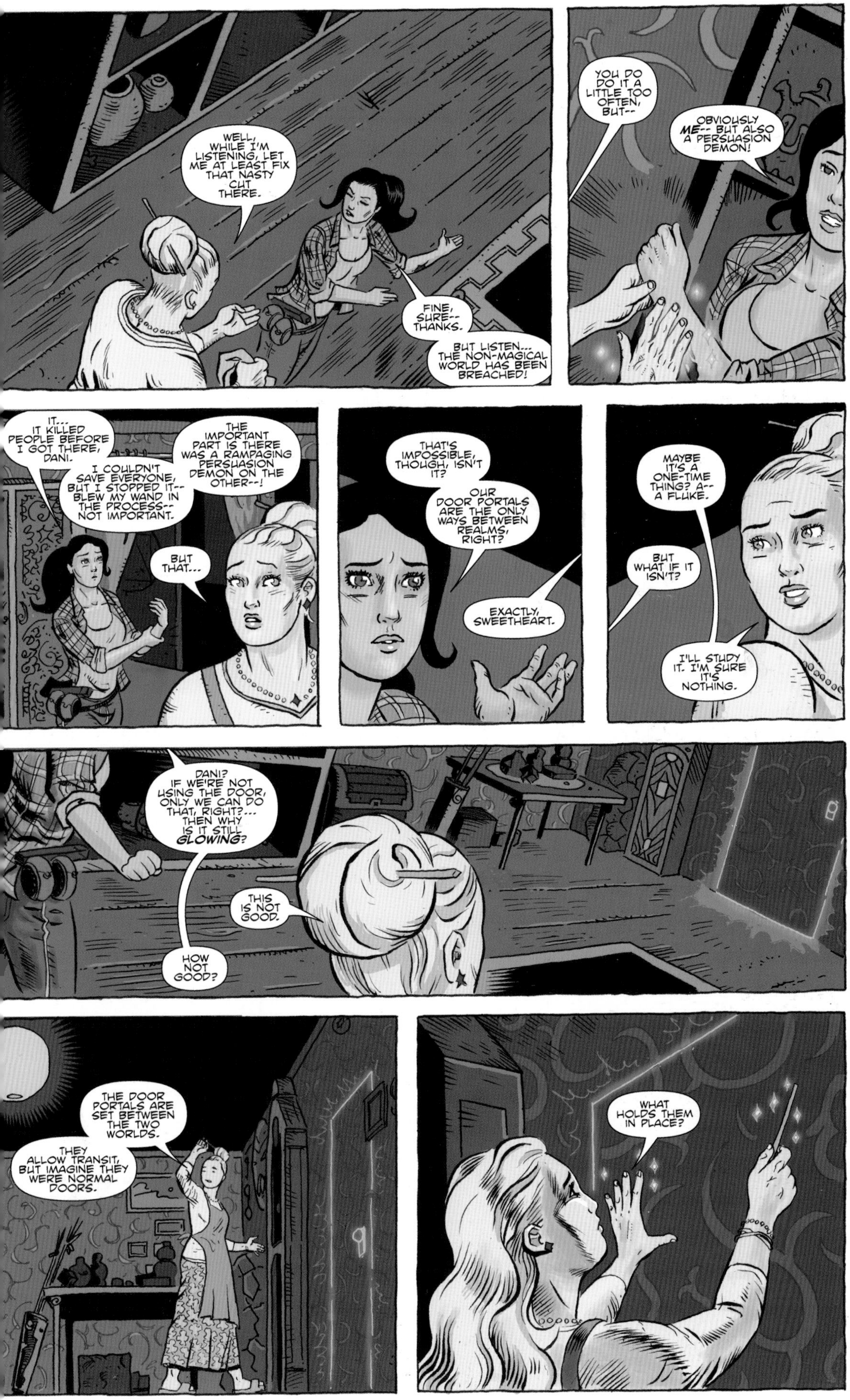
WELL, WHILE I'M LISTENING, LET ME AT LEAST FIX THAT NASTY CUT THERE.
FINE, SURE-- THANKS.
BUT LISTEN... THE NON-MAGICAL WORLD HAS BEEN BREACHED!
OBVIOUSLY ME-- BUT ALSO A PERSUASION DEMON!
YOU DO DO IT A LITTLE TOO OFTEN, BUT--
THE IMPORTANT PART IS THERE WAS A RAMPAGING PERSUASION DEMON ON THE OTHER--!
IT... IT KILLED PEOPLE BEFORE I GOT THERE, DANI.
I COULDN'T SAVE EVERYONE, BUT I STOPPED IT-- BLEW MY WAND IN THE PROCESS-- NOT IMPORTANT.
BUT THAT...
THAT'S IMPOSSIBLE, THOUGH, ISN'T IT?
OUR DOOR PORTALS ARE THE ONLY WAYS BETWEEN REALMS, RIGHT?
EXACTLY, SWEETHEART.
MAYBE IT'S A ONE-TIME THING? A-- A FLUKE.
BUT WHAT IF IT ISN'T?
I'LL STUDY IT. I'M SURE IT'S NOTHING.
DANI? IF WE'RE NOT USING THE DOOR, ONLY WE CAN DO THAT, RIGHT?... THEN WHY IS IT STILL GLOWING?
THIS IS NOT GOOD.
HOW NOT GOOD?
THE DOOR PORTALS ARE SET BETWEEN THE TWO WORLDS.
THEY ALLOW TRANSIT, BUT IMAGINE THEY WERE NORMAL DOORS.
WHAT HOLDS THEM IN PLACE?

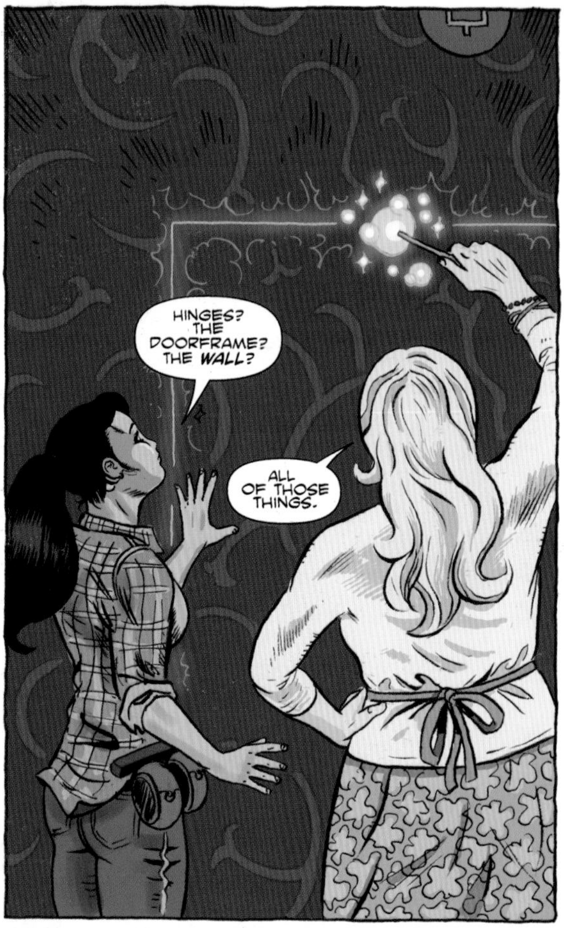
HINGES? THE DOORFRAME? THE WALL?
ALL OF THOSE THINGS.

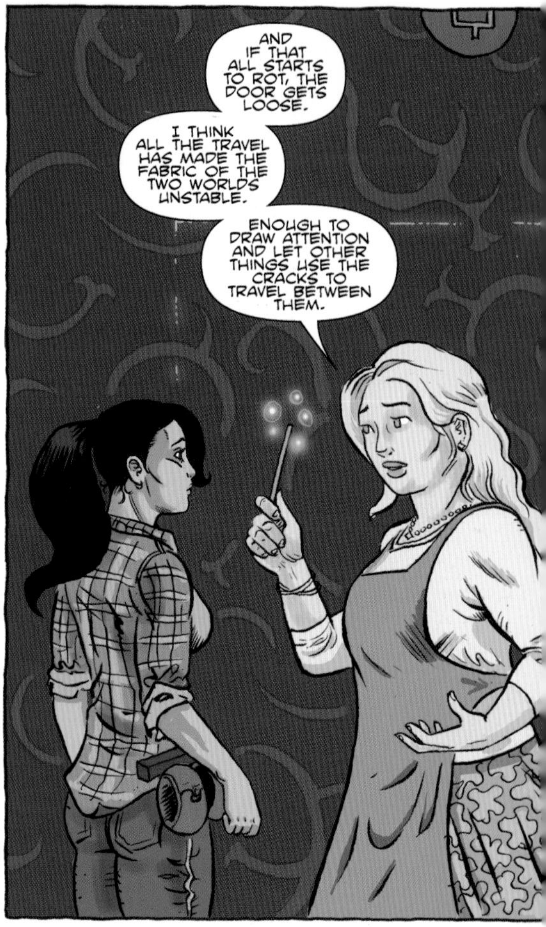
AND IF THAT ALL STARTS TO ROT, THE DOOR GETS LOOSE.
I THINK ALL THE TRAVEL HAS MADE THE FABRIC OF THE TWO WORLDS UNSTABLE.
ENOUGH TO DRAW ATTENTION AND LET OTHER THINGS USE THE CRACKS TO TRAVEL BETWEEN THEM.

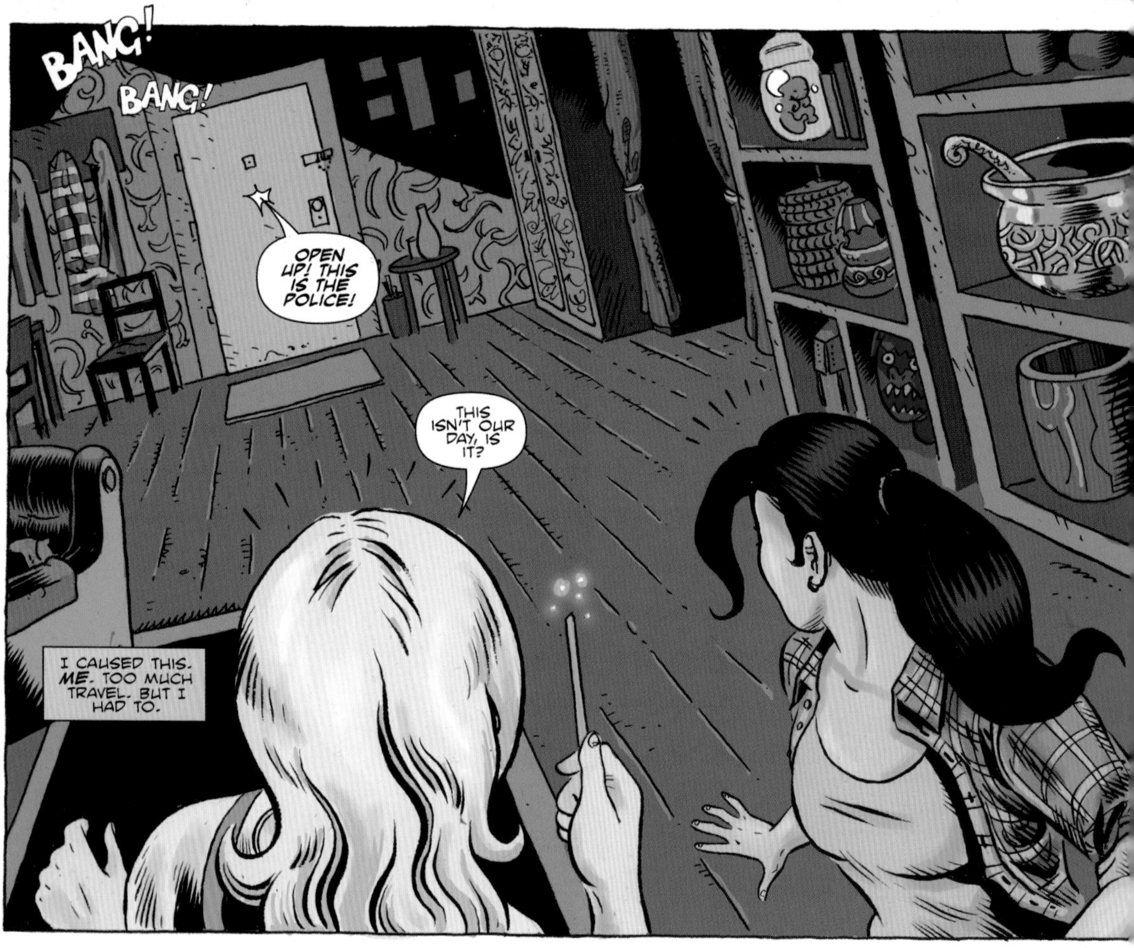
BANG!
BANG!
OPEN UP! THIS IS THE POLICE!
THIS ISN'T OUR DAY, IS IT?
I CAUSED THIS. ME. TOO MUCH TRAVEL. BUT I HAD TO.

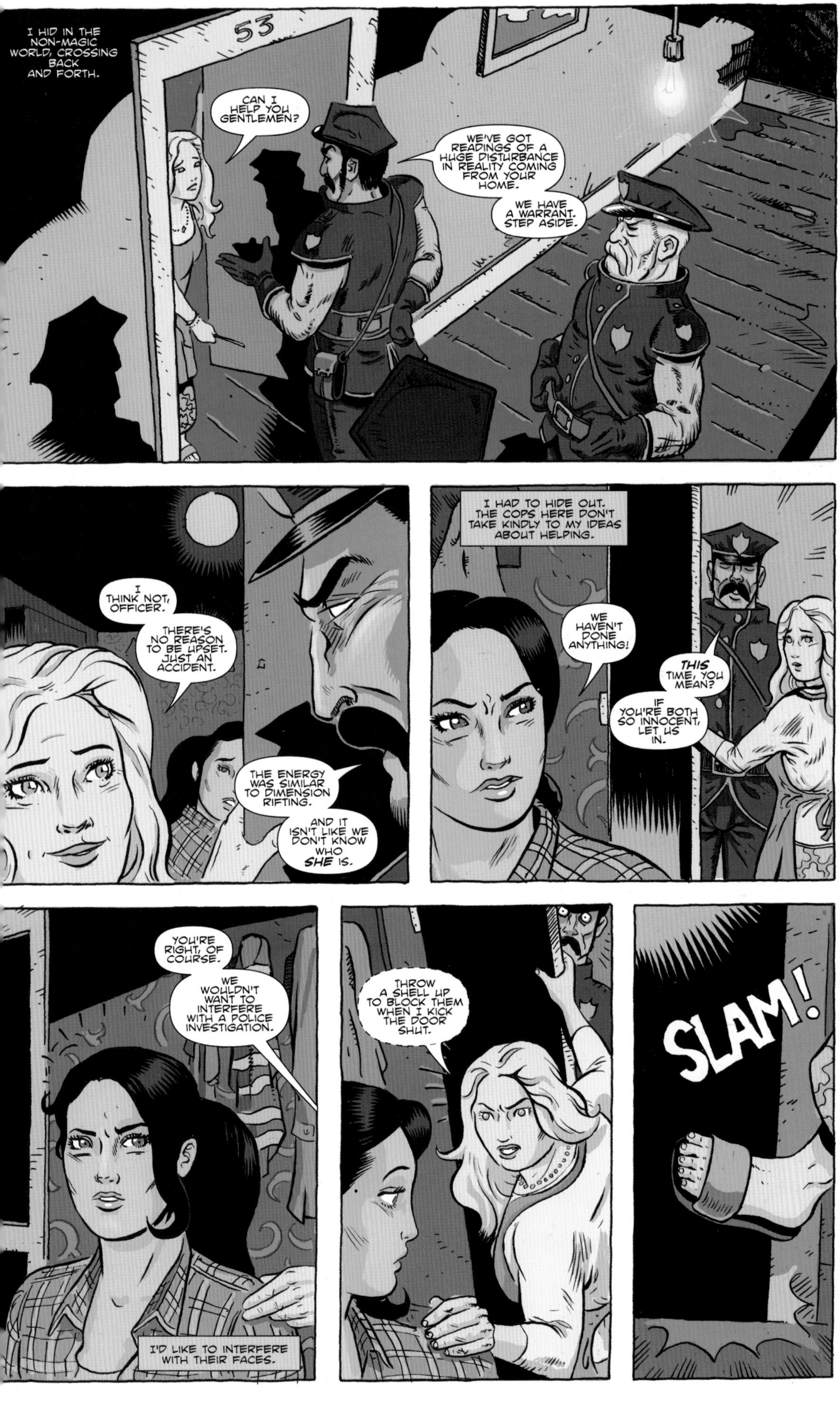
I HID IN THE NON-MAGIC WORLD, CROSSING BACK AND FORTH.
53
CAN I HELP YOU GENTLEMEN?
WE'VE GOT READINGS OF A HUGE DISTURBANCE IN REALITY COMING FROM YOUR HOME.
WE HAVE A WARRANT. STEP ASIDE.
I THINK NOT, OFFICER.
THERE'S NO REASON TO BE UPSET. JUST AN ACCIDENT.
THE ENERGY WAS SIMILAR TO DIMENSION RIFTING.
AND IT ISN'T LIKE WE DON'T KNOW WHO *SHE* IS.
I HAD TO HIDE OUT. THE COPS HERE DON'T TAKE KINDLY TO MY IDEAS ABOUT HELPING.
WE HAVEN'T DONE ANYTHING!
THIS TIME, YOU MEAN?
IF YOU'RE BOTH SO INNOCENT, LET US IN.
YOU'RE RIGHT, OF COURSE.
WE WOULDN'T WANT TO INTERFERE WITH A POLICE INVESTIGATION.
I'D LIKE TO INTERFERE WITH THEIR FACES.
THROW A SHELL UP TO BLOCK THEM WHEN I KICK THE DOOR SHUT.
SLAM!

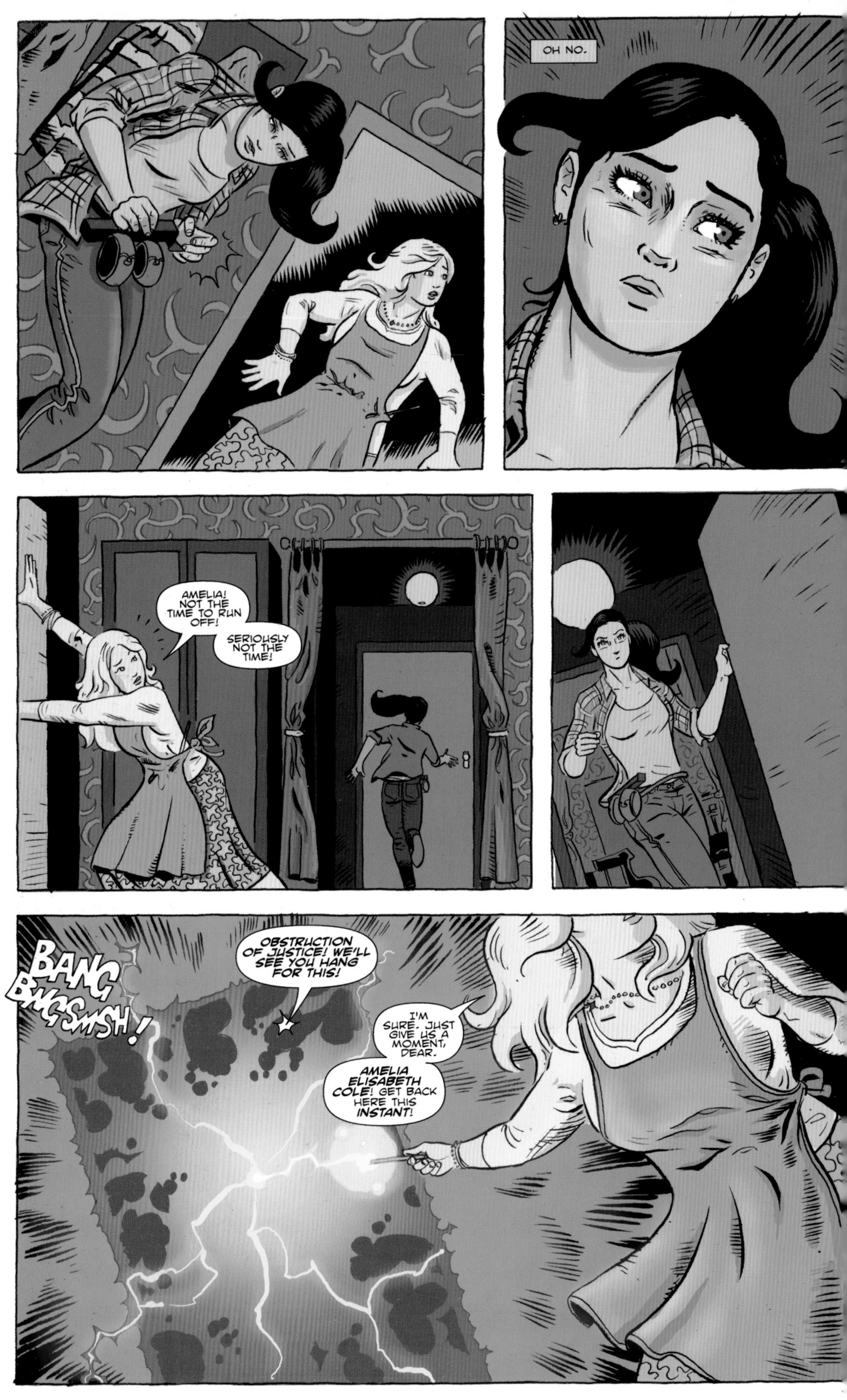
OH NO.
AMELIA! NOT THE TIME TO RUN OFF!
SERIOUSLY NOT THE TIME!
BANG BANG SMSH!
OBSTRUCTION OF JUSTICE! WE'LL SEE YOU HANG FOR THIS!
I'M SURE. JUST GIVE US A MOMENT, DEAR.
AMELIA ELISABETH COLE! GET BACK HERE THIS INSTANT!

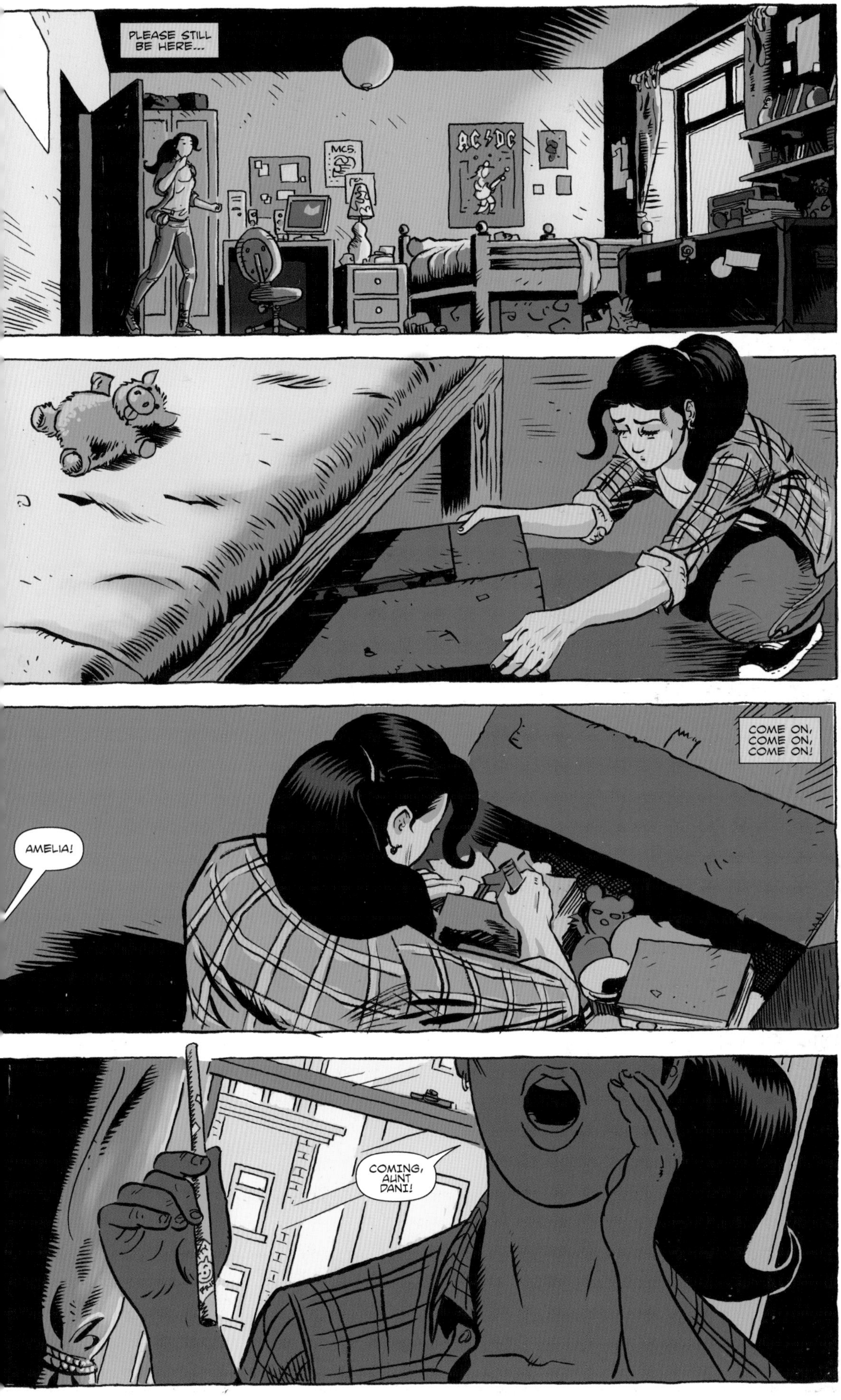
PLEASE STILL BE HERE...
AC/DC
MC5
COME ON, COME ON, COME ON!
AMELIA!
COMING, AUNT DANI!

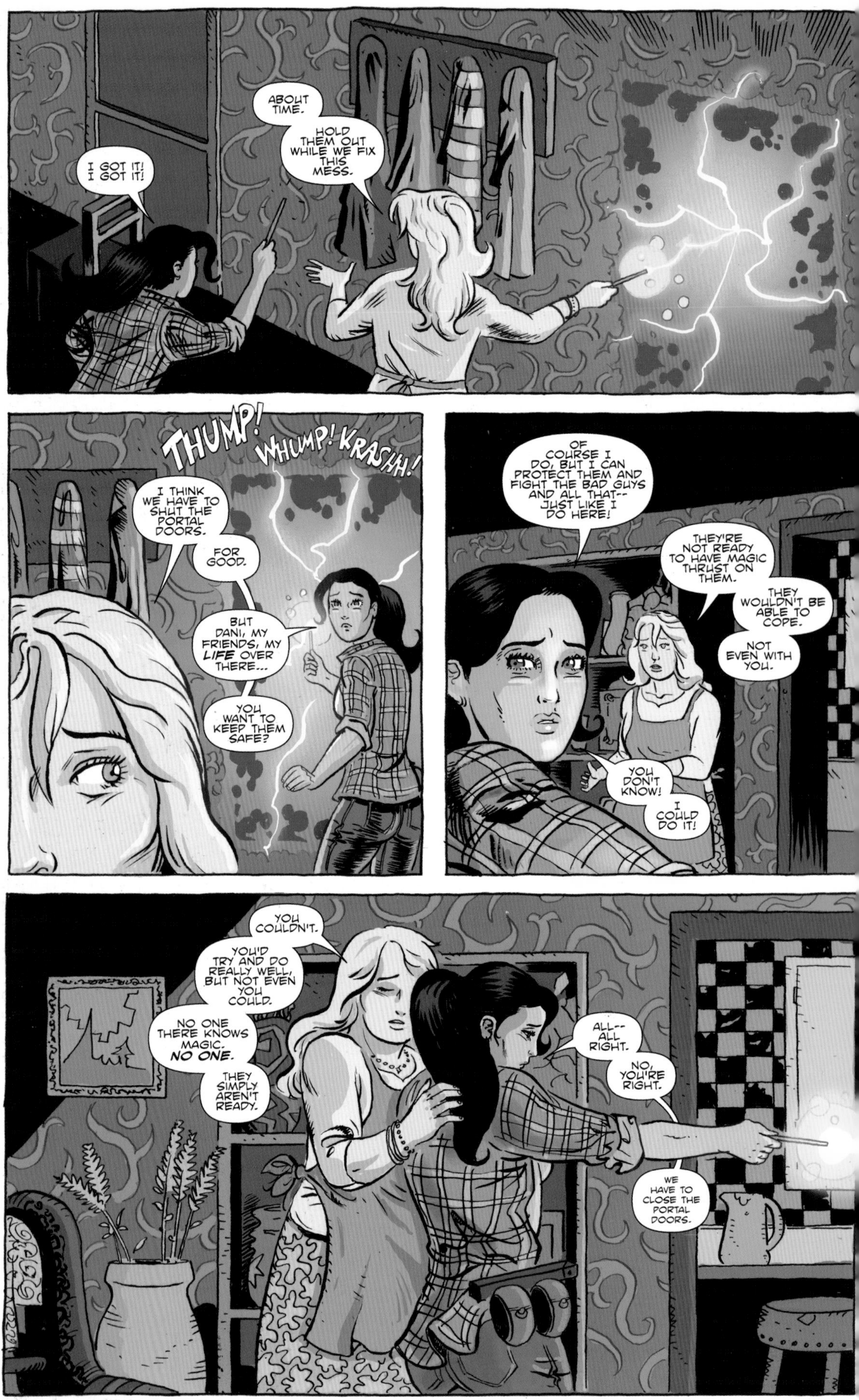

I GOT IT! I GOT IT!
ABOUT TIME.
HOLD THEM OUT WHILE WE FIX THIS MESS.
THUMP! WHUMP! KRASHH!
I THINK WE HAVE TO SHUT THE PORTAL DOORS.
FOR GOOD.
BUT DANI, MY FRIENDS, MY LIFE OVER THERE...
YOU WANT TO KEEP THEM SAFE?
OF COURSE I DO, BUT I CAN PROTECT THEM AND FIGHT THE BAD GUYS AND ALL THAT-- JUST LIKE I DO HERE!
THEY'RE NOT READY TO HAVE MAGIC THRUST ON THEM.
THEY WOULDN'T BE ABLE TO COPE.
NOT EVEN WITH YOU.
YOU DON'T KNOW!
I COULD DO IT!
YOU COULDN'T.
YOU'D TRY AND DO REALLY WELL, BUT NOT EVEN YOU COULD.
NO ONE THERE KNOWS MAGIC. NO ONE.
THEY SIMPLY AREN'T READY.
ALL-- ALL RIGHT.
NO, YOU'RE RIGHT.
WE HAVE TO CLOSE THE PORTAL DOORS.

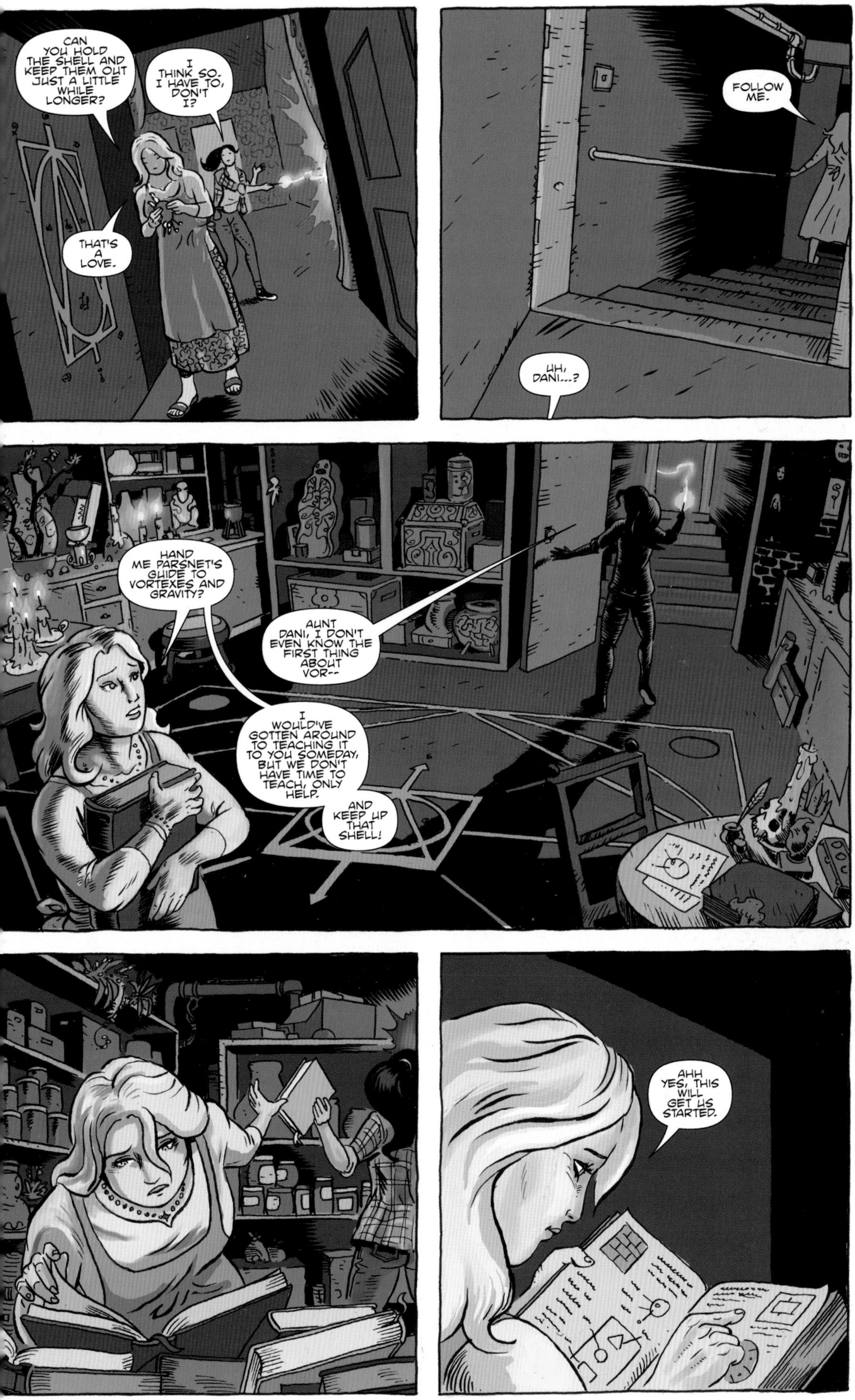
CAN YOU HOLD THE SHELL AND KEEP THEM OUT JUST A LITTLE WHILE LONGER?
I THINK SO. I HAVE TO, DON'T I?
THAT'S A LOVE.
FOLLOW ME.
UH, DANI...?
HAND ME PARSNET'S GUIDE TO VORTEXES AND GRAVITY?
AUNT DANI, I DON'T EVEN KNOW THE FIRST THING ABOUT VOR--
I WOULD'VE GOTTEN AROUND TO TEACHING IT TO YOU SOMEDAY, BUT WE DON'T HAVE TIME TO TEACH, ONLY HELP.
AND KEEP UP THAT SHELL!
AHH YES, THIS WILL GET US STARTED.

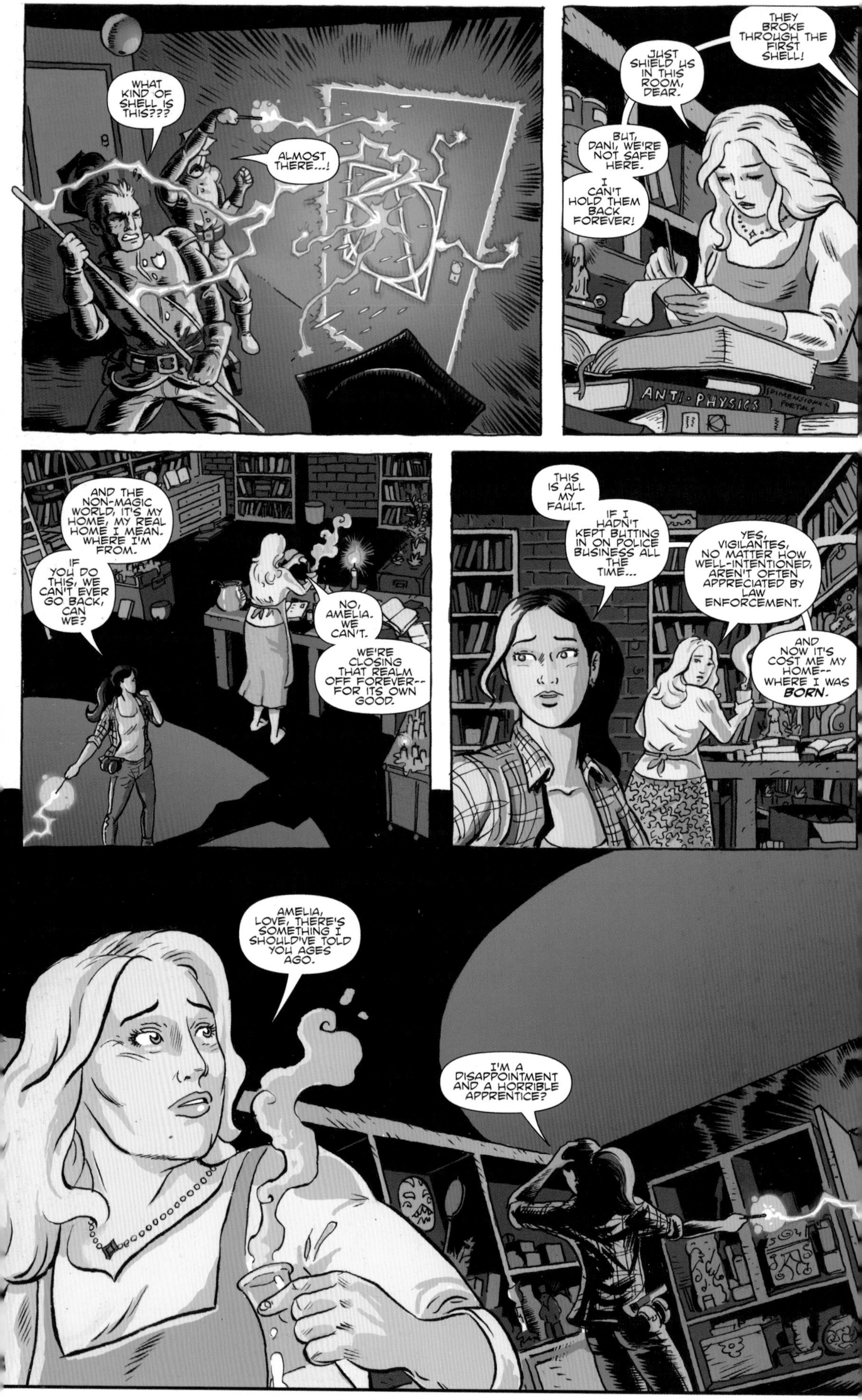
WHAT KIND OF SHELL IS THIS???
ALMOST THERE...!
THEY BROKE THROUGH THE FIRST SHELL!
JUST SHIELD US IN THIS ROOM, DEAR.
BUT, DANI, WE'RE NOT SAFE HERE.
I CAN'T HOLD THEM BACK FOREVER!
ANTI-PHYSICS
DIMENSIONAL PORTALS
AND THE NON-MAGIC WORLD, IT'S MY HOME, MY REAL HOME I MEAN. WHERE I'M FROM.
IF YOU DO THIS, WE CAN'T EVER GO BACK, CAN WE?
NO, AMELIA. WE CAN'T.
WE'RE CLOSING THAT REALM OFF FOREVER--FOR ITS OWN GOOD.
THIS IS ALL MY FAULT.
IF I HADN'T KEPT BUTTING IN ON POLICE BUSINESS ALL THE TIME...
YES, VIGILANTES, NO MATTER HOW WELL-INTENTIONED, AREN'T OFTEN APPRECIATED BY LAW ENFORCEMENT.
AND NOW IT'S COST ME MY HOME--WHERE I WAS **BORN**.
AMELIA, LOVE, THERE'S SOMETHING I SHOULD'VE TOLD YOU AGES AGO.
I'M A DISAPPOINTMENT AND A HORRIBLE APPRENTICE?

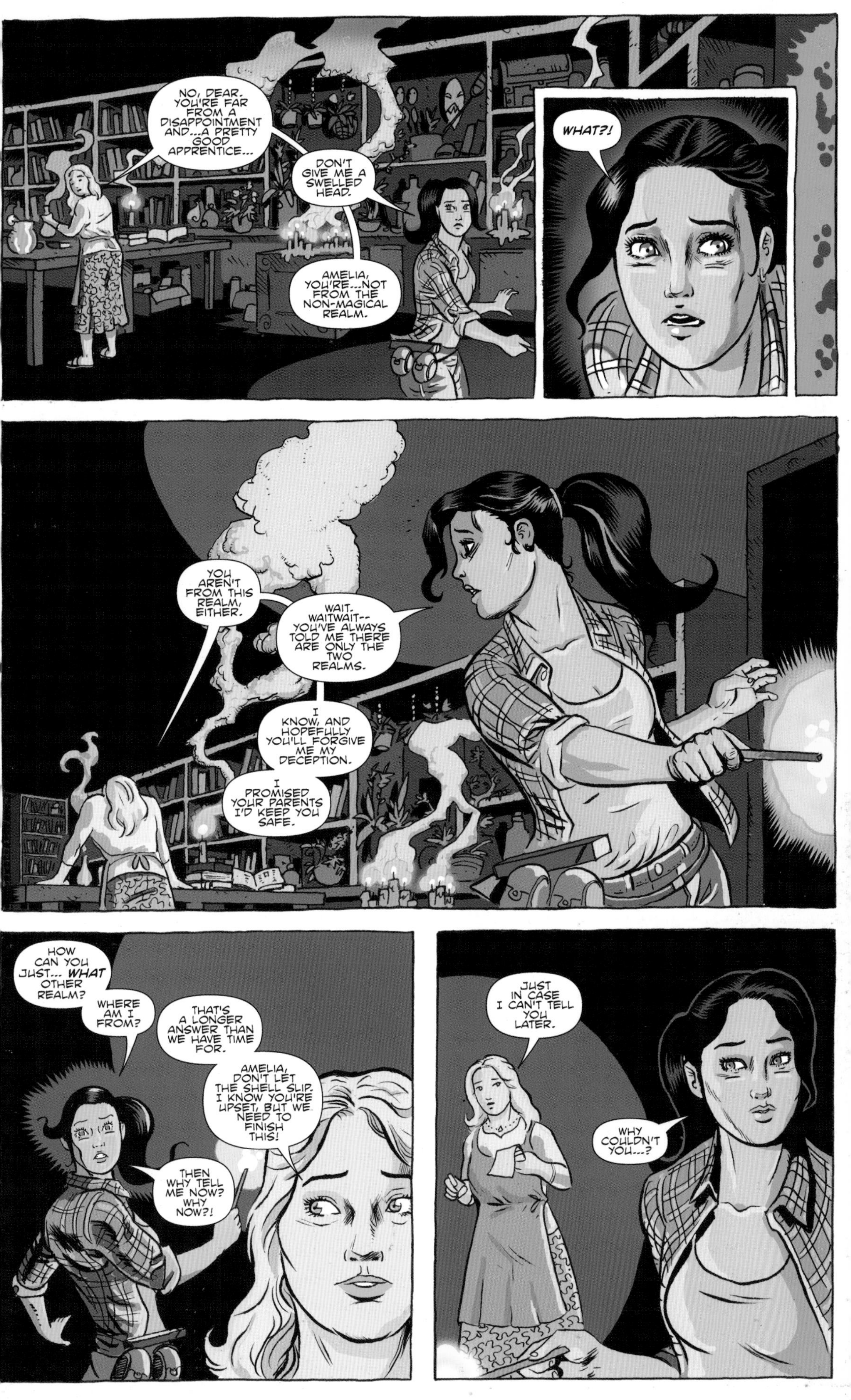

NO, DEAR. YOU'RE FAR FROM A DISAPPOINTMENT AND...A PRETTY GOOD APPRENTICE...
DON'T GIVE ME A SWELLED HEAD.
AMELIA, YOU'RE...NOT FROM THE NON-MAGICAL REALM.
WHAT?!
YOU AREN'T FROM THIS REALM, EITHER.
WAIT. WAITWAIT-- YOU'VE ALWAYS TOLD ME THERE ARE ONLY THE TWO REALMS.
I KNOW, AND HOPEFULLY YOU'LL FORGIVE ME MY DECEPTION.
I PROMISED YOUR PARENTS I'D KEEP YOU SAFE.
HOW CAN YOU JUST... WHAT OTHER REALM?
WHERE AM I FROM?
THAT'S A LONGER ANSWER THAN WE HAVE TIME FOR.
AMELIA, DON'T LET THE SHELL SLIP. I KNOW YOU'RE UPSET, BUT WE NEED TO FINISH THIS!
THEN WHY TELL ME NOW? WHY NOW?!
JUST IN CASE I CAN'T TELL YOU LATER.
WHY COULDN'T YOU...?

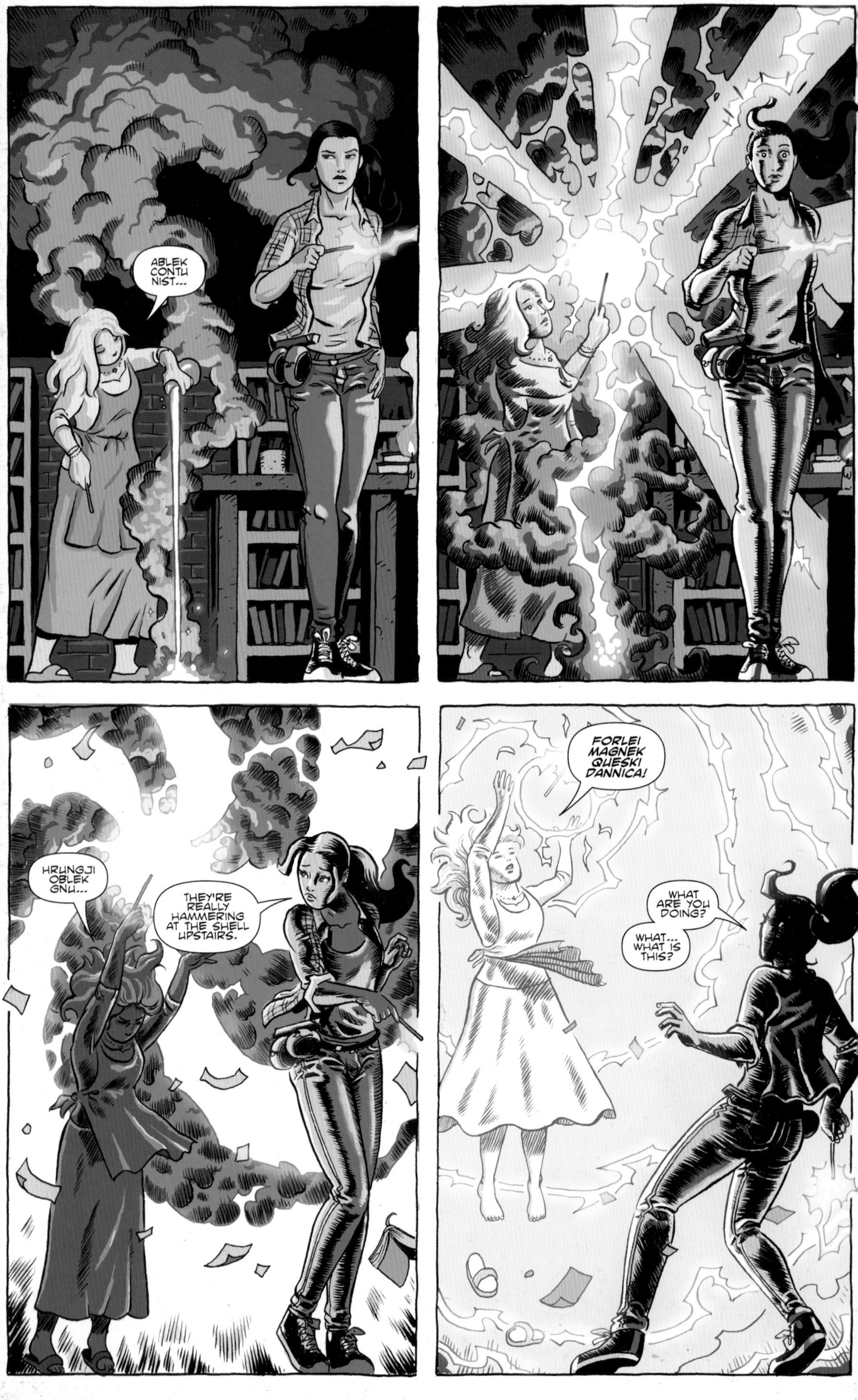
ABLEK CONTUI NIST...
HRUNGJI OBLEK GNU...
THEY'RE REALLY HAMMERING AT THE SHELL UPSTAIRS.
FORLEI MAGNEK QUESKI DANNICA!
WHAT ARE YOU DOING?
WHAT... WHAT IS THIS?

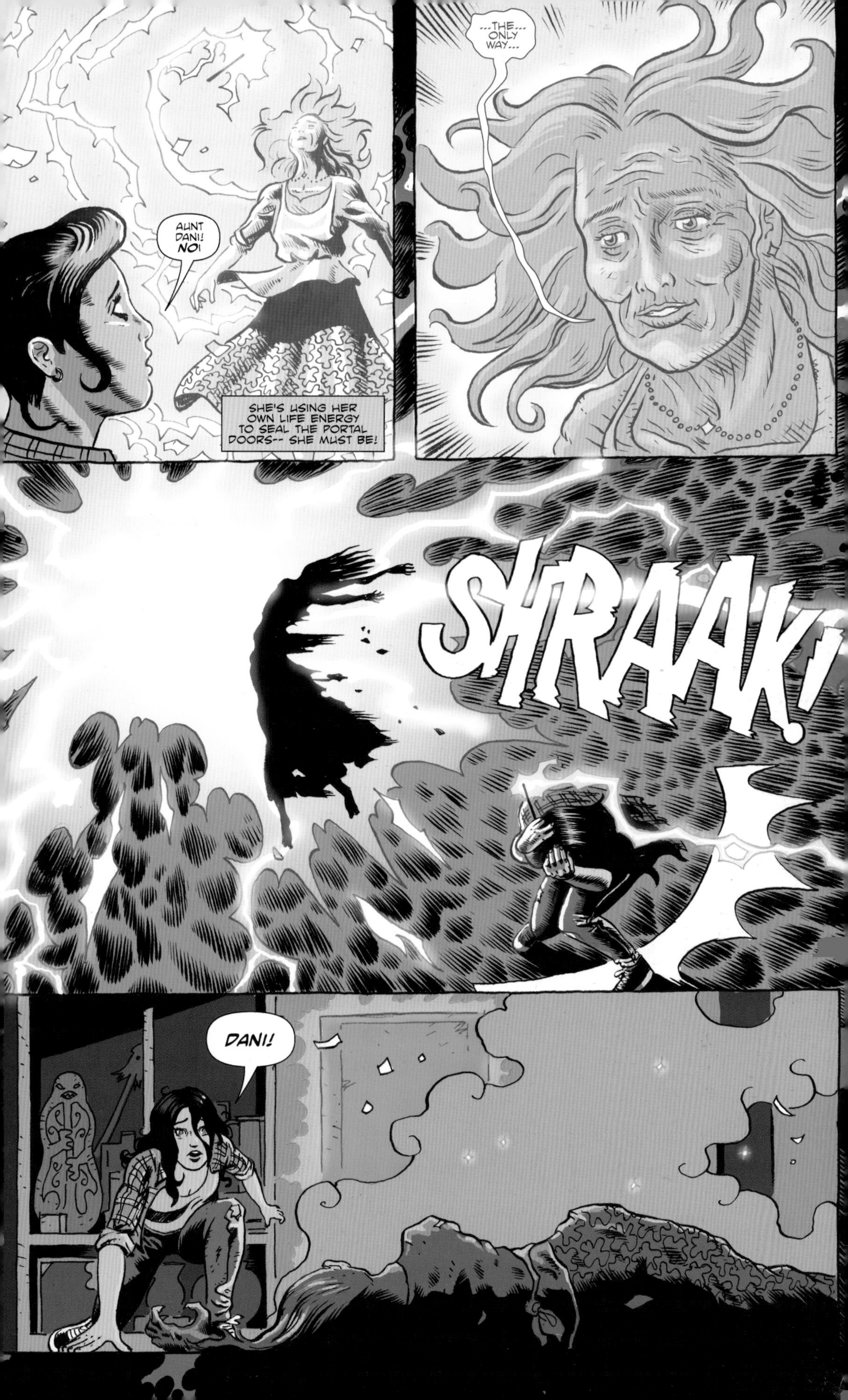
AUNT DANI! NO!
SHE'S USING HER OWN LIFE ENERGY TO SEAL THE PORTAL DOORS-- SHE MUST BE!
...THE... ONLY WAY...
SHRAAK!
DANI!

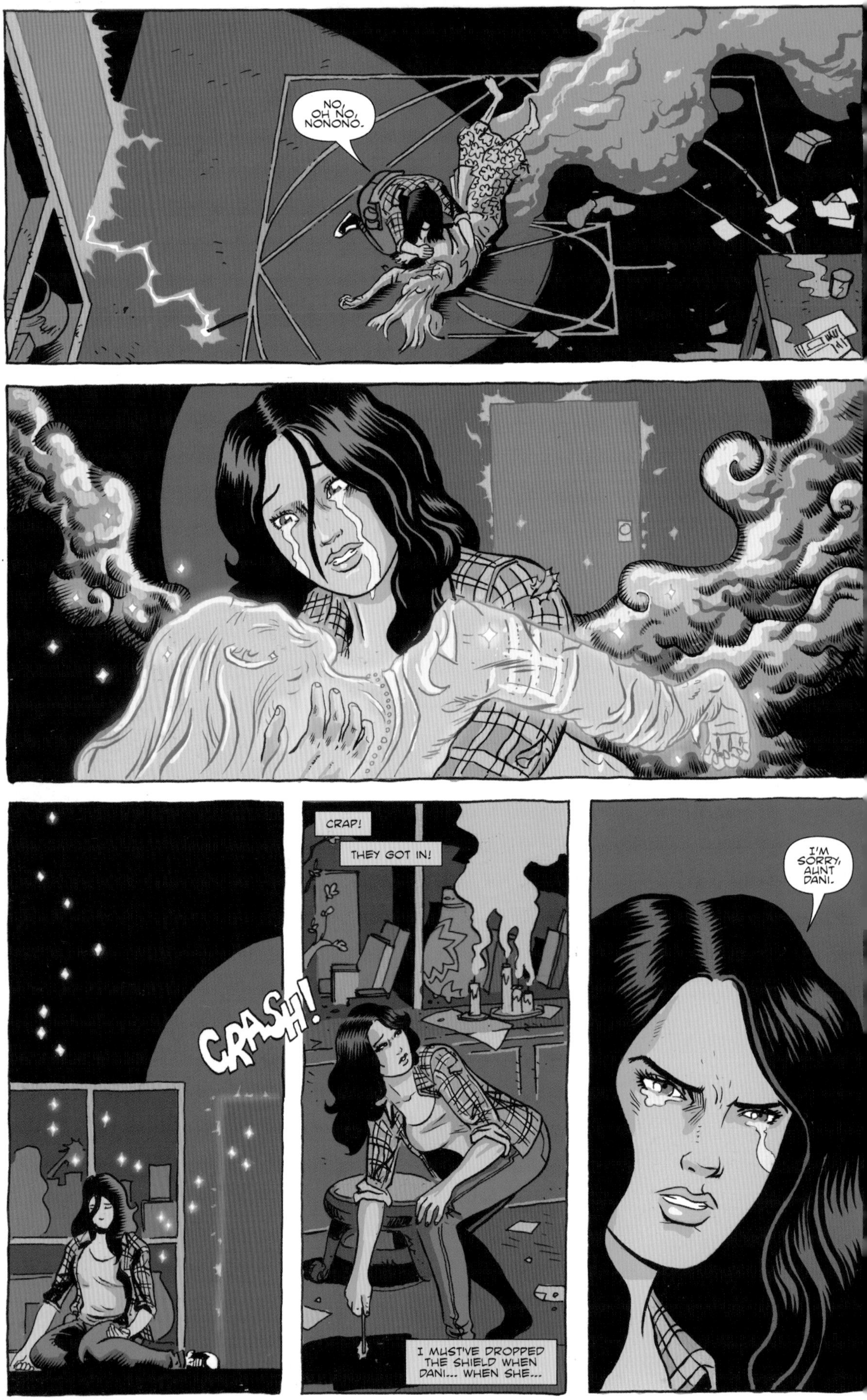
NO, OH NO, NONONO.
CRASH!
CRAP!
THEY GOT IN!
I MUST'VE DROPPED THE SHIELD WHEN DANI... WHEN SHE...
I'M SORRY, AUNT DANI.

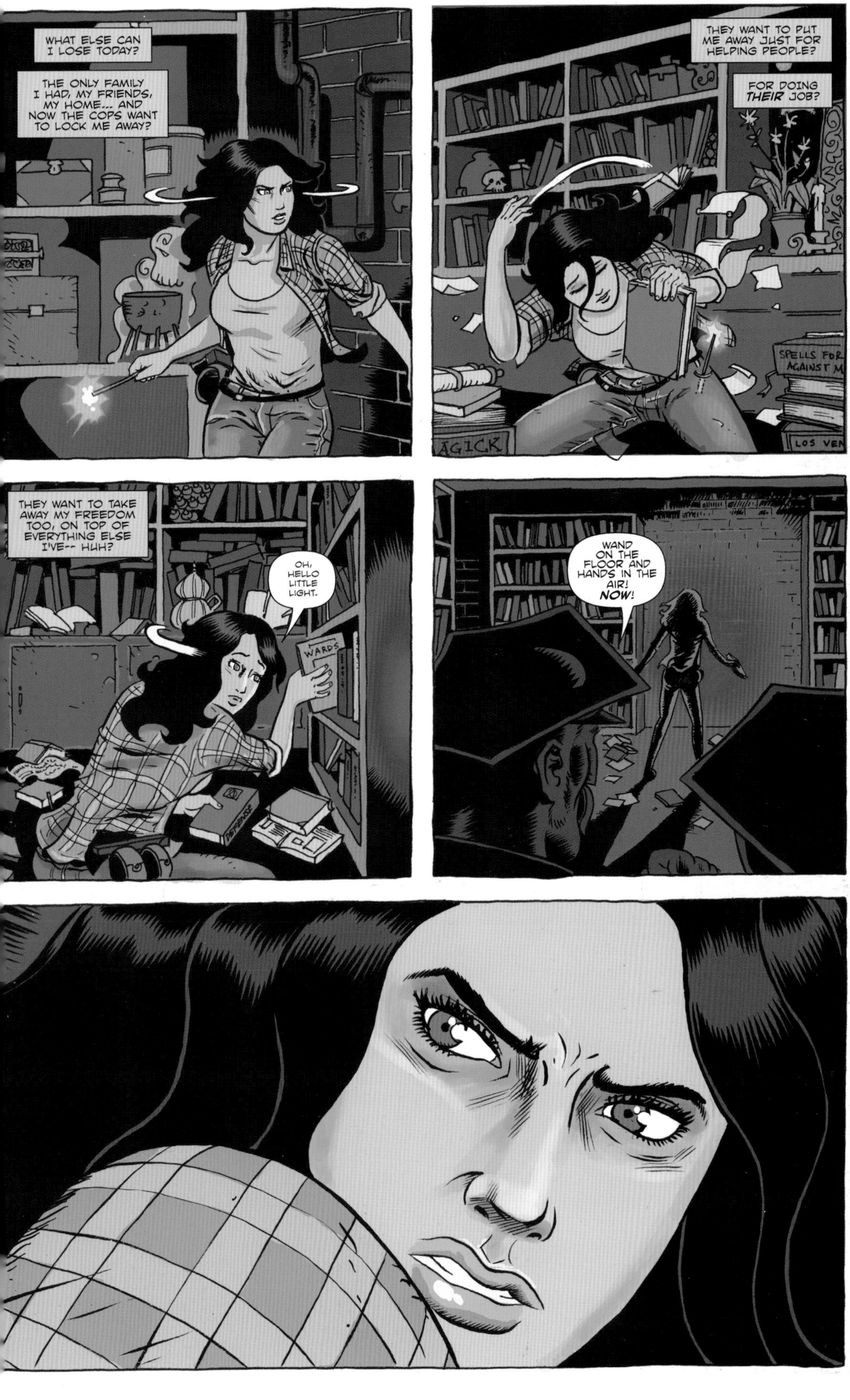
WHAT ELSE CAN I LOSE TODAY?
THE ONLY FAMILY I HAD, MY FRIENDS, MY HOME... AND NOW THE COPS WANT TO LOCK ME AWAY?
THEY WANT TO PUT ME AWAY JUST FOR HELPING PEOPLE?
FOR DOING THEIR JOB?
SPELLS FOR AGAINST M
AGICK
LOS VEN
THEY WANT TO TAKE AWAY MY FREEDOM TOO, ON TOP OF EVERYTHING ELSE I'VE-- HUH?
OH, HELLO LITTLE LIGHT.
WARDS
DEFENSE
WAND ON THE FLOOR AND HANDS IN THE AIR! NOW!

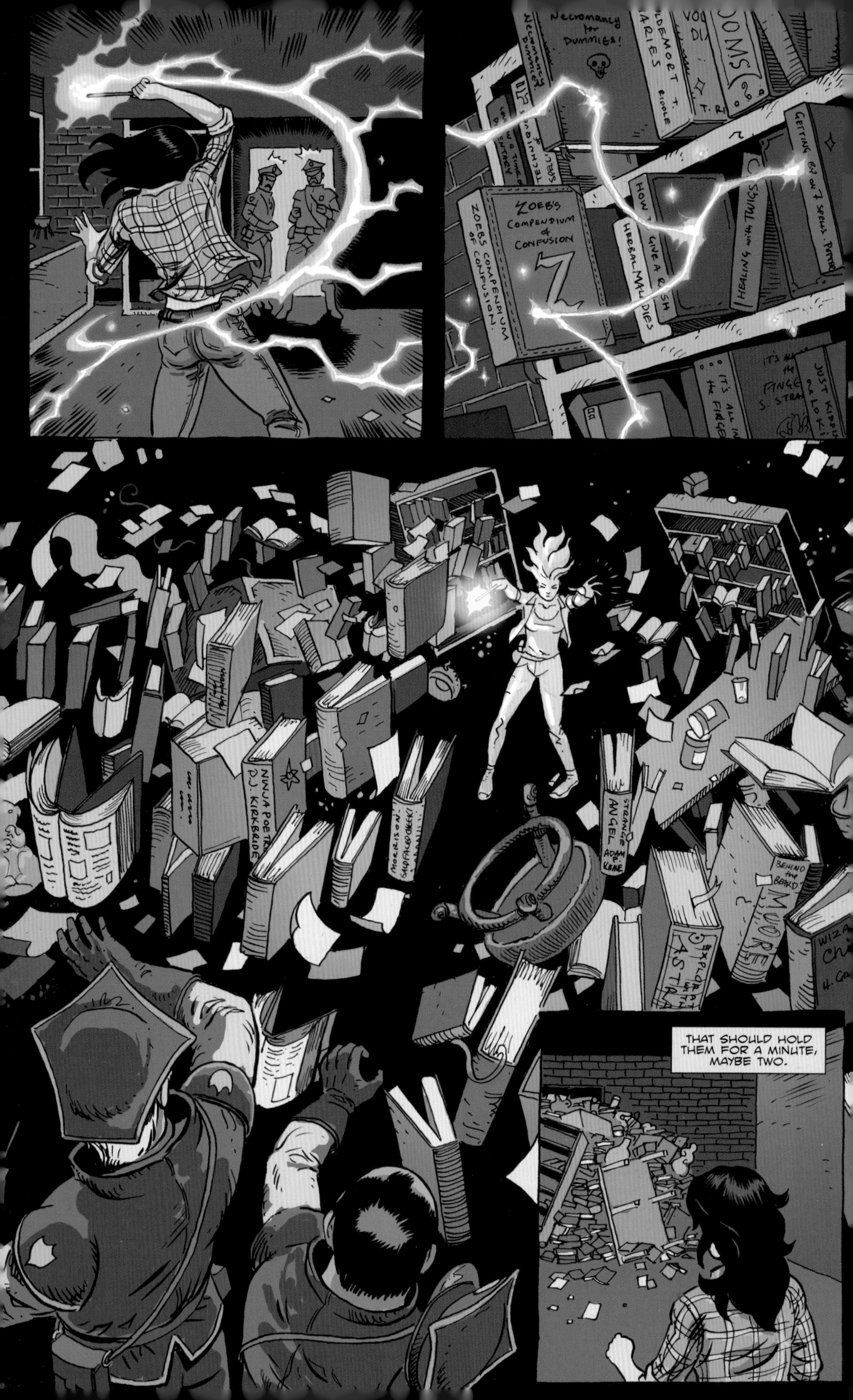
Necromancy for DUMMIES!
ZOEB'S COMPENDIUM of CONFUSION
ZOEB'S COMPENDIUM OF CONFUSION
HERBAL MALADIES
HEALING with TWIGS
GETTING BY on 7 SPELLS. POTTER
NINJA POETRY D.J. KIRKBRIDE
STRANGE ANGEL ADAM P. KNAVE
BEHIND the BOARD
MOORE
THAT SHOULD HOLD THEM FOR A MINUTE, MAYBE TWO.

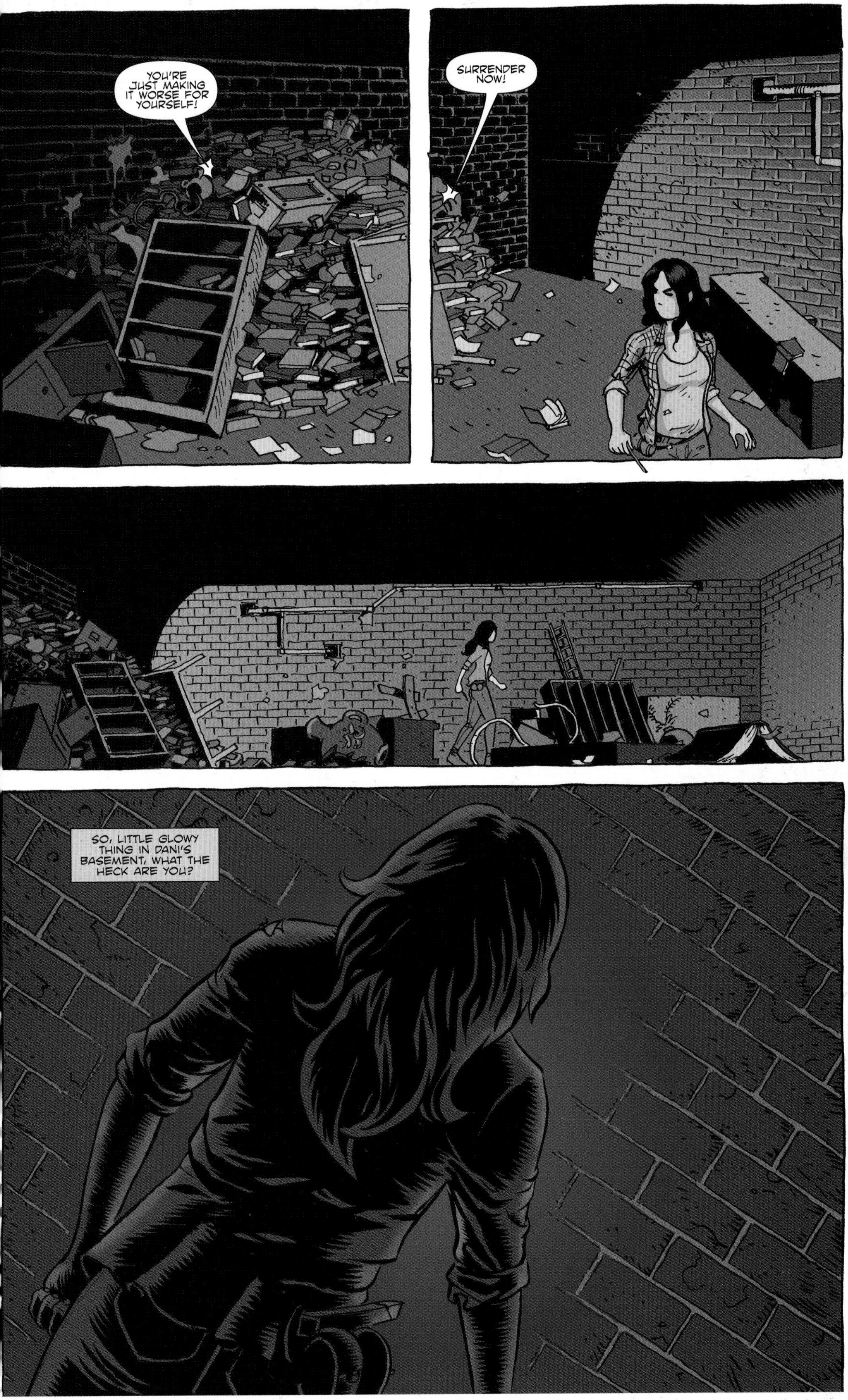
YOU'RE JUST MAKING IT WORSE FOR YOURSELF!
SURRENDER NOW!
SO, LITTLE GLOWY THING IN DANI'S BASEMENT, WHAT THE HECK ARE YOU?

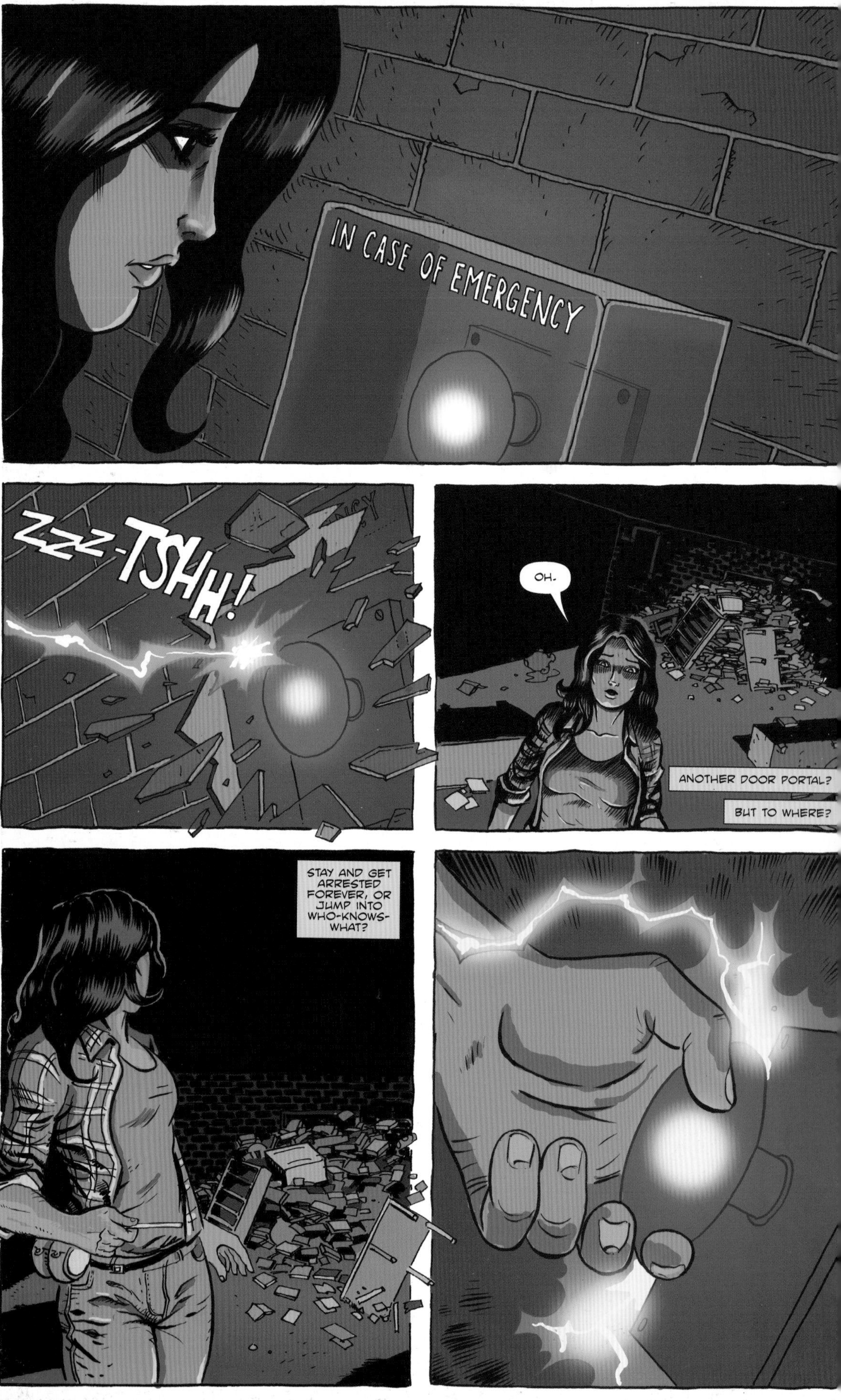
IN CASE OF EMERGENCY
ZZZ-TSHH!
OH.
ANOTHER DOOR PORTAL?
BUT TO WHERE?
STAY AND GET ARRESTED FOREVER, OR JUMP INTO WHO-KNOWS-WHAT?

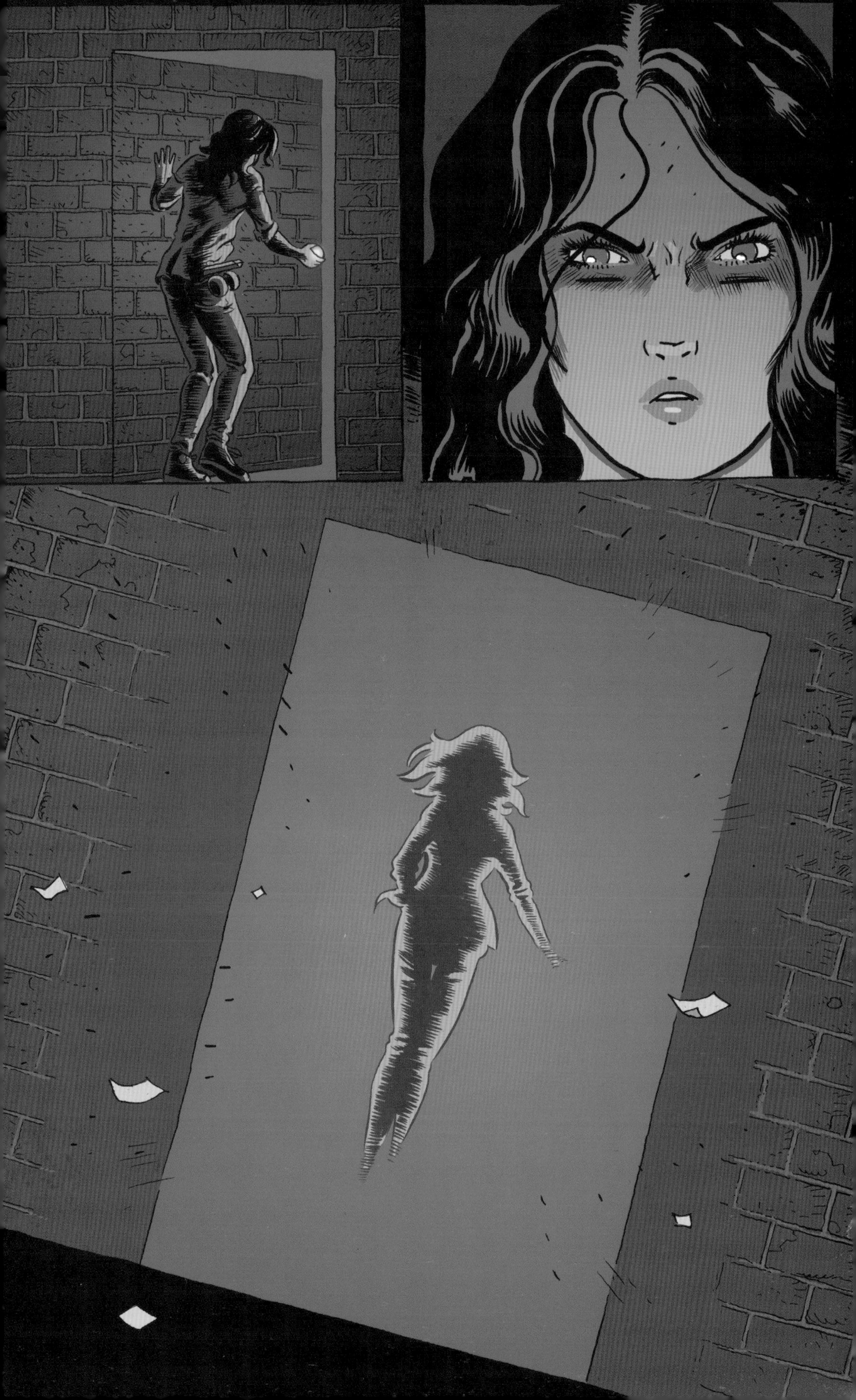

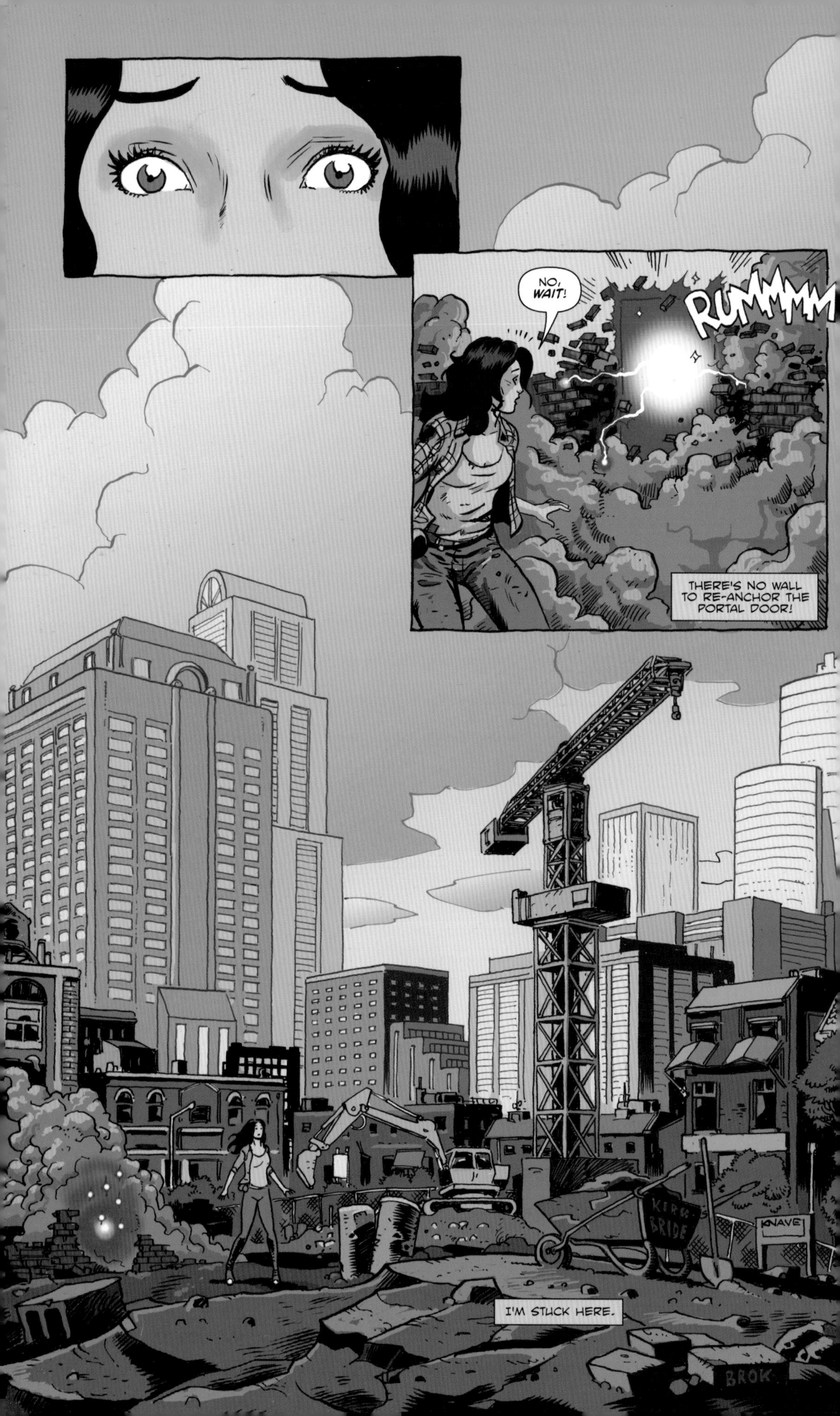

NO, WAIT!
RUMMMM
THERE'S NO WALL TO RE-ANCHOR THE PORTAL DOOR!
KNAVE
I'M STUCK HERE.
BROK

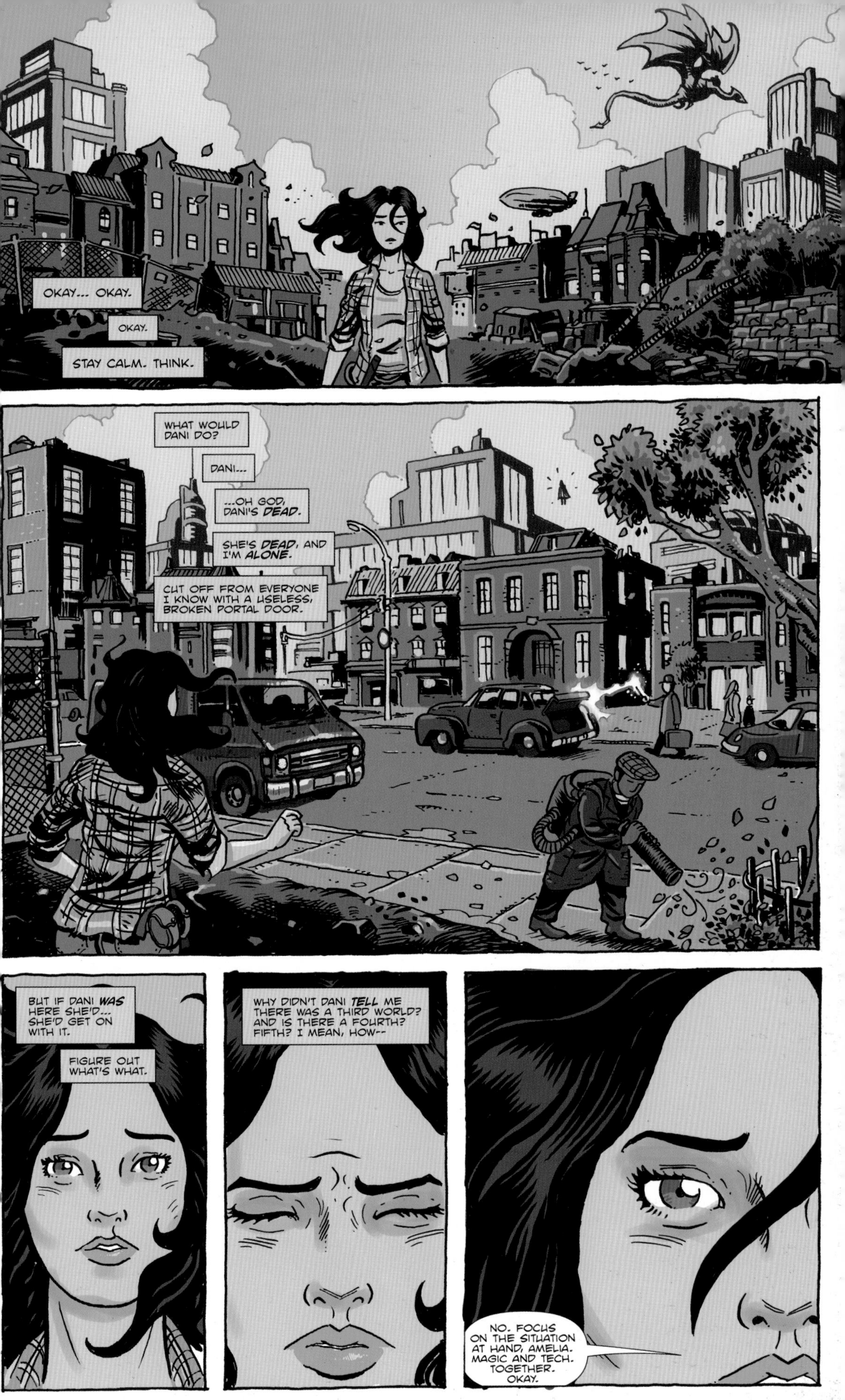
OKAY... OKAY.
OKAY.
STAY CALM. THINK.
WHAT WOULD DANI DO?
DANI...
...OH GOD, DANI'S *DEAD*.
SHE'S *DEAD*, AND I'M *ALONE*.
CUT OFF FROM EVERYONE I KNOW WITH A USELESS, BROKEN PORTAL DOOR.
BUT IF DANI *WAS* HERE SHE'D... SHE'D GET ON WITH IT.
FIGURE OUT WHAT'S WHAT.
WHY DIDN'T DANI *TELL* ME THERE WAS A THIRD WORLD? AND IS THERE A FOURTH? FIFTH? I MEAN, HOW--
NO. FOCUS ON THE SITUATION AT HAND, AMELIA. MAGIC AND TECH. TOGETHER. OKAY.

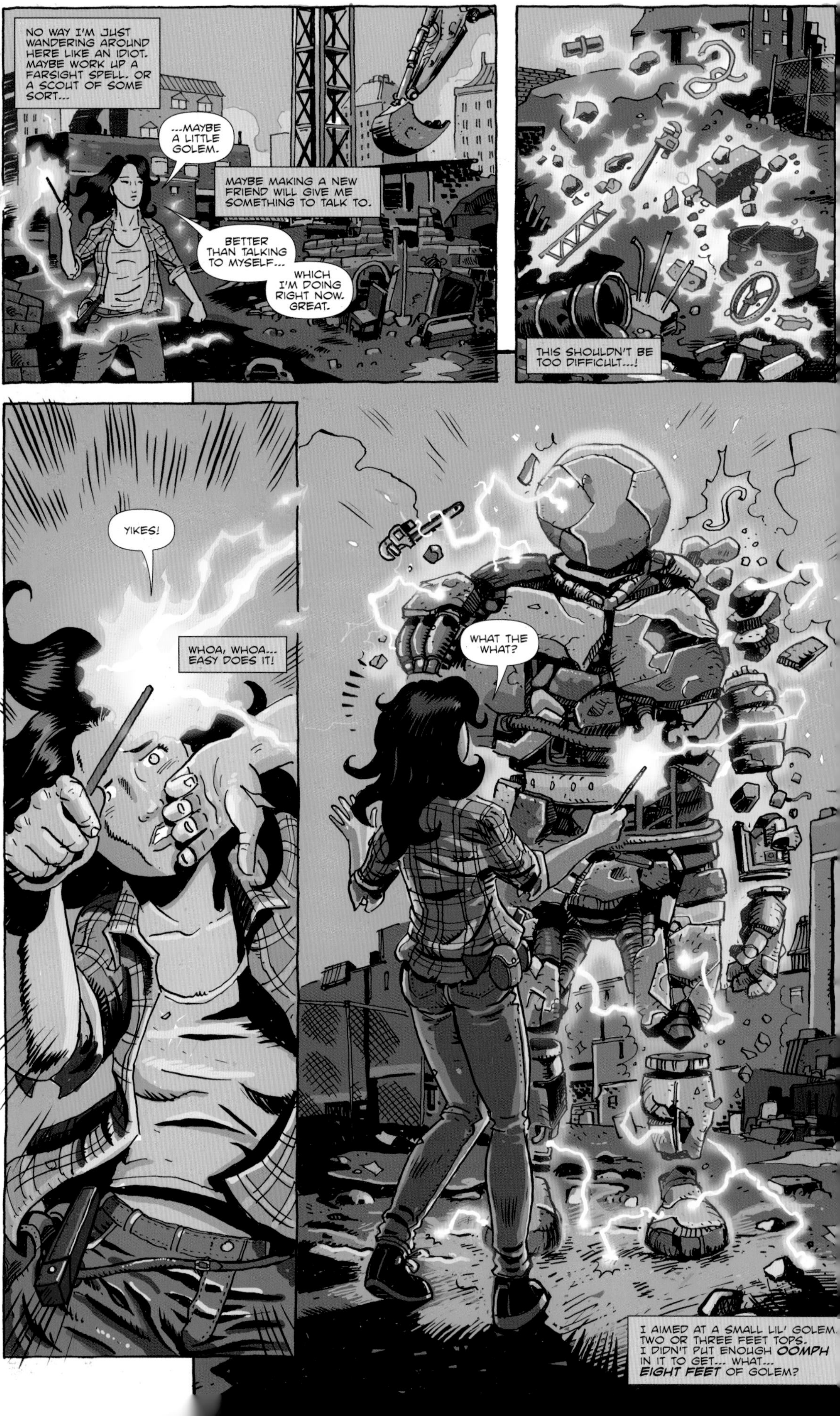
NO WAY I'M JUST WANDERING AROUND HERE LIKE AN IDIOT. MAYBE WORK UP A FARSIGHT SPELL. OR A SCOUT OF SOME SORT...
...MAYBE A LITTLE GOLEM.
MAYBE MAKING A NEW FRIEND WILL GIVE ME SOMETHING TO TALK TO.
BETTER THAN TALKING TO MYSELF...
WHICH I'M DOING RIGHT NOW. GREAT.
THIS SHOULDN'T BE TOO DIFFICULT...!
YIKES!
WHOA, WHOA... EASY DOES IT!
WHAT THE WHAT?
I AIMED AT A SMALL LIL' GOLEM. TWO OR THREE FEET TOPS. I DIDN'T PUT ENOUGH OOMPH IN IT TO GET... WHAT... EIGHT FEET OF GOLEM?

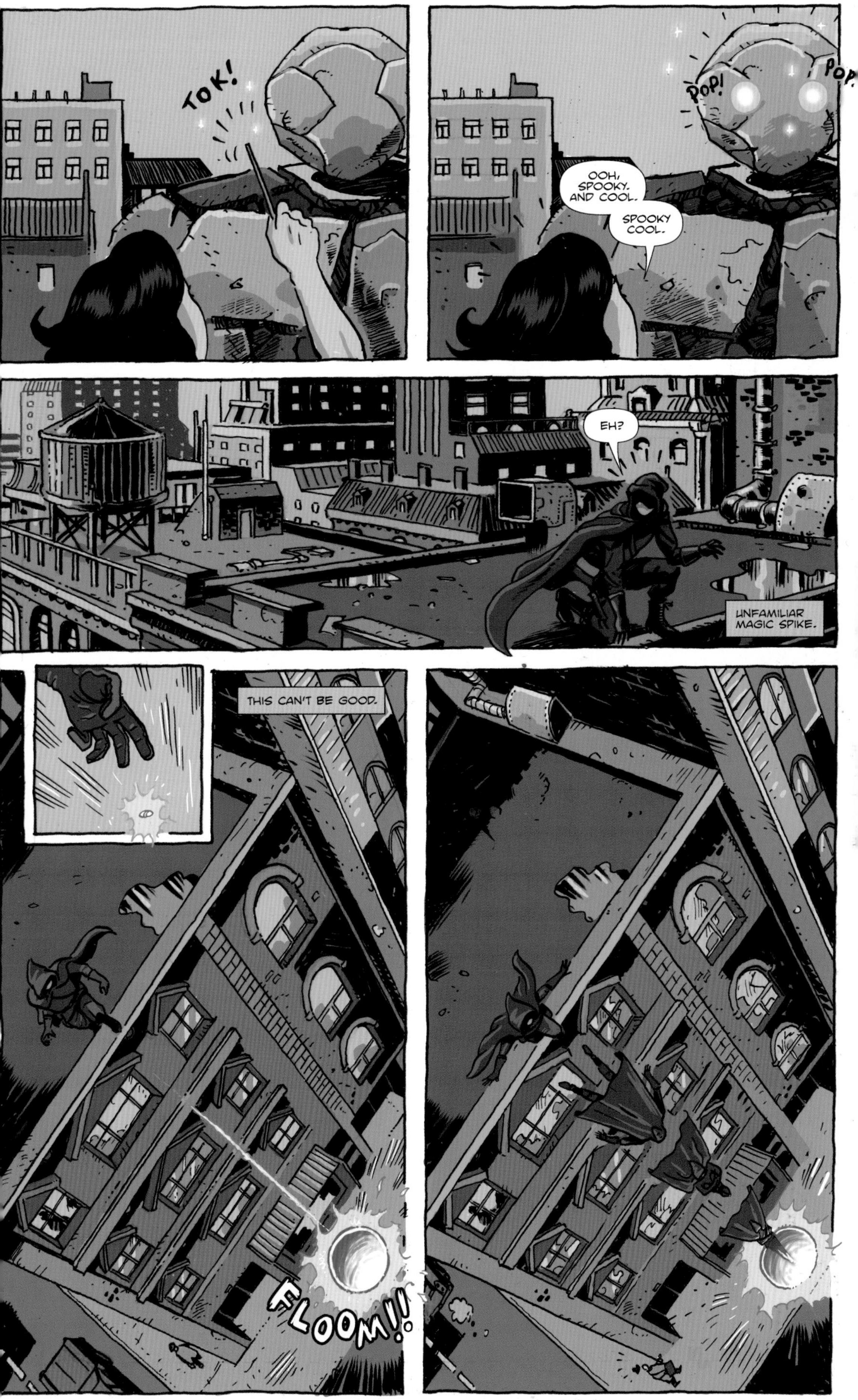
TOK!
POP! POP.
OOH, SPOOKY. AND COOL.
SPOOKY COOL.
EH?
UNFAMILIAR MAGIC SPIKE.
THIS CAN'T BE GOOD.
FLOOM!!

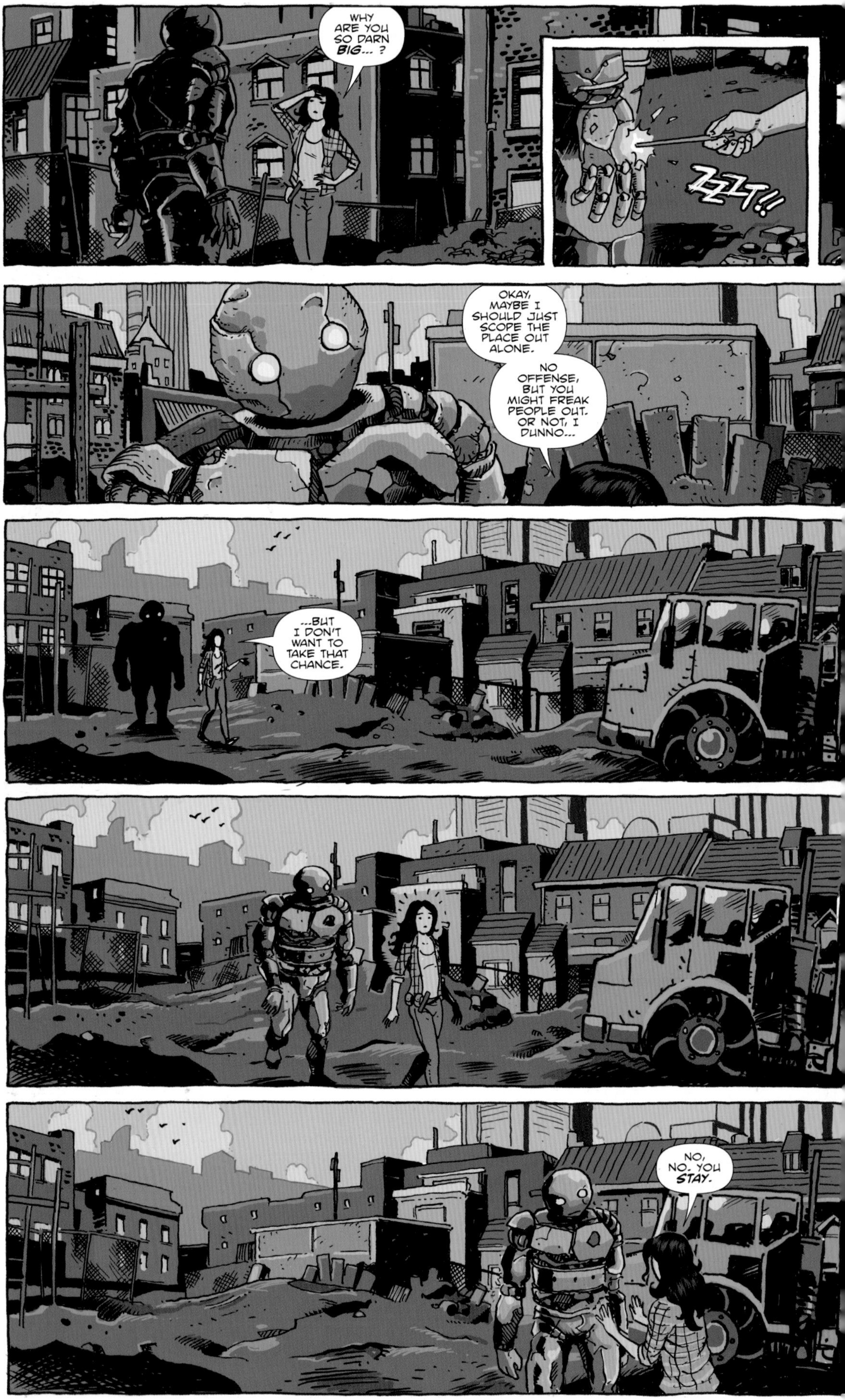
WHY ARE YOU SO DARN BIG... ?
ZZZT!!
OKAY, MAYBE I SHOULD JUST SCOPE THE PLACE OUT ALONE.
NO OFFENSE, BUT YOU MIGHT FREAK PEOPLE OUT. OR NOT, I DUNNO...
...BUT I DON'T WANT TO TAKE THAT CHANCE.
NO, NO. YOU STAY.

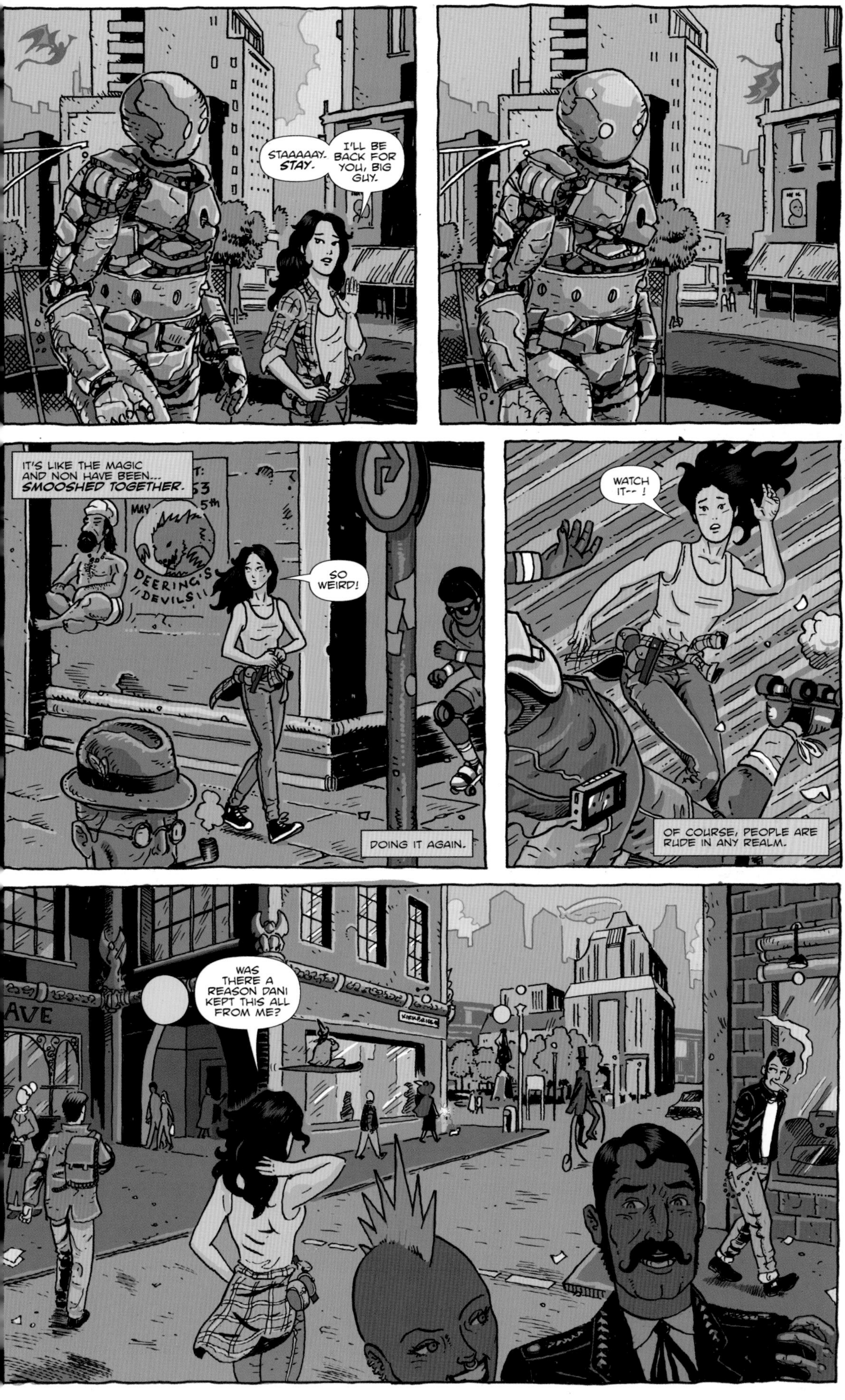
STAAAAAY. STAY.
I'LL BE BACK FOR YOU, BIG GUY.
IT'S LIKE THE MAGIC AND NON HAVE BEEN... SMOOSHED TOGETHER.
MAY
5th
DEERING'S DEVILS
SO WEIRD!
DOING IT AGAIN.
WATCH IT-- !
OF COURSE, PEOPLE ARE RUDE IN ANY REALM.
AVE
WAS THERE A REASON DANI KEPT THIS ALL FROM ME?

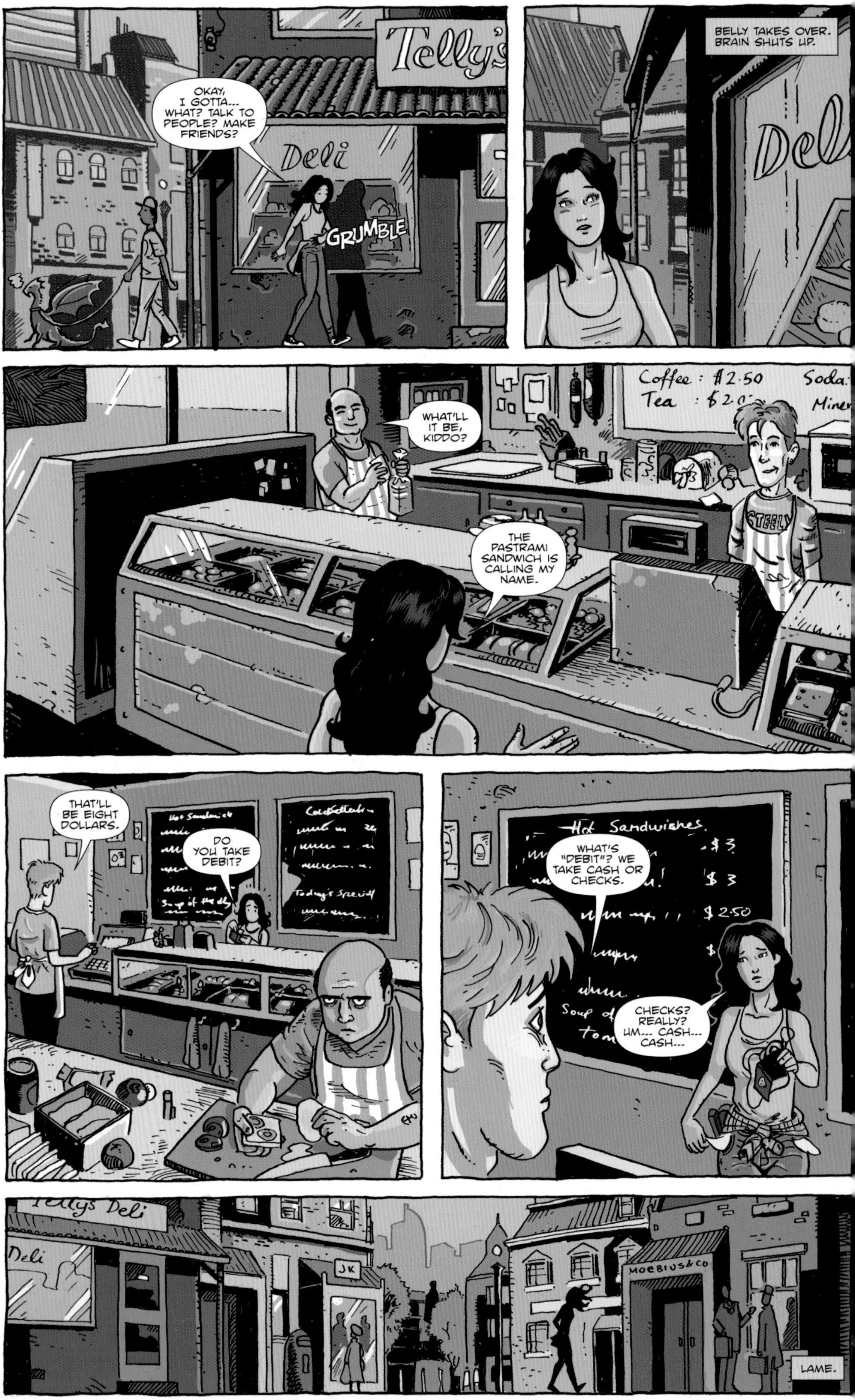
Telly's
Deli
OKAY, I GOTTA... WHAT? TALK TO PEOPLE? MAKE FRIENDS?
GRUMBLE
BELLY TAKES OVER. BRAIN SHUTS UP.
Coffee : $2.50
Tea : $2.0
WHAT'LL IT BE, KIDDO?
THE PASTRAMI SANDWICH IS CALLING MY NAME.
STEELY
THAT'LL BE EIGHT DOLLARS.
DO YOU TAKE DEBIT?
Hot Sandwiches
WHAT'S "DEBIT"? WE TAKE CASH OR CHECKS.
CHECKS? REALLY? UM... CASH... CASH...
Telly's Deli
Deli
JK
MOEBIUS & CO
LAME.

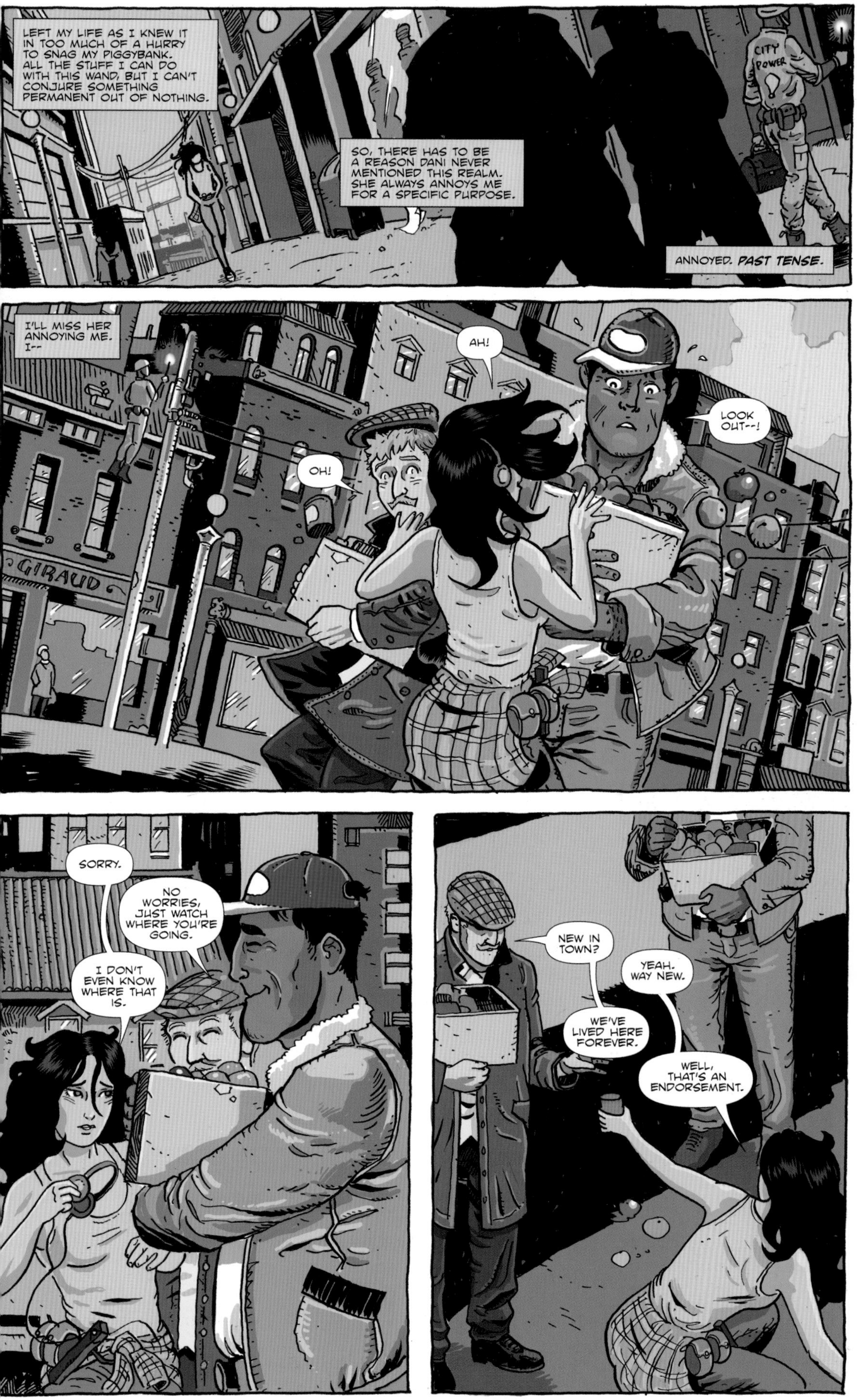
LEFT MY LIFE AS I KNEW IT IN TOO MUCH OF A HURRY TO SNAG MY PIGGYBANK. ALL THE STUFF I CAN DO WITH THIS WAND, BUT I CAN'T CONJURE SOMETHING PERMANENT OUT OF NOTHING.
CITY POWER
SO, THERE HAS TO BE A REASON DANI NEVER MENTIONED THIS REALM. SHE ALWAYS ANNOYS ME FOR A SPECIFIC PURPOSE.
ANNOYED. PAST TENSE.
I'LL MISS HER ANNOYING ME. I--
AH!
LOOK OUT--!
OH!
GIRAUD
SORRY.
NO WORRIES, JUST WATCH WHERE YOU'RE GOING.
I DON'T EVEN KNOW WHERE THAT IS.
NEW IN TOWN?
YEAH. WAY NEW.
WE'VE LIVED HERE FOREVER.
WELL, THAT'S AN ENDORSEMENT.

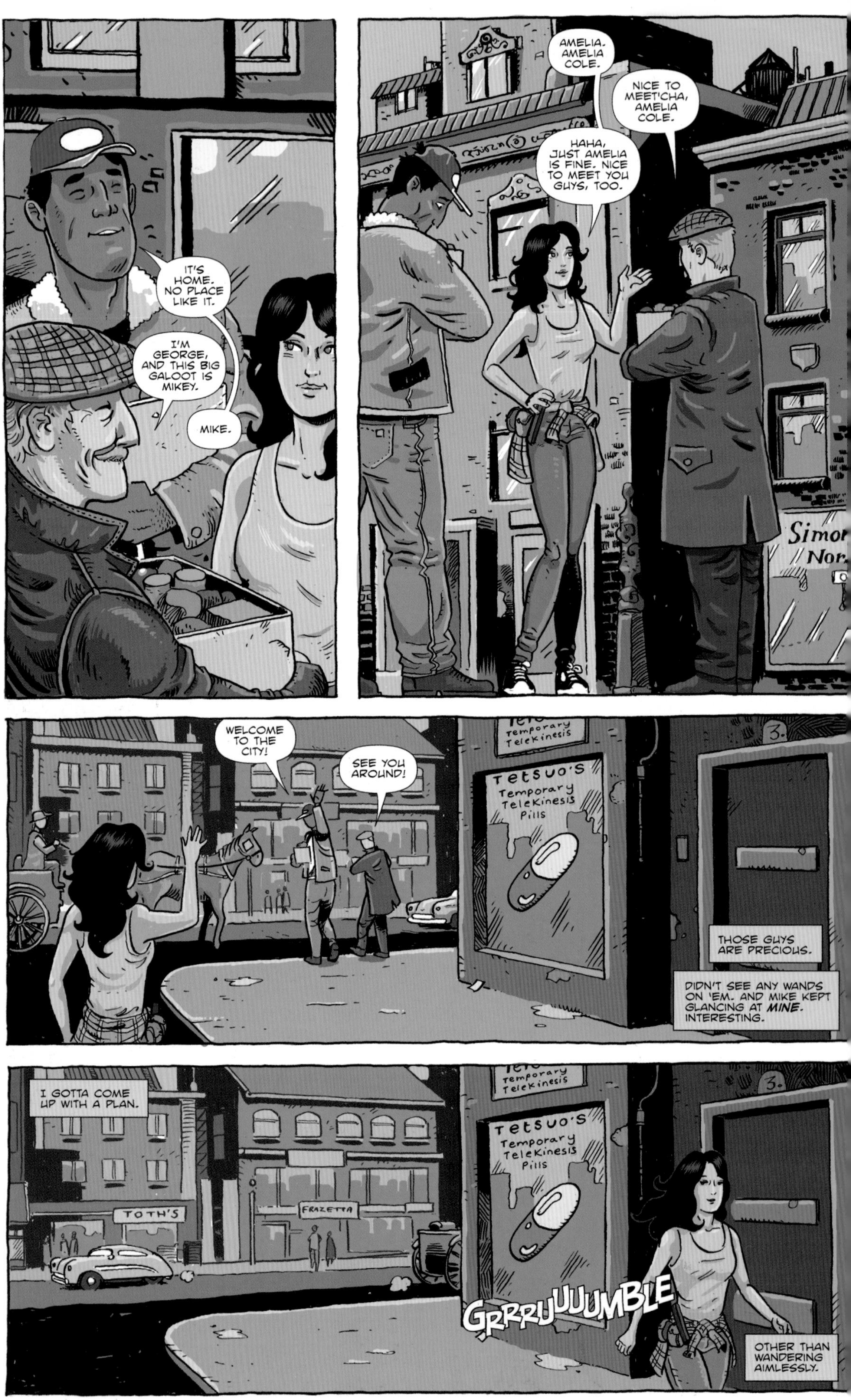
IT'S HOME. NO PLACE LIKE IT.
I'M GEORGE, AND THIS BIG GALOOT IS MIKEY.
MIKE.
AMELIA. AMELIA COLE.
NICE TO MEET'CHA, AMELIA COLE.
HAHA, JUST AMELIA IS FINE. NICE TO MEET YOU GUYS, TOO.
WELCOME TO THE CITY!
SEE YOU AROUND!
Tetsuo's Temporary TeleKinesis Pills
3.
THOSE GUYS ARE PRECIOUS.
DIDN'T SEE ANY WANDS ON 'EM. AND MIKE KEPT GLANCING AT **MINE**. INTERESTING.
I GOTTA COME UP WITH A PLAN.
TOTH'S
FRAZETTA
Tetsuo's Temporary TeleKinesis Pills
GRRRUUUUMBLE
OTHER THAN WANDERING AIMLESSLY.

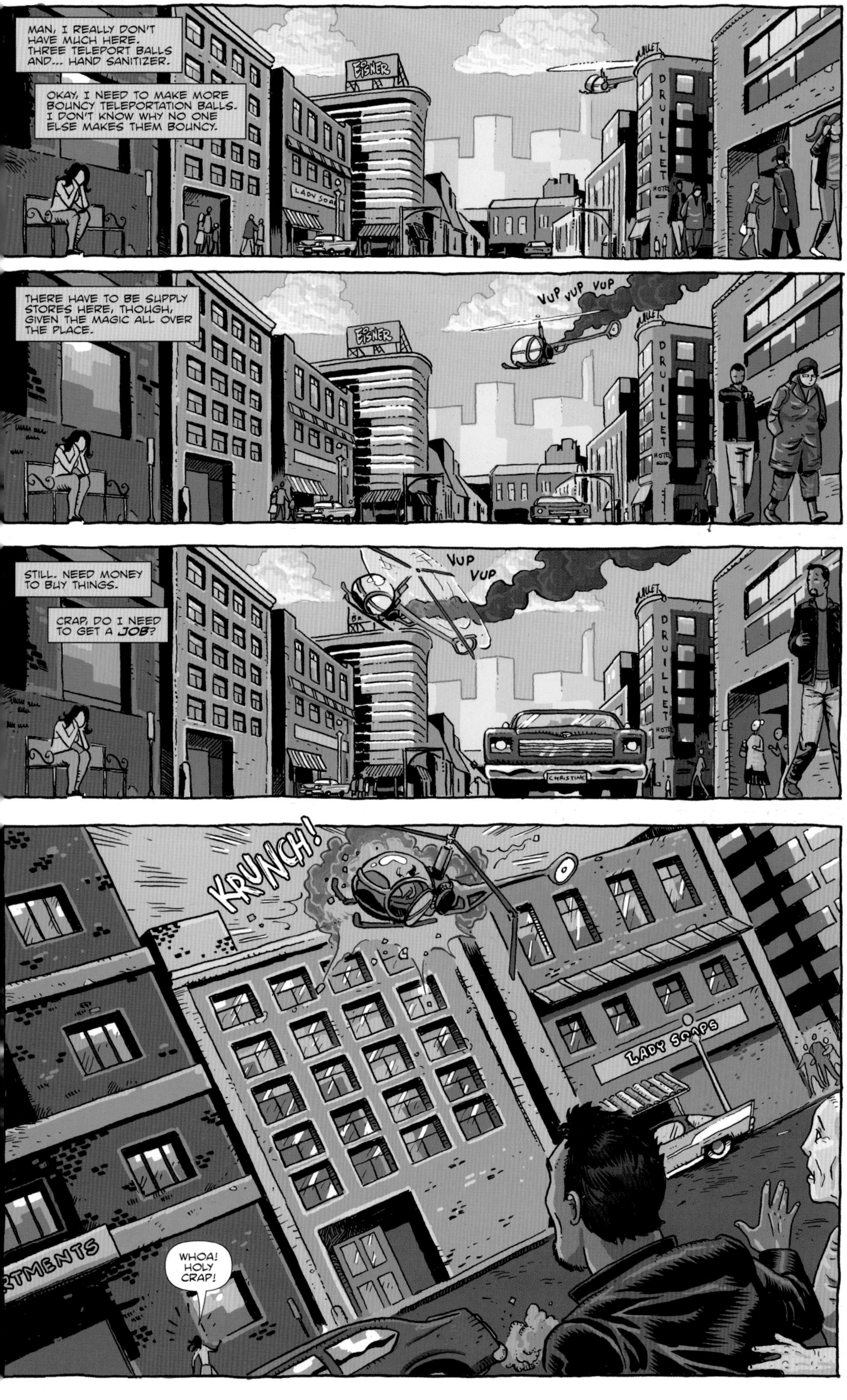
MAN, I REALLY DON'T HAVE MUCH HERE. THREE TELEPORT BALLS AND... HAND SANITIZER.
OKAY, I NEED TO MAKE MORE BOUNCY TELEPORTATION BALLS. I DON'T KNOW WHY NO ONE ELSE MAKES THEM BOUNCY.
EISNER
DRUILLET HOTEL
LADY SOAP
THERE HAVE TO BE SUPPLY STORES HERE, THOUGH, GIVEN THE MAGIC ALL OVER THE PLACE.
VUP VUP VUP
STILL. NEED MONEY TO BUY THINGS.
CRAP, DO I NEED TO GET A *JOB*?
VUP
VUP
CHRISTINE
KRUNCH!
LADY SOAPS
RTMENTS
WHOA! HOLY CRAP!

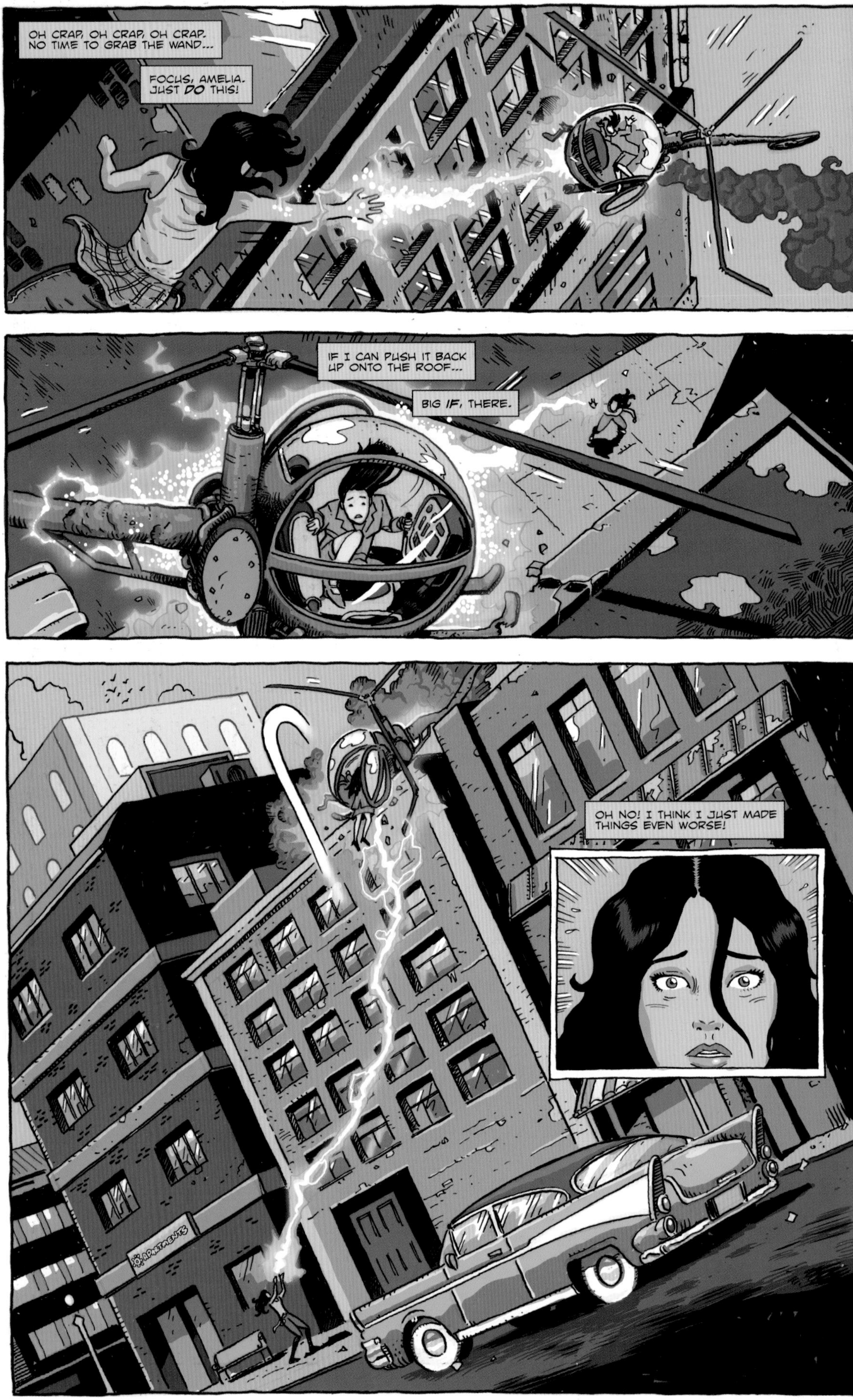
OH CRAP, OH CRAP, OH CRAP. NO TIME TO GRAB THE WAND...
FOCUS, AMELIA. JUST DO THIS!
IF I CAN PUSH IT BACK UP ONTO THE ROOF...
BIG IF, THERE.
OH NO! I THINK I JUST MADE THINGS EVEN WORSE!
APARTMENTS

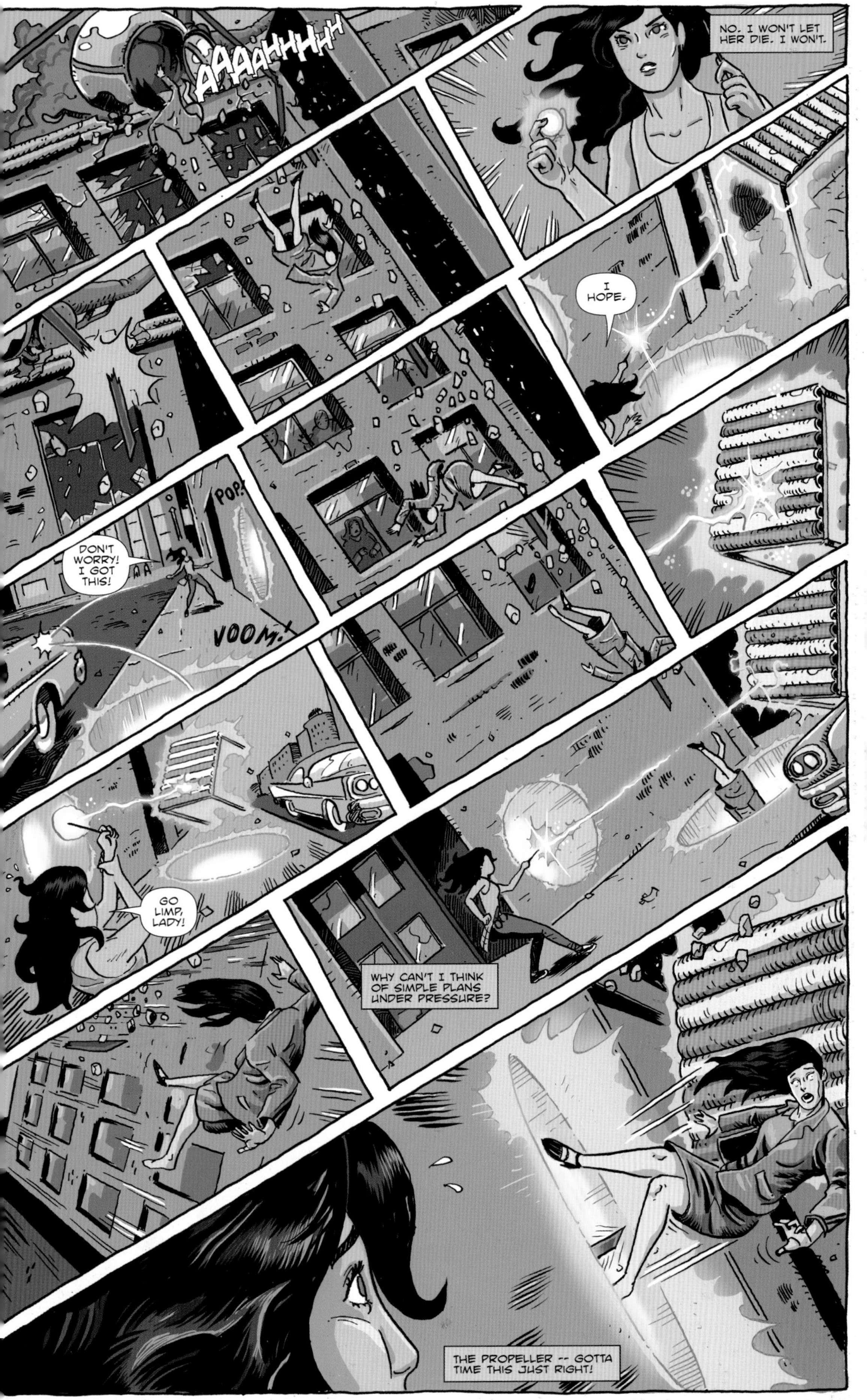
AAAAHHHHH
NO. I WON'T LET HER DIE. I WON'T.
I HOPE.
POP!
DON'T WORRY! I GOT THIS!
VOOM!
GO LIMP, LADY!
WHY CAN'T I THINK OF SIMPLE PLANS UNDER PRESSURE?
THE PROPELLER -- GOTTA TIME THIS JUST RIGHT!

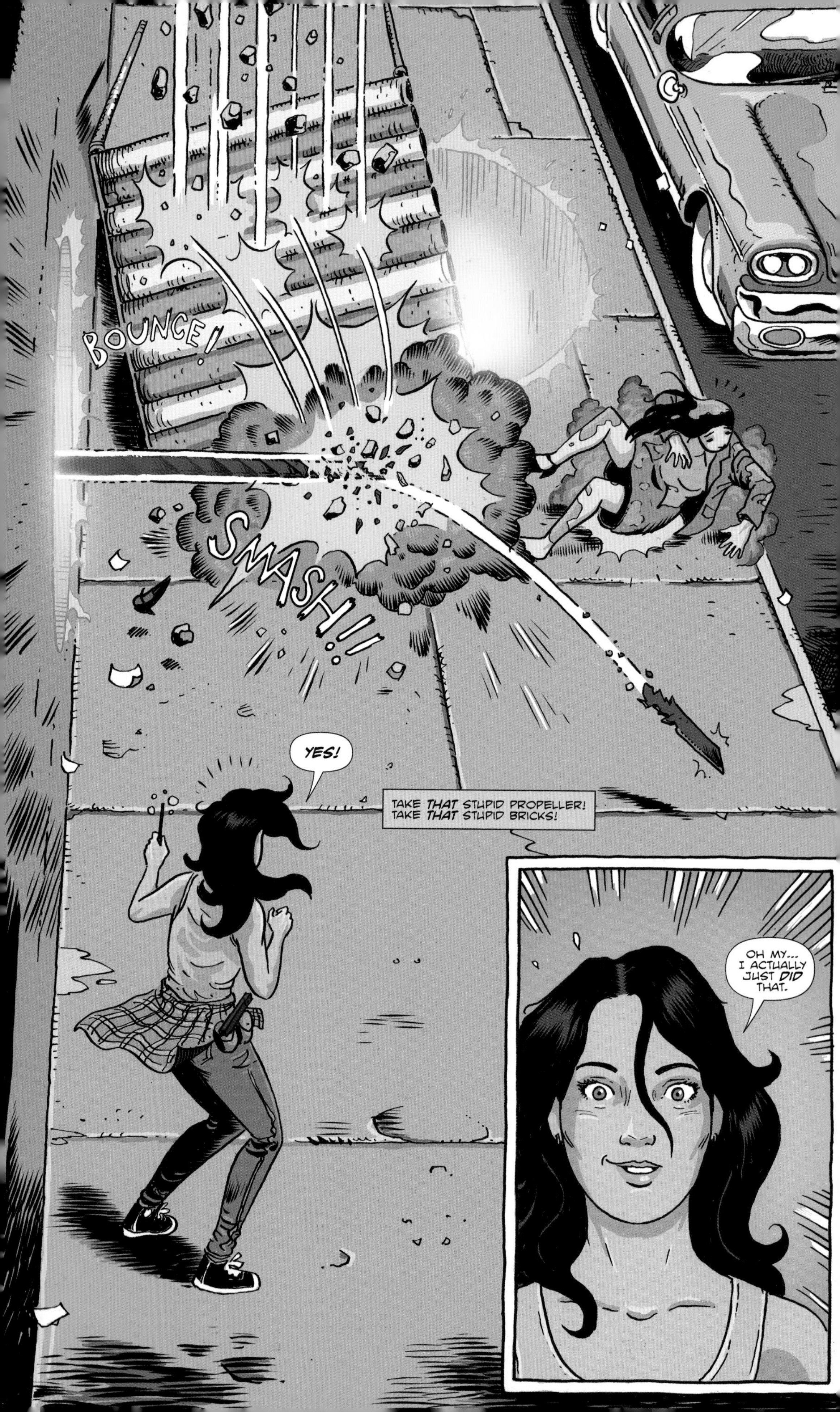
BOUNCE!
SMASH!!!
YES!
TAKE THAT STUPID PROPELLER! TAKE THAT STUPID BRICKS!
OH MY... I ACTUALLY JUST DID THAT.

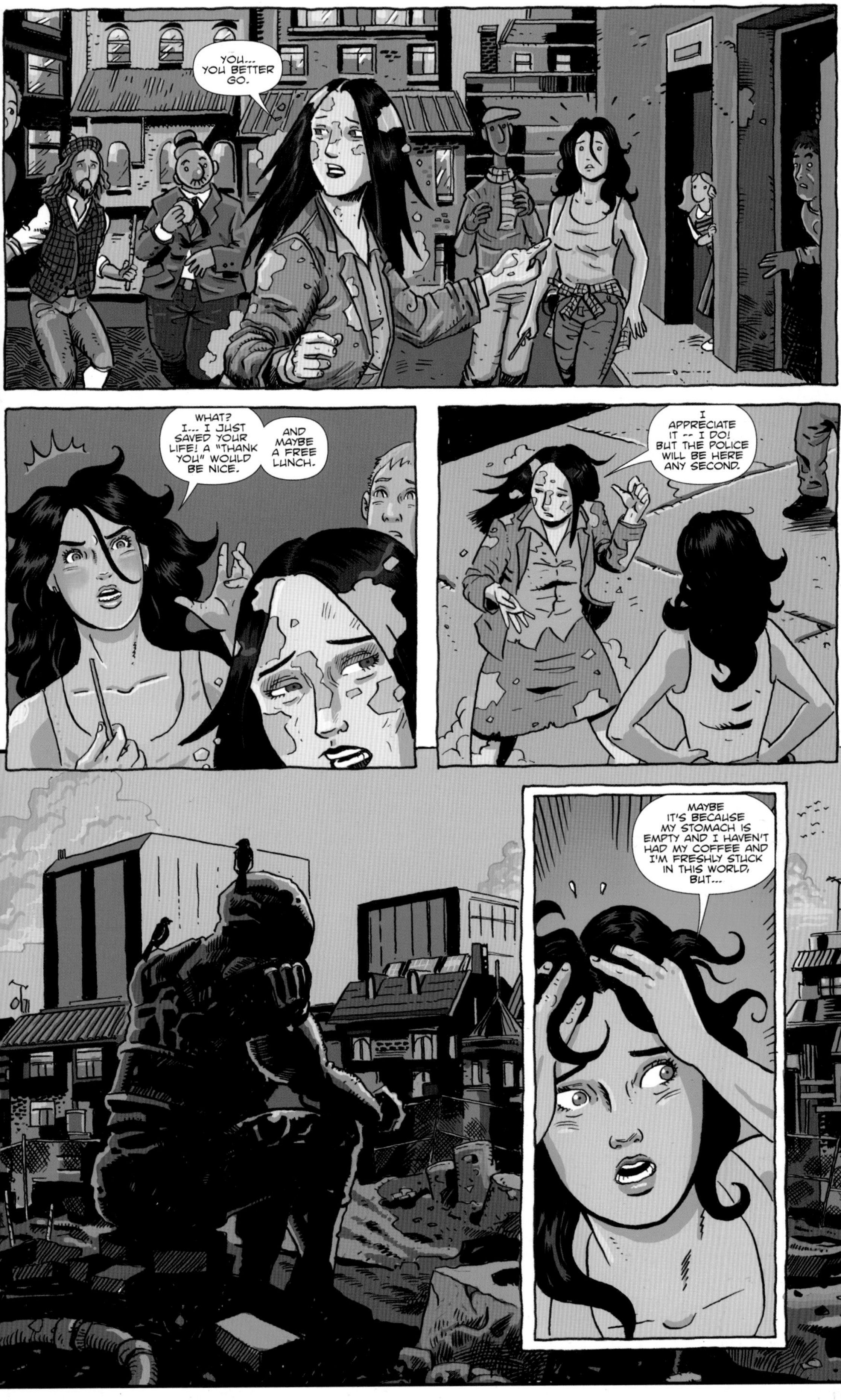
YOU... YOU BETTER GO.
WHAT? I... I JUST SAVED YOUR LIFE! A "THANK YOU" WOULD BE NICE.
AND MAYBE A FREE LUNCH.
I APPRECIATE IT -- I DO! BUT THE POLICE WILL BE HERE ANY SECOND.
MAYBE IT'S BECAUSE MY STOMACH IS EMPTY AND I HAVEN'T HAD MY COFFEE AND I'M FRESHLY STUCK IN THIS WORLD, BUT...

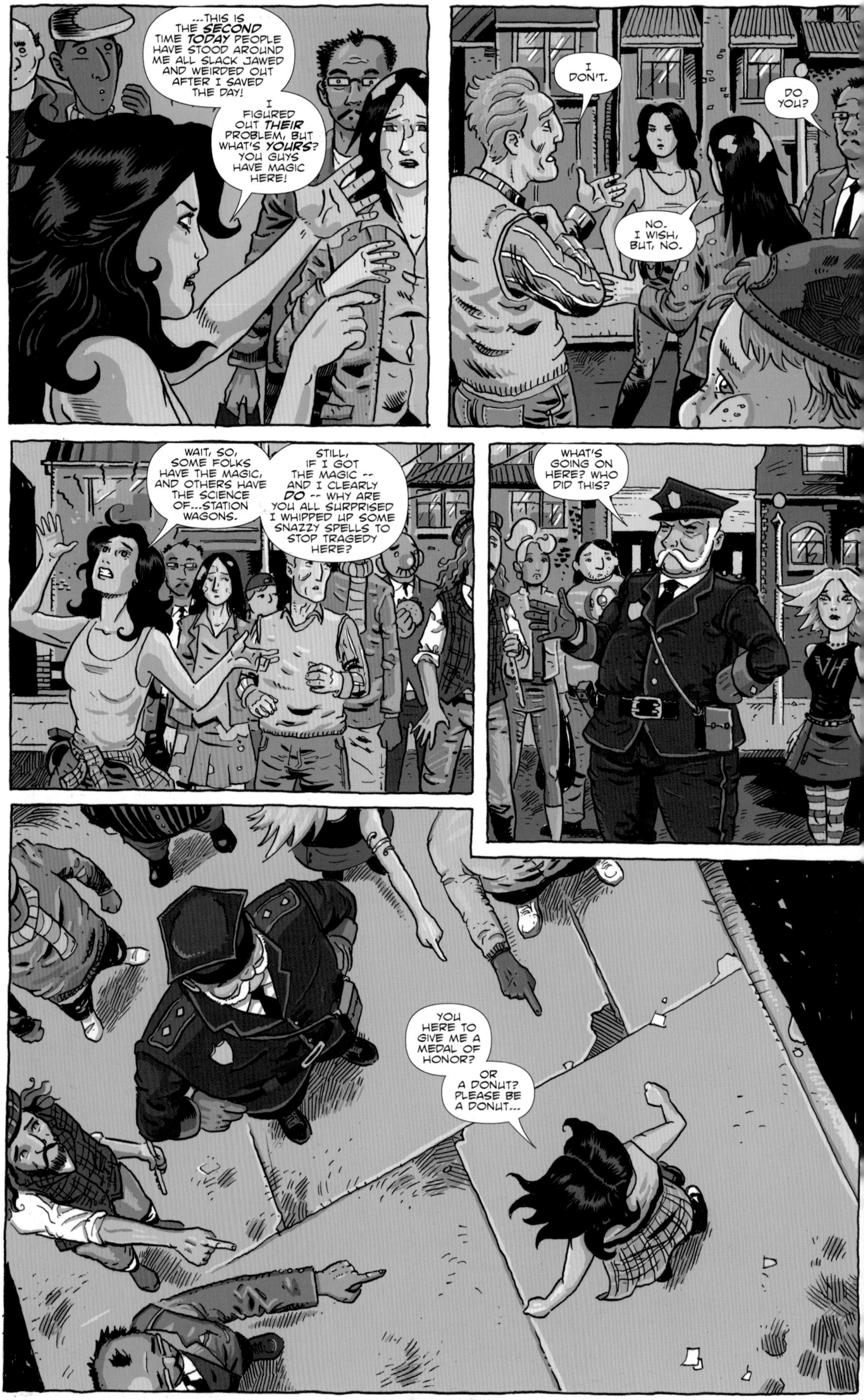
...THIS IS THE SECOND TIME TODAY PEOPLE HAVE STOOD AROUND ME ALL SLACK JAWED AND WEIRDED OUT AFTER I SAVED THE DAY!
I FIGURED OUT THEIR PROBLEM, BUT WHAT'S YOURS? YOU GUYS HAVE MAGIC HERE!
I DON'T.
DO YOU?
NO. I WISH, BUT, NO.
WAIT, SO, SOME FOLKS HAVE THE MAGIC, AND OTHERS HAVE THE SCIENCE OF...STATION WAGONS.
STILL, IF I GOT THE MAGIC -- AND I CLEARLY DO -- WHY ARE YOU ALL SURPRISED I WHIPPED UP SOME SNAZZY SPELLS TO STOP TRAGEDY HERE?
WHAT'S GOING ON HERE? WHO DID THIS?
YOU HERE TO GIVE ME A MEDAL OF HONOR?
OR A DONUT? PLEASE BE A DONUT...

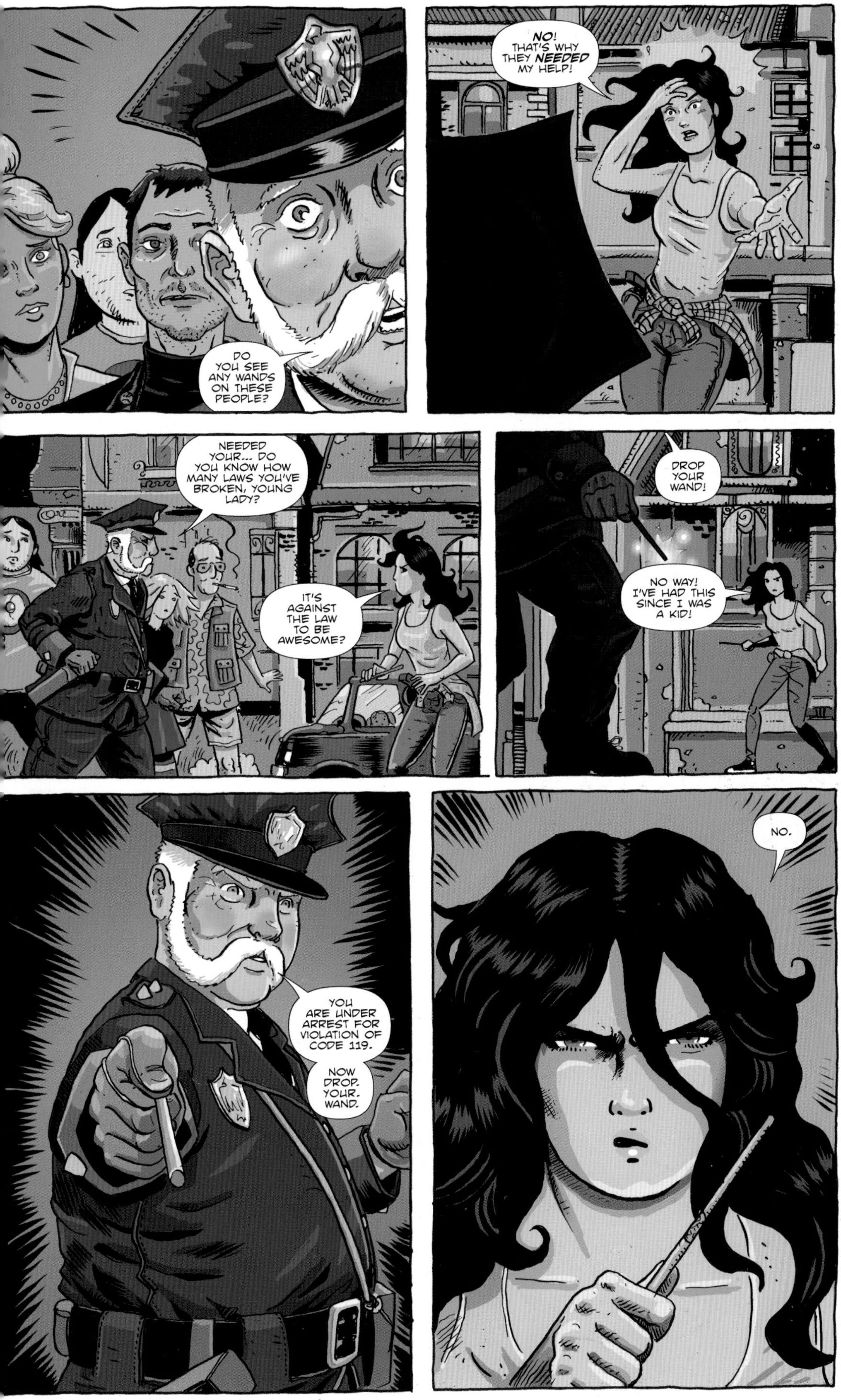
DO YOU SEE ANY WANDS ON THESE PEOPLE?
NO! THAT'S WHY THEY NEEDED MY HELP!
NEEDED YOUR... DO YOU KNOW HOW MANY LAWS YOU'VE BROKEN, YOUNG LADY?
IT'S AGAINST THE LAW TO BE AWESOME?
DROP YOUR WAND!
NO WAY! I'VE HAD THIS SINCE I WAS A KID!
YOU ARE UNDER ARREST FOR VIOLATION OF CODE 119.
NOW DROP. YOUR. WAND.
NO.

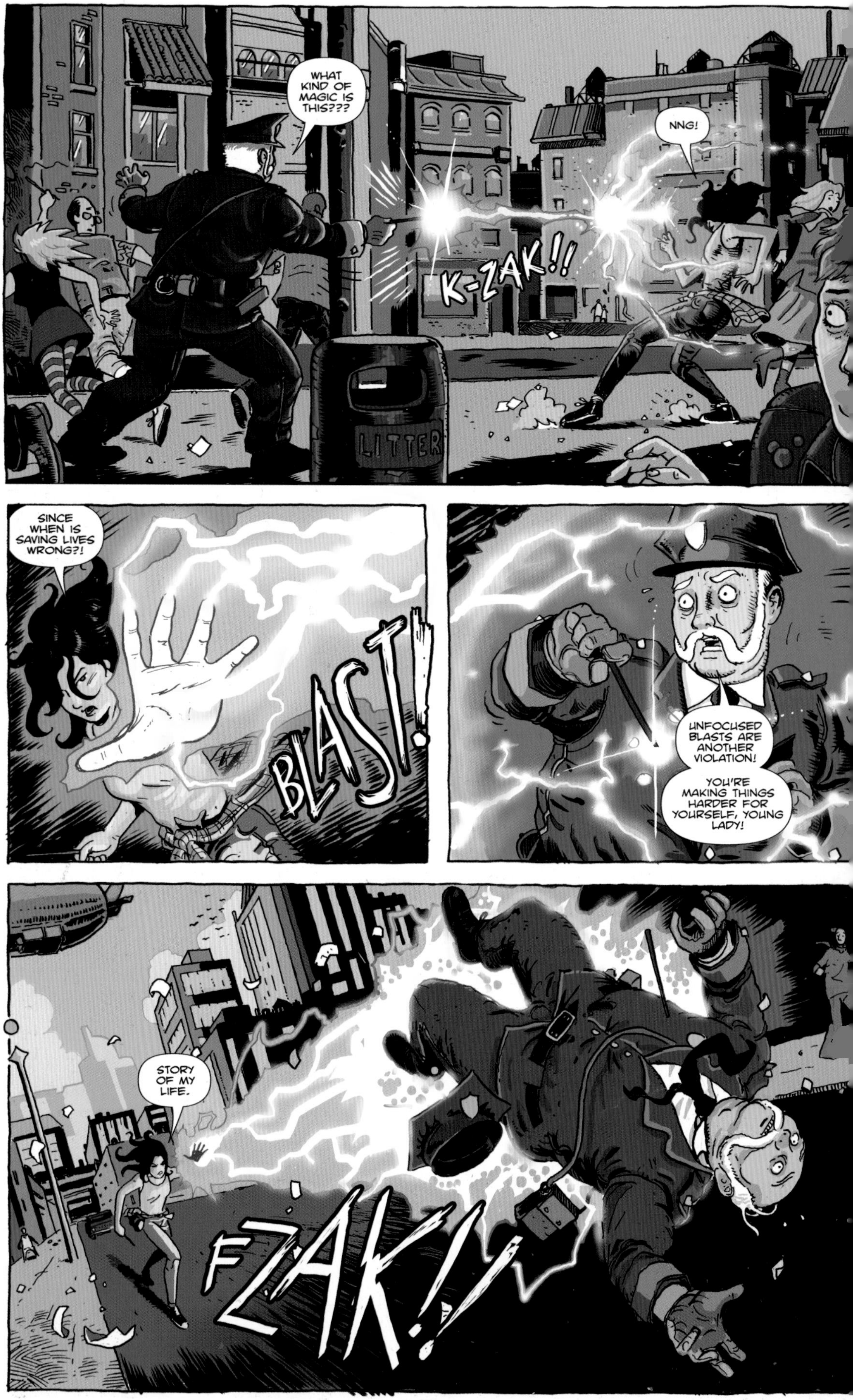
WHAT KIND OF MAGIC IS THIS???
NNG!
K-ZAK!!
SINCE WHEN IS SAVING LIVES WRONG?!
BLAST!
UNFOCUSED BLASTS ARE ANOTHER VIOLATION!
YOU'RE MAKING THINGS HARDER FOR YOURSELF, YOUNG LADY!
STORY OF MY LIFE.
FZAK!!

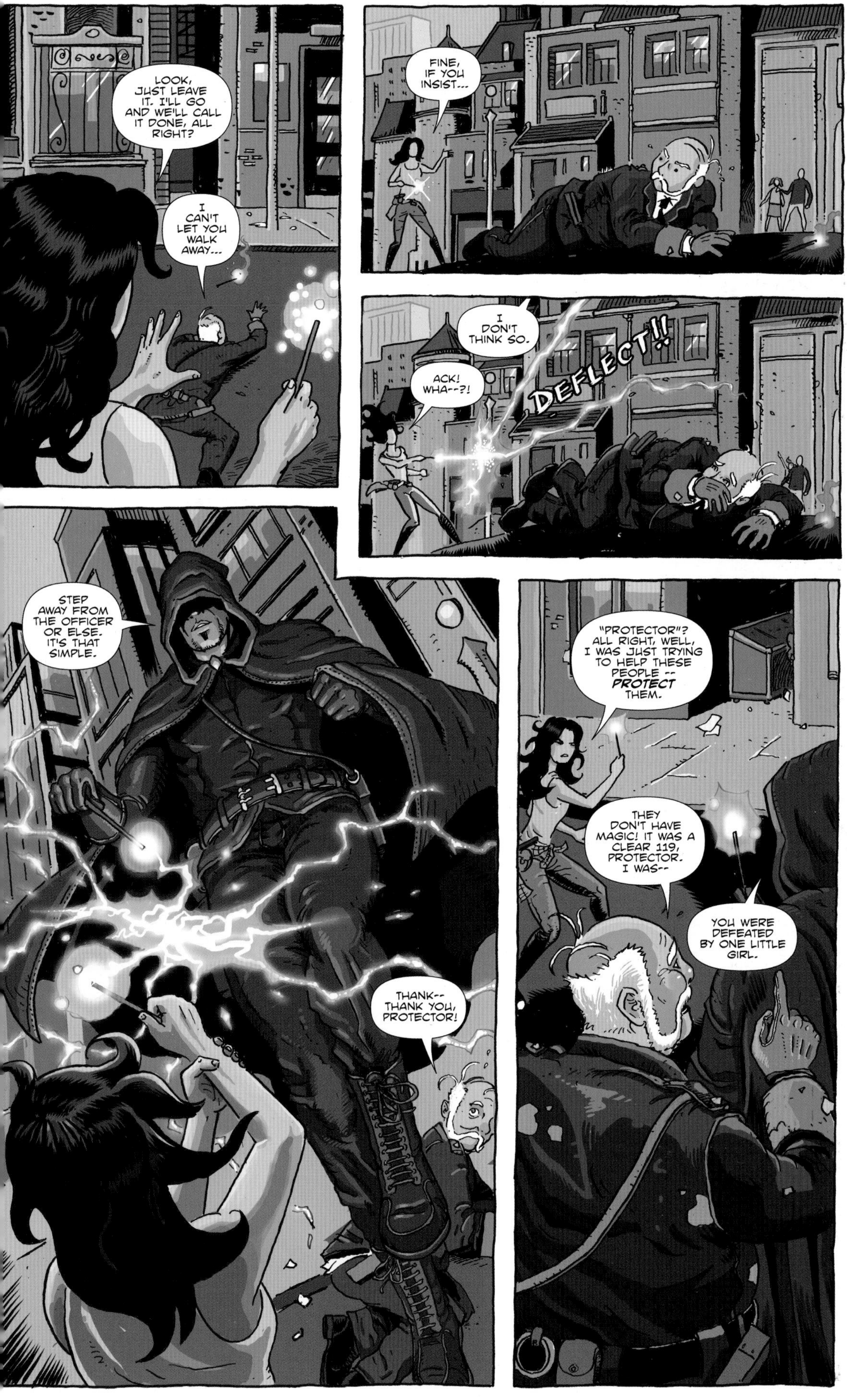
LOOK, JUST LEAVE IT. I'LL GO AND WE'LL CALL IT DONE, ALL RIGHT?
I CAN'T LET YOU WALK AWAY...
FINE, IF YOU INSIST...
I DON'T THINK SO.
ACK! WHA--?!
DEFLECT!!
STEP AWAY FROM THE OFFICER OR ELSE. IT'S THAT SIMPLE.
THANK-- THANK YOU, PROTECTOR!
"PROTECTOR"? ALL RIGHT, WELL, I WAS JUST TRYING TO HELP THESE PEOPLE -- *PROTECT* THEM.
THEY DON'T HAVE MAGIC! IT WAS A CLEAR 119, PROTECTOR. I WAS--
YOU WERE DEFEATED BY ONE LITTLE GIRL.

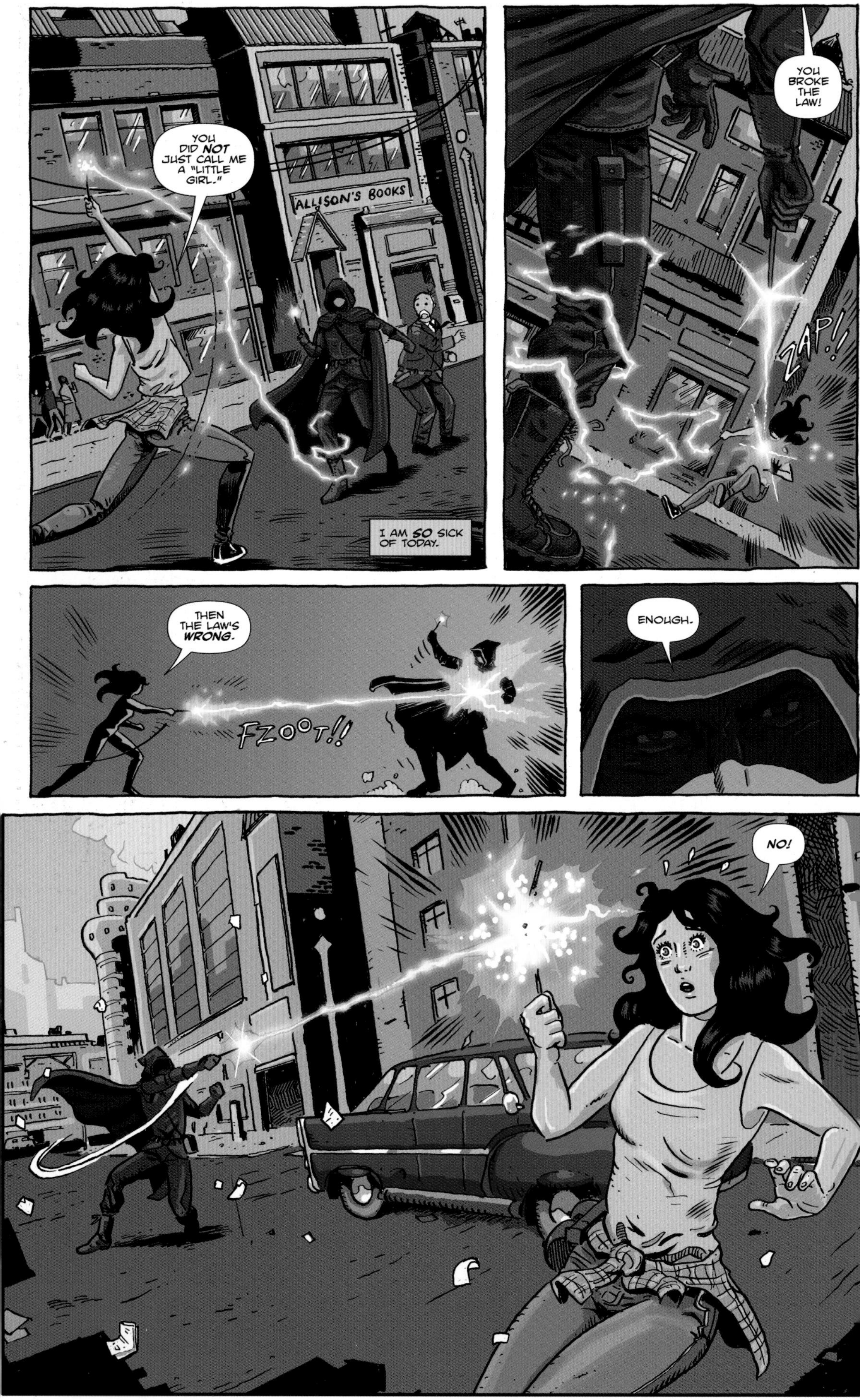
YOU DID NOT JUST CALL ME A "LITTLE GIRL."
ALLISON'S BOOKS
I AM SO SICK OF TODAY.
YOU BROKE THE LAW!
ZAP!!
THEN THE LAW'S WRONG.
FZOOT!!
ENOUGH.
NO!

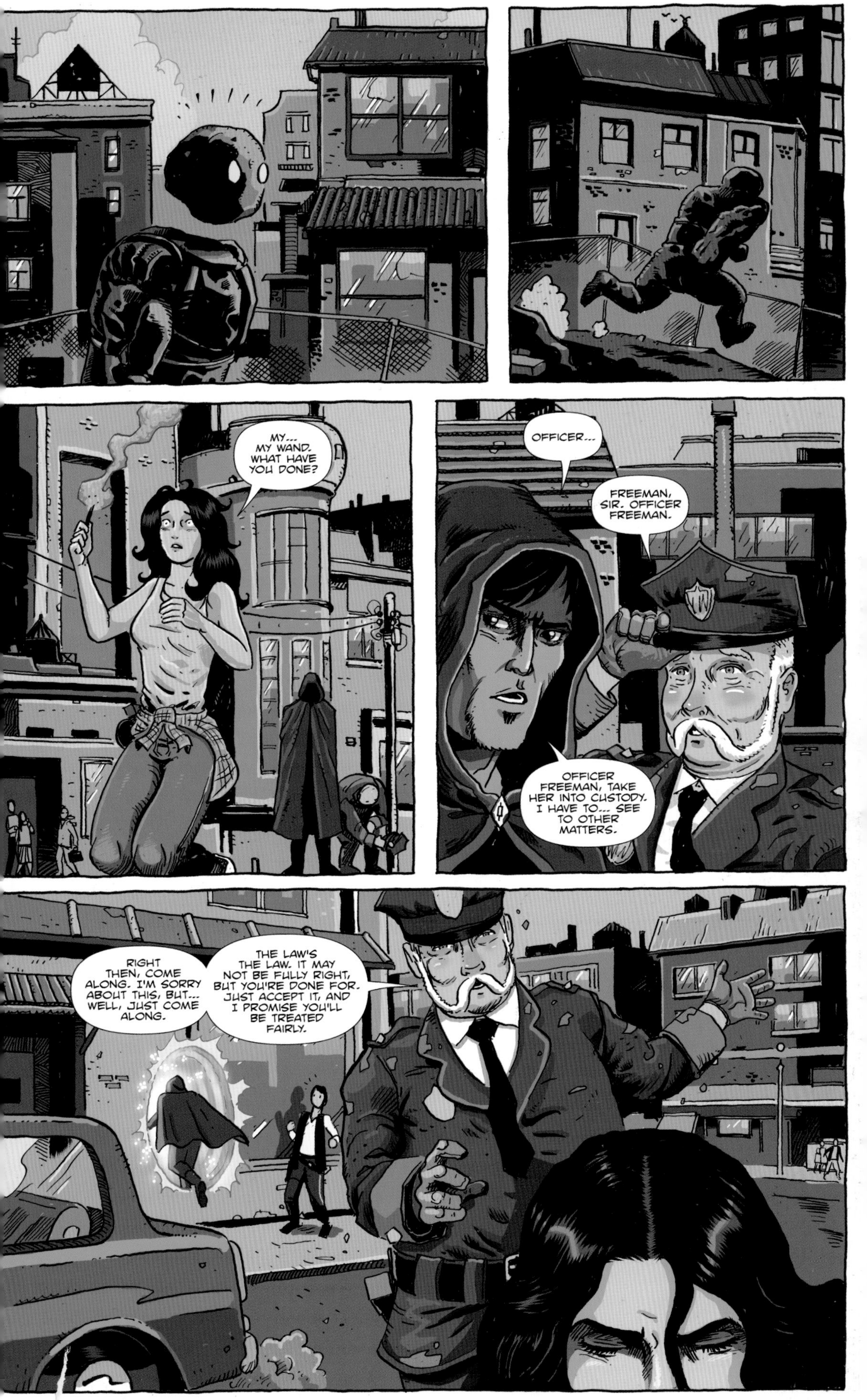
MY... MY WAND. WHAT HAVE YOU DONE?
OFFICER...
FREEMAN, SIR. OFFICER FREEMAN.
OFFICER FREEMAN, TAKE HER INTO CUSTODY. I HAVE TO... SEE TO OTHER MATTERS.
RIGHT THEN, COME ALONG. I'M SORRY ABOUT THIS, BUT... WELL, JUST COME ALONG.
THE LAW'S THE LAW. IT MAY NOT BE FULLY RIGHT, BUT YOU'RE DONE FOR. JUST ACCEPT IT, AND I PROMISE YOU'LL BE TREATED FAIRLY.

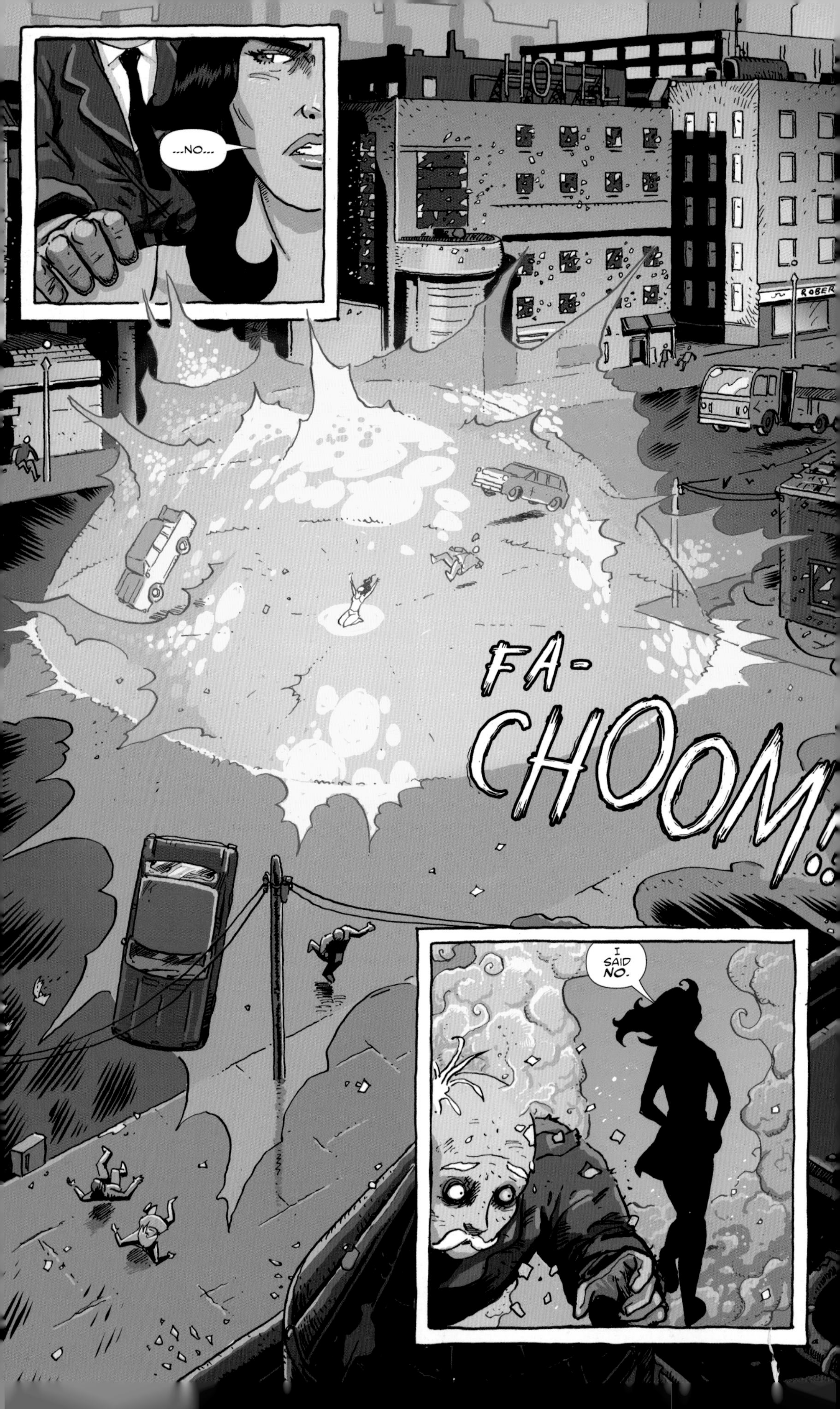
...NO...
HOTEL
FA-CHOOM!!
I SAID NO.

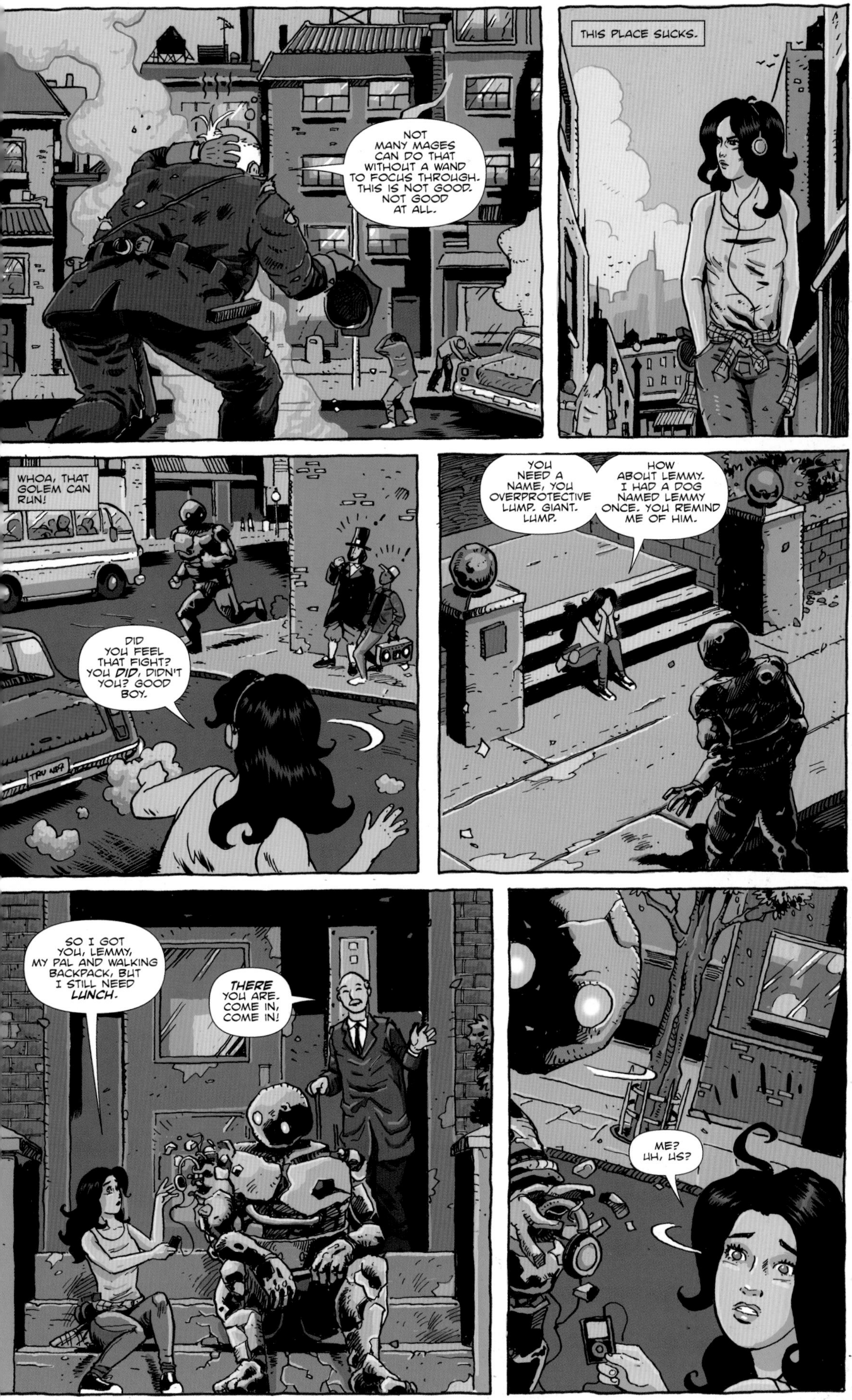
NOT MANY MAGES CAN DO THAT WITHOUT A WAND TO FOCUS THROUGH. THIS IS NOT GOOD. NOT GOOD AT ALL.
THIS PLACE SUCKS.
WHOA, THAT GOLEM CAN RUN!
DID YOU FEEL THAT FIGHT? YOU *DID*, DIDN'T YOU? GOOD BOY.
YOU NEED A NAME, YOU OVERPROTECTIVE LUMP. GIANT. LUMP.
HOW ABOUT LEMMY. I HAD A DOG NAMED LEMMY ONCE. YOU REMIND ME OF HIM.
SO I GOT YOU, LEMMY, MY PAL AND WALKING BACKPACK, BUT I STILL NEED ***LUNCH.***
THERE YOU ARE. COME IN, COME IN!
ME? UH, US?

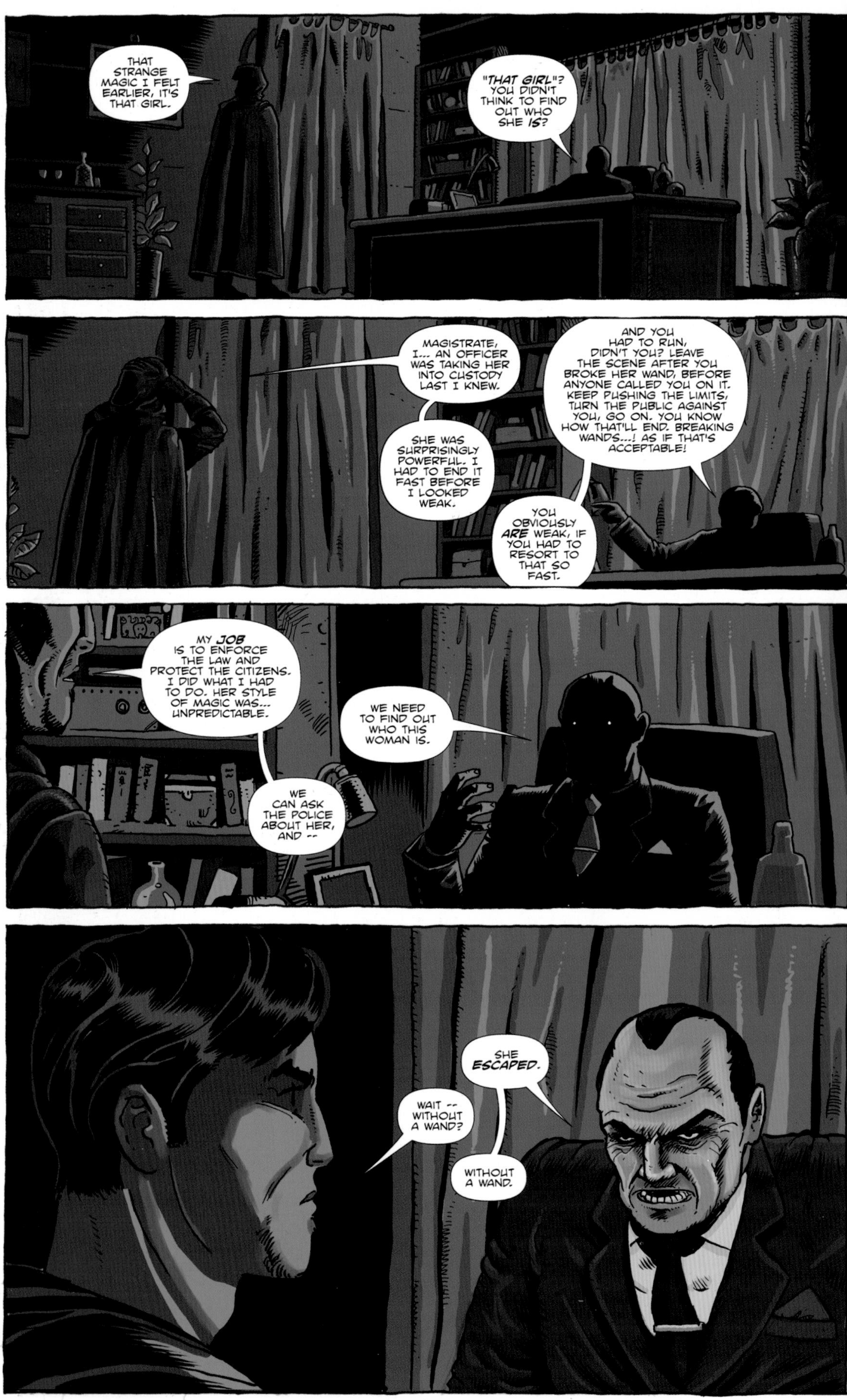
THAT STRANGE MAGIC I FELT EARLIER, IT'S THAT GIRL.
"THAT GIRL"? YOU DIDN'T THINK TO FIND OUT WHO SHE IS?
MAGISTRATE, I... AN OFFICER WAS TAKING HER INTO CUSTODY LAST I KNEW.
SHE WAS SURPRISINGLY POWERFUL. I HAD TO END IT FAST BEFORE I LOOKED WEAK.
AND YOU HAD TO RUN, DIDN'T YOU? LEAVE THE SCENE AFTER YOU BROKE HER WAND, BEFORE ANYONE CALLED YOU ON IT. KEEP PUSHING THE LIMITS, TURN THE PUBLIC AGAINST YOU, GO ON. YOU KNOW HOW THAT'LL END. BREAKING WANDS...! AS IF THAT'S ACCEPTABLE!
YOU OBVIOUSLY ARE WEAK, IF YOU HAD TO RESORT TO THAT SO FAST.
MY JOB IS TO ENFORCE THE LAW AND PROTECT THE CITIZENS. I DID WHAT I HAD TO DO. HER STYLE OF MAGIC WAS... UNPREDICTABLE.
WE CAN ASK THE POLICE ABOUT HER, AND --
WE NEED TO FIND OUT WHO THIS WOMAN IS.
SHE ESCAPED.
WAIT -- WITHOUT A WAND?
WITHOUT A WAND.

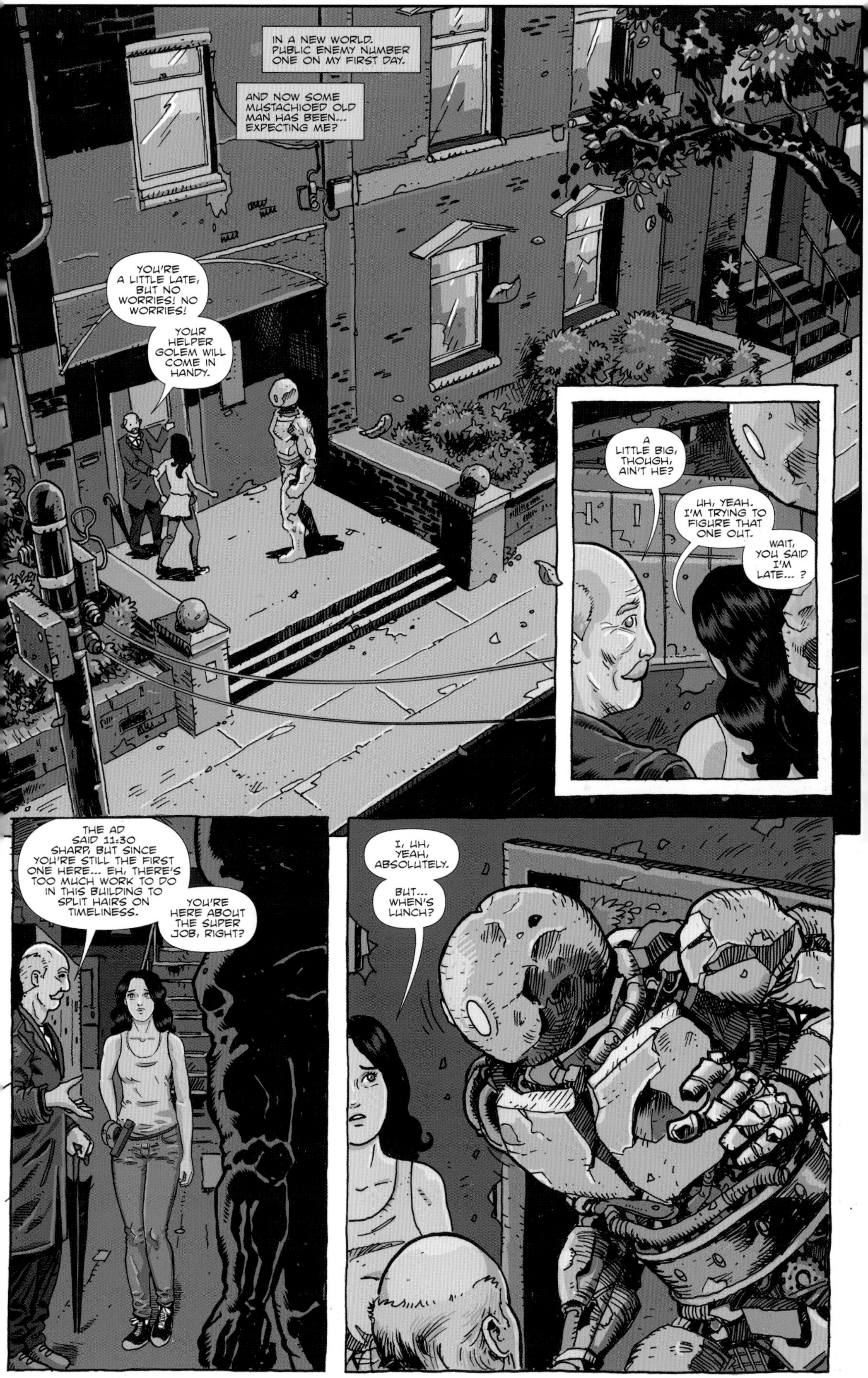
IN A NEW WORLD. PUBLIC ENEMY NUMBER ONE ON MY FIRST DAY.
AND NOW SOME MUSTACHIOED OLD MAN HAS BEEN... EXPECTING ME?
YOU'RE A LITTLE LATE, BUT NO WORRIES! NO WORRIES!
YOUR HELPER GOLEM WILL COME IN HANDY.
A LITTLE BIG, THOUGH, AIN'T HE?
UH, YEAH. I'M TRYING TO FIGURE THAT ONE OUT.
WAIT, YOU SAID I'M LATE... ?
THE AD SAID 11:30 SHARP, BUT SINCE YOU'RE STILL THE FIRST ONE HERE... EH, THERE'S TOO MUCH WORK TO DO IN THIS BUILDING TO SPLIT HAIRS ON TIMELINESS.
YOU'RE HERE ABOUT THE SUPER JOB, RIGHT?
I, UH, YEAH, ABSOLUTELY.
BUT... WHEN'S LUNCH?

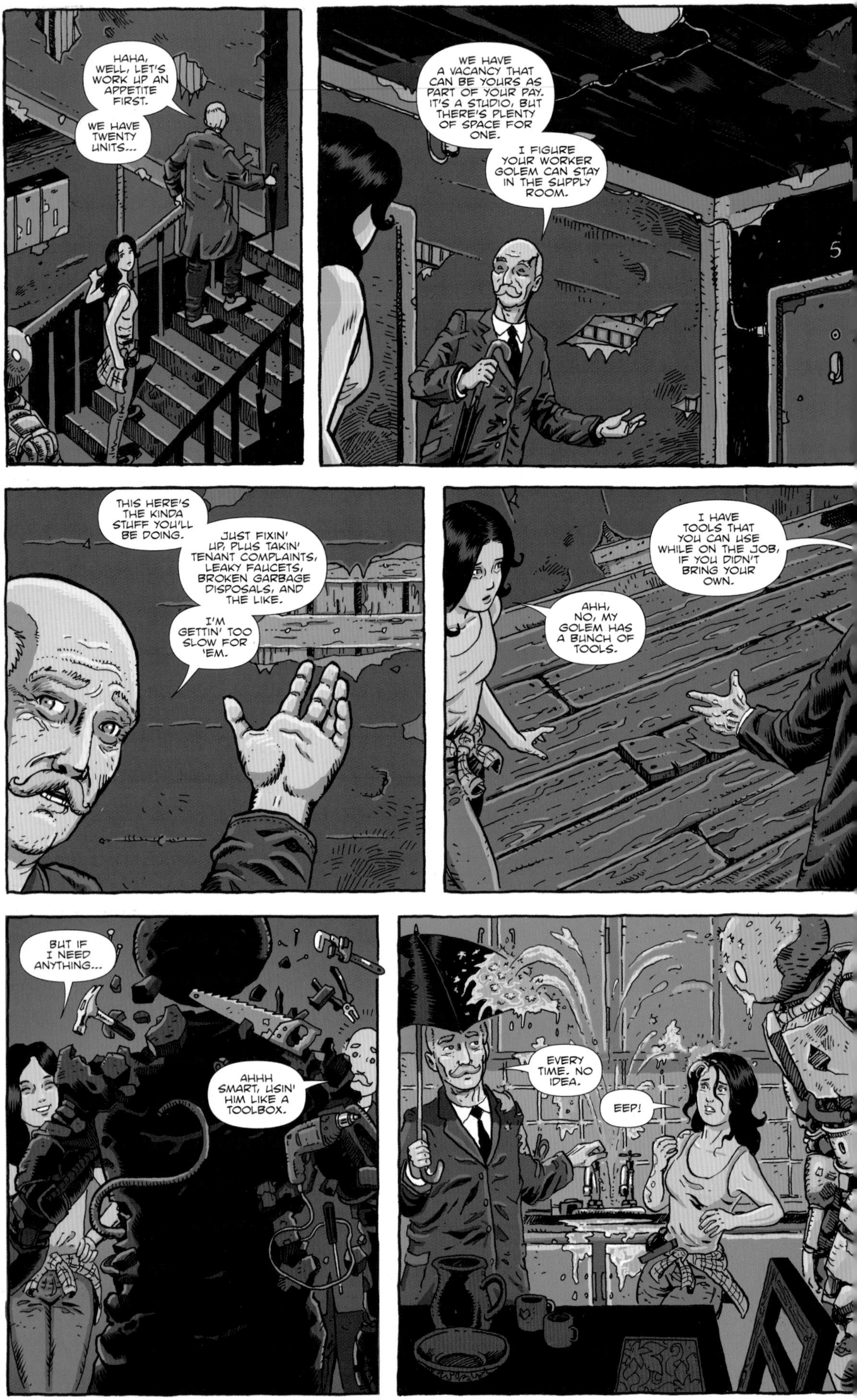
HAHA, WELL, LET'S WORK UP AN APPETITE FIRST.
WE HAVE TWENTY UNITS...
WE HAVE A VACANCY THAT CAN BE YOURS AS PART OF YOUR PAY. IT'S A STUDIO, BUT THERE'S PLENTY OF SPACE FOR ONE.
I FIGURE YOUR WORKER GOLEM CAN STAY IN THE SUPPLY ROOM.
5
THIS HERE'S THE KINDA STUFF YOU'LL BE DOING.
JUST FIXIN' UP, PLUS TAKIN' TENANT COMPLAINTS, LEAKY FAUCETS, BROKEN GARBAGE DISPOSALS, AND THE LIKE.
I'M GETTIN' TOO SLOW FOR 'EM.
I HAVE TOOLS THAT YOU CAN USE WHILE ON THE JOB, IF YOU DIDN'T BRING YOUR OWN.
AHH, NO, MY GOLEM HAS A BUNCH OF TOOLS.
BUT IF I NEED ANYTHING...
AHHH SMART, USIN' HIM LIKE A TOOLBOX.
EVERY TIME. NO IDEA.
EEP!

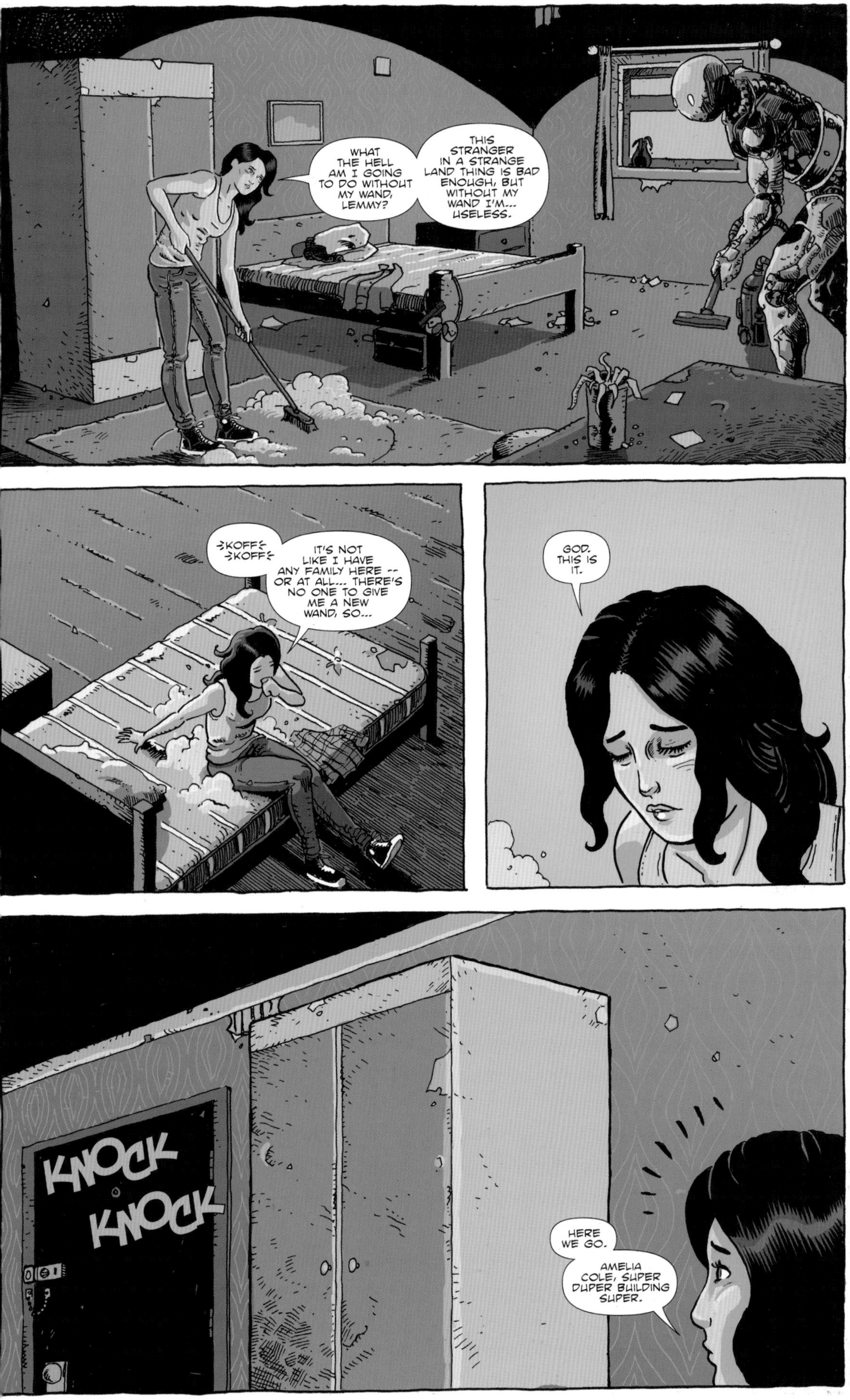
WHAT THE HELL AM I GOING TO DO WITHOUT MY WAND, LEMMY?
THIS STRANGER IN A STRANGE LAND THING IS BAD ENOUGH, BUT WITHOUT MY WAND I'M... USELESS.
-KOFF- -KOFF-
IT'S NOT LIKE I HAVE ANY FAMILY HERE -- OR AT ALL... THERE'S NO ONE TO GIVE ME A NEW WAND, SO...
GOD. THIS IS IT.
KNOCK KNOCK
HERE WE GO.
AMELIA COLE, SUPER DUPER BUILDING SUPER.

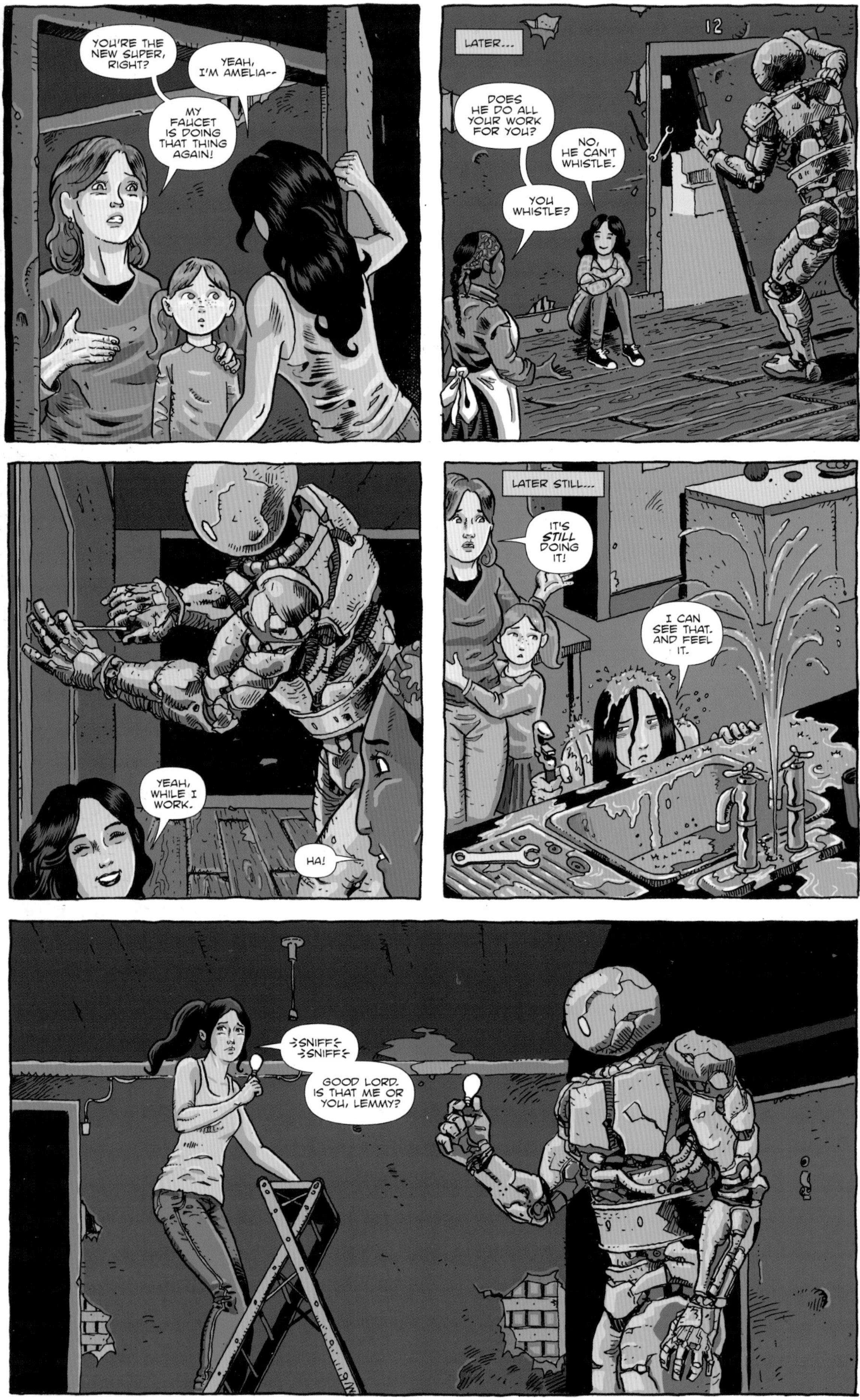
YOU'RE THE NEW SUPER, RIGHT?
YEAH, I'M AMELIA--
MY FAUCET IS DOING THAT THING AGAIN!
12
LATER...
DOES HE DO ALL YOUR WORK FOR YOU?
NO, HE CAN'T WHISTLE.
YOU WHISTLE?
YEAH, WHILE I WORK.
HA!
LATER STILL...
IT'S *STILL* DOING IT!
I CAN SEE THAT. AND FEEL IT.
SNIFF SNIFF
GOOD LORD. IS THAT ME OR YOU, LEMMY?

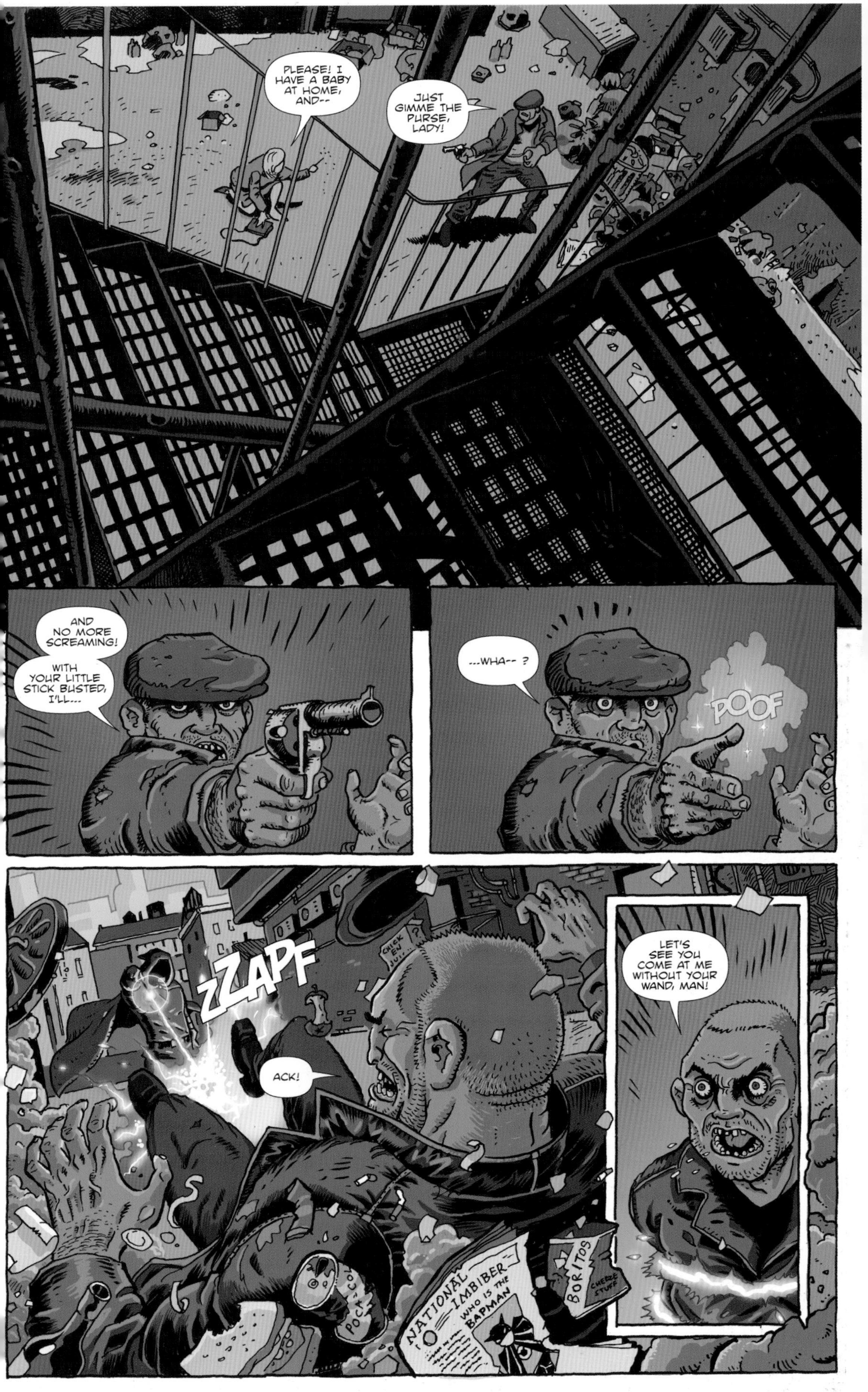
PLEASE! I HAVE A BABY AT HOME, AND--
JUST GIMME THE PURSE, LADY!
AND NO MORE SCREAMING!
WITH YOUR LITTLE STICK BUSTED, I'LL...
...WHA-- ?
POOF
ZZAPF
ACK!
NATIONAL IMBIBER
WHO IS THE BAPMAN
BORITOS
LET'S SEE YOU COME AT ME WITHOUT YOUR WAND, MAN!

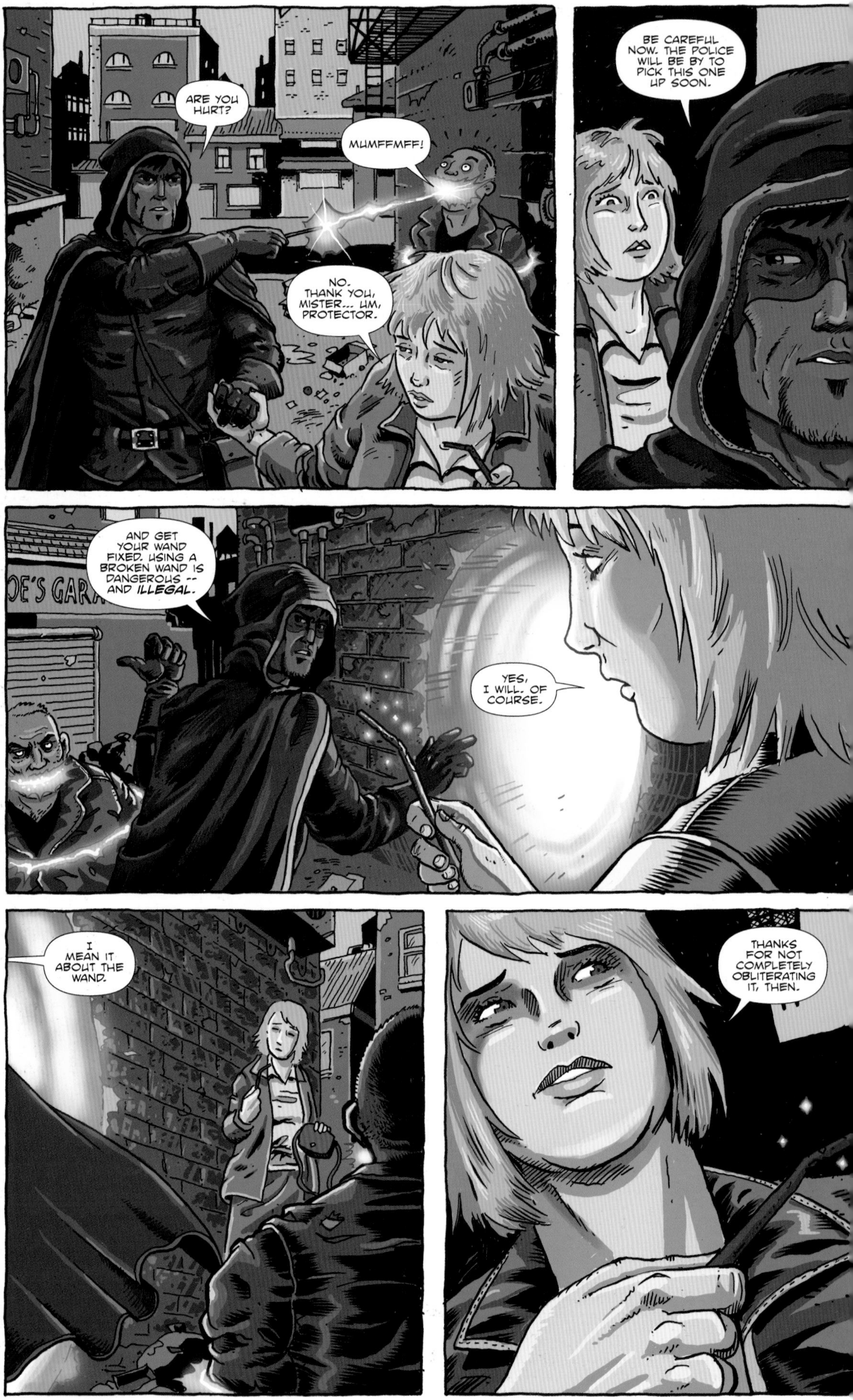

ARE YOU HURT?
MUMFFMFF!
NO. THANK YOU, MISTER... UM, PROTECTOR.
BE CAREFUL NOW. THE POLICE WILL BE BY TO PICK THIS ONE UP SOON.
AND GET YOUR WAND FIXED. USING A BROKEN WAND IS DANGEROUS -- AND *ILLEGAL*.
OE'S GARA
YES, I WILL. OF COURSE.
I MEAN IT ABOUT THE WAND.
THANKS FOR NOT COMPLETELY OBLITERATING IT, THEN.

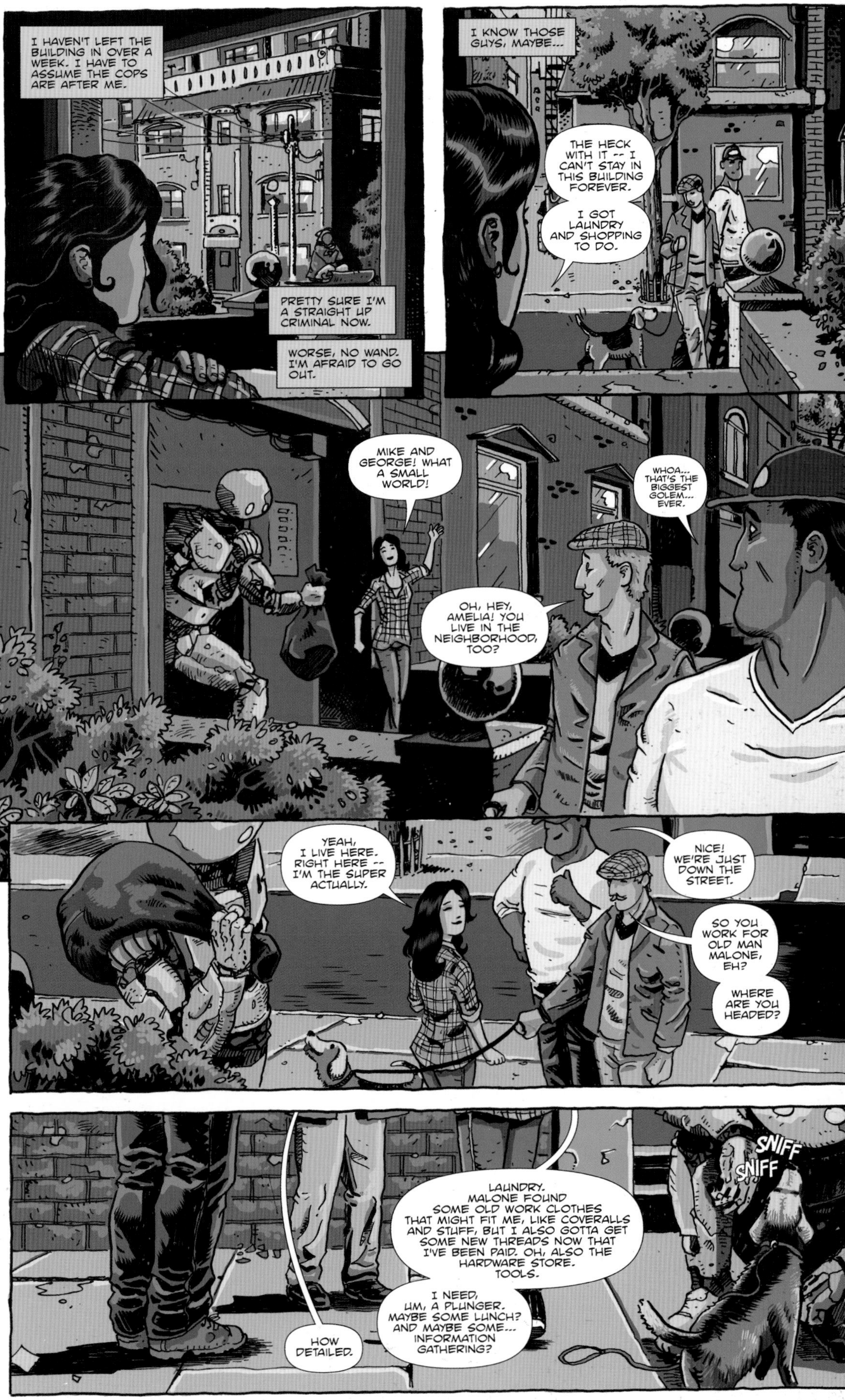
I HAVEN'T LEFT THE BUILDING IN OVER A WEEK. I HAVE TO ASSUME THE COPS ARE AFTER ME.
PRETTY SURE I'M A STRAIGHT UP CRIMINAL NOW.
WORSE, NO WAND. I'M AFRAID TO GO OUT.
I KNOW THOSE GUYS, MAYBE...
THE HECK WITH IT -- I CAN'T STAY IN THIS BUILDING FOREVER.
I GOT LAUNDRY AND SHOPPING TO DO.
MIKE AND GEORGE! WHAT A SMALL WORLD!
WHOA... THAT'S THE BIGGEST GOLEM... EVER.
OH, HEY, AMELIA! YOU LIVE IN THE NEIGHBORHOOD, TOO?
YEAH, I LIVE HERE. RIGHT HERE -- I'M THE SUPER ACTUALLY.
NICE! WE'RE JUST DOWN THE STREET.
SO YOU WORK FOR OLD MAN MALONE, EH?
WHERE ARE YOU HEADED?
LAUNDRY. MALONE FOUND SOME OLD WORK CLOTHES THAT MIGHT FIT ME, LIKE COVERALLS AND STUFF, BUT I ALSO GOTTA GET SOME NEW THREADS NOW THAT I'VE BEEN PAID. OH, ALSO THE HARDWARE STORE. TOOLS.
I NEED, UM, A PLUNGER. MAYBE SOME LUNCH? AND MAYBE SOME... INFORMATION GATHERING?
HOW DETAILED.
SNIFF
SNIFF

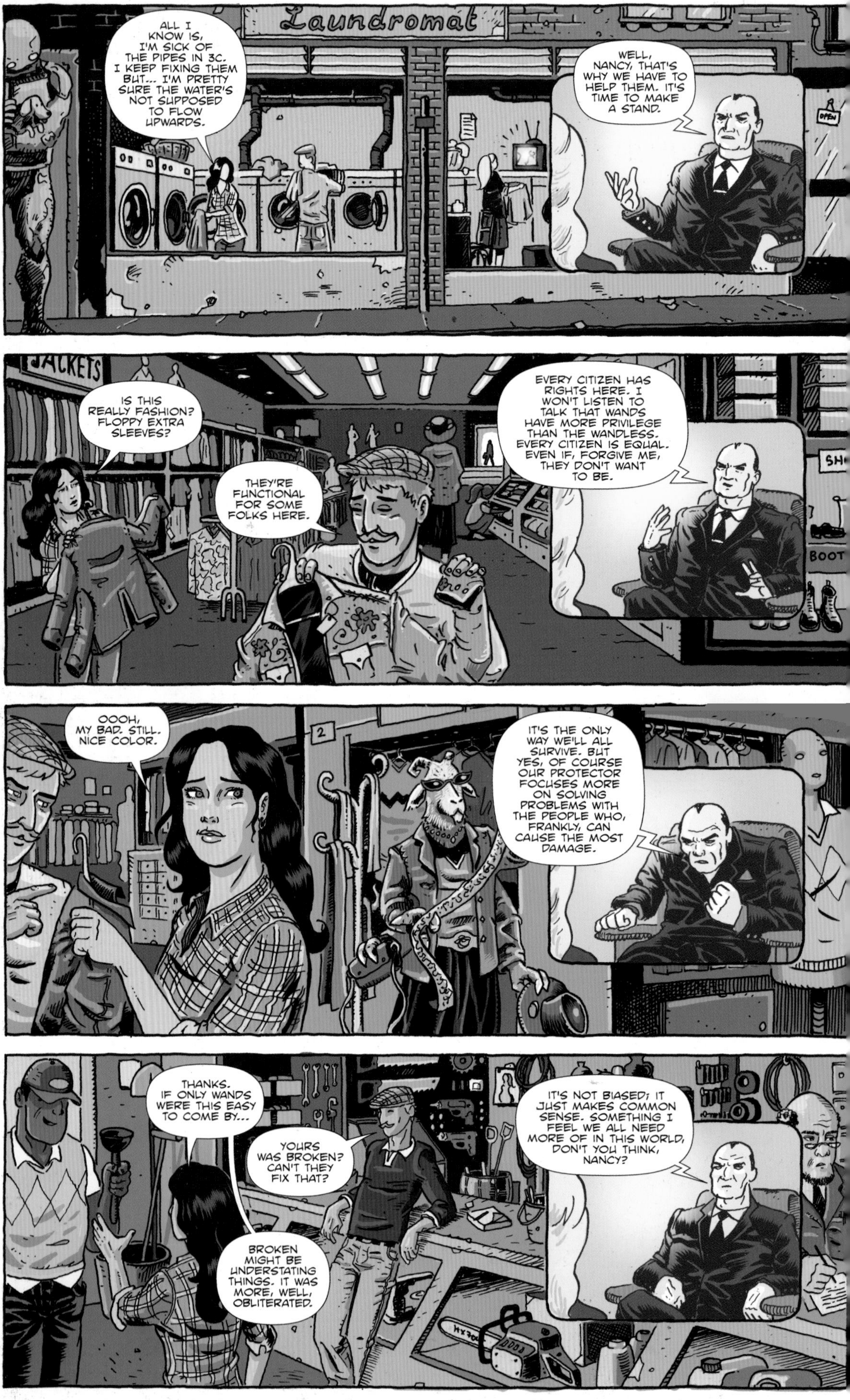
Laundromat
ALL I KNOW IS, I'M SICK OF THE PIPES IN 3C. I KEEP FIXING THEM BUT... I'M PRETTY SURE THE WATER'S NOT SUPPOSED TO FLOW UPWARDS.
WELL, NANCY, THAT'S WHY WE HAVE TO HELP THEM. IT'S TIME TO MAKE A STAND.
OPEN
JACKETS
IS THIS REALLY FASHION? FLOPPY EXTRA SLEEVES?
THEY'RE FUNCTIONAL FOR SOME FOLKS HERE.
EVERY CITIZEN HAS RIGHTS HERE. I WON'T LISTEN TO TALK THAT WANDS HAVE MORE PRIVILEGE THAN THE WANDLESS. EVERY CITIZEN IS EQUAL. EVEN IF, FORGIVE ME, THEY DON'T WANT TO BE.
BOOT
OOOH, MY BAD. STILL. NICE COLOR.
2
IT'S THE ONLY WAY WE'LL ALL SURVIVE. BUT YES, OF COURSE OUR PROTECTOR FOCUSES MORE ON SOLVING PROBLEMS WITH THE PEOPLE WHO, FRANKLY, CAN CAUSE THE MOST DAMAGE.
THANKS. IF ONLY WANDS WERE THIS EASY TO COME BY...
YOURS WAS BROKEN? CAN'T THEY FIX THAT?
BROKEN MIGHT BE UNDERSTATING THINGS. IT WAS MORE, WELL, OBLITERATED.
IT'S NOT BIASED; IT JUST MAKES COMMON SENSE. SOMETHING I FEEL WE ALL NEED MORE OF IN THIS WORLD, DON'T YOU THINK, NANCY?

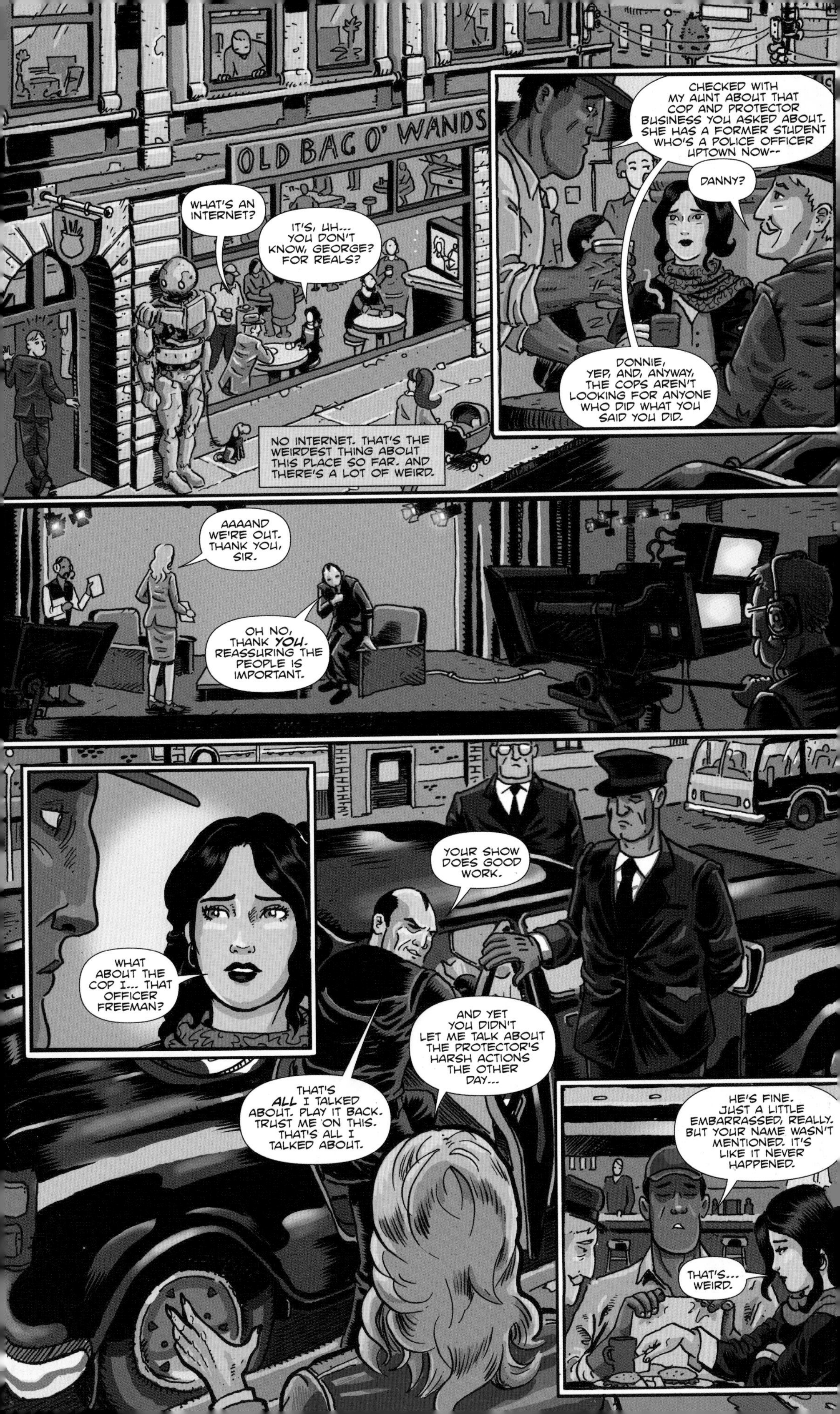
OLD BAG O' WANDS
WHAT'S AN INTERNET?
IT'S, UH... YOU DON'T KNOW, GEORGE? FOR REALS?
NO INTERNET. THAT'S THE WEIRDEST THING ABOUT THIS PLACE SO FAR. AND THERE'S A LOT OF WEIRD.
CHECKED WITH MY AUNT ABOUT THAT COP AND PROTECTOR BUSINESS YOU ASKED ABOUT. SHE HAS A FORMER STUDENT WHO'S A POLICE OFFICER UPTOWN NOW--
DANNY?
DONNIE, YEP, AND, ANYWAY, THE COPS AREN'T LOOKING FOR ANYONE WHO DID WHAT YOU SAID YOU DID.
AAAAND WE'RE OUT. THANK YOU, SIR.
OH NO, THANK *YOU*. REASSURING THE PEOPLE IS IMPORTANT.
WHAT ABOUT THE COP I... THAT OFFICER FREEMAN?
YOUR SHOW DOES GOOD WORK.
AND YET YOU DIDN'T LET ME TALK ABOUT THE PROTECTOR'S HARSH ACTIONS THE OTHER DAY...
THAT'S *ALL* I TALKED ABOUT. PLAY IT BACK. TRUST ME ON THIS. THAT'S ALL I TALKED ABOUT.
HE'S FINE. JUST A LITTLE EMBARRASSED, REALLY. BUT YOUR NAME WASN'T MENTIONED. IT'S LIKE IT NEVER HAPPENED.
THAT'S... WEIRD.

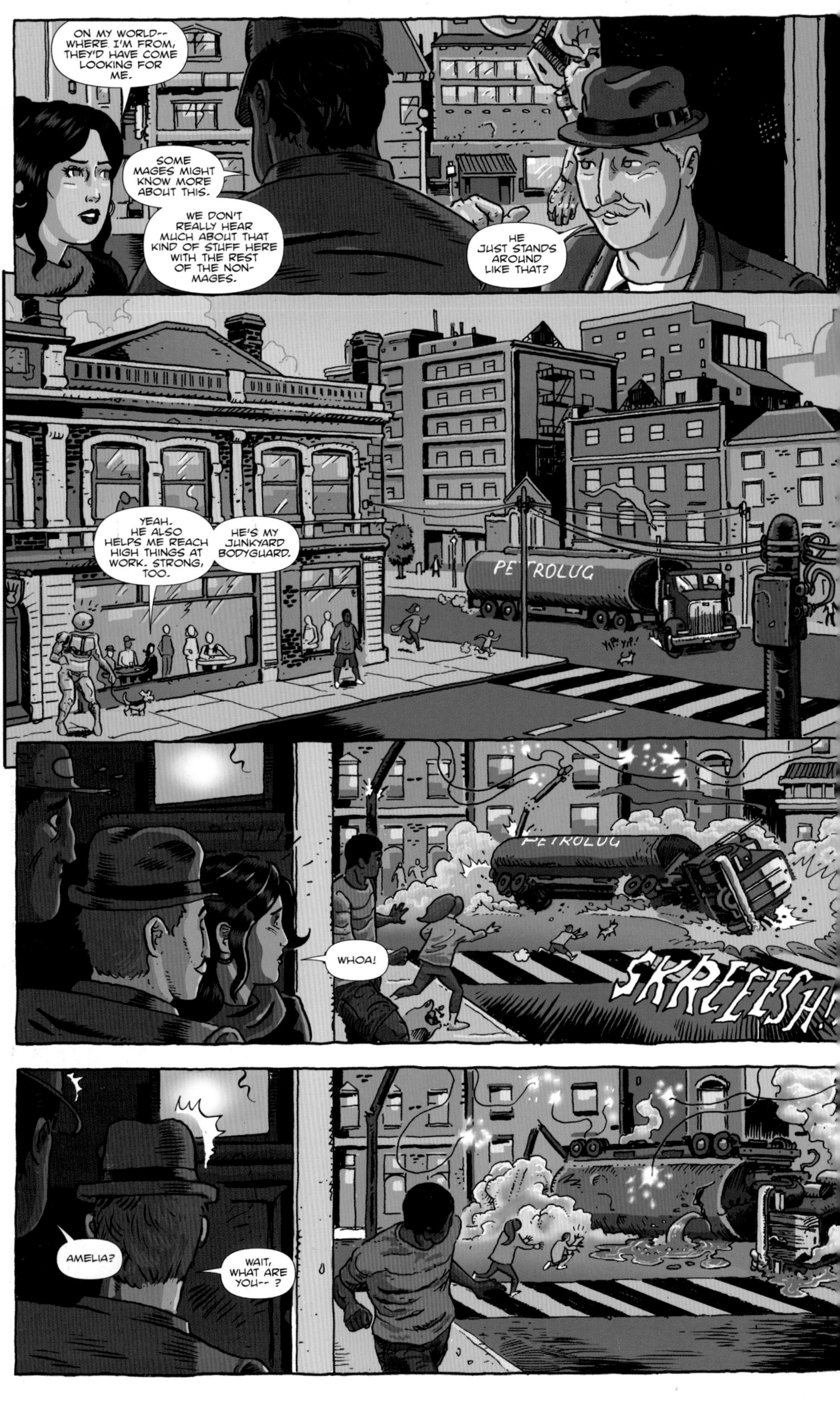
ON MY WORLD-- WHERE I'M FROM, THEY'D HAVE COME LOOKING FOR ME.
SOME MAGES MIGHT KNOW MORE ABOUT THIS.
WE DON'T REALLY HEAR MUCH ABOUT THAT KIND OF STUFF HERE WITH THE REST OF THE NON-MAGES.
HE JUST STANDS AROUND LIKE THAT?
YEAH. HE ALSO HELPS ME REACH HIGH THINGS AT WORK. STRONG, TOO.
HE'S MY JUNKYARD BODYGUARD.
PETROLUG
YIP! YIP!
PETROLUG
WHOA!
SKREEESH!
AMELIA?
WAIT, WHAT ARE YOU-- ?

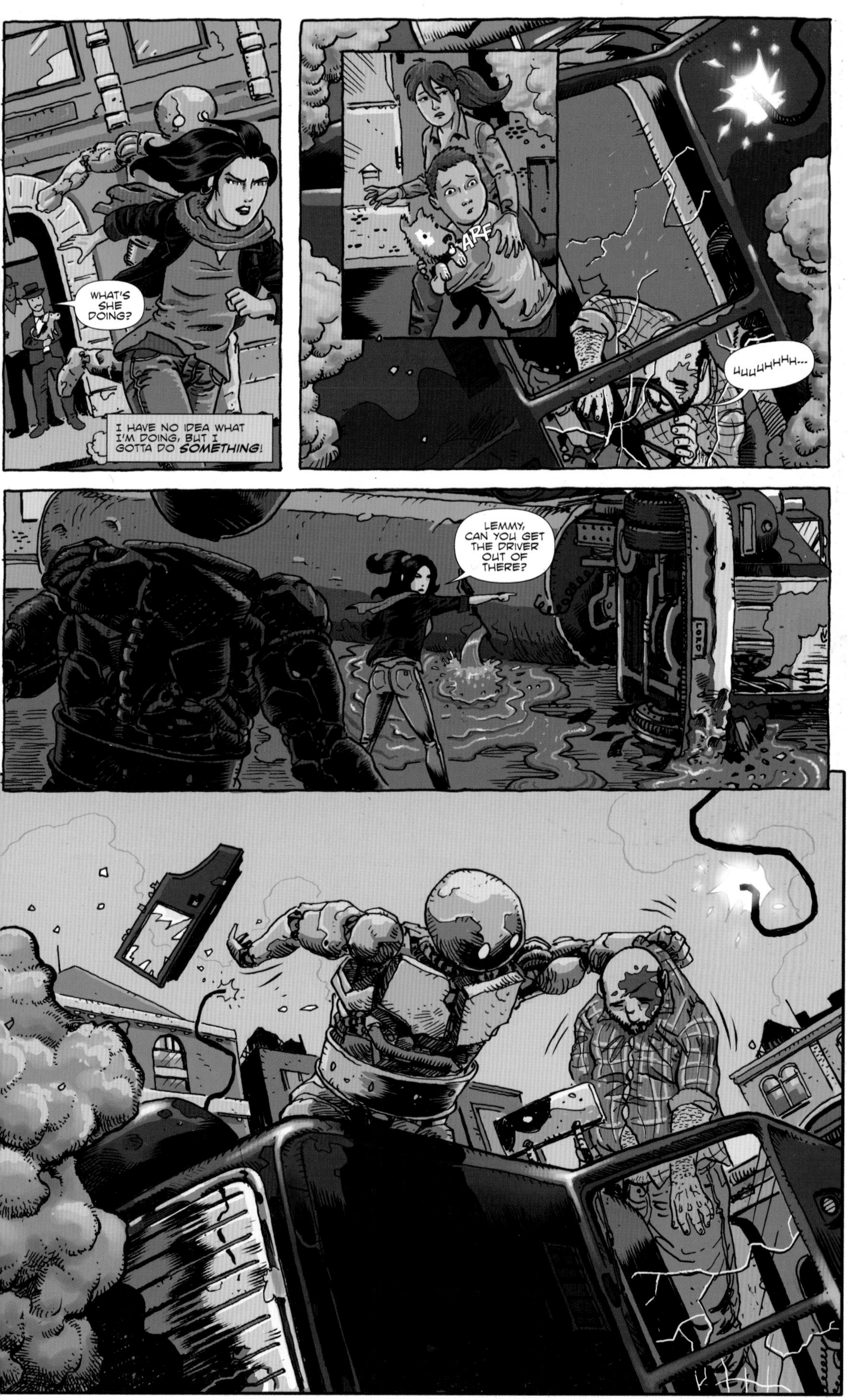
WHAT'S SHE DOING?
I HAVE NO IDEA WHAT I'M DOING, BUT I GOTTA DO SOMETHING!
ARF
UUUHHHHH...
LEMMY, CAN YOU GET THE DRIVER OUT OF THERE?

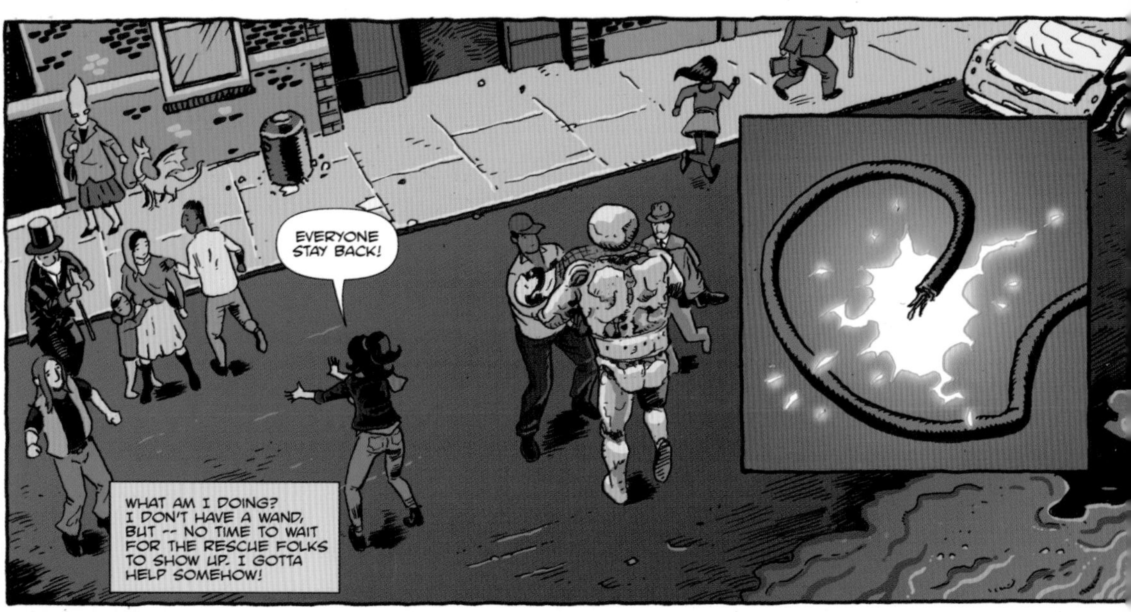
EVERYONE STAY BACK!
WHAT AM I DOING? I DON'T HAVE A WAND, BUT -- NO TIME TO WAIT FOR THE RESCUE FOLKS TO SHOW UP. I GOTTA HELP SOMEHOW!

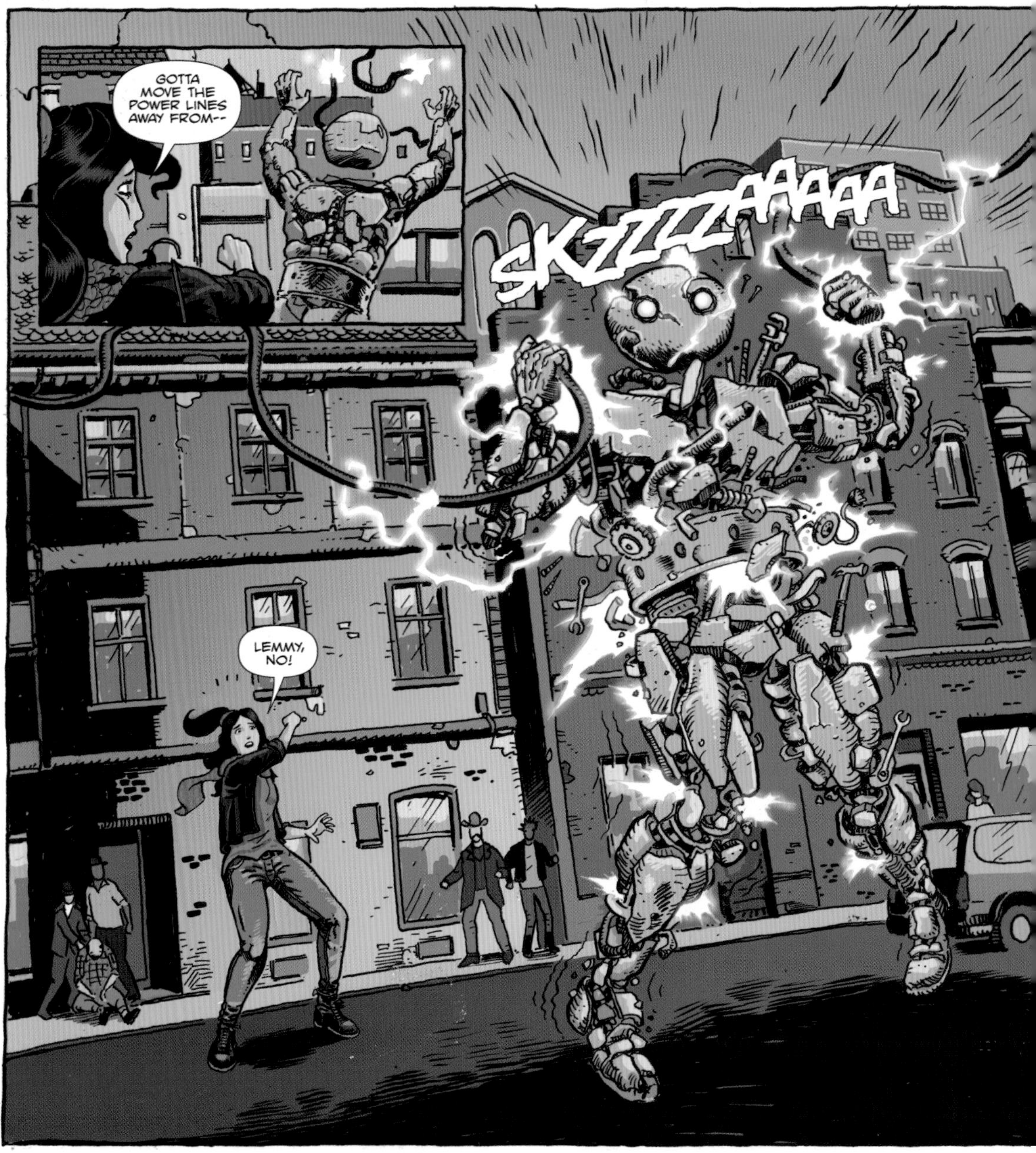
GOTTA MOVE THE POWER LINES AWAY FROM--
SKZZZZAAAAA
LEMMY, NO!

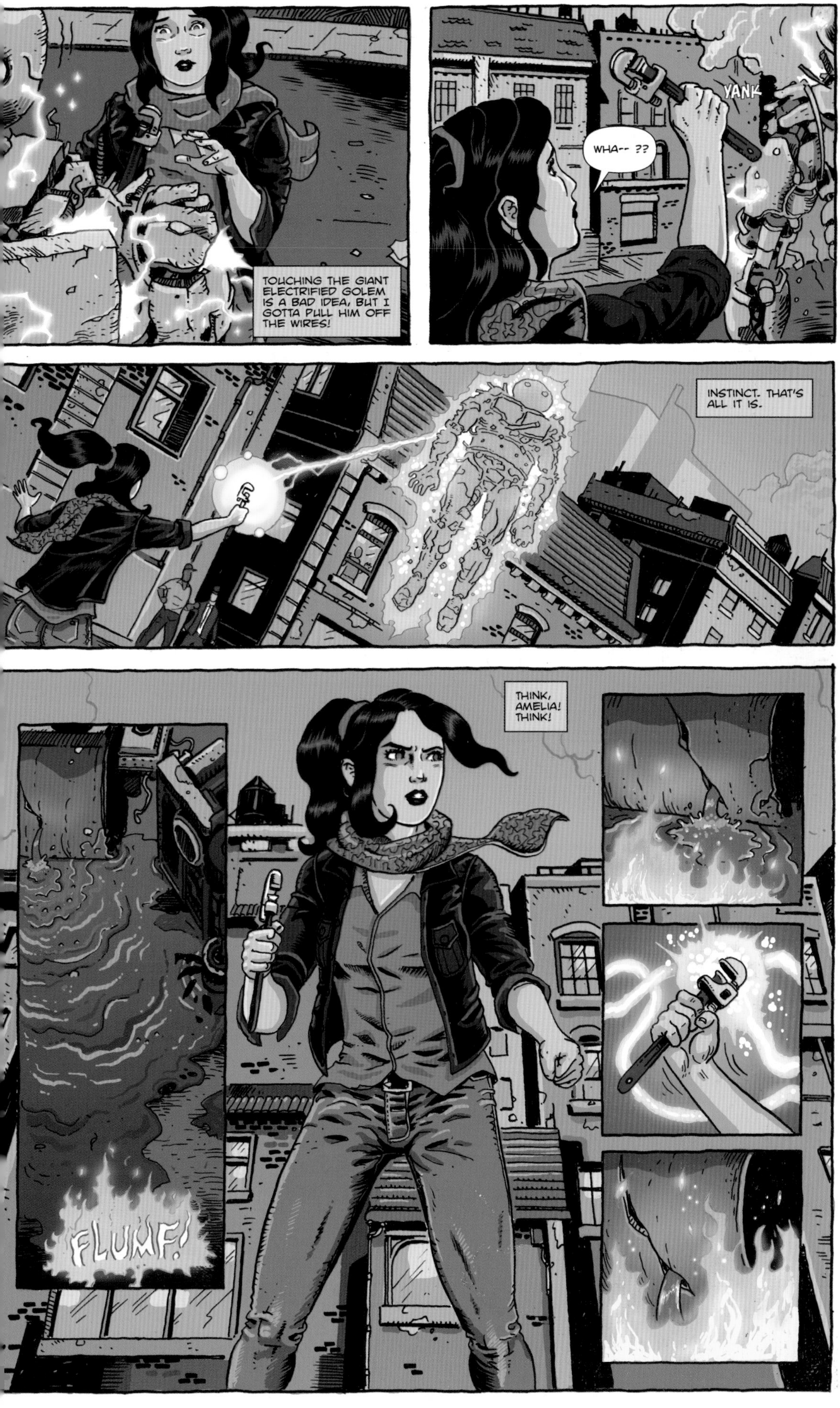
TOUCHING THE GIANT ELECTRIFIED GOLEM IS A BAD IDEA, BUT I GOTTA PULL HIM OFF THE WIRES!
YANK
WHA-- ??
INSTINCT. THAT'S ALL IT IS.
THINK, AMELIA! THINK!
FLUMF!

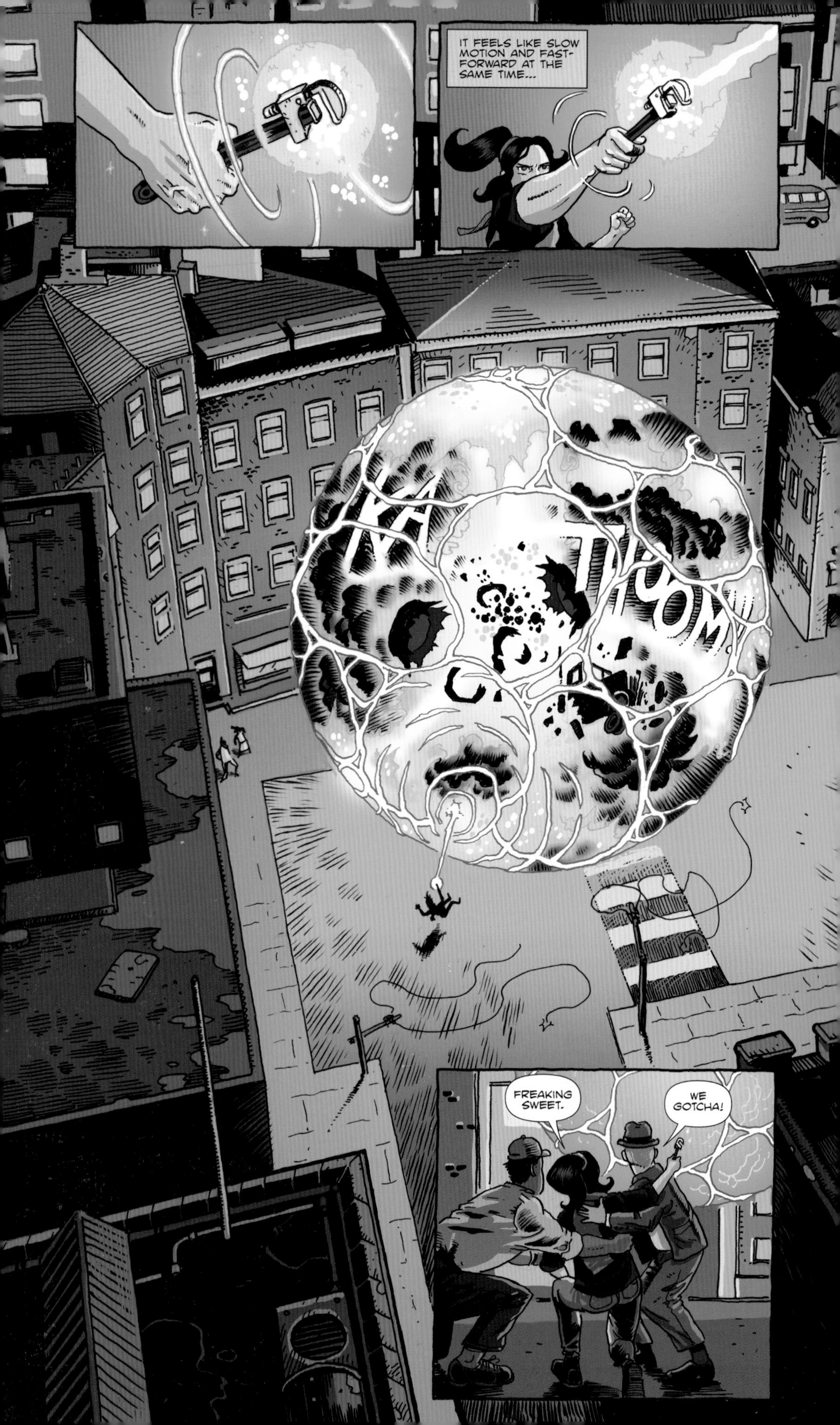

IT FEELS LIKE SLOW MOTION AND FAST-FORWARD AT THE SAME TIME...
KA
THOOM
FREAKING SWEET.
WE GOTCHA!

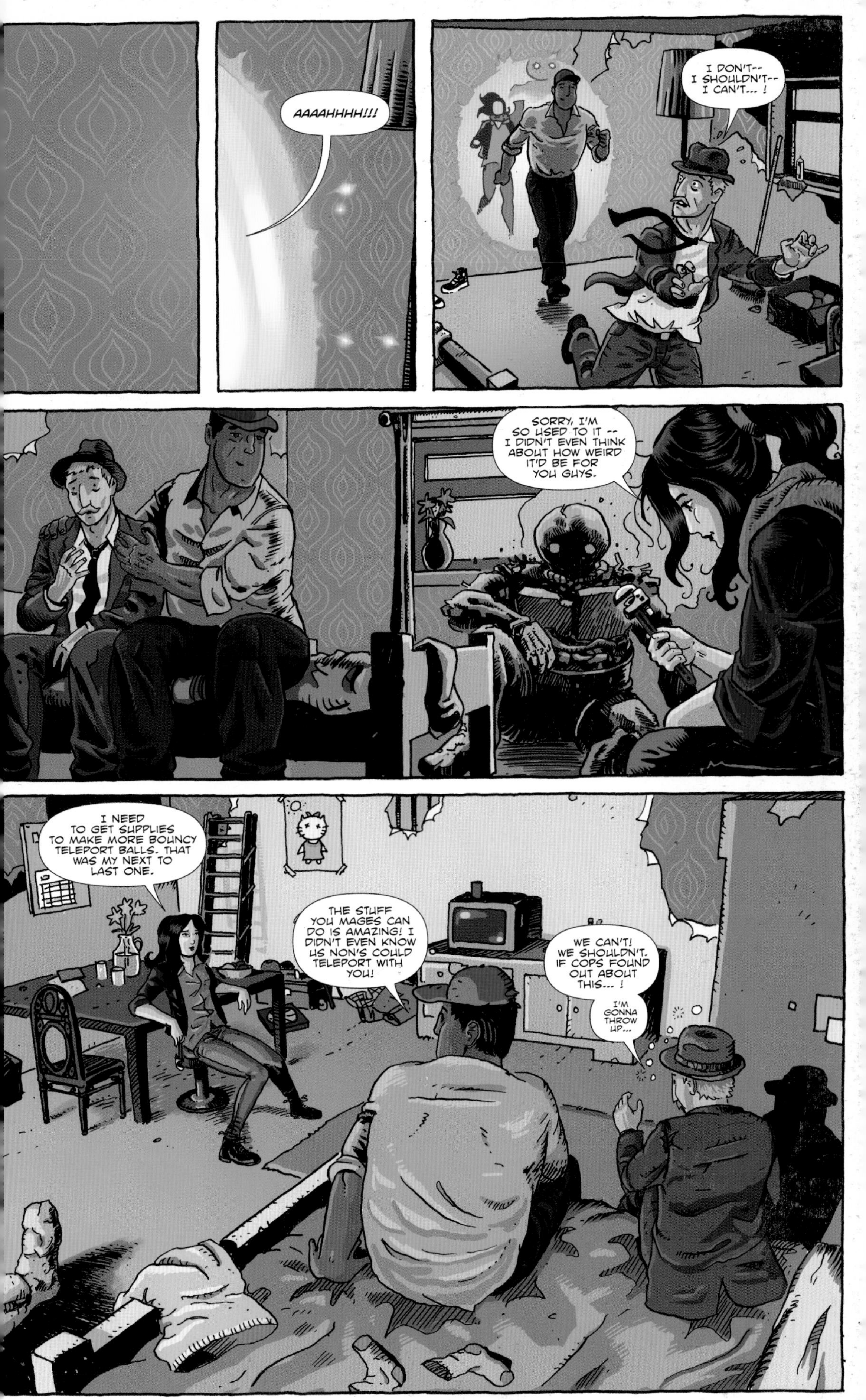

AAAAHHHH!!!
I DON'T-- I SHOULDN'T-- I CAN'T... !
SORRY, I'M SO USED TO IT -- I DIDN'T EVEN THINK ABOUT HOW WEIRD IT'D BE FOR YOU GUYS.
I NEED TO GET SUPPLIES TO MAKE MORE BOUNCY TELEPORT BALLS. THAT WAS MY NEXT TO LAST ONE.
THE STUFF YOU MAGES CAN DO IS AMAZING! I DIDN'T EVEN KNOW US NON'S COULD TELEPORT WITH YOU!
WE CAN'T! WE SHOULDN'T. IF COPS FOUND OUT ABOUT THIS... !
I'M GONNA THROW UP...

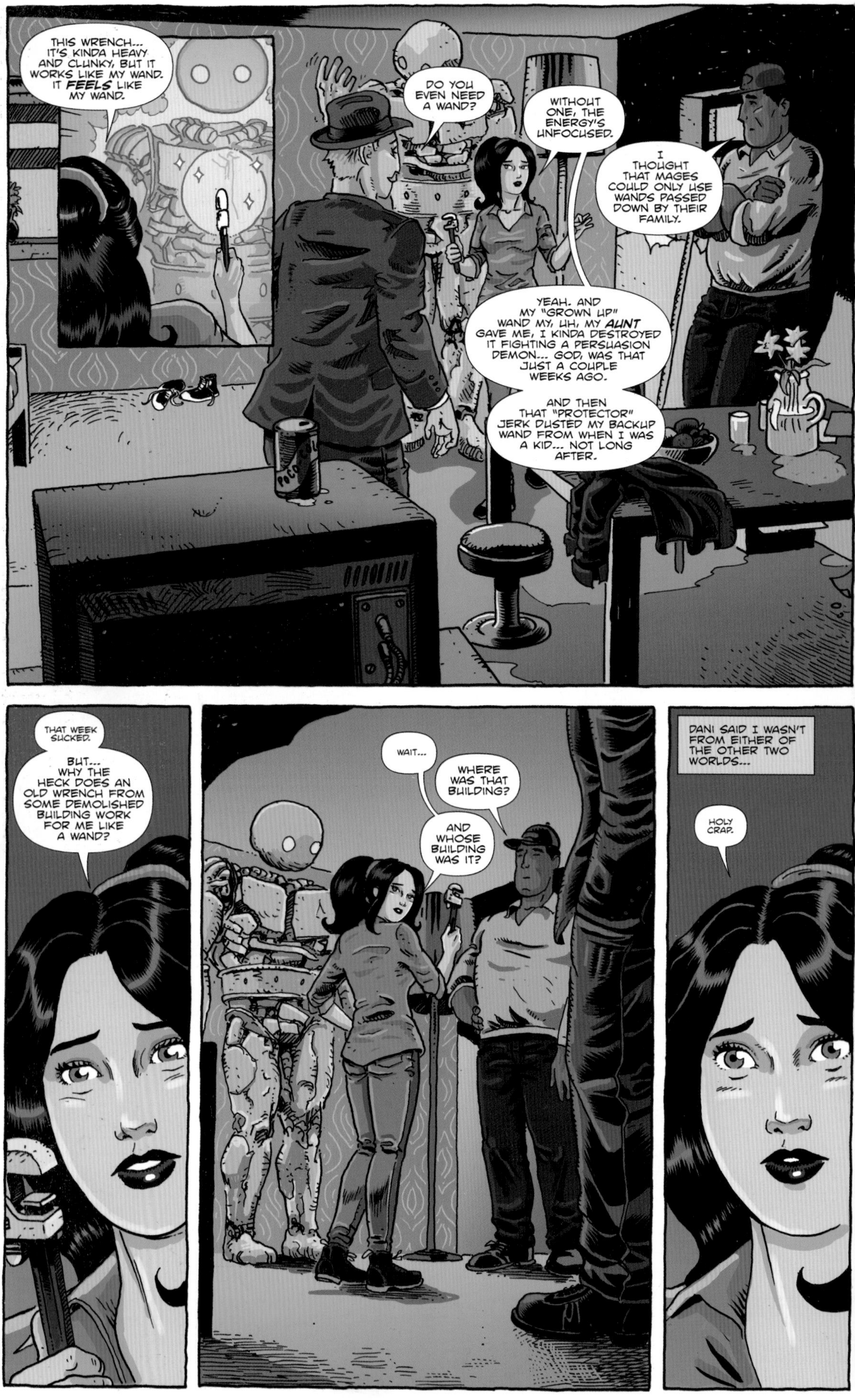
THIS WRENCH... IT'S KINDA HEAVY AND CLUNKY, BUT IT WORKS LIKE MY WAND. IT FEELS LIKE MY WAND.
DO YOU EVEN NEED A WAND?
WITHOUT ONE, THE ENERGY'S UNFOCUSED.
I THOUGHT THAT MAGES COULD ONLY USE WANDS PASSED DOWN BY THEIR FAMILY.
YEAH. AND MY "GROWN UP" WAND MY, UH, MY AUNT GAVE ME, I KINDA DESTROYED IT FIGHTING A PERSUASION DEMON... GOD, WAS THAT JUST A COUPLE WEEKS AGO.
AND THEN THAT "PROTECTOR" JERK DUSTED MY BACKUP WAND FROM WHEN I WAS A KID... NOT LONG AFTER.
THAT WEEK SUCKED.
BUT... WHY THE HECK DOES AN OLD WRENCH FROM SOME DEMOLISHED BUILDING WORK FOR ME LIKE A WAND?
WAIT...
WHERE WAS THAT BUILDING?
AND WHOSE BUILDING WAS IT?
DANI SAID I WASN'T FROM EITHER OF THE OTHER TWO WORLDS...
HOLY CRAP.

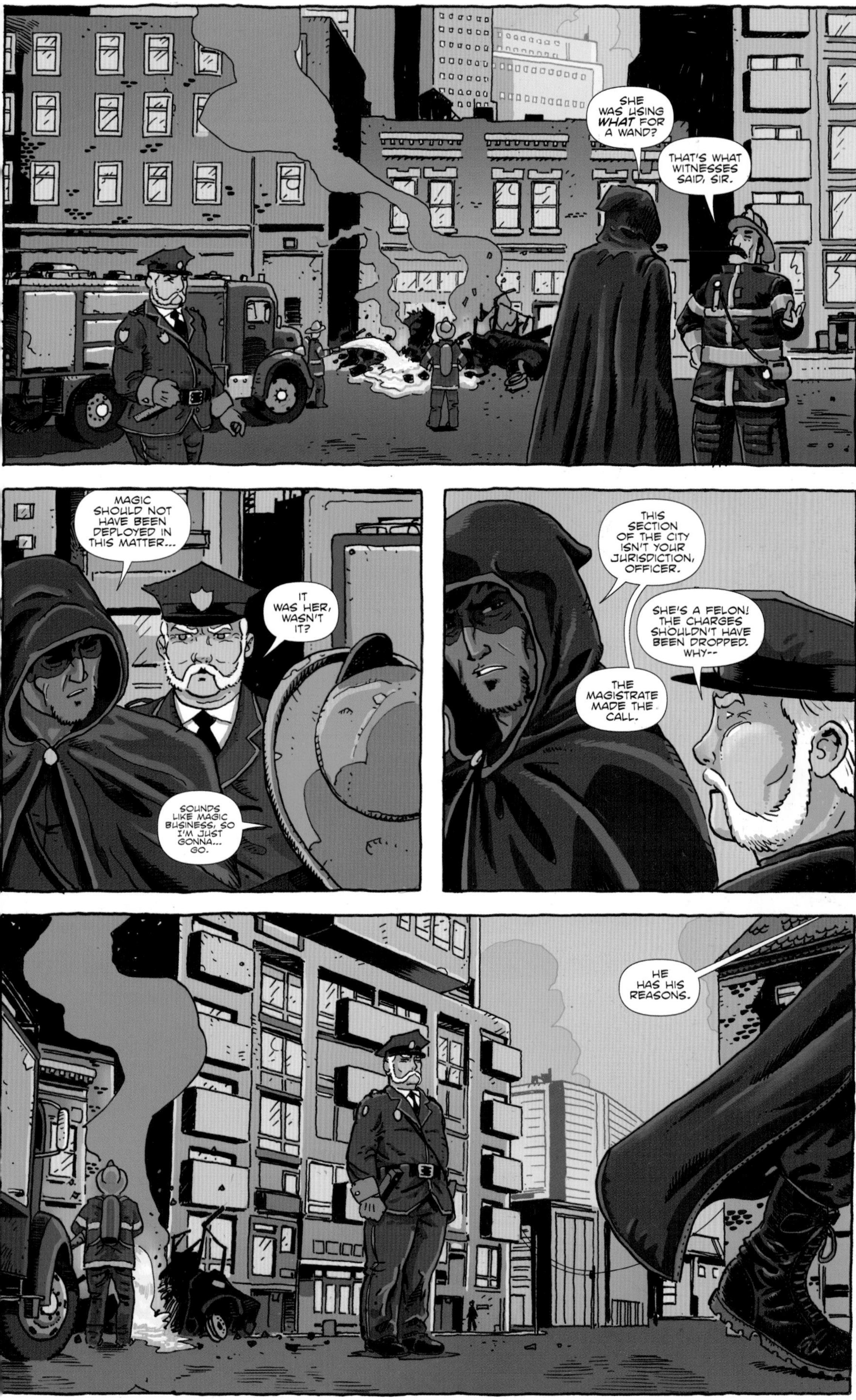
SHE WAS USING *WHAT* FOR A WAND?
THAT'S WHAT WITNESSES SAID, SIR.
MAGIC SHOULD NOT HAVE BEEN DEPLOYED IN THIS MATTER...
IT WAS HER, WASN'T IT?
SOUNDS LIKE MAGIC BUSINESS, SO I'M JUST GONNA... GO.
THIS SECTION OF THE CITY ISN'T YOUR JURISDICTION, OFFICER.
SHE'S A FELON! THE CHARGES SHOULDN'T HAVE BEEN DROPPED. WHY--
THE MAGISTRATE MADE THE CALL.
HE HAS HIS REASONS.

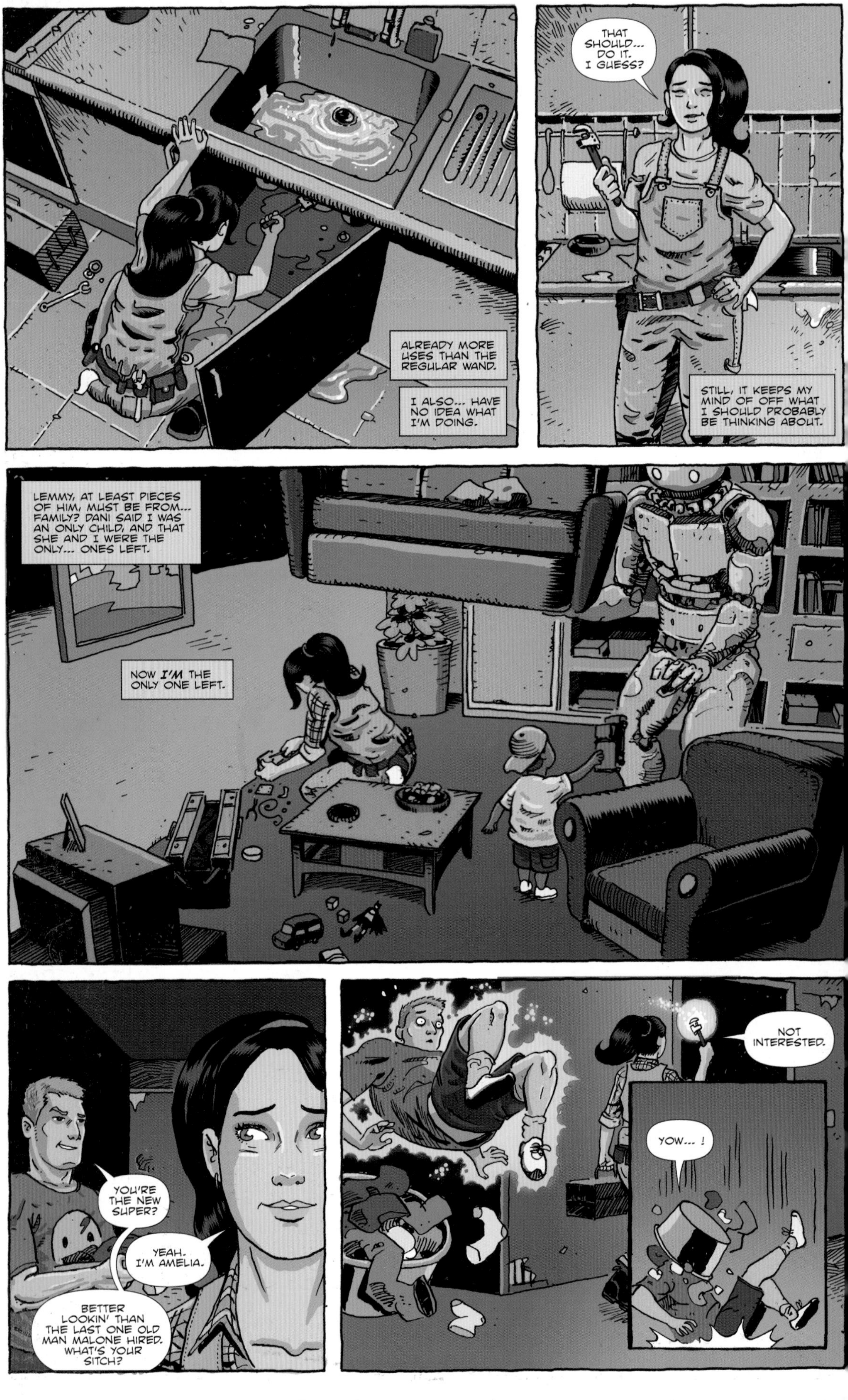
ALREADY MORE USES THAN THE REGULAR WAND.
I ALSO... HAVE NO IDEA WHAT I'M DOING.
THAT SHOULD... DO IT. I GUESS?
STILL, IT KEEPS MY MIND OF OFF WHAT I SHOULD PROBABLY BE THINKING ABOUT.
LEMMY, AT LEAST PIECES OF HIM, MUST BE FROM... FAMILY? DANI SAID I WAS AN ONLY CHILD, AND THAT SHE AND I WERE THE ONLY... ONES LEFT.
NOW I'M THE ONLY ONE LEFT.
YOU'RE THE NEW SUPER?
YEAH. I'M AMELIA.
BETTER LOOKIN' THAN THE LAST ONE OLD MAN MALONE HIRED. WHAT'S YOUR SITCH?
NOT INTERESTED.
YOW... !

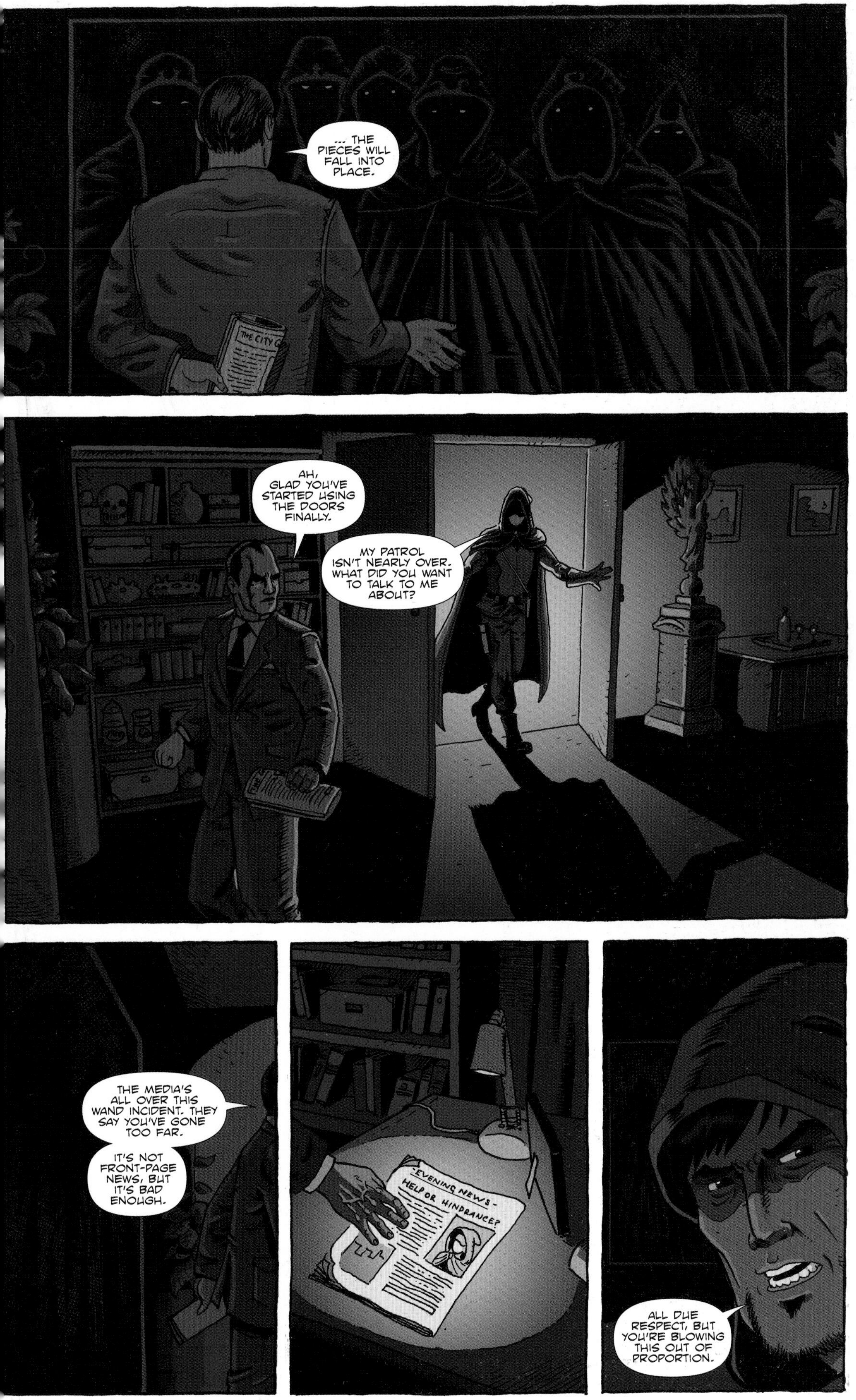

... THE PIECES WILL FALL INTO PLACE.
THE CITY
AH, GLAD YOU'VE STARTED USING THE DOORS FINALLY.
MY PATROL ISN'T NEARLY OVER. WHAT DID YOU WANT TO TALK TO ME ABOUT?
THE MEDIA'S ALL OVER THIS WAND INCIDENT. THEY SAY YOU'VE GONE TOO FAR.
IT'S NOT FRONT-PAGE NEWS, BUT IT'S BAD ENOUGH.
-EVENING NEWS-
HELP OR HINDRANCE?
ALL DUE RESPECT, BUT YOU'RE BLOWING THIS OUT OF PROPORTION.

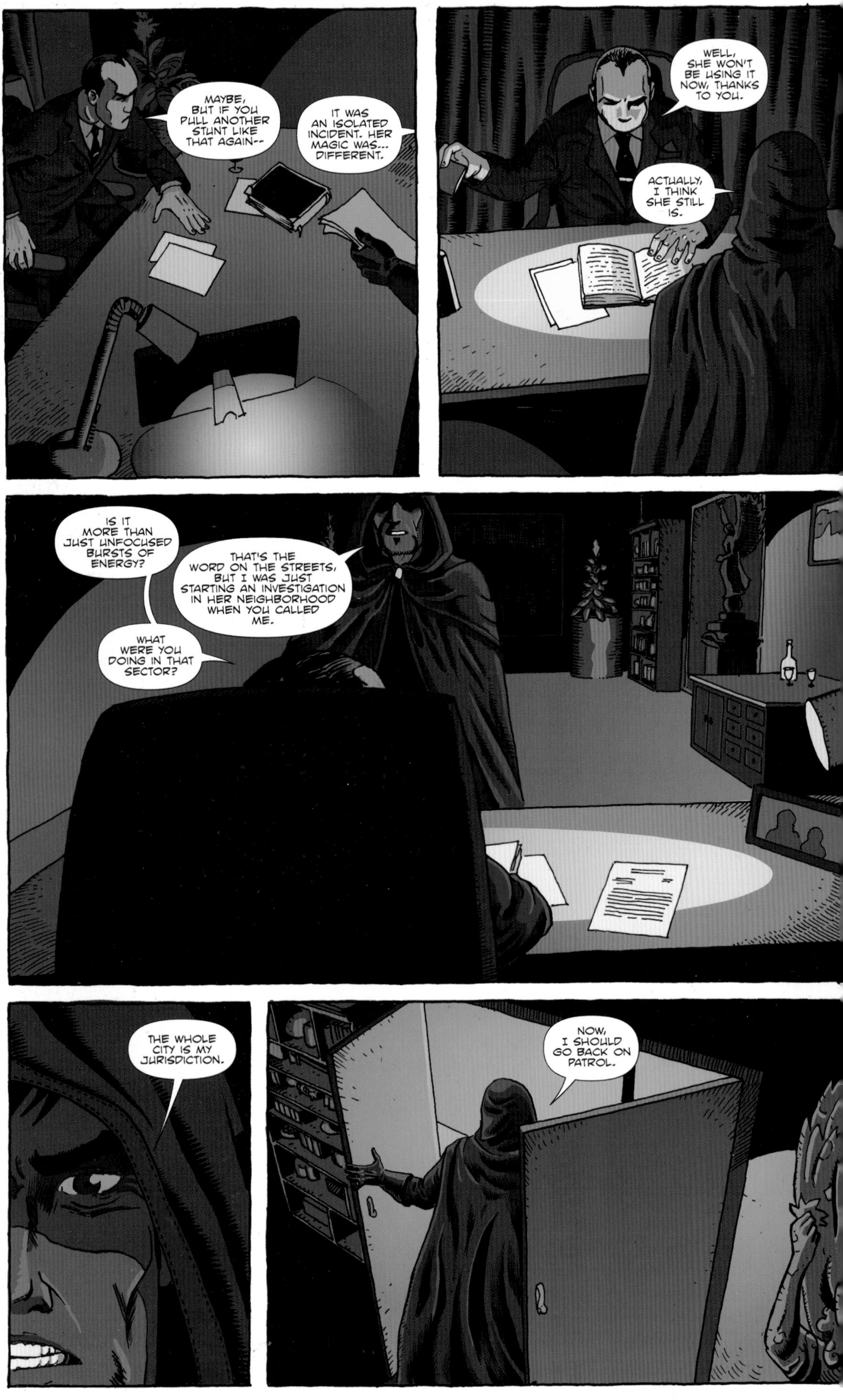

MAYBE, BUT IF YOU PULL ANOTHER STUNT LIKE THAT AGAIN--
IT WAS AN ISOLATED INCIDENT. HER MAGIC WAS... DIFFERENT.
WELL, SHE WON'T BE USING IT NOW, THANKS TO YOU.
ACTUALLY, I THINK SHE STILL IS.
IS IT MORE THAN JUST UNFOCUSED BURSTS OF ENERGY?
THAT'S THE WORD ON THE STREETS, BUT I WAS JUST STARTING AN INVESTIGATION IN HER NEIGHBORHOOD WHEN YOU CALLED ME.
WHAT WERE YOU DOING IN THAT SECTOR?
THE WHOLE CITY IS MY JURISDICTION.
NOW, I SHOULD GO BACK ON PATROL.

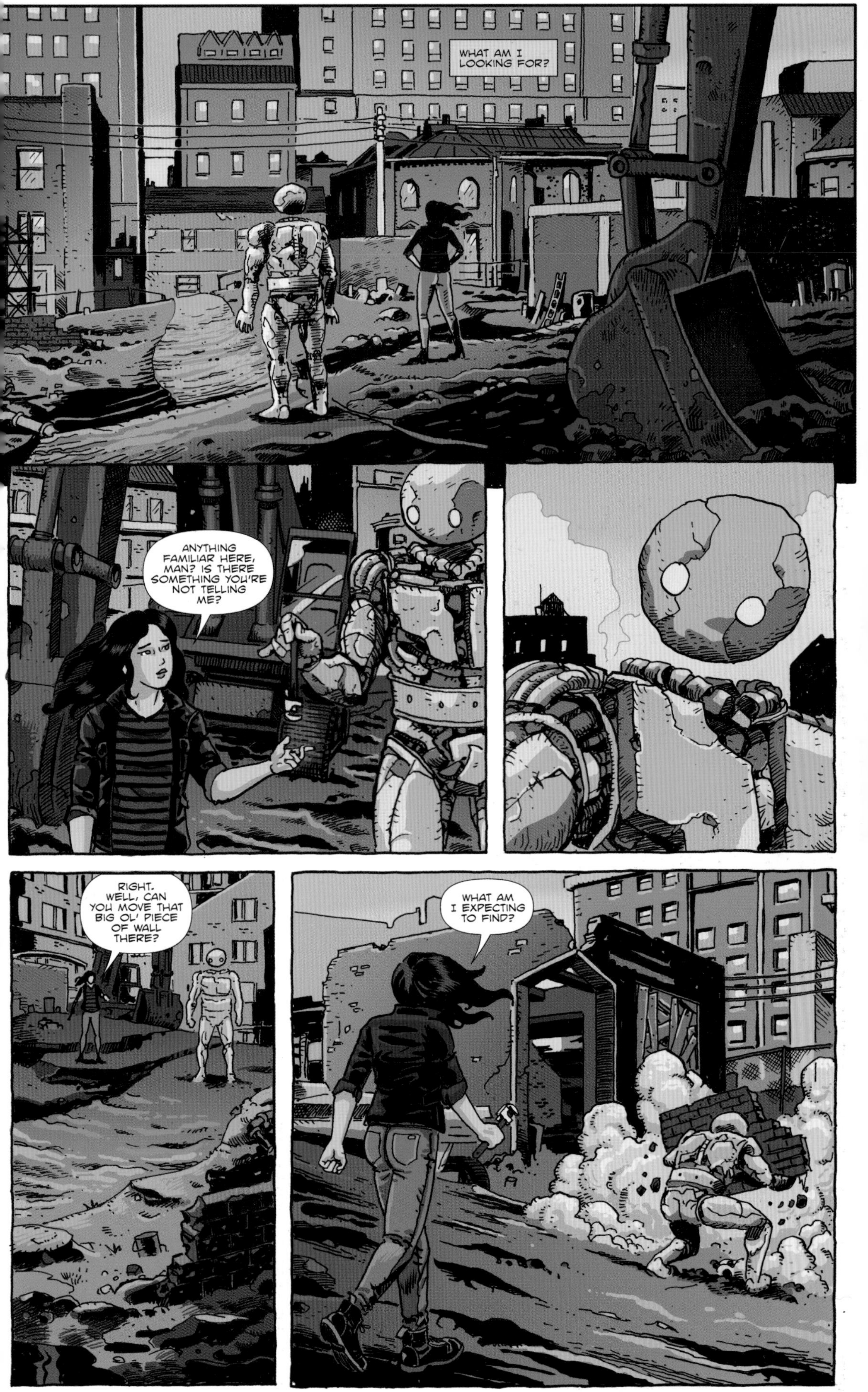
WHAT AM I LOOKING FOR?
ANYTHING FAMILIAR HERE, MAN? IS THERE SOMETHING YOU'RE NOT TELLING ME?
RIGHT. WELL, CAN YOU MOVE THAT BIG OL' PIECE OF WALL THERE?
WHAT AM I EXPECTING TO FIND?

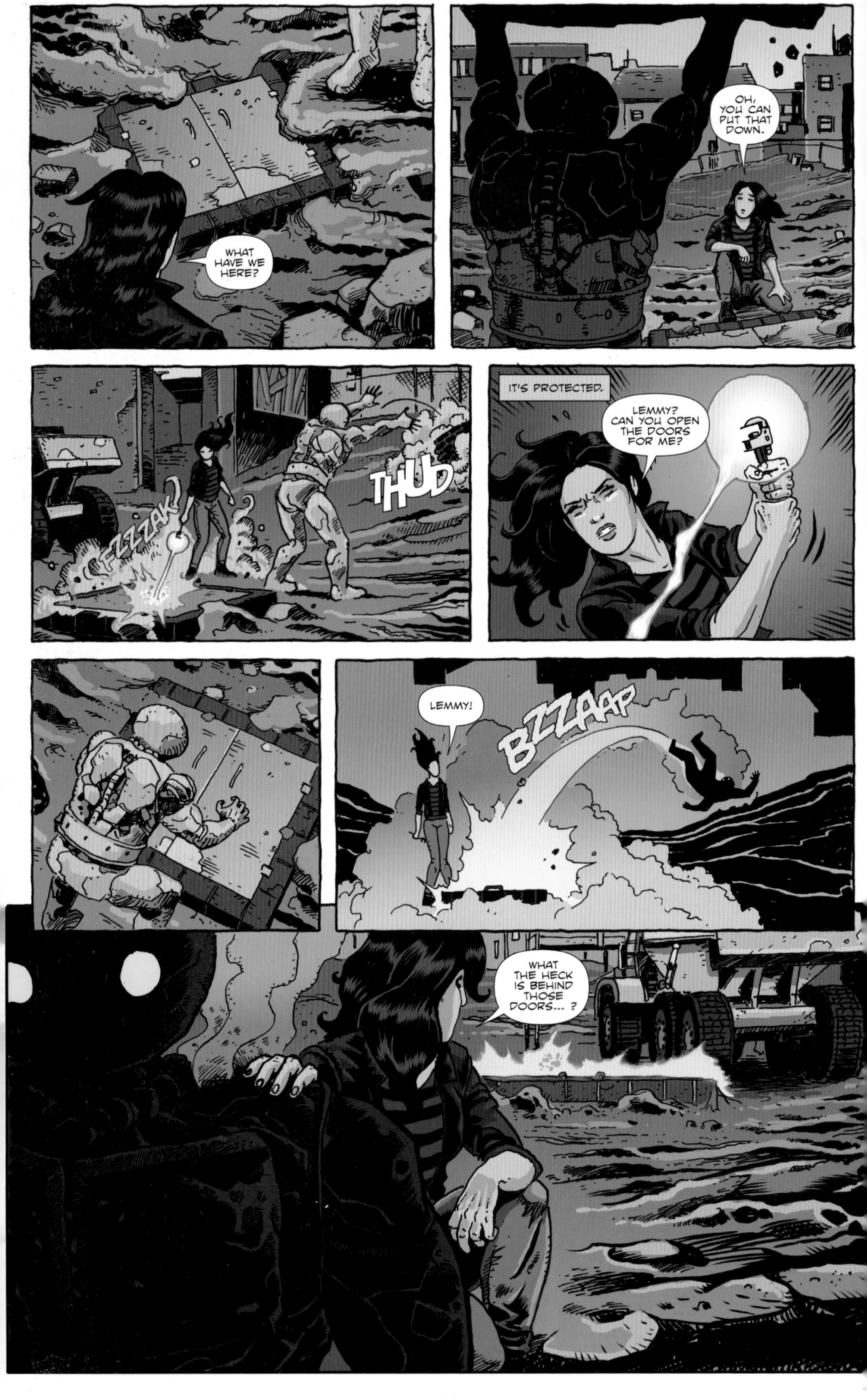
WHAT HAVE WE HERE?
OH, YOU CAN PUT THAT DOWN.
FZZZAK
THUD
IT'S PROTECTED.
LEMMY? CAN YOU OPEN THE DOORS FOR ME?
LEMMY!
BZZAAP
WHAT THE HECK IS BEHIND THOSE DOORS... ?

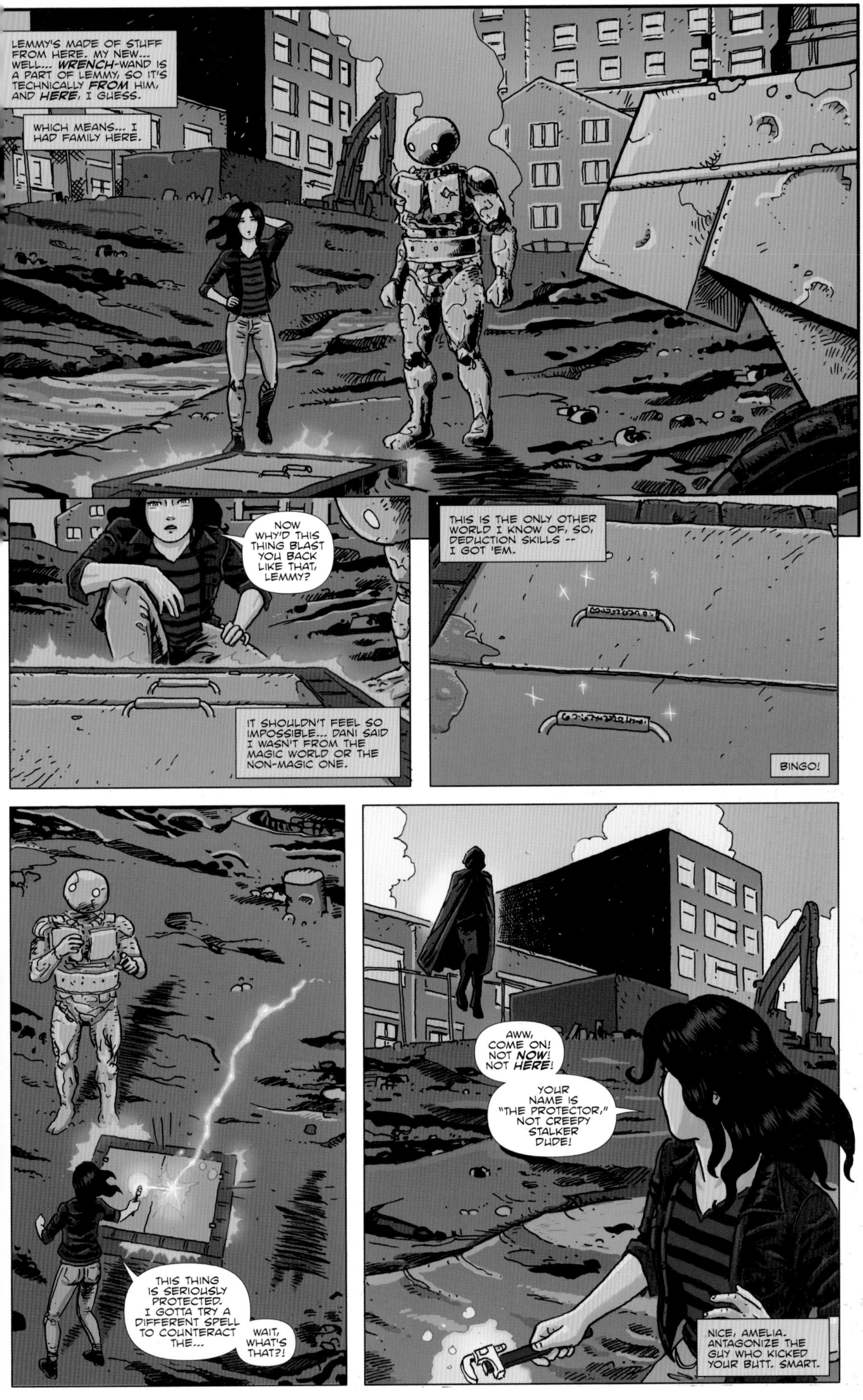
LEMMY'S MADE OF STUFF FROM HERE. MY NEW... WELL... WRENCH-WAND IS A PART OF LEMMY, SO IT'S TECHNICALLY FROM HIM, AND HERE, I GUESS.
WHICH MEANS... I HAD FAMILY HERE.
NOW WHY'D THIS THING BLAST YOU BACK LIKE THAT, LEMMY?
IT SHOULDN'T FEEL SO IMPOSSIBLE... DANI SAID I WASN'T FROM THE MAGIC WORLD OR THE NON-MAGIC ONE.
THIS IS THE ONLY OTHER WORLD I KNOW OF, SO, DEDUCTION SKILLS -- I GOT 'EM.
BINGO!
THIS THING IS SERIOUSLY PROTECTED. I GOTTA TRY A DIFFERENT SPELL TO COUNTERACT THE...
WAIT, WHAT'S THAT?!
AWW, COME ON! NOT NOW! NOT HERE!
YOUR NAME IS "THE PROTECTOR," NOT CREEPY STALKER DUDE!
NICE, AMELIA. ANTAGONIZE THE GUY WHO KICKED YOUR BUTT. SMART.

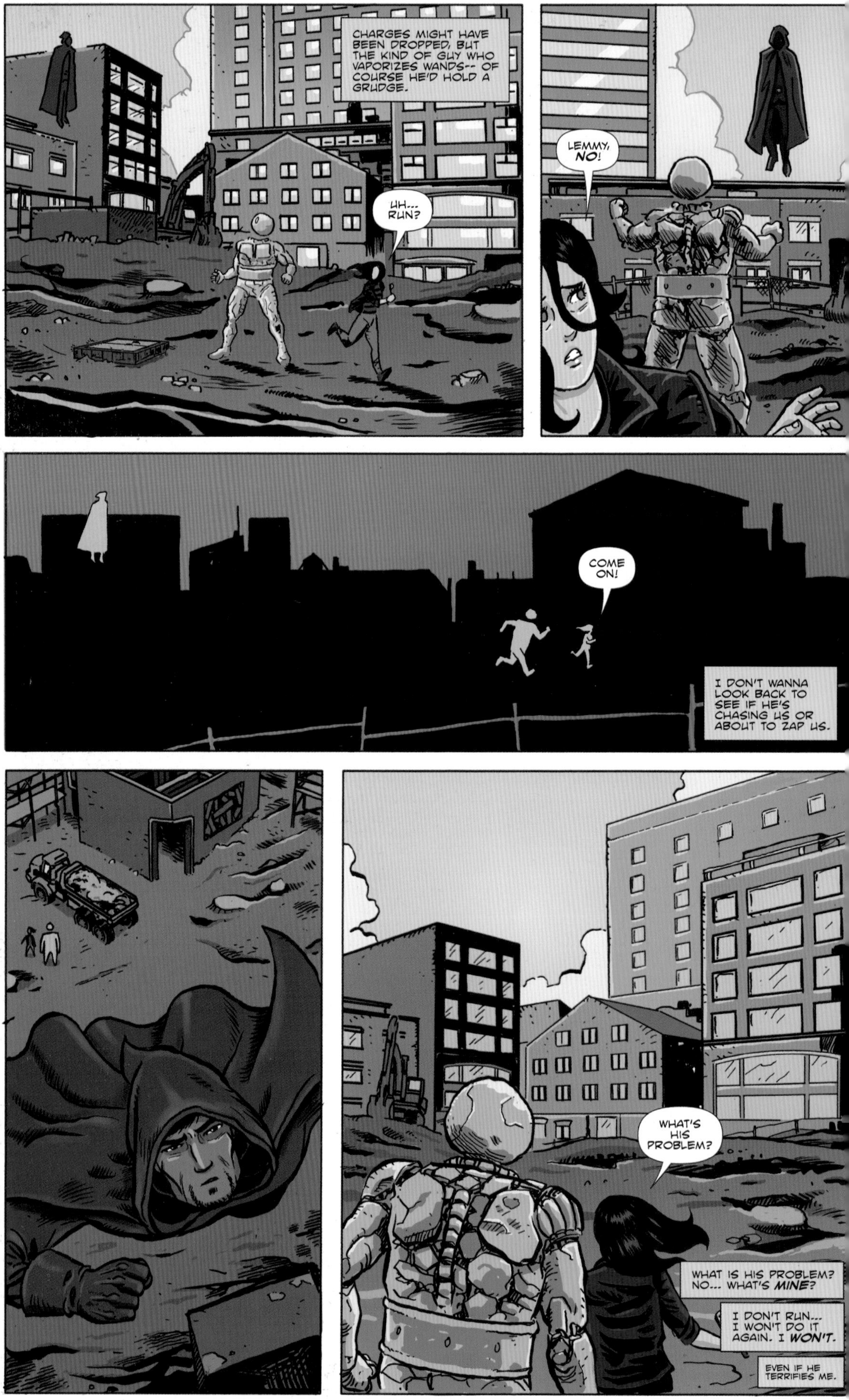
CHARGES MIGHT HAVE BEEN DROPPED, BUT THE KIND OF GUY WHO VAPORIZES WANDS-- OF COURSE HE'D HOLD A GRUDGE.
UH... RUN?
LEMMY, NO!
COME ON!
I DON'T WANNA LOOK BACK TO SEE IF HE'S CHASING US OR ABOUT TO ZAP US.
WHAT'S HIS PROBLEM?
WHAT IS HIS PROBLEM? NO... WHAT'S MINE?
I DON'T RUN... I WON'T DO IT AGAIN. I WON'T.
EVEN IF HE TERRIFIES ME.

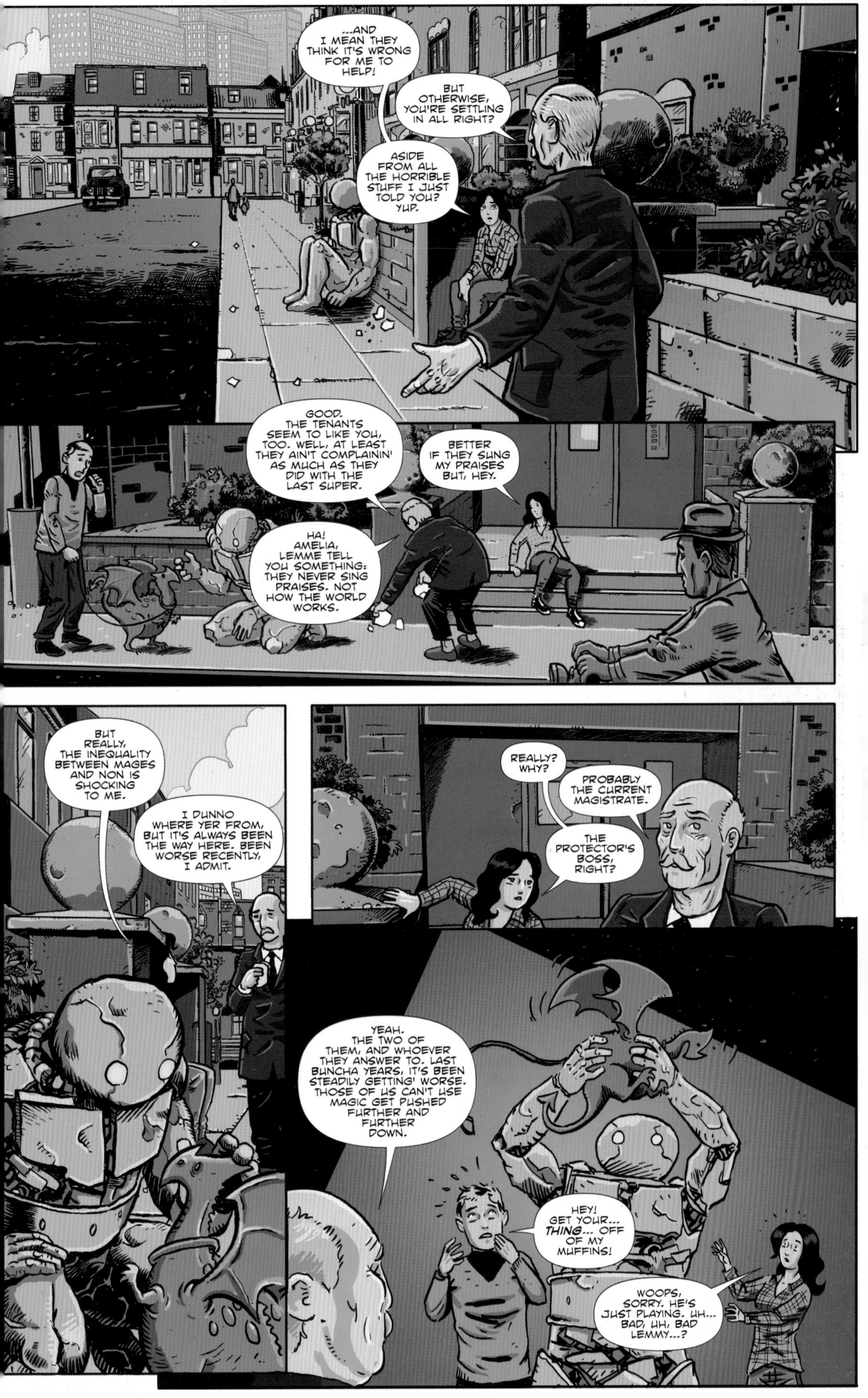
...AND I MEAN THEY THINK IT'S WRONG FOR ME TO HELP!
BUT OTHERWISE, YOU'RE SETTLING IN ALL RIGHT?
ASIDE FROM ALL THE HORRIBLE STUFF I JUST TOLD YOU? YUP.
GOOD. THE TENANTS SEEM TO LIKE YOU, TOO. WELL, AT LEAST THEY AIN'T COMPLAININ' AS MUCH AS THEY DID WITH THE LAST SUPER.
BETTER IF THEY SUNG MY PRAISES BUT, HEY.
HA! AMELIA, LEMME TELL YOU SOMETHING: THEY NEVER SING PRAISES. NOT HOW THE WORLD WORKS.
BUT REALLY, THE INEQUALITY BETWEEN MAGES AND NON IS SHOCKING TO ME.
I DUNNO WHERE YER FROM, BUT IT'S ALWAYS BEEN THE WAY HERE. BEEN WORSE RECENTLY, I ADMIT.
REALLY? WHY?
PROBABLY THE CURRENT MAGISTRATE.
THE PROTECTOR'S BOSS, RIGHT?
YEAH. THE TWO OF THEM, AND WHOEVER THEY ANSWER TO. LAST BUNCHA YEARS, IT'S BEEN STEADILY GETTING' WORSE. THOSE OF US CAN'T USE MAGIC GET PUSHED FURTHER AND FURTHER DOWN.
HEY! GET YOUR... *THING*... OFF OF MY MUFFINS!
WOOPS, SORRY. HE'S JUST PLAYING. UH... BAD, UH, BAD LEMMY...?

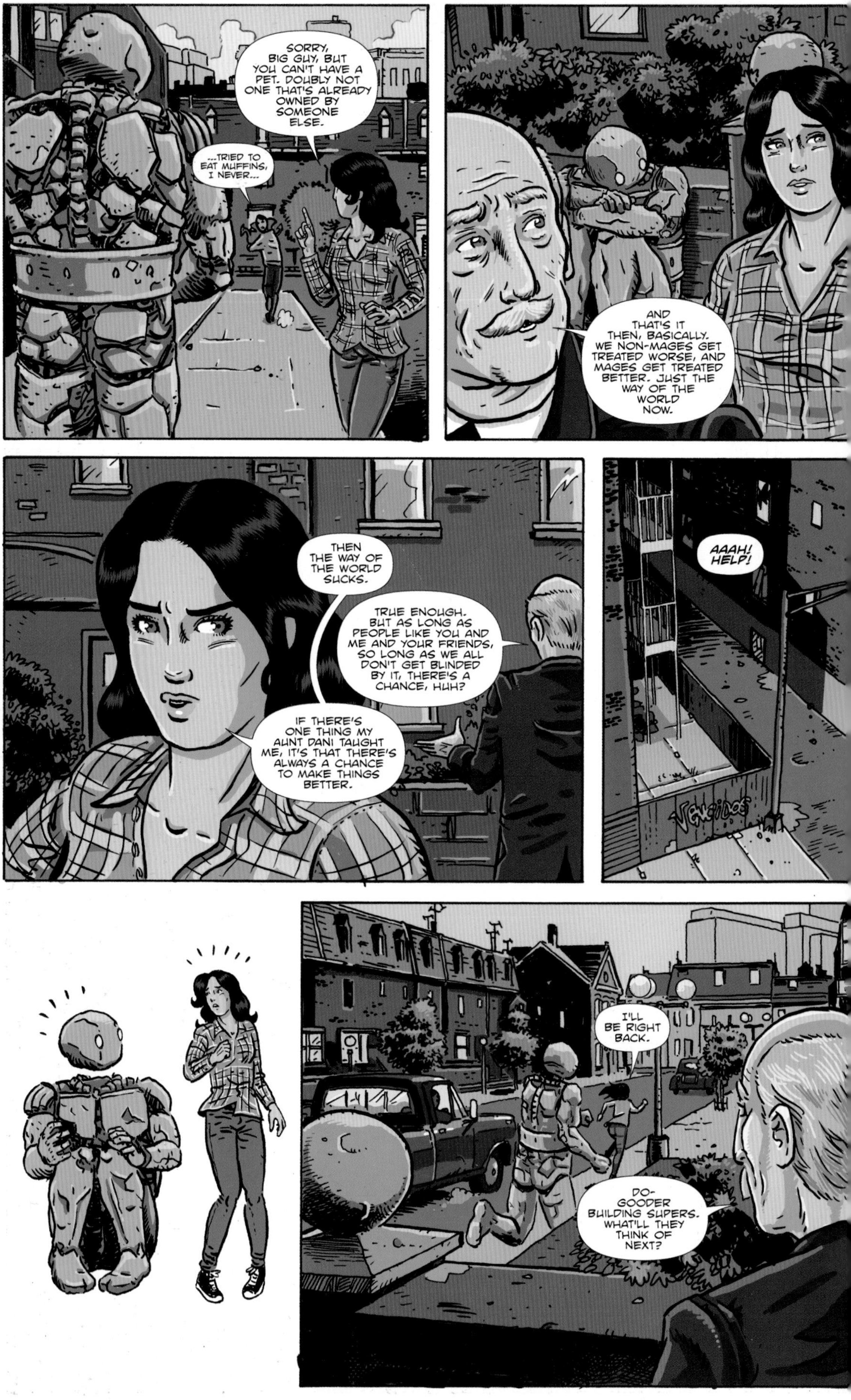
SORRY, BIG GUY, BUT YOU CAN'T HAVE A PET. DOUBLY NOT ONE THAT'S ALREADY OWNED BY SOMEONE ELSE.
...TRIED TO EAT MUFFINS, I NEVER...
AND THAT'S IT THEN, BASICALLY. WE NON-MAGES GET TREATED WORSE, AND MAGES GET TREATED BETTER. JUST THE WAY OF THE WORLD NOW.
THEN THE WAY OF THE WORLD SUCKS.
TRUE ENOUGH. BUT AS LONG AS PEOPLE LIKE YOU AND ME AND YOUR FRIENDS, SO LONG AS WE ALL DON'T GET BLINDED BY IT, THERE'S A CHANCE, HUH?
IF THERE'S ONE THING MY AUNT DANI TAUGHT ME, IT'S THAT THERE'S ALWAYS A CHANCE TO MAKE THINGS BETTER.
AAAH! HELP!
I'LL BE RIGHT BACK.
DO-GOODER BUILDING SUPERS. WHAT'LL THEY THINK OF NEXT?

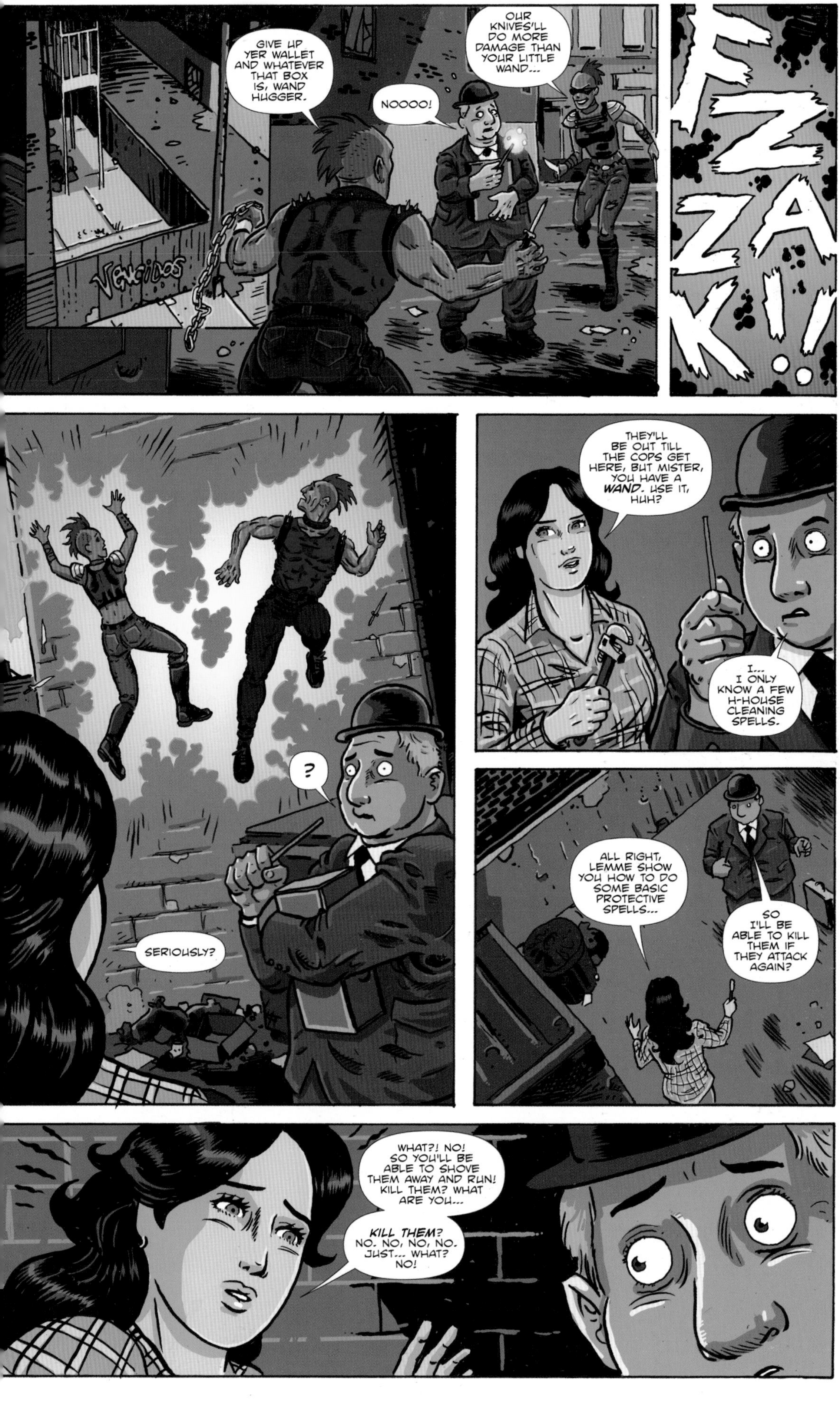
GIVE UP YER WALLET AND WHATEVER THAT BOX IS, WAND HUGGER.
NOOOO!
OUR KNIVES'LL DO MORE DAMAGE THAN YOUR LITTLE WAND...
VENCIDOS
FZZAK!!
?
SERIOUSLY?
THEY'LL BE OUT TILL THE COPS GET HERE, BUT MISTER, YOU HAVE A WAND. USE IT, HUH?
I... I ONLY KNOW A FEW H-HOUSE CLEANING SPELLS.
ALL RIGHT, LEMME SHOW YOU HOW TO DO SOME BASIC PROTECTIVE SPELLS...
SO I'LL BE ABLE TO KILL THEM IF THEY ATTACK AGAIN?
WHAT?! NO! SO YOU'LL BE ABLE TO SHOVE THEM AWAY AND RUN! KILL THEM? WHAT ARE YOU...
KILL THEM? NO. NO, NO, NO. JUST... WHAT? NO!

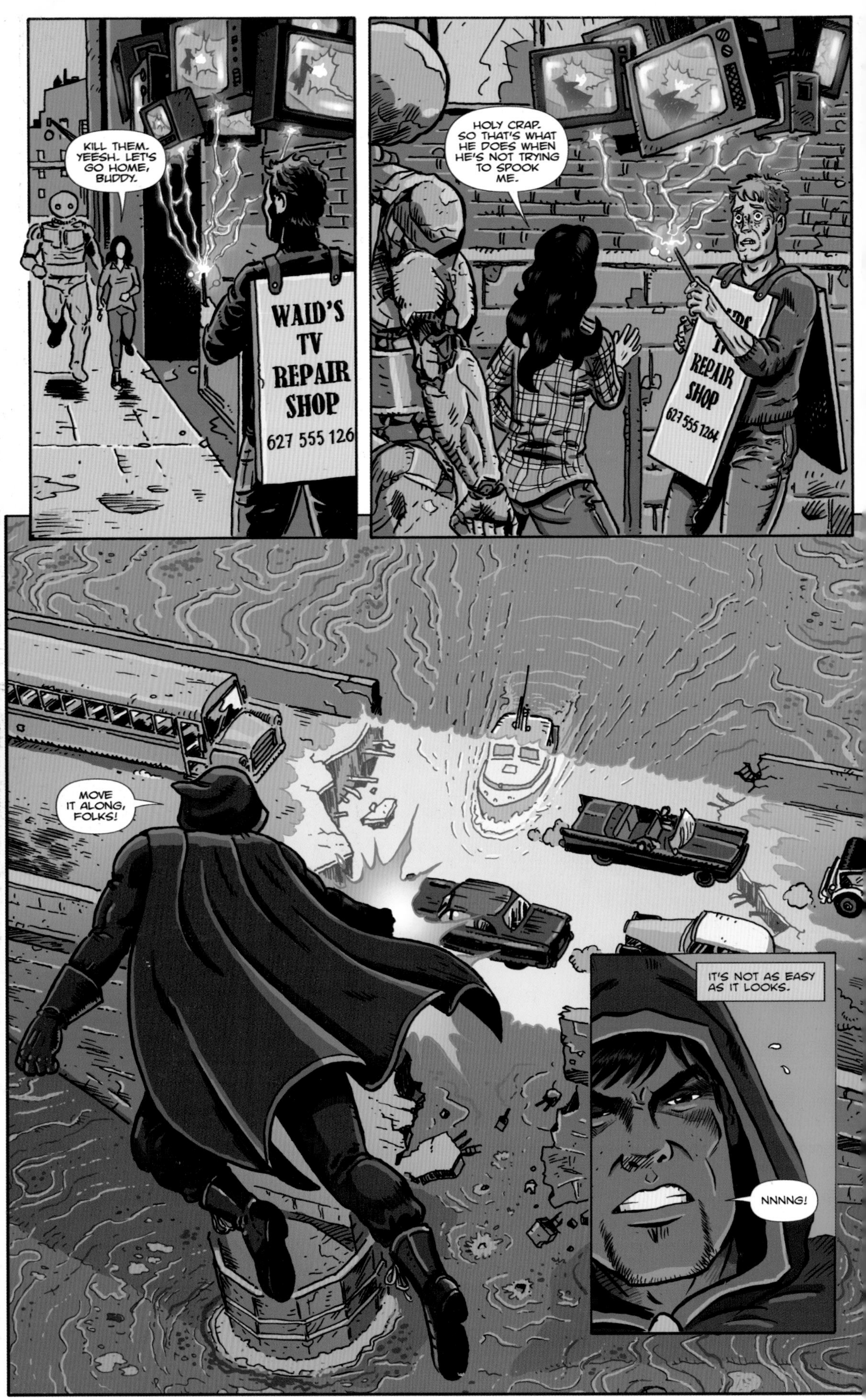
KILL THEM. YEESH. LET'S GO HOME, BUDDY.
WAID'S TV REPAIR SHOP
627 555 126
HOLY CRAP. SO THAT'S WHAT HE DOES WHEN HE'S NOT TRYING TO SPOOK ME.
REPAIR SHOP
627 555 1264
MOVE IT ALONG, FOLKS!
IT'S NOT AS EASY AS IT LOOKS.
NNNNG!

MAGIC -- WAND WIELDING OR FIGURING OUT A SPELL -- IS ALL WELL AND GOOD, BUT BRUTE FORCE IS SOMETIMES JUST FASTER.

TO WIT, THE DOOR'S WARDED AGAINST OPENINGS, BUT MAGIC AGAINST, OH I DON'T KNOW, A *TRUCK*, MIGHT JUST DO THE TRICK.

THERE SHOULD BE A BIGGER CROWD.

ANYWAY...

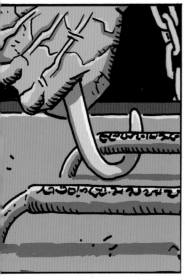

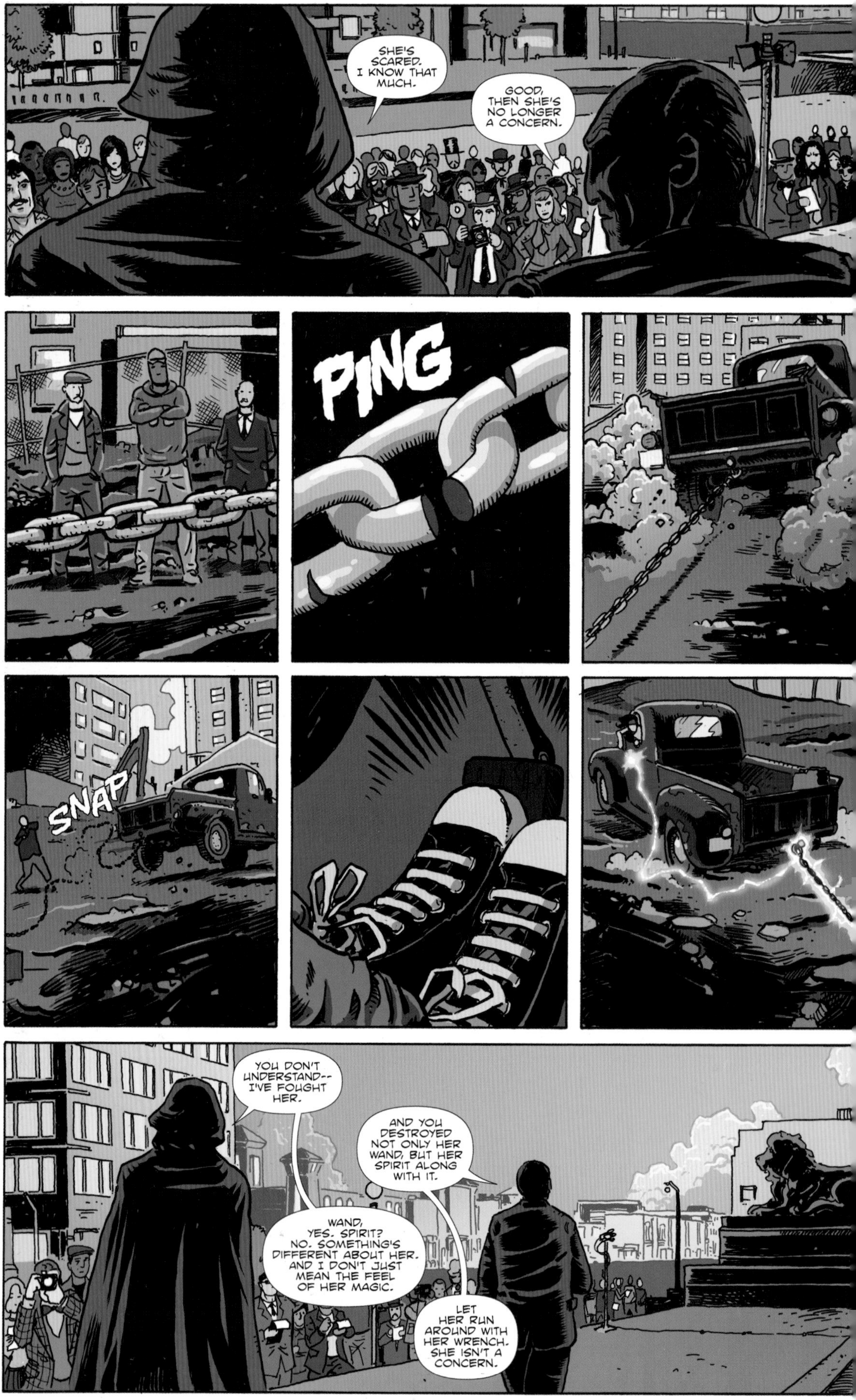
SHE'S SCARED. I KNOW THAT MUCH.
GOOD, THEN SHE'S NO LONGER A CONCERN.
PING
SNAP
YOU DON'T UNDERSTAND-- I'VE FOUGHT HER.
AND YOU DESTROYED NOT ONLY HER WAND, BUT HER SPIRIT ALONG WITH IT.
WAND, YES. SPIRIT? NO. SOMETHING'S DIFFERENT ABOUT HER. AND I DON'T JUST MEAN THE FEEL OF HER MAGIC.
LET HER RUN AROUND WITH HER WRENCH. SHE ISN'T A CONCERN.

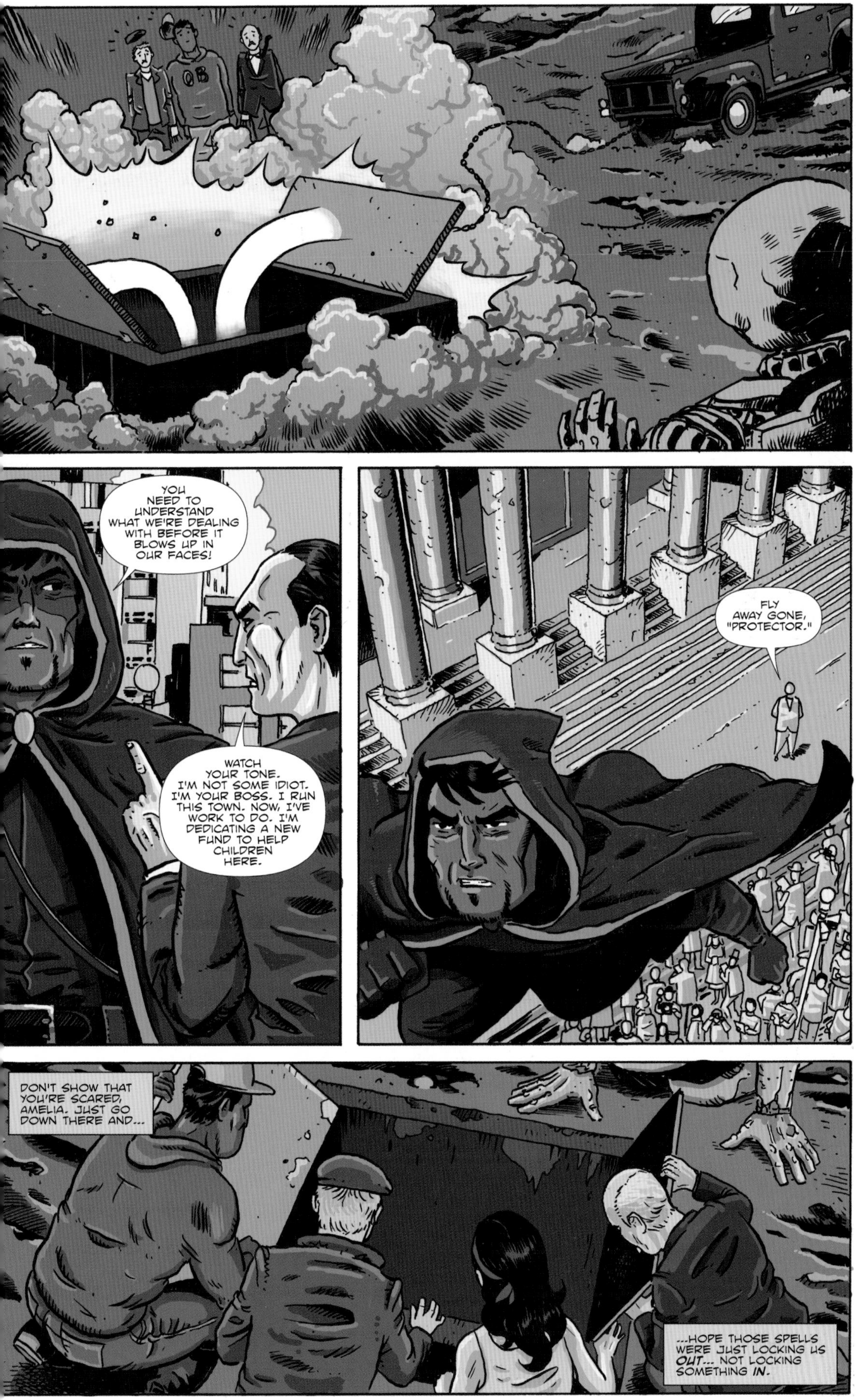
YOU NEED TO UNDERSTAND WHAT WE'RE DEALING WITH BEFORE IT BLOWS UP IN OUR FACES!
WATCH YOUR TONE. I'M NOT SOME IDIOT. I'M YOUR BOSS. I RUN THIS TOWN. NOW, I'VE WORK TO DO. I'M DEDICATING A NEW FUND TO HELP CHILDREN HERE.
FLY AWAY GONE, "PROTECTOR."
DON'T SHOW THAT YOU'RE SCARED, AMELIA. JUST GO DOWN THERE AND...
...HOPE THOSE SPELLS WERE JUST LOCKING US *OUT*... NOT LOCKING SOMETHING *IN*.

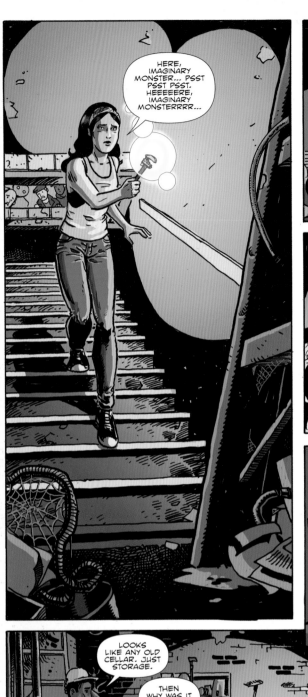

HERE, IMAGINARY MONSTER... PSST PSST PSST. HEEEEERE, IMAGINARY MONSTERRRR...

FELLOW CITIZENS, WE'RE HERE TODAY TO HELP THE CHILDREN -- OUR MOST PRECIOUS RESOURCE.

OUR FUTURE!

MONSTER...?

PLEASE DON'T PUT IDEAS IN HIS HEAD.

IF THERE IS SOMETHING HERE, I'D RATHER FIND IT NOW THAN WHEN IT REACHES OUT FROM HIDING TO SCARE THE CRAP OUT OF US.

OR EATS US.

WE MUST ENSURE THAT FUTURE BY HELPING THOSE CHILDREN NOW. BUT YOU KNOW ALL THAT. IT'S WHY WE'RE ALL HERE.

LET'S DEDICATE THIS FUND AND START HELPING, NOT JUST MAKING SPEECHES. THOUGH I AM GOOD AT THAT, AREN'T I?

LOOKS LIKE ANY OLD CELLAR. JUST STORAGE.

THEN WHY WAS IT WARDED SO HARD?

MAGES WANTING TO KEEP NON-MAGES OUT?

MAYBE...

...BUT, NO, I DON'T THINK SO. THAT WARD WAS... GUYS, IT WAS LIKE BUYING A BANK SAFE TO LOCK DOWN A SOCK DRAWER.

MAYBE THEY TOOK THEIR SOCKS SERIOUSLY.

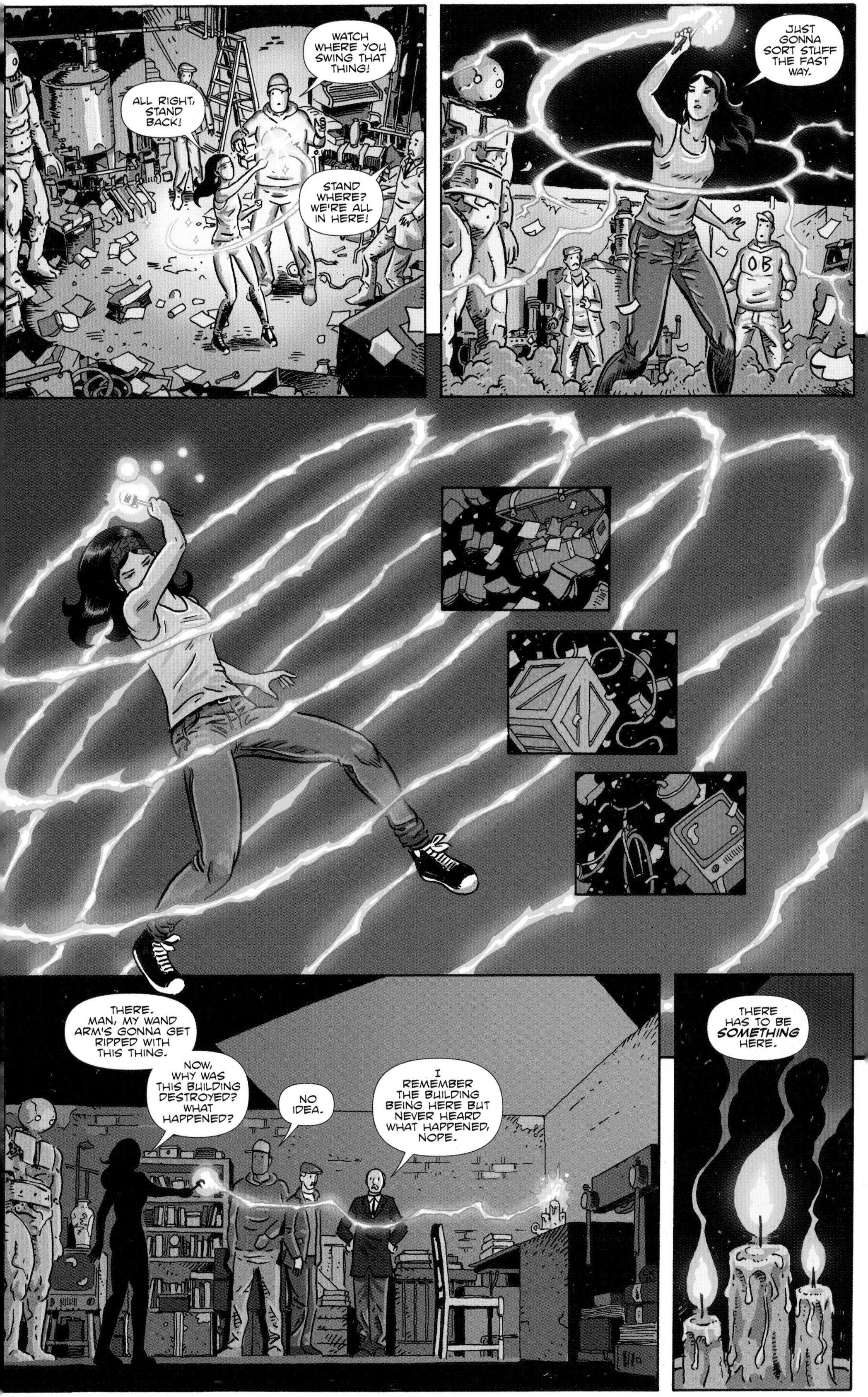
ALL RIGHT, STAND BACK!
WATCH WHERE YOU SWING THAT THING!
STAND WHERE? WE'RE ALL IN HERE!
JUST GONNA SORT STUFF THE FAST WAY.
OB
THERE. MAN, MY WAND ARM'S GONNA GET RIPPED WITH THIS THING.
NOW, WHY WAS THIS BUILDING DESTROYED? WHAT HAPPENED?
NO IDEA.
I REMEMBER THE BUILDING BEING HERE BUT NEVER HEARD WHAT HAPPENED, NOPE.
THERE HAS TO BE *SOMETHING* HERE.

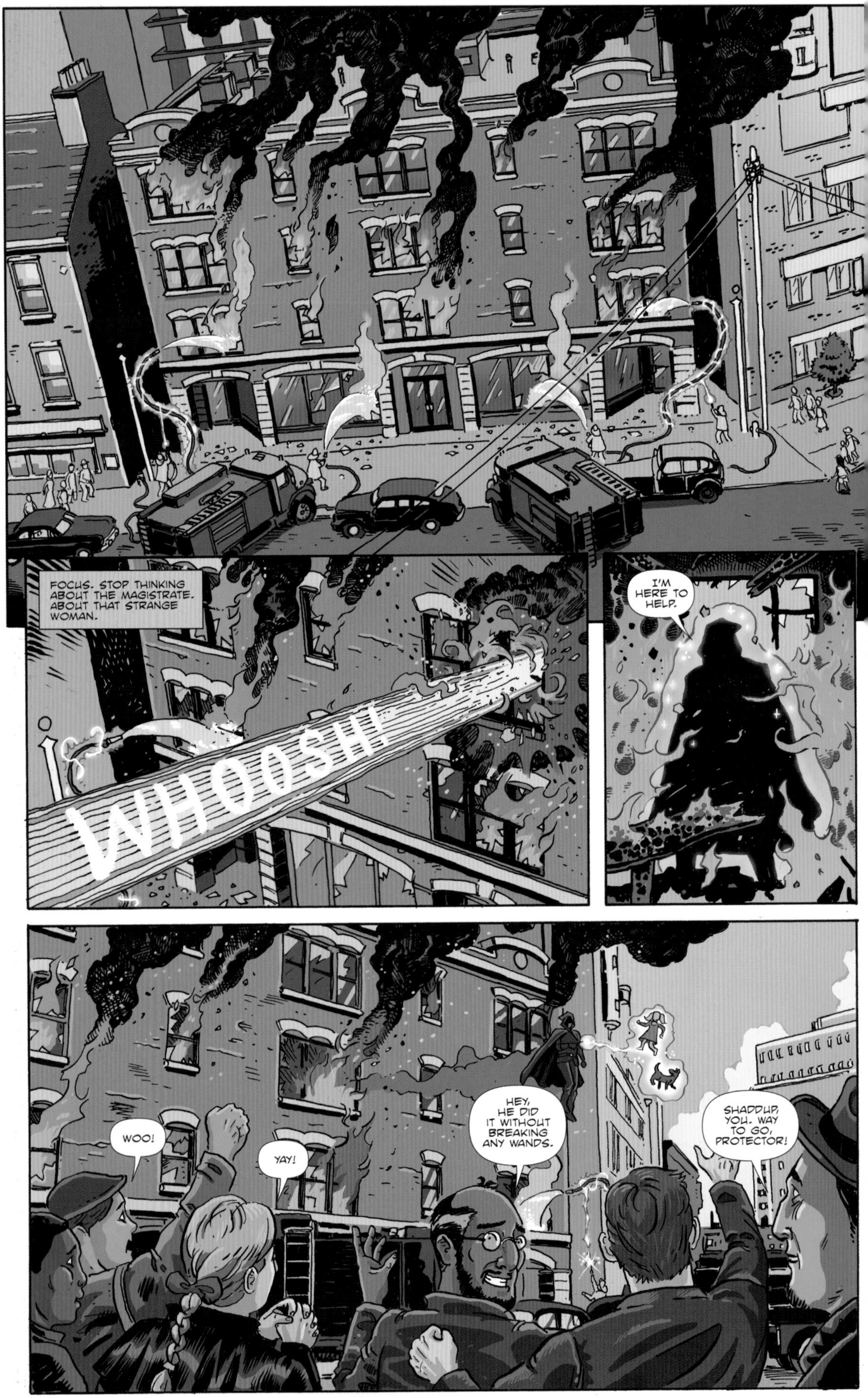
FOCUS. STOP THINKING ABOUT THE MAGISTRATE. ABOUT THAT STRANGE WOMAN.
WHOOSH!
I'M HERE TO HELP.
WOO!
YAY!
HEY, HE DID IT WITHOUT BREAKING ANY WANDS.
SHADDUP, YOU. WAY TO GO, PROTECTOR!

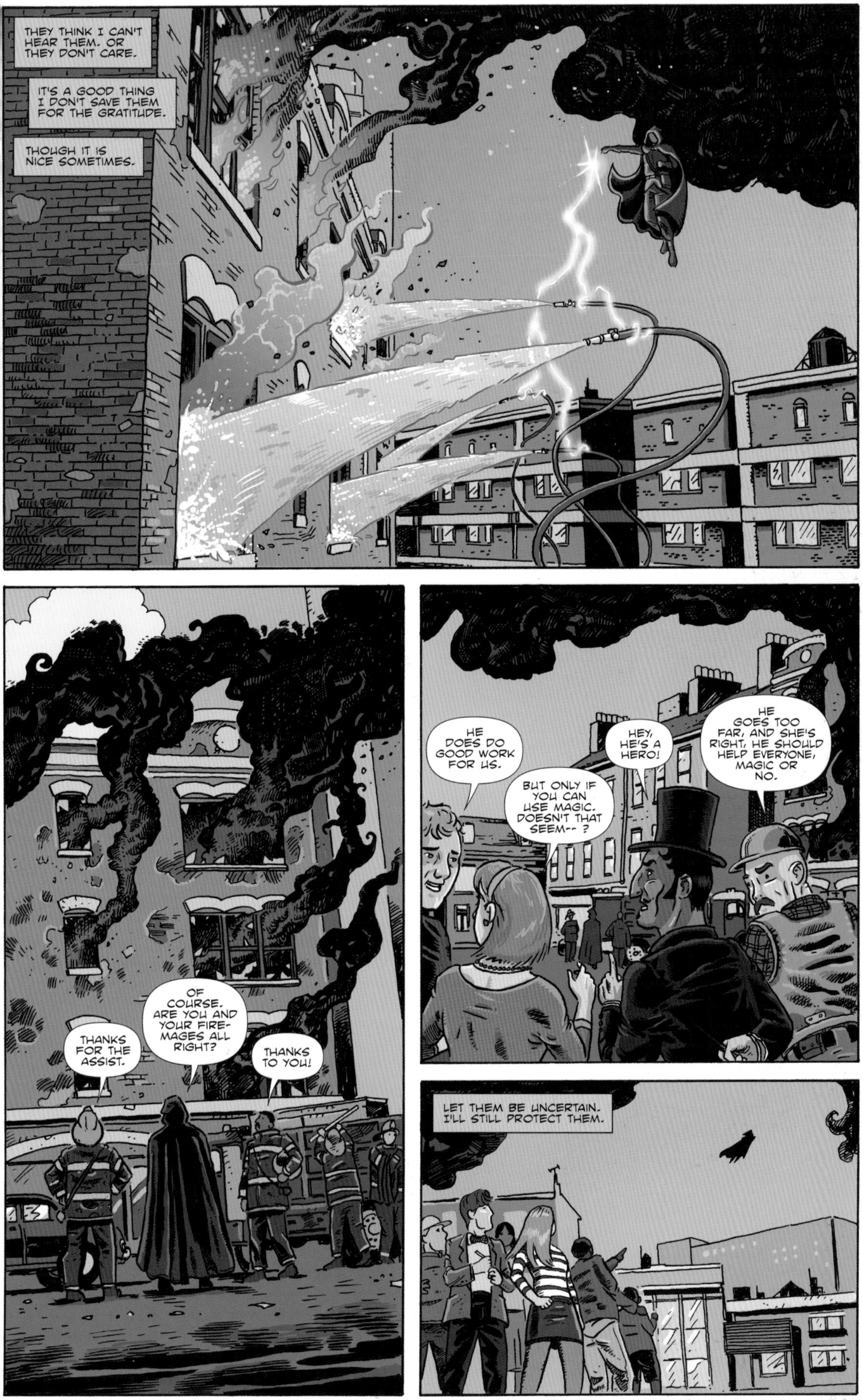
THEY THINK I CAN'T HEAR THEM. OR THEY DON'T CARE.
IT'S A GOOD THING I DON'T SAVE THEM FOR THE GRATITUDE.
THOUGH IT IS NICE SOMETIMES.
THANKS FOR THE ASSIST.
OF COURSE. ARE YOU AND YOUR FIRE-MAGES ALL RIGHT?
THANKS TO YOU!
HE DOES DO GOOD WORK FOR US.
BUT ONLY IF YOU CAN USE MAGIC. DOESN'T THAT SEEM-- ?
HEY, HE'S A HERO!
HE GOES TOO FAR, AND SHE'S RIGHT, HE SHOULD HELP EVERYONE, MAGIC OR NO.
LET THEM BE UNCERTAIN. I'LL STILL PROTECT THEM.

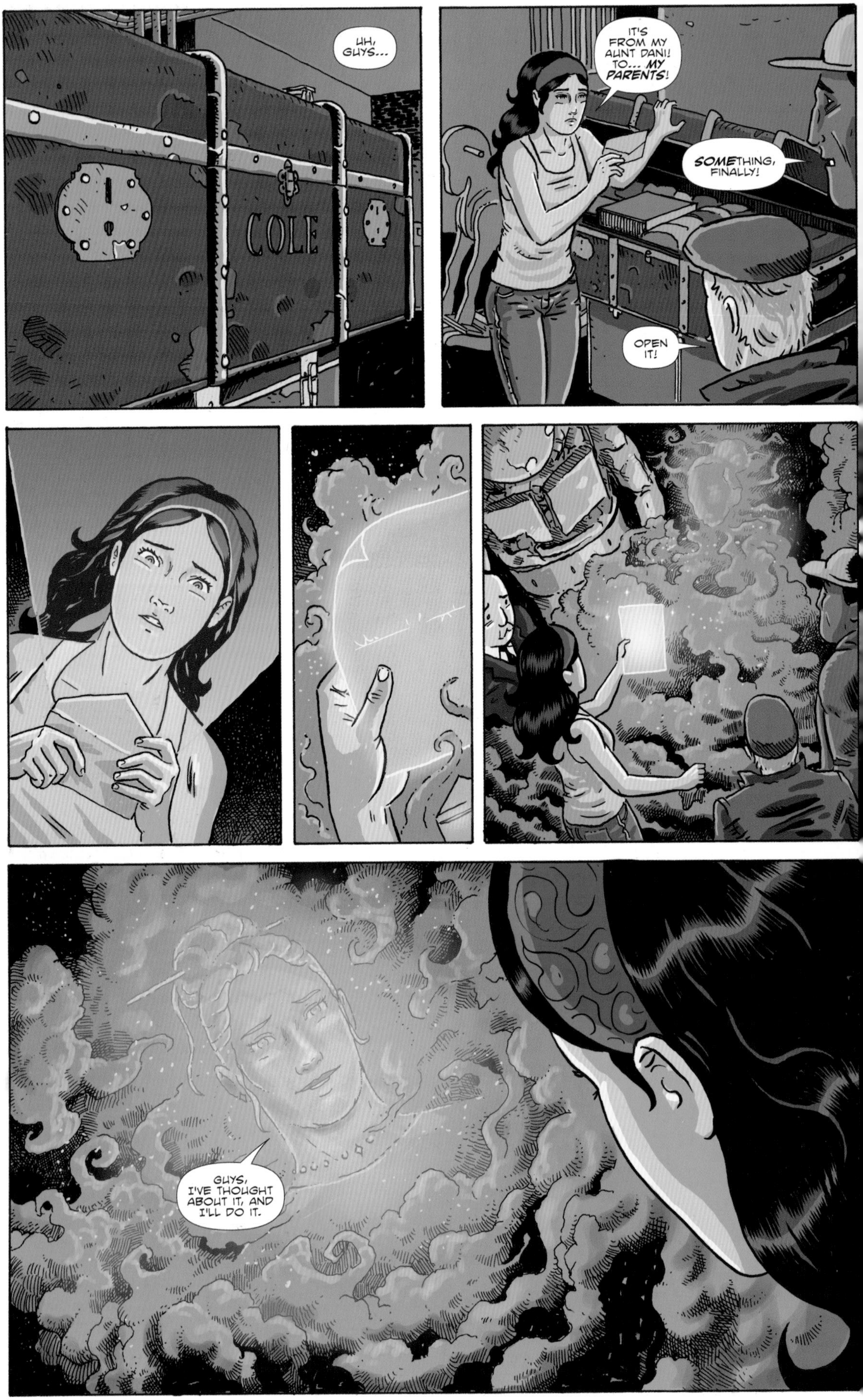
UH, GUYS...
IT'S FROM MY AUNT DANI! TO... MY PARENTS!
SOMETHING, FINALLY!
OPEN IT!
COLE
GUYS, I'VE THOUGHT ABOUT IT, AND I'LL DO IT.

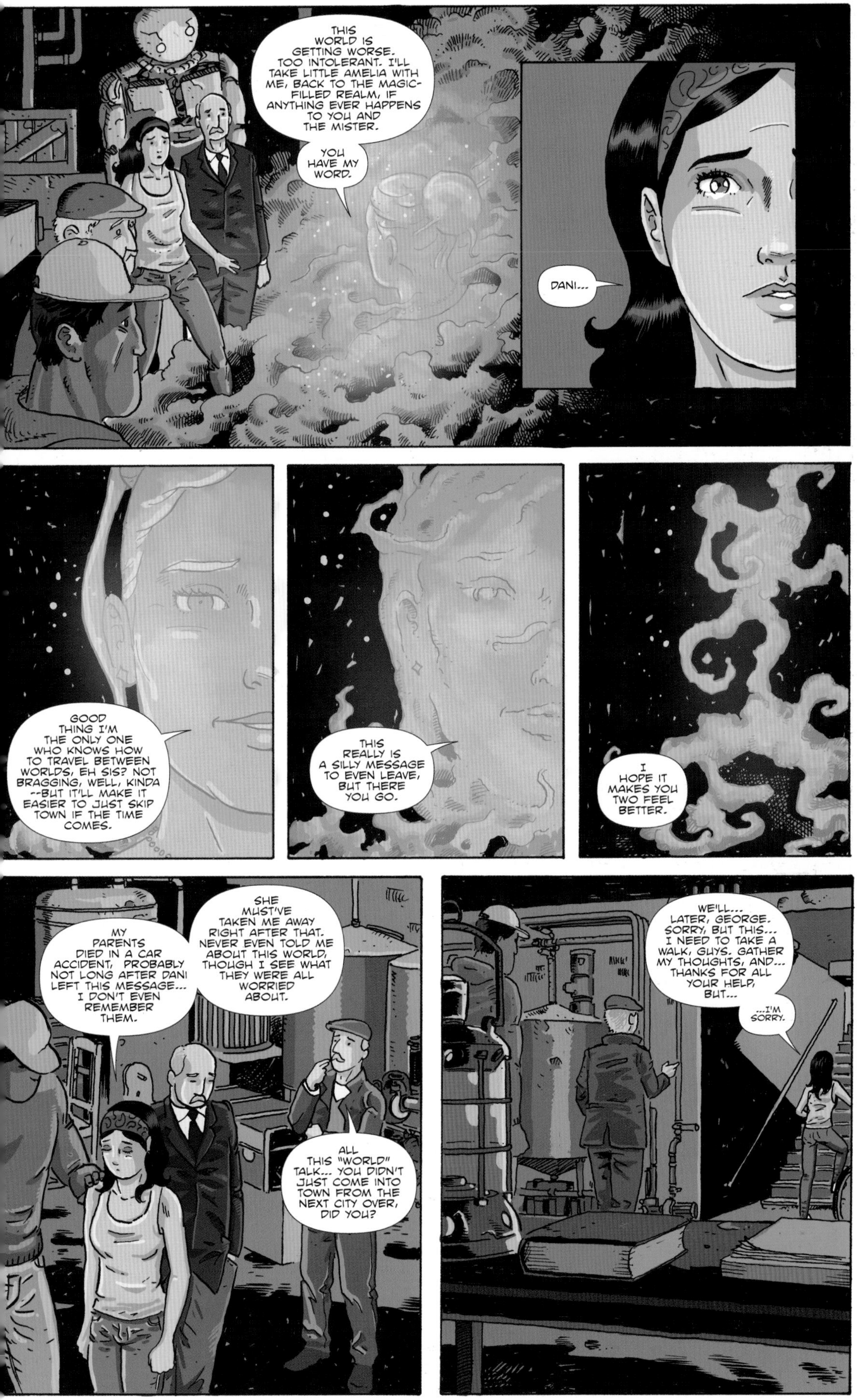
THIS WORLD IS GETTING WORSE. TOO INTOLERANT. I'LL TAKE LITTLE AMELIA WITH ME, BACK TO THE MAGIC-FILLED REALM, IF ANYTHING EVER HAPPENS TO YOU AND THE MISTER.
YOU HAVE MY WORD.
DANI...
GOOD THING I'M THE ONLY ONE WHO KNOWS HOW TO TRAVEL BETWEEN WORLDS, EH SIS? NOT BRAGGING, WELL, KINDA --BUT IT'LL MAKE IT EASIER TO JUST SKIP TOWN IF THE TIME COMES.
THIS REALLY IS A SILLY MESSAGE TO EVEN LEAVE, BUT THERE YOU GO.
I HOPE IT MAKES YOU TWO FEEL BETTER.
MY PARENTS DIED IN A CAR ACCIDENT, PROBABLY NOT LONG AFTER DANI LEFT THIS MESSAGE... I DON'T EVEN REMEMBER THEM.
SHE MUST'VE TAKEN ME AWAY RIGHT AFTER THAT. NEVER EVEN TOLD ME ABOUT THIS WORLD, THOUGH I SEE WHAT THEY WERE ALL WORRIED ABOUT.
ALL THIS "WORLD" TALK... YOU DIDN'T JUST COME INTO TOWN FROM THE NEXT CITY OVER, DID YOU?
WE'LL... LATER, GEORGE. SORRY, BUT THIS... I NEED TO TAKE A WALK, GUYS. GATHER MY THOUGHTS, AND... THANKS FOR ALL YOUR HELP, BUT...
...I'M SORRY.

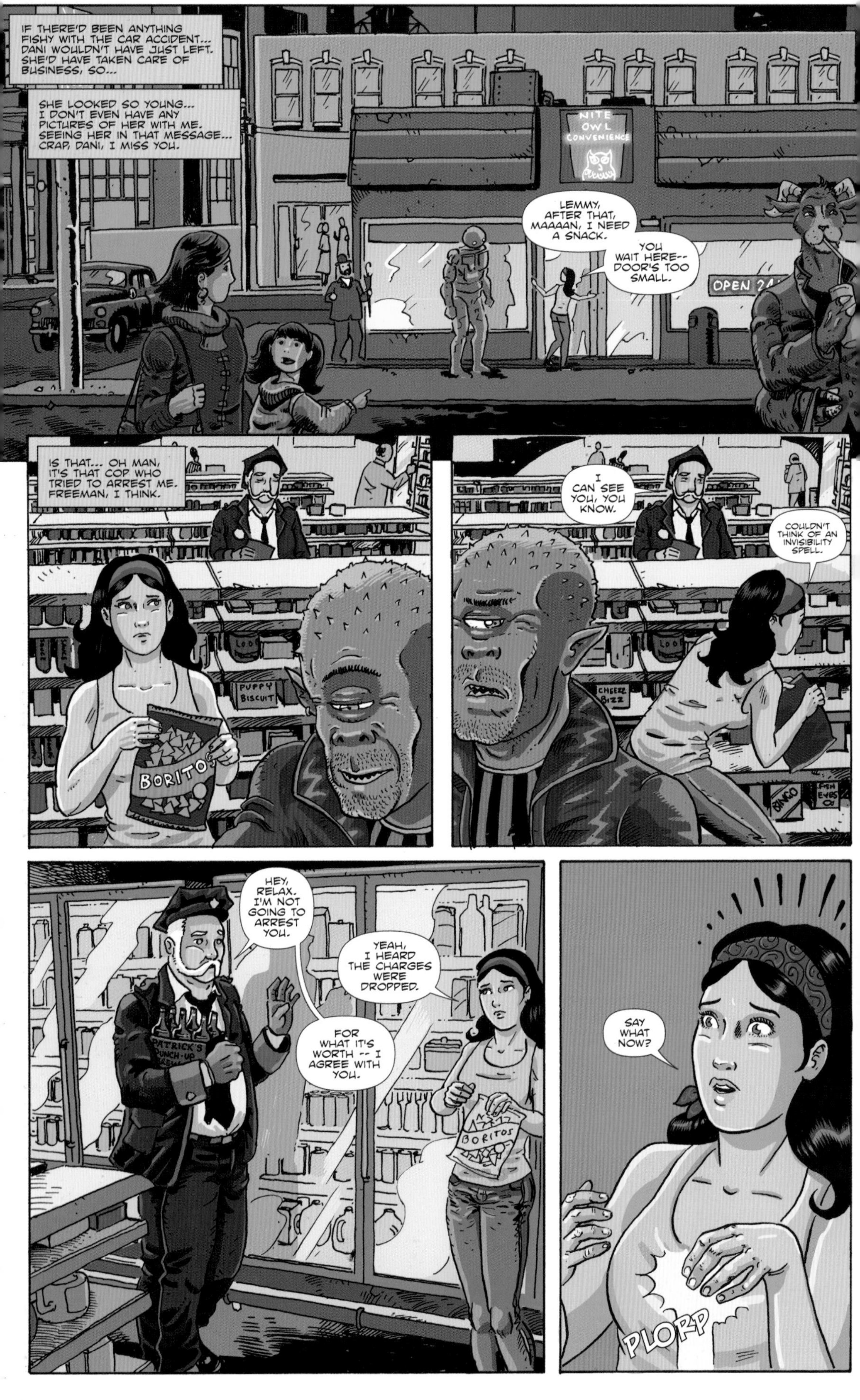
IF THERE'D BEEN ANYTHING FISHY WITH THE CAR ACCIDENT... DANI WOULDN'T HAVE JUST LEFT. SHE'D HAVE TAKEN CARE OF BUSINESS, SO...
SHE LOOKED SO YOUNG... I DON'T EVEN HAVE ANY PICTURES OF HER WITH ME. SEEING HER IN THAT MESSAGE... CRAP, DANI, I MISS YOU.
NITE OWL CONVENIENCE
LEMMY, AFTER THAT, MAAAAN, I NEED A SNACK.
YOU WAIT HERE-- DOOR'S TOO SMALL.
OPEN 24
IS THAT... OH MAN, IT'S THAT COP WHO TRIED TO ARREST ME. FREEMAN, I THINK.
PUPPY BISCUIT
BORITOS
I CAN SEE YOU, YOU KNOW.
COULDN'T THINK OF AN INVISIBILITY SPELL.
CHEEZE BIZZ
BINGO
FISH EYES
HEY, RELAX. I'M NOT GOING TO ARREST YOU.
YEAH, I HEARD THE CHARGES WERE DROPPED.
FOR WHAT IT'S WORTH -- I AGREE WITH YOU.
PATRICK'S PUNCH-UP BREW
BORITOS
SAY WHAT NOW?
PLORP

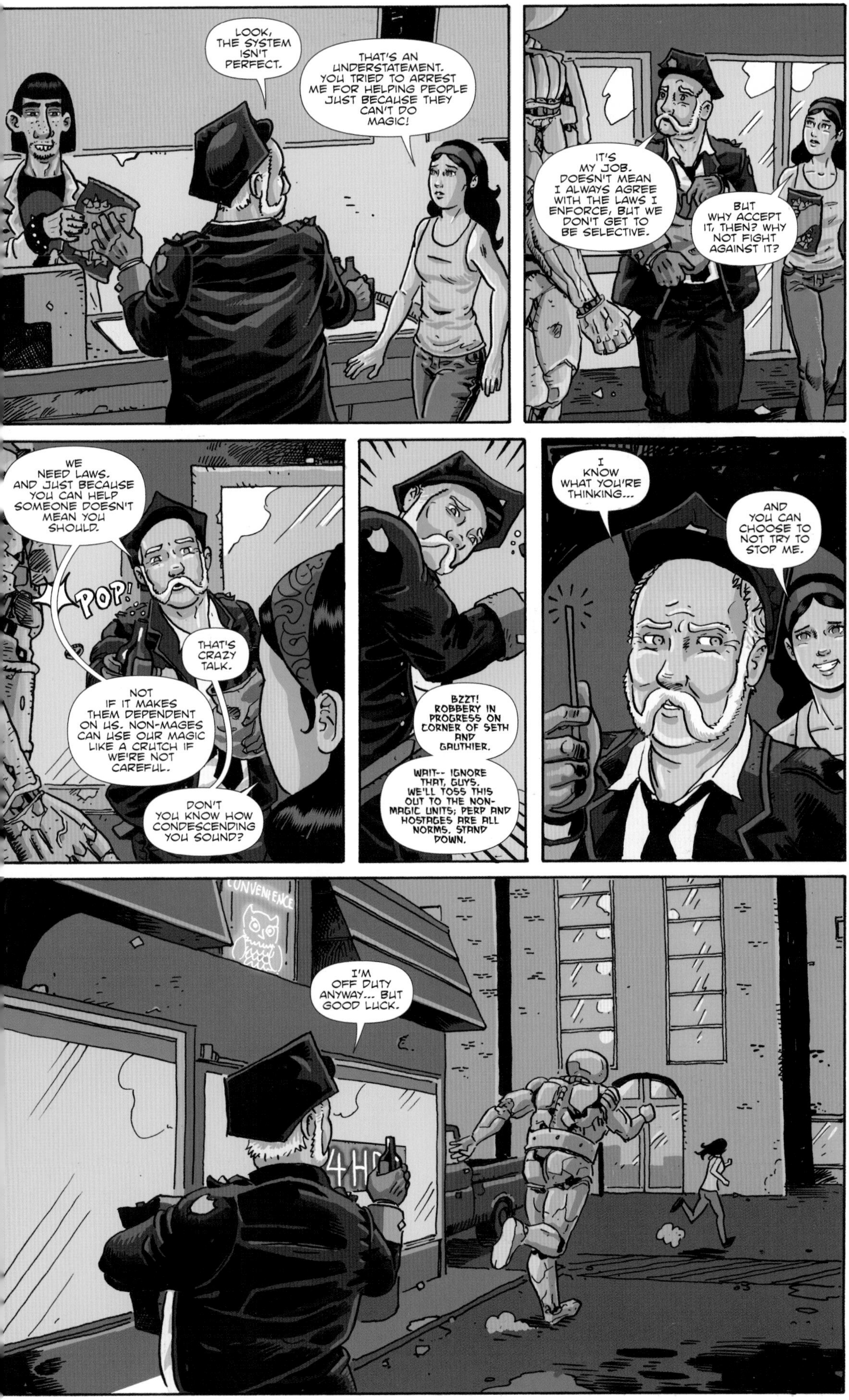
LOOK, THE SYSTEM ISN'T PERFECT.
THAT'S AN UNDERSTATEMENT. YOU TRIED TO ARREST ME FOR HELPING PEOPLE JUST BECAUSE THEY CAN'T DO MAGIC!
IT'S MY JOB. DOESN'T MEAN I ALWAYS AGREE WITH THE LAWS I ENFORCE, BUT WE DON'T GET TO BE SELECTIVE.
BUT WHY ACCEPT IT, THEN? WHY NOT FIGHT AGAINST IT?
WE NEED LAWS. AND JUST BECAUSE YOU CAN HELP SOMEONE DOESN'T MEAN YOU SHOULD.
POP!
THAT'S CRAZY TALK.
NOT IF IT MAKES THEM DEPENDENT ON US. NON-MAGES CAN USE OUR MAGIC LIKE A CRUTCH IF WE'RE NOT CAREFUL.
DON'T YOU KNOW HOW CONDESCENDING YOU SOUND?
BZZT! ROBBERY IN PROGRESS ON CORNER OF SETH AND GAUTHIER.
WAIT-- IGNORE THAT, GUYS. WE'LL TOSS THIS OUT TO THE NON-MAGIC UNITS; PERP AND HOSTAGES ARE ALL NORMS. STAND DOWN.
I KNOW WHAT YOU'RE THINKING...
AND YOU CAN CHOOSE TO NOT TRY TO STOP ME.
CONVENIENCE
I'M OFF DUTY ANYWAY... BUT GOOD LUCK.

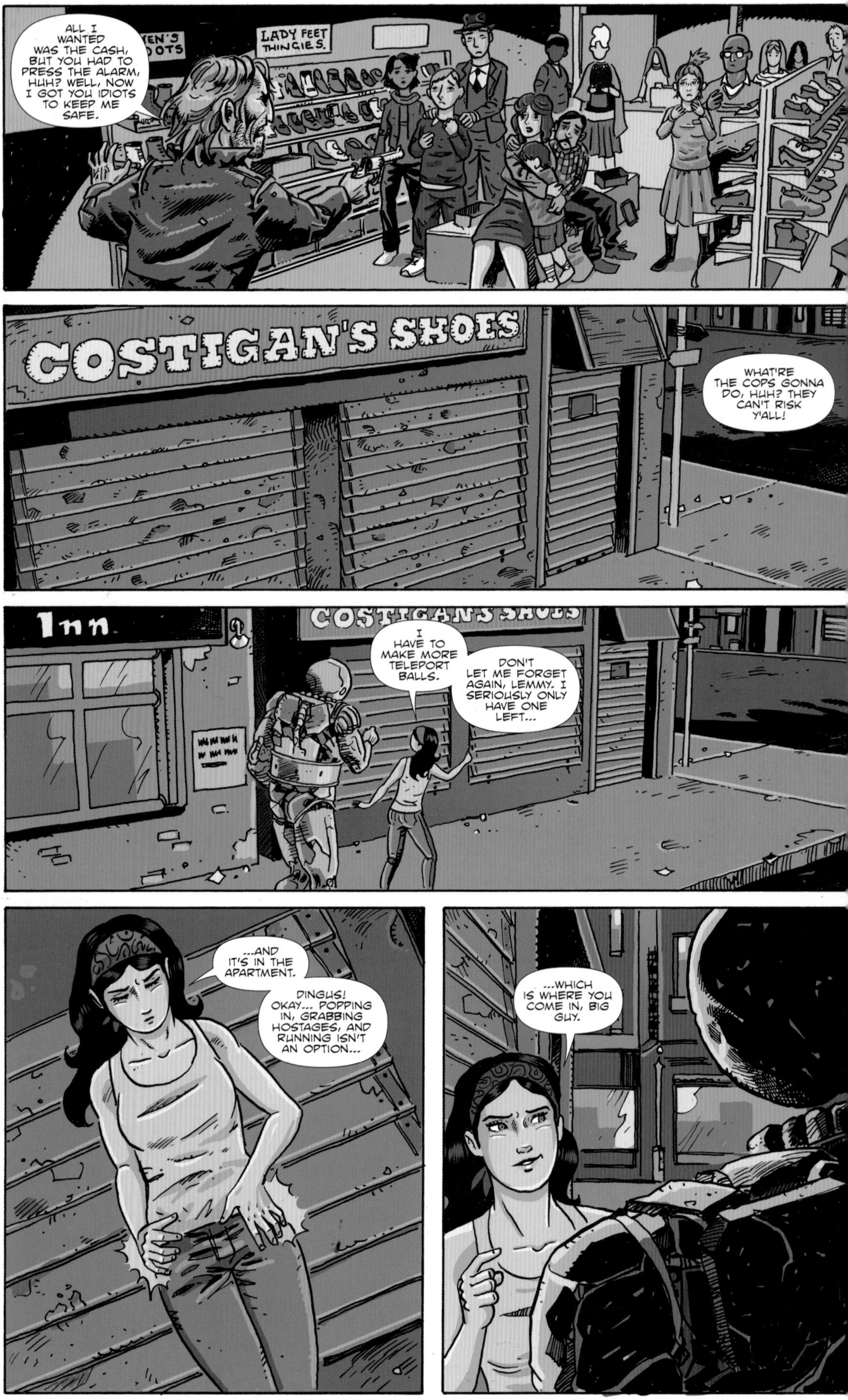

ALL I WANTED WAS THE CASH, BUT YOU HAD TO PRESS THE ALARM, HUH? WELL, NOW I GOT YOU IDIOTS TO KEEP ME SAFE.
LADY FEET THINGIES.
COSTIGAN'S SHOES
WHAT'RE THE COPS GONNA DO, HUH? THEY CAN'T RISK Y'ALL!
Inn
COSTIGAN'S SHOES
I HAVE TO MAKE MORE TELEPORT BALLS.
DON'T LET ME FORGET AGAIN, LEMMY. I SERIOUSLY ONLY HAVE ONE LEFT...
...AND IT'S IN THE APARTMENT.
DINGUS! OKAY... POPPING IN, GRABBING HOSTAGES, AND RUNNING ISN'T AN OPTION...
...WHICH IS WHERE YOU COME IN, BIG GUY.

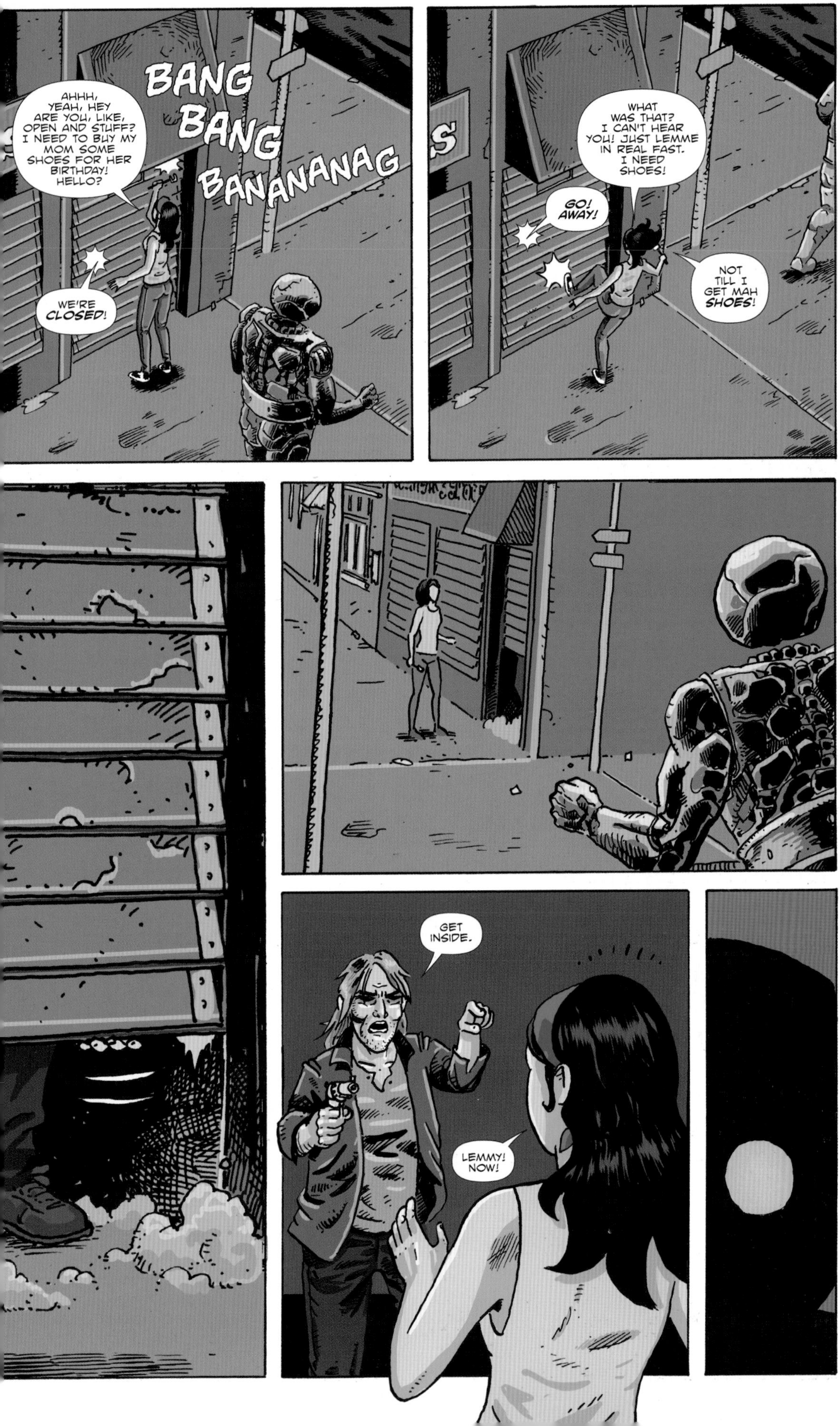
BANG
BANG
BANANANAG
AHHH, YEAH, HEY ARE YOU, LIKE, OPEN AND STUFF? I NEED TO BUY MY MOM SOME SHOES FOR HER BIRTHDAY! HELLO?
WE'RE CLOSED!
WHAT WAS THAT? I CAN'T HEAR YOU! JUST LEMME IN REAL FAST. I NEED SHOES!
GO! AWAY!
NOT TILL I GET MAH SHOES!
GET INSIDE.
LEMMY! NOW!

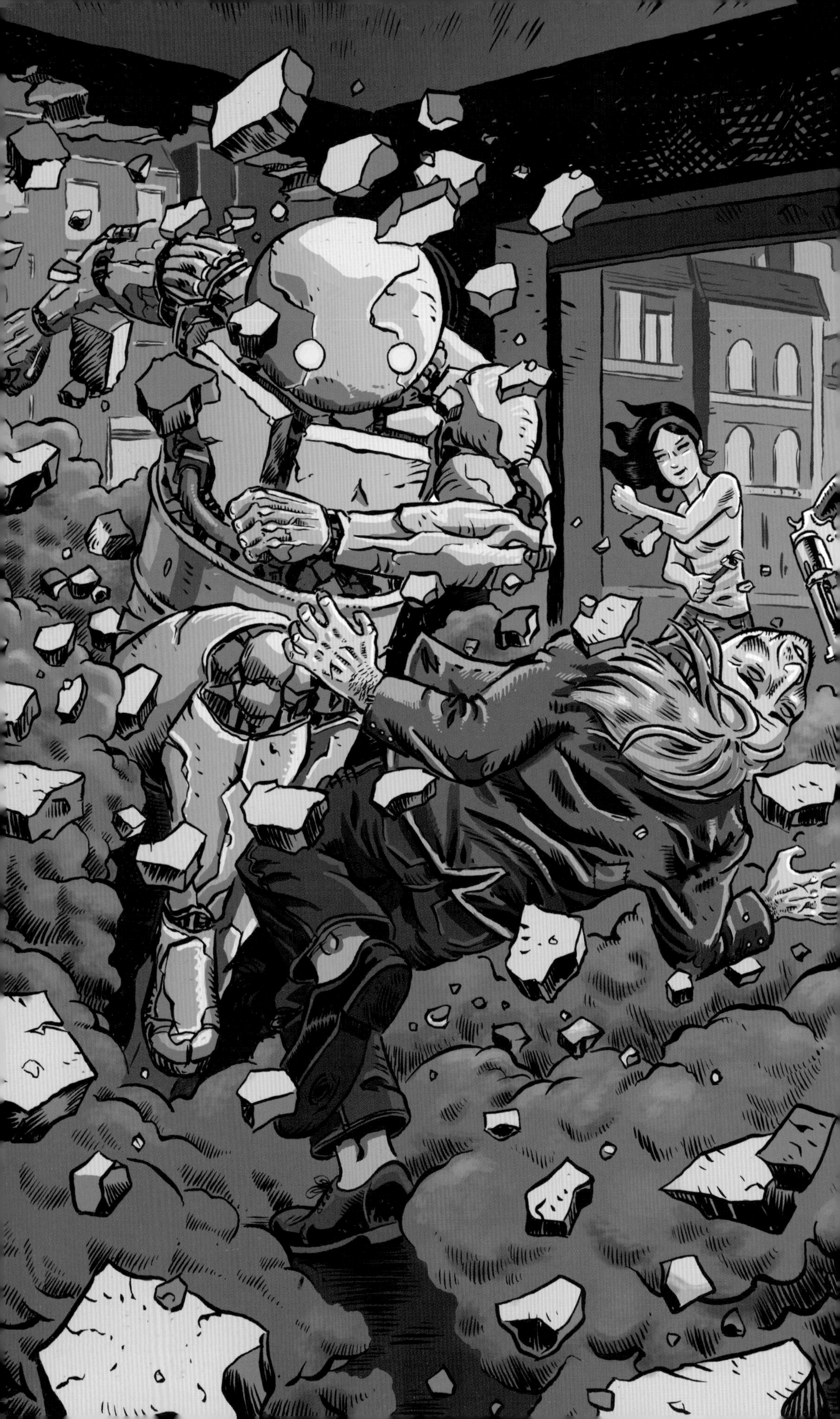

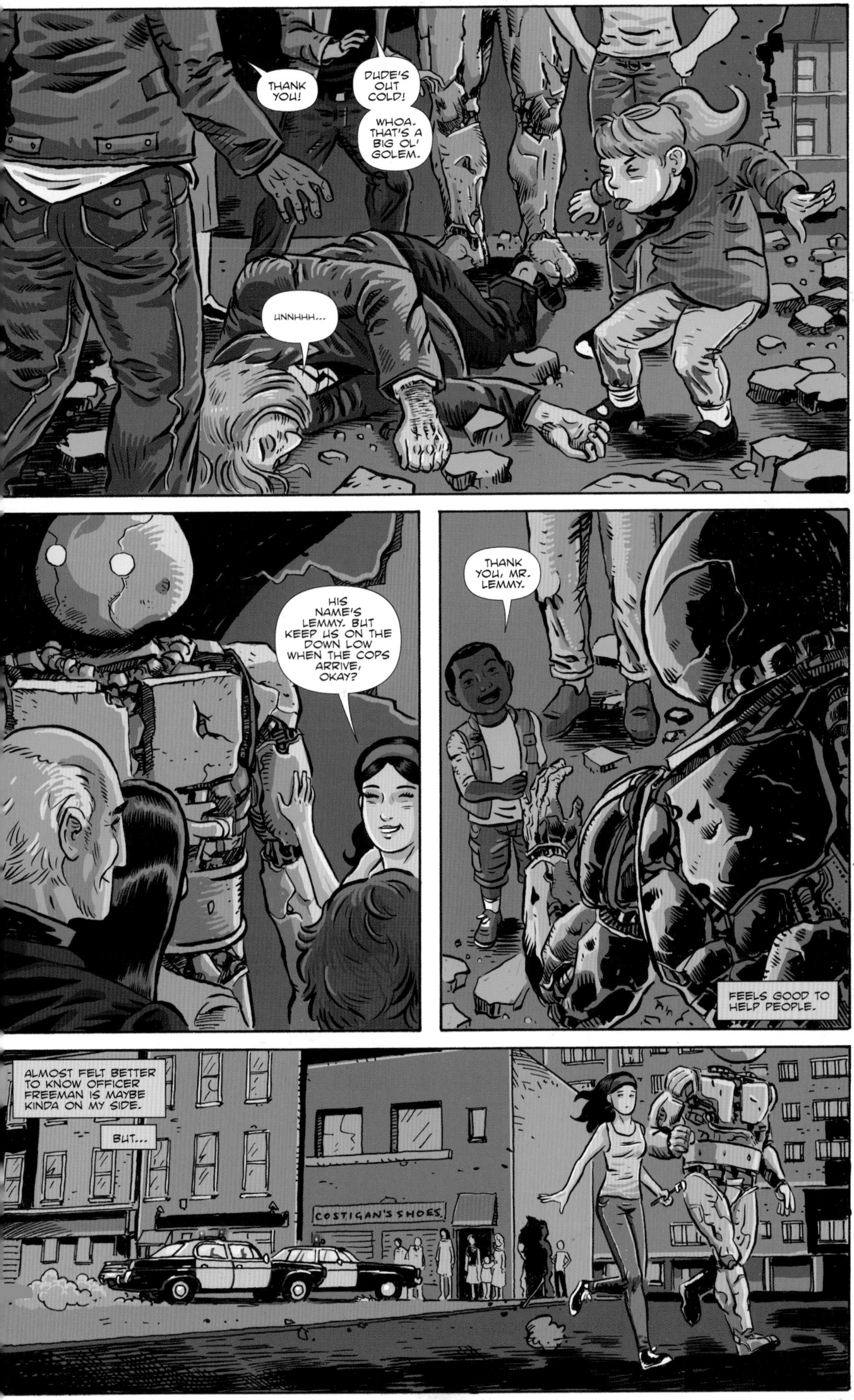
THANK YOU!
DUDE'S OUT COLD!
WHOA. THAT'S A BIG OL' GOLEM.
UNNHHH...
HIS NAME'S LEMMY. BUT KEEP US ON THE DOWN LOW WHEN THE COPS ARRIVE, OKAY?
THANK YOU, MR. LEMMY.
FEELS GOOD TO HELP PEOPLE.
ALMOST FELT BETTER TO KNOW OFFICER FREEMAN IS MAYBE KINDA ON MY SIDE.
BUT...
COSTIGAN'S SHOES

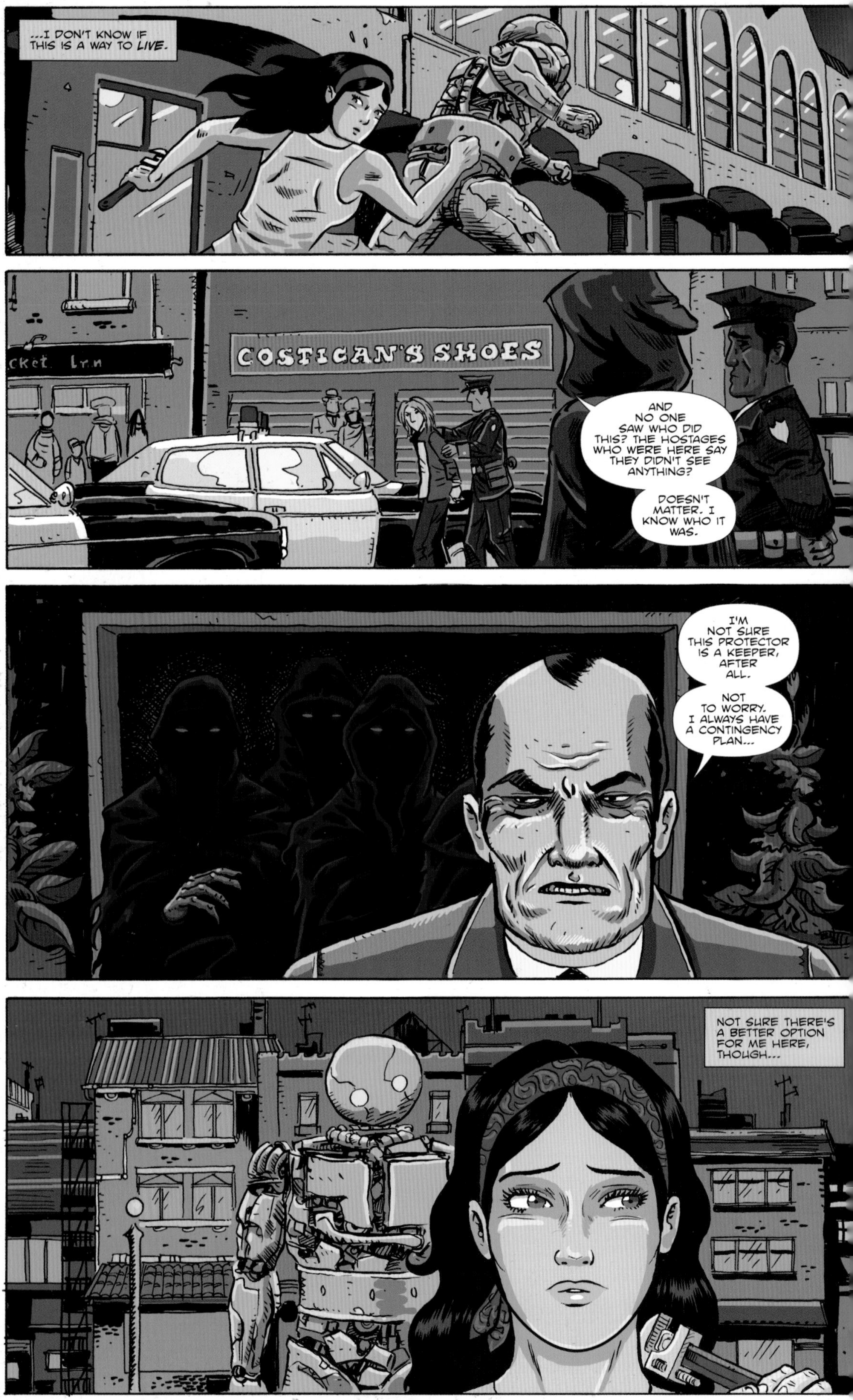
...I DON'T KNOW IF THIS IS A WAY TO *LIVE*.
COSTIGAN'S SHOES
AND NO ONE SAW WHO DID THIS? THE HOSTAGES WHO WERE HERE SAY THEY DIDN'T SEE ANYTHING?
DOESN'T MATTER. I KNOW WHO IT WAS.
I'M NOT SURE THIS PROTECTOR IS A KEEPER, AFTER ALL.
NOT TO WORRY. I ALWAYS HAVE A CONTINGENCY PLAN...
NOT SURE THERE'S A BETTER OPTION FOR ME HERE, THOUGH...

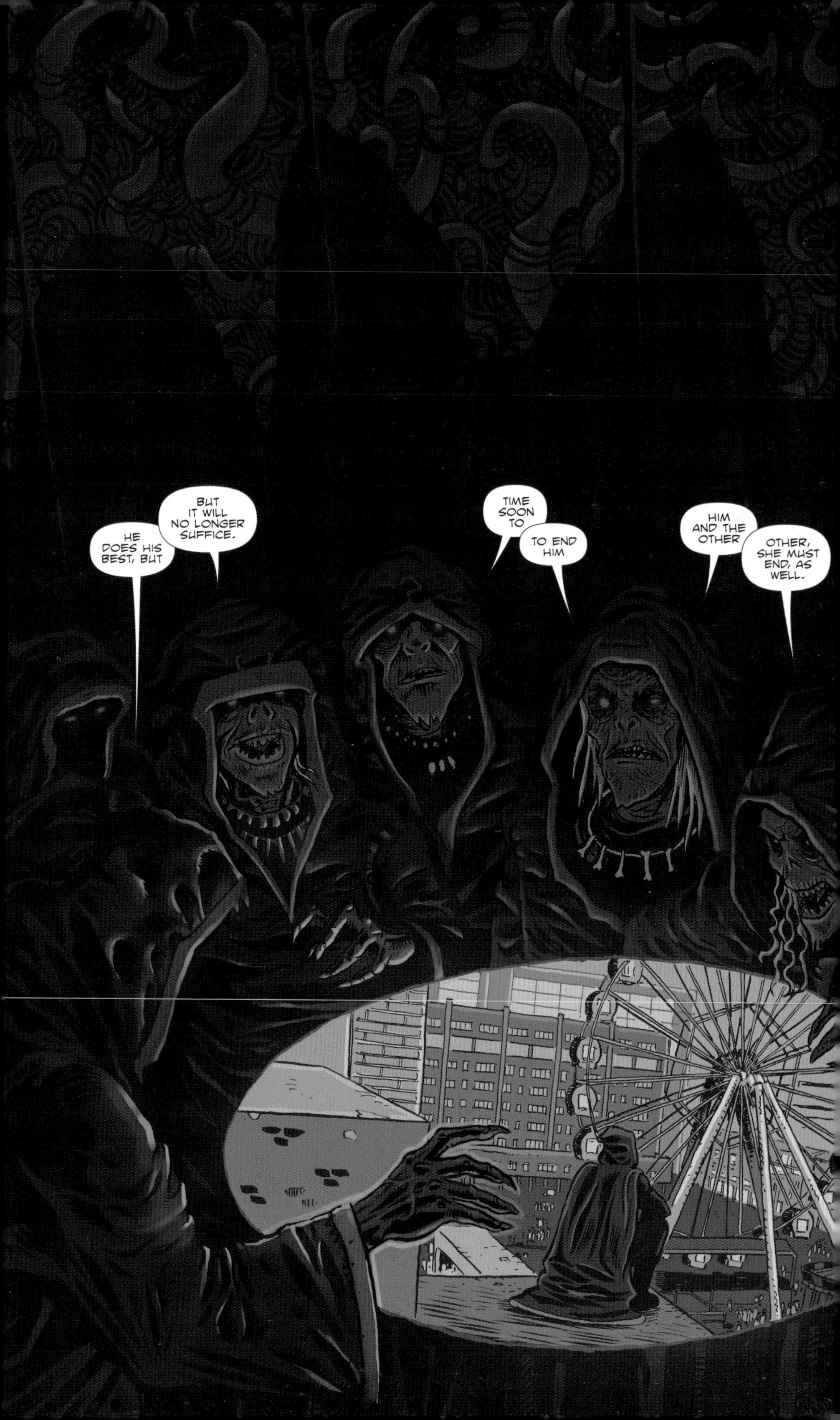
HE DOES HIS BEST, BUT
BUT IT WILL NO LONGER SUFFICE.
TIME SOON TO
TO END HIM
HIM AND THE OTHER
OTHER, SHE MUST END, AS WELL.

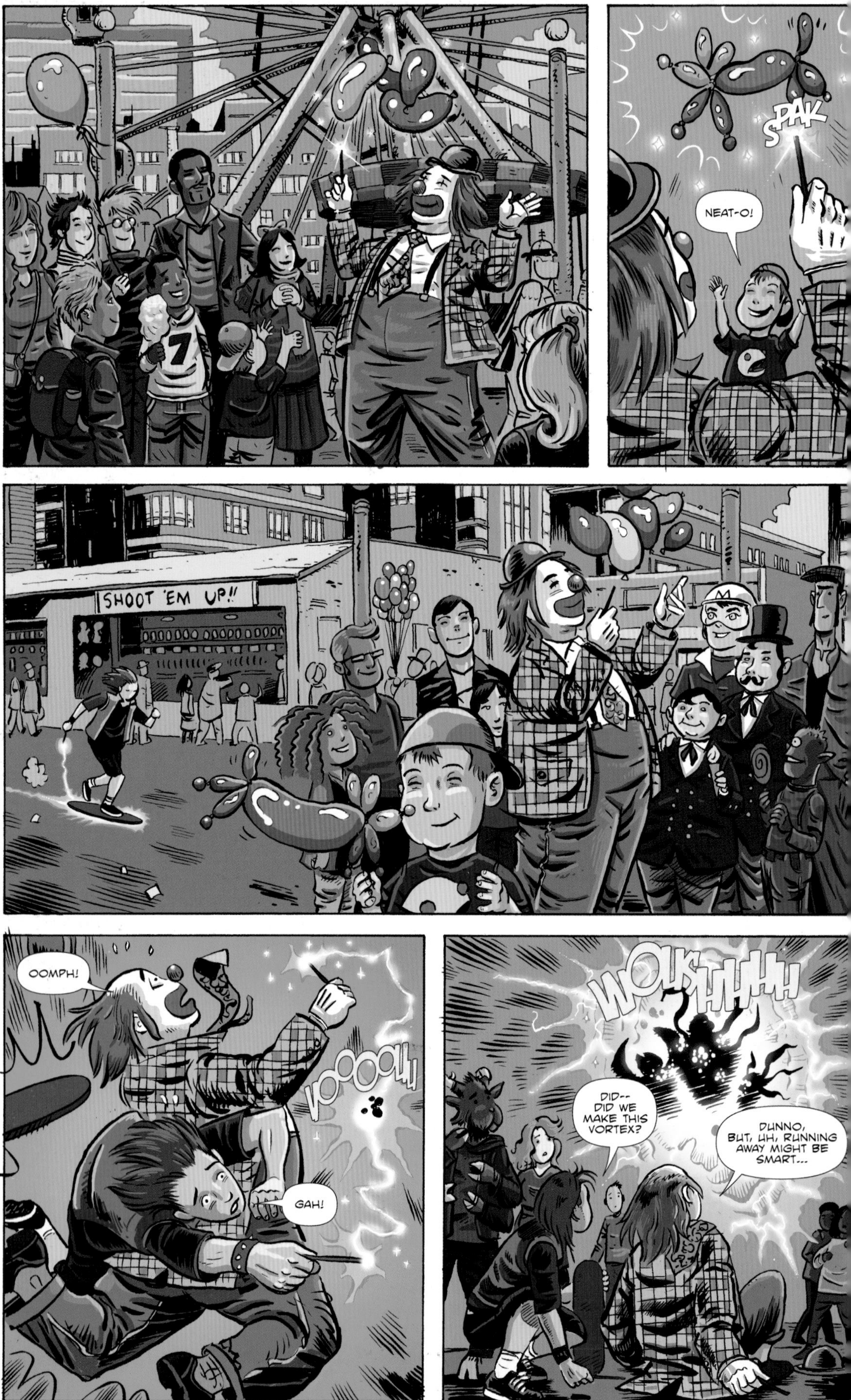
SPAK
NEAT-O!
SHOOT 'EM UP!!
OOMPH!
VOOOOUH
GAH!
WOUSHHHHH
DID-- DID WE MAKE THIS VORTEX?
DUNNO, BUT, UH, RUNNING AWAY MIGHT BE SMART...

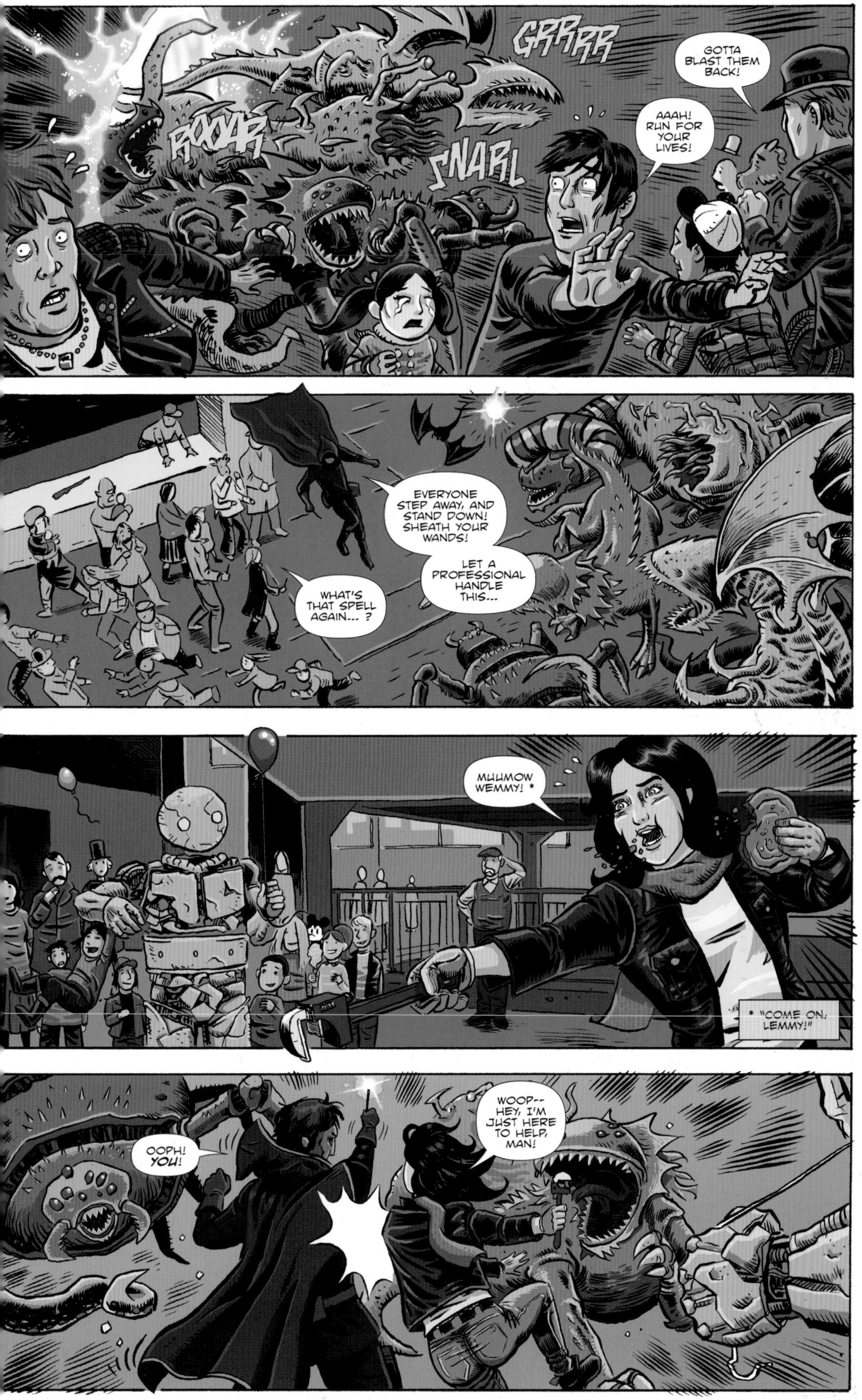
GRRRR
ROOAR
SNARL
GOTTA BLAST THEM BACK!
AAAH! RUN FOR YOUR LIVES!
EVERYONE STEP AWAY, AND STAND DOWN! SHEATH YOUR WANDS!
LET A PROFESSIONAL HANDLE THIS...
WHAT'S THAT SPELL AGAIN... ?
MUUMOW WEMMY! *
* "COME ON, LEMMY!"
OOPH! YOU!
WOOP-- HEY, I'M JUST HERE TO HELP, MAN!

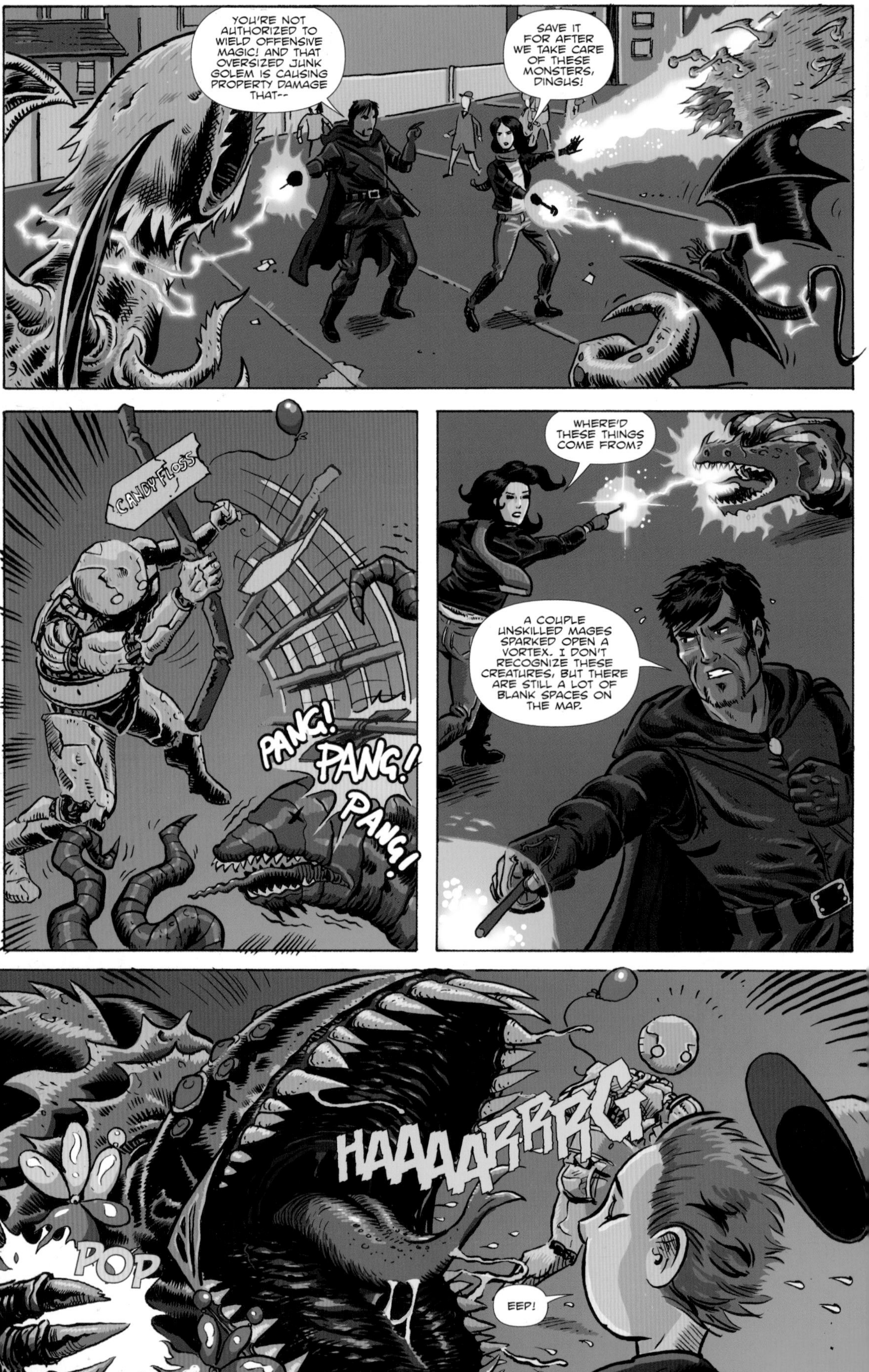
YOU'RE NOT AUTHORIZED TO WIELD OFFENSIVE MAGIC! AND THAT OVERSIZED JUNK GOLEM IS CAUSING PROPERTY DAMAGE THAT--
SAVE IT FOR AFTER WE TAKE CARE OF THESE MONSTERS, DINGUS!
CANDY FLOSS
PANG!
PANG!
PANG!
WHERE'D THESE THINGS COME FROM?
A COUPLE UNSKILLED MAGES SPARKED OPEN A VORTEX. I DON'T RECOGNIZE THESE CREATURES, BUT THERE ARE STILL A LOT OF BLANK SPACES ON THE MAP.
HAAAARRRG
POP
EEP!

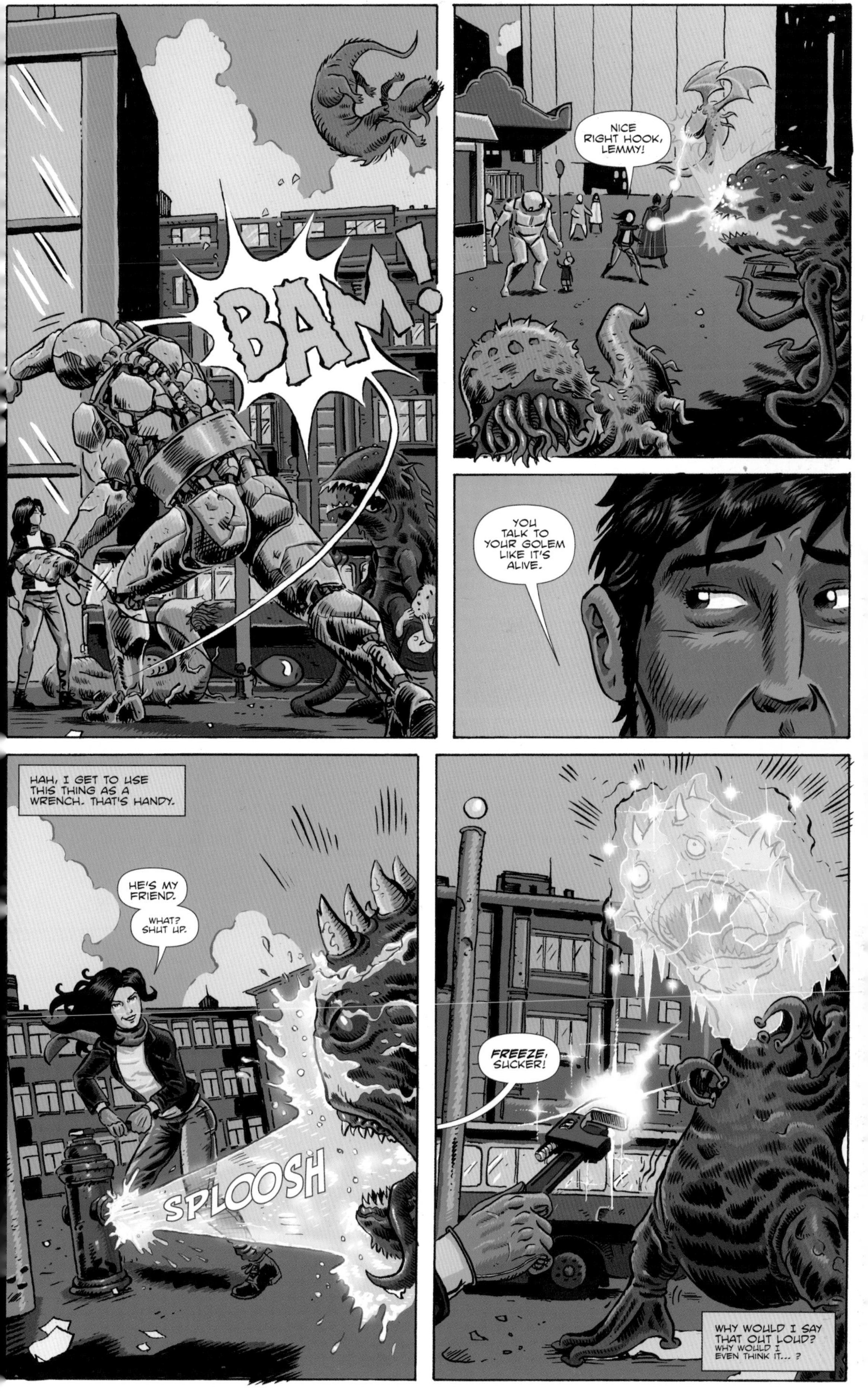

BAM!
NICE RIGHT HOOK, LEMMY!
YOU TALK TO YOUR GOLEM LIKE IT'S ALIVE.
HAH, I GET TO USE THIS THING AS A WRENCH. THAT'S HANDY.
HE'S MY FRIEND.
WHAT? SHUT UP.
SPLOOSH
FREEZE, SUCKER!
WHY WOULD I SAY THAT OUT LOUD? WHY WOULD I EVEN THINK IT... ?

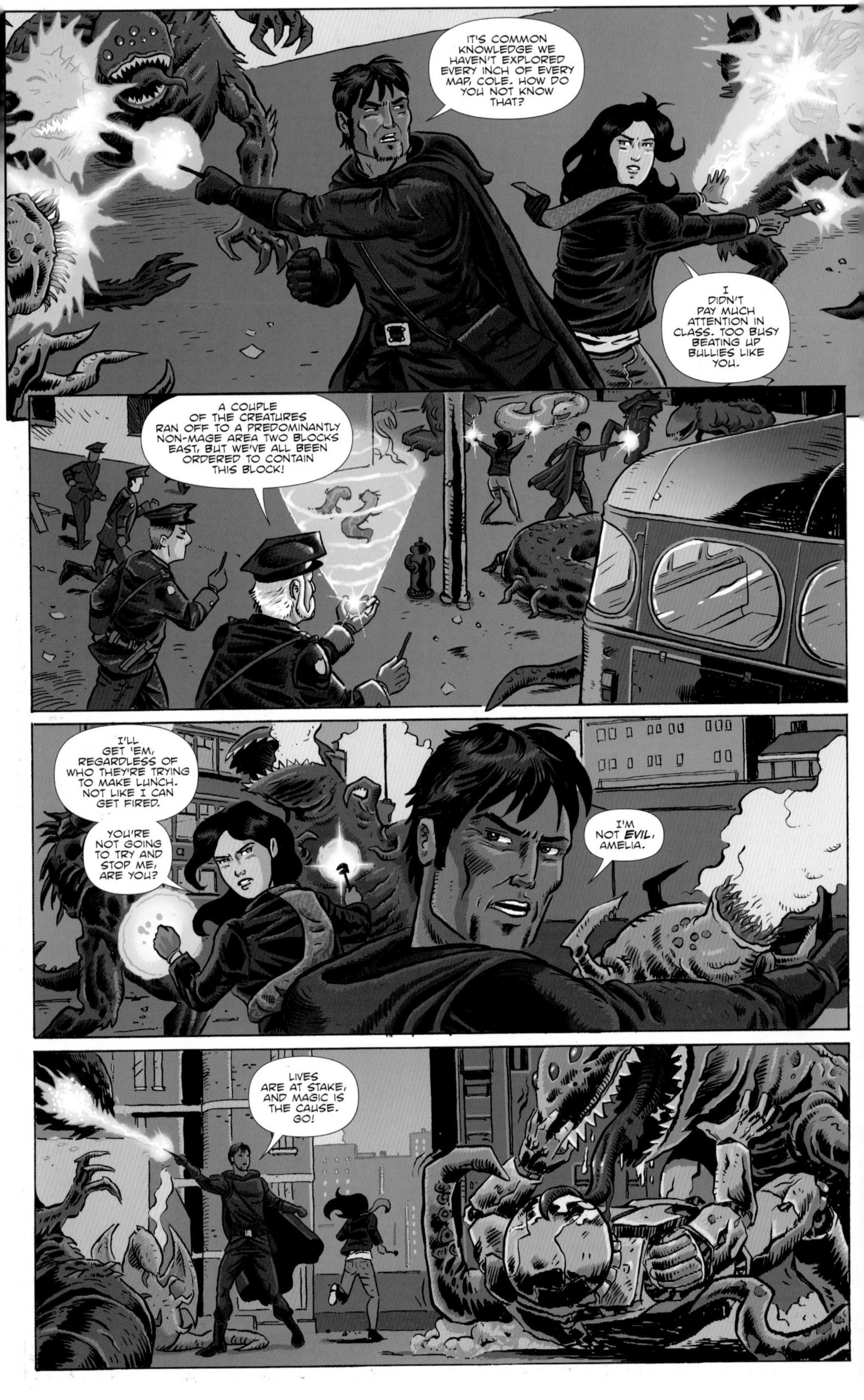
IT'S COMMON KNOWLEDGE WE HAVEN'T EXPLORED EVERY INCH OF EVERY MAP, COLE. HOW DO YOU NOT KNOW THAT?
I DIDN'T PAY MUCH ATTENTION IN CLASS. TOO BUSY BEATING UP BULLIES LIKE YOU.
A COUPLE OF THE CREATURES RAN OFF TO A PREDOMINANTLY NON-MAGE AREA TWO BLOCKS EAST, BUT WE'VE ALL BEEN ORDERED TO CONTAIN THIS BLOCK!
I'LL GET 'EM, REGARDLESS OF WHO THEY'RE TRYING TO MAKE LUNCH. NOT LIKE I CAN GET FIRED.
YOU'RE NOT GOING TO TRY AND STOP ME, ARE YOU?
I'M NOT EVIL, AMELIA.
LIVES ARE AT STAKE, AND MAGIC IS THE CAUSE. GO!

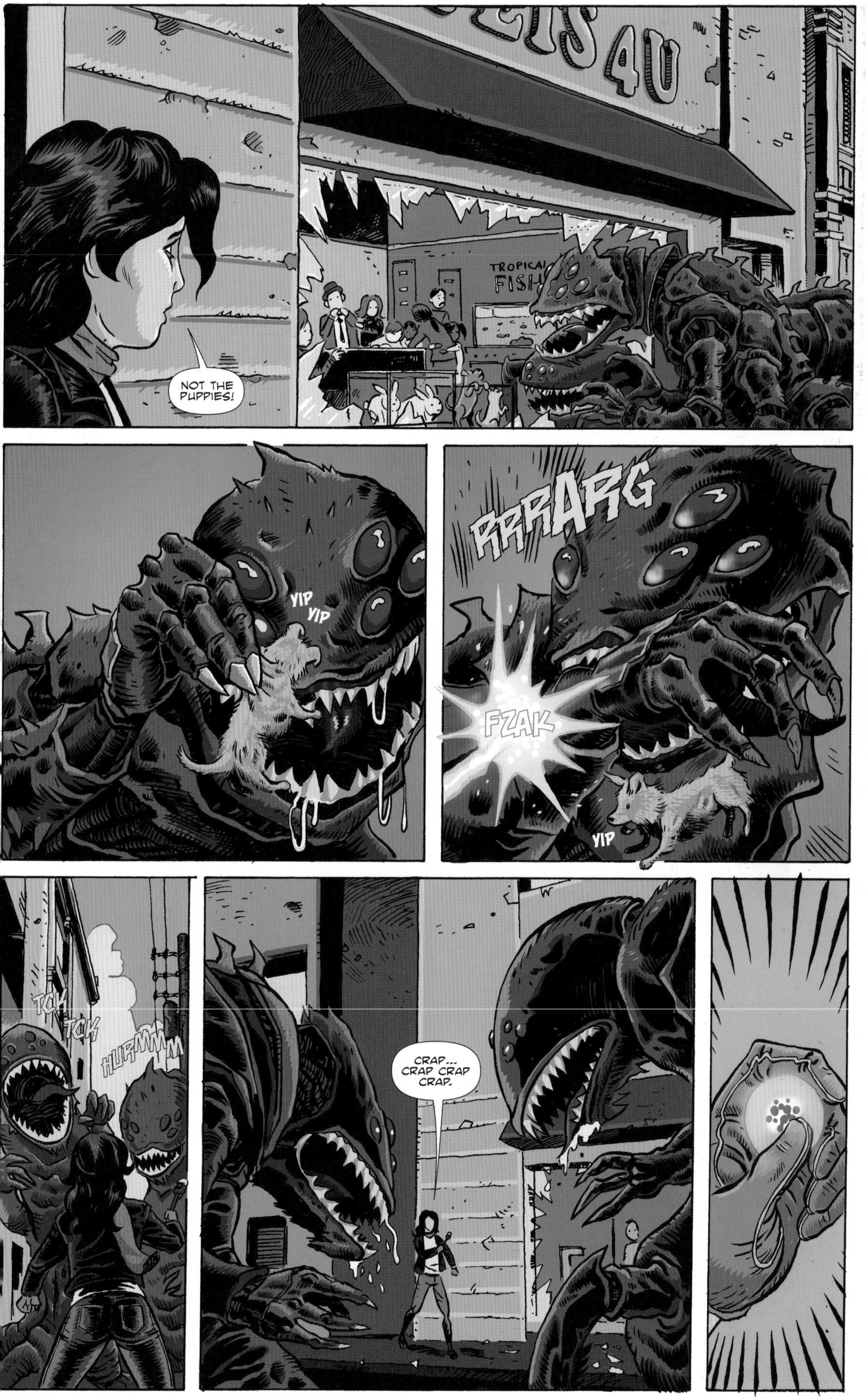
PETS 4U
TROPICAL FISH
NOT THE PUPPIES!
YIP YIP
RRRARG
FZAK
YIP
TCK TCK
HURMMMM
CRAP... CRAP CRAP CRAP.

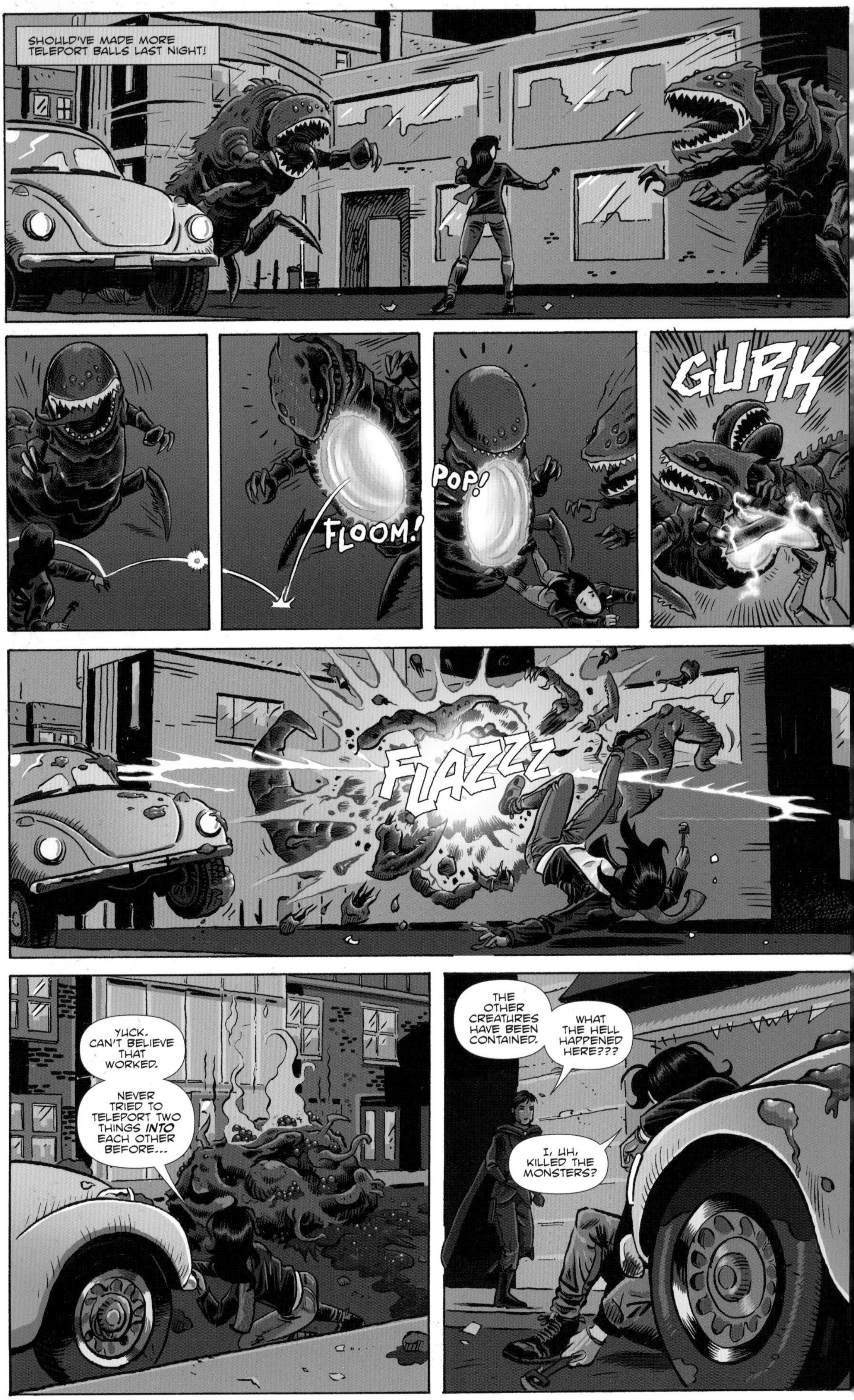
SHOULD'VE MADE MORE TELEPORT BALLS LAST NIGHT!
FLOOM!
POP!
GURK
FLAZZZ
YUCK. CAN'T BELIEVE THAT WORKED.
NEVER TRIED TO TELEPORT TWO THINGS *INTO* EACH OTHER BEFORE...
THE OTHER CREATURES HAVE BEEN CONTAINED.
WHAT THE HELL HAPPENED HERE???
I, UH, KILLED THE MONSTERS?

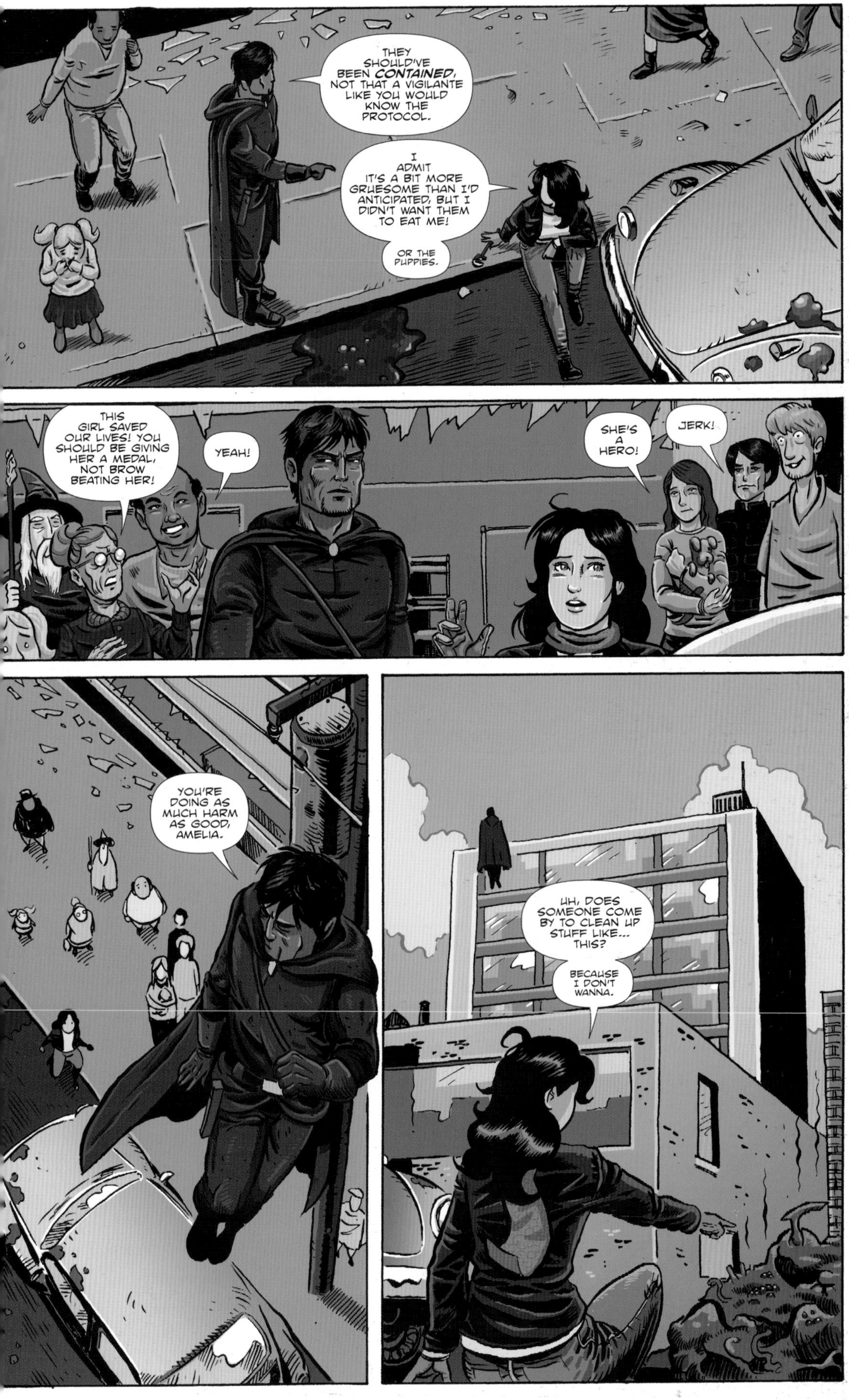
THEY SHOULD'VE BEEN CONTAINED, NOT THAT A VIGILANTE LIKE YOU WOULD KNOW THE PROTOCOL.
I ADMIT IT'S A BIT MORE GRUESOME THAN I'D ANTICIPATED, BUT I DIDN'T WANT THEM TO EAT ME!
OR THE PUPPIES.
THIS GIRL SAVED OUR LIVES! YOU SHOULD BE GIVING HER A MEDAL, NOT BROW BEATING HER!
YEAH!
SHE'S A HERO!
JERK!
YOU'RE DOING AS MUCH HARM AS GOOD, AMELIA.
UH, DOES SOMEONE COME BY TO CLEAN UP STUFF LIKE... THIS?
BECAUSE I DON'T WANNA.

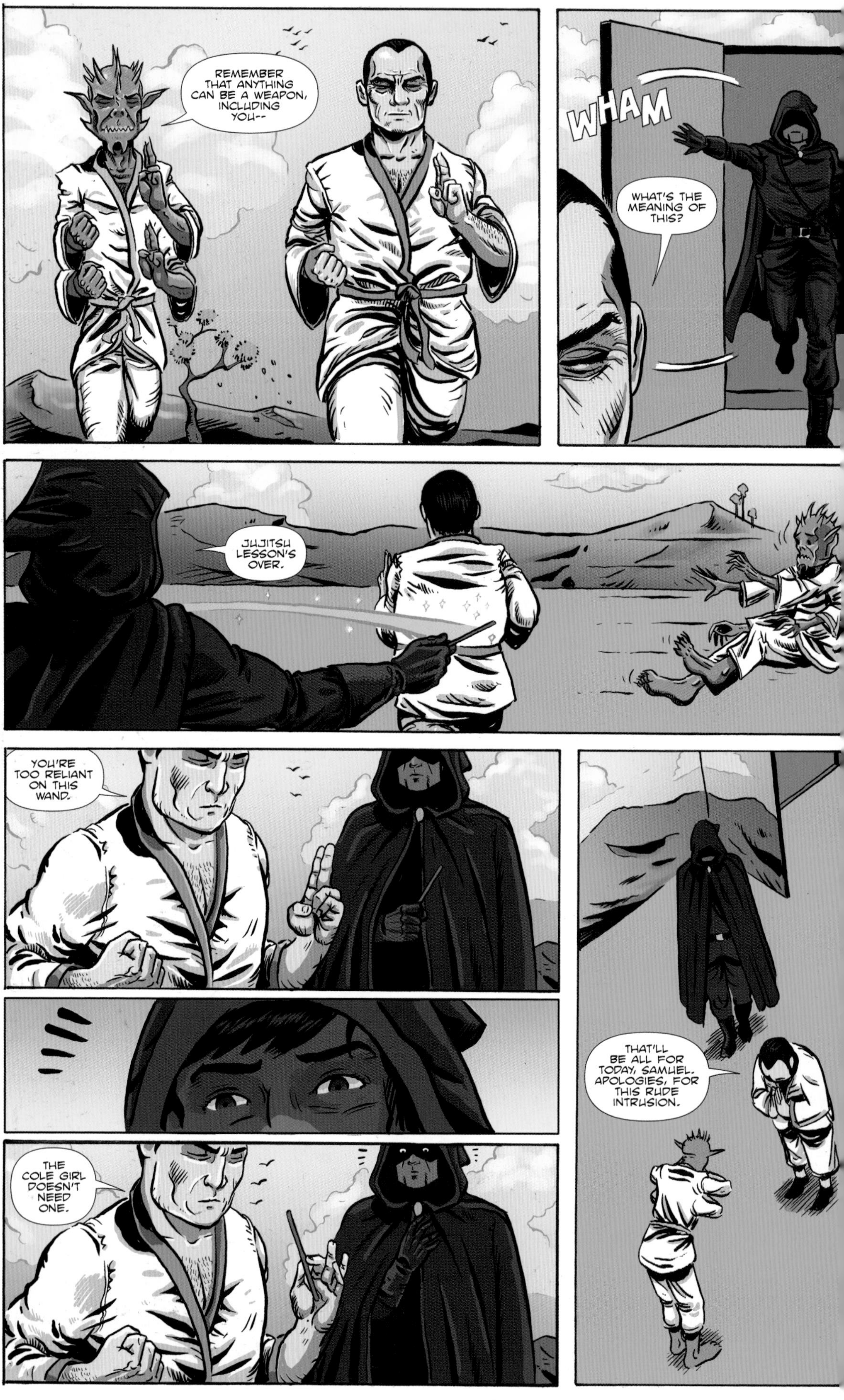
REMEMBER THAT ANYTHING CAN BE A WEAPON, INCLUDING YOU--
WHAM
WHAT'S THE MEANING OF THIS?
JUJITSU LESSON'S OVER.
YOU'RE TOO RELIANT ON THIS WAND.
THE COLE GIRL DOESN'T NEED ONE.
THAT'LL BE ALL FOR TODAY, SAMUEL. APOLOGIES, FOR THIS RUDE INTRUSION.

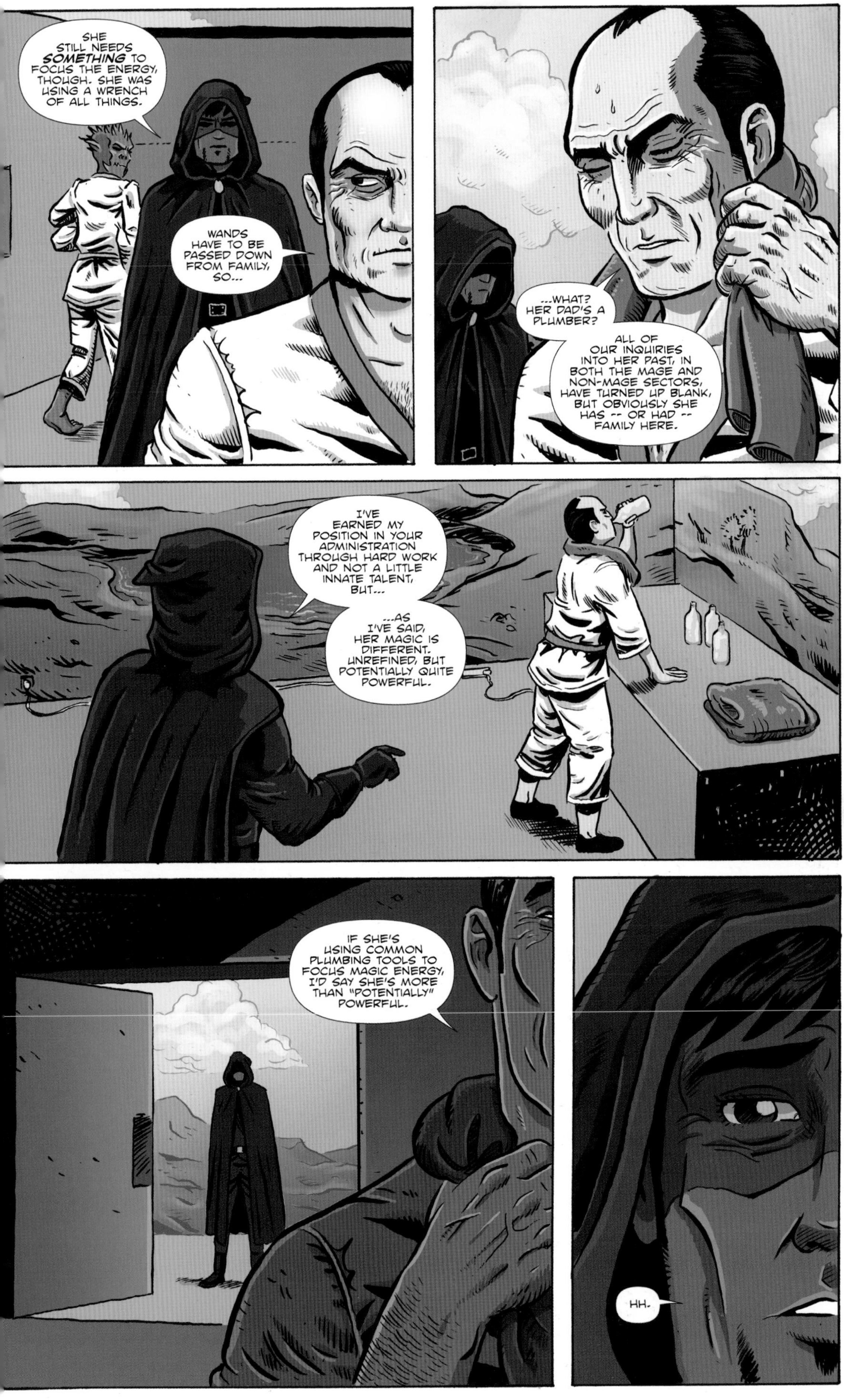
SHE STILL NEEDS *SOMETHING* TO FOCUS THE ENERGY, THOUGH. SHE WAS USING A WRENCH OF ALL THINGS.
WANDS HAVE TO BE PASSED DOWN FROM FAMILY, SO...
...WHAT? HER DAD'S A PLUMBER?
ALL OF OUR INQUIRIES INTO HER PAST, IN BOTH THE MAGE AND NON-MAGE SECTORS, HAVE TURNED UP BLANK, BUT OBVIOUSLY SHE HAS -- OR HAD -- FAMILY HERE.
I'VE EARNED MY POSITION IN YOUR ADMINISTRATION THROUGH HARD WORK AND NOT A LITTLE INNATE TALENT, BUT...
...AS I'VE SAID, HER MAGIC IS DIFFERENT. UNREFINED, BUT POTENTIALLY QUITE POWERFUL.
IF SHE'S USING COMMON PLUMBING TOOLS TO FOCUS MAGIC ENERGY, I'D SAY SHE'S MORE THAN "POTENTIALLY" POWERFUL.
HH.

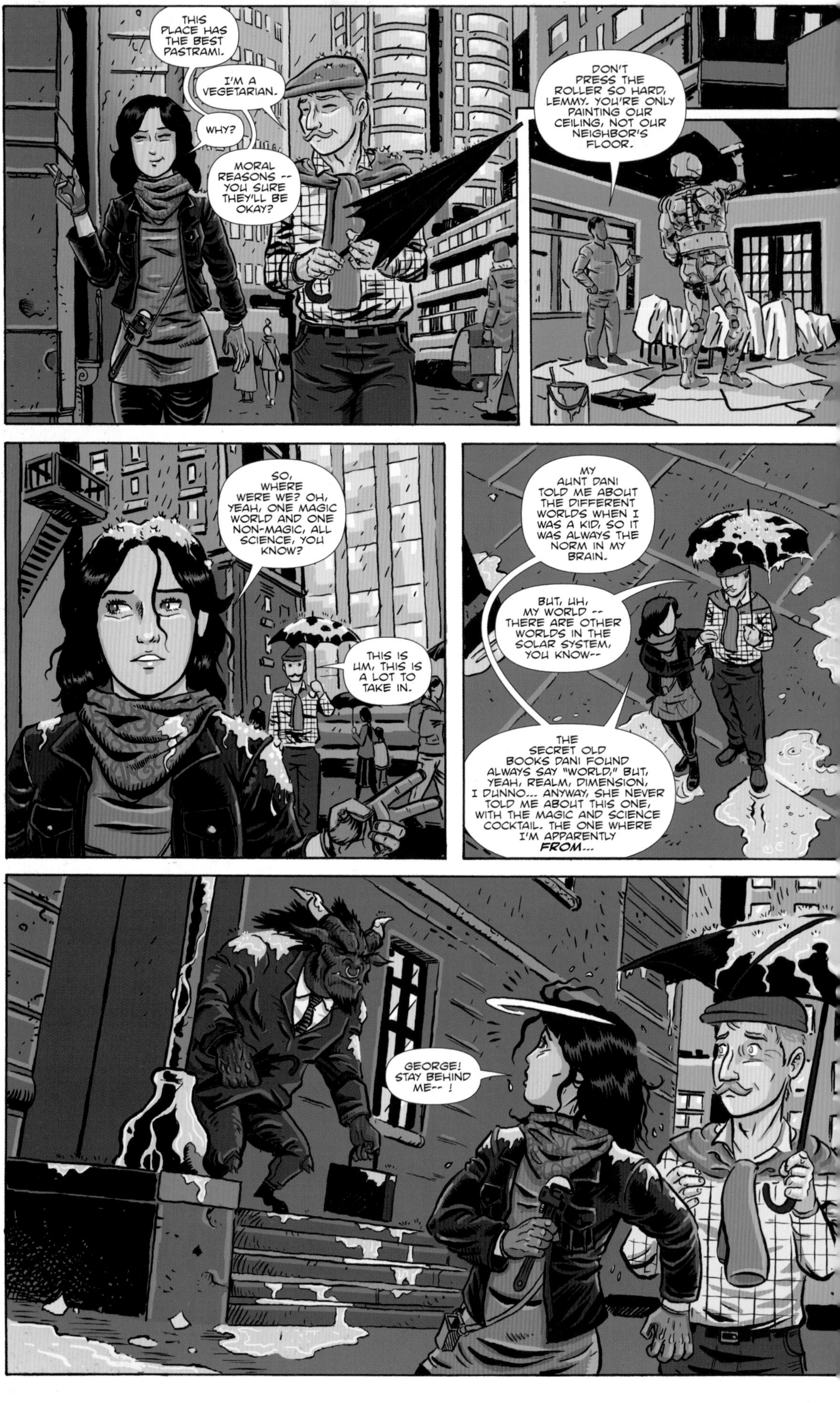
THIS PLACE HAS THE BEST PASTRAMI.
I'M A VEGETARIAN.
WHY?
MORAL REASONS -- YOU SURE THEY'LL BE OKAY?
DON'T PRESS THE ROLLER SO HARD, LEMMY. YOU'RE ONLY PAINTING OUR CEILING, NOT OUR NEIGHBOR'S FLOOR.
SO, WHERE WERE WE? OH, YEAH, ONE MAGIC WORLD AND ONE NON-MAGIC, ALL SCIENCE, YOU KNOW?
THIS IS UM, THIS IS A LOT TO TAKE IN.
MY AUNT DANI TOLD ME ABOUT THE DIFFERENT WORLDS WHEN I WAS A KID, SO IT WAS ALWAYS THE NORM IN MY BRAIN.
BUT, UH, MY WORLD -- THERE ARE OTHER WORLDS IN THE SOLAR SYSTEM, YOU KNOW--
THE SECRET OLD BOOKS DANI FOUND ALWAYS SAY "WORLD," BUT, YEAH, REALM, DIMENSION, I DUNNO... ANYWAY, SHE NEVER TOLD ME ABOUT THIS ONE, WITH THE MAGIC AND SCIENCE COCKTAIL. THE ONE WHERE I'M APPARENTLY FROM...
GEORGE! STAY BEHIND ME-- !

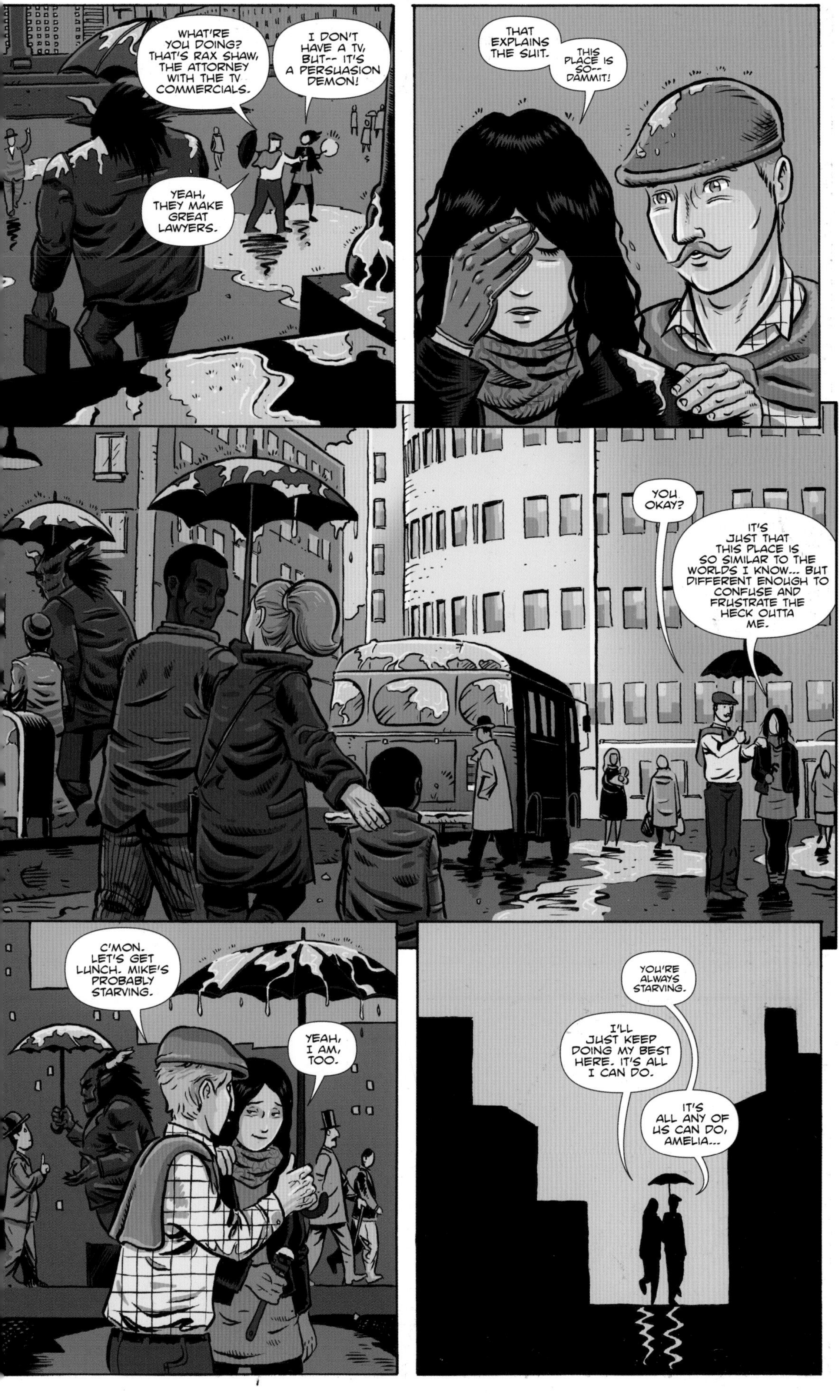

WHAT'RE YOU DOING? THAT'S RAX SHAW, THE ATTORNEY WITH THE TV COMMERCIALS.
I DON'T HAVE A TV, BUT-- IT'S A PERSUASION DEMON!
YEAH, THEY MAKE GREAT LAWYERS.
THAT EXPLAINS THE SUIT.
THIS PLACE IS SO-- DAMMIT!
YOU OKAY?
IT'S JUST THAT THIS PLACE IS SO SIMILAR TO THE WORLDS I KNOW... BUT DIFFERENT ENOUGH TO CONFUSE AND FRUSTRATE THE HECK OUTTA ME.
C'MON. LET'S GET LUNCH. MIKE'S PROBABLY STARVING.
YEAH, I AM, TOO.
YOU'RE ALWAYS STARVING.
I'LL JUST KEEP DOING MY BEST HERE. IT'S ALL I CAN DO.
IT'S ALL ANY OF US CAN DO, AMELIA...

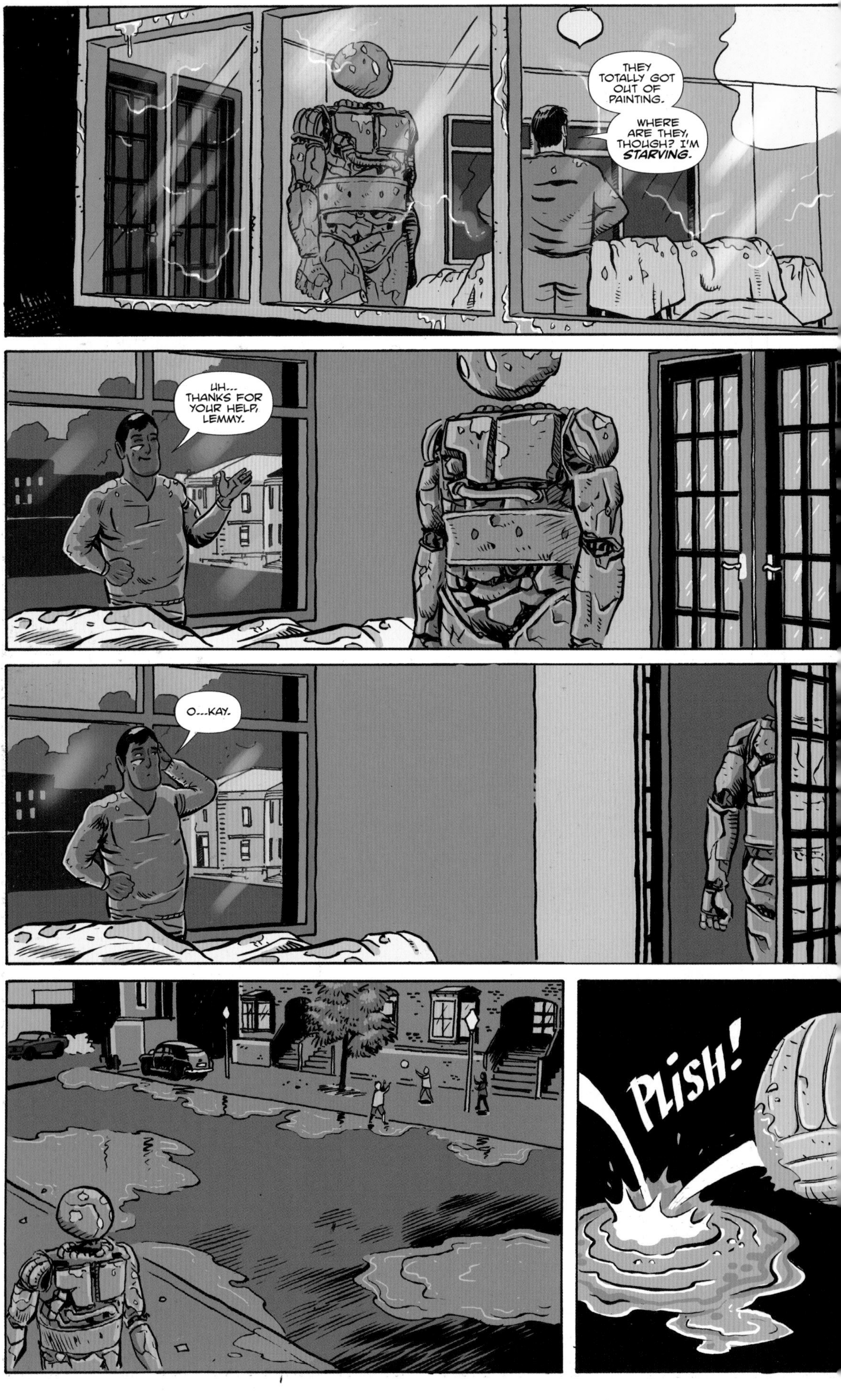
THEY TOTALLY GOT OUT OF PAINTING.
WHERE ARE THEY, THOUGH? I'M STARVING.
UH... THANKS FOR YOUR HELP, LEMMY.
O...KAY.
PLISH!

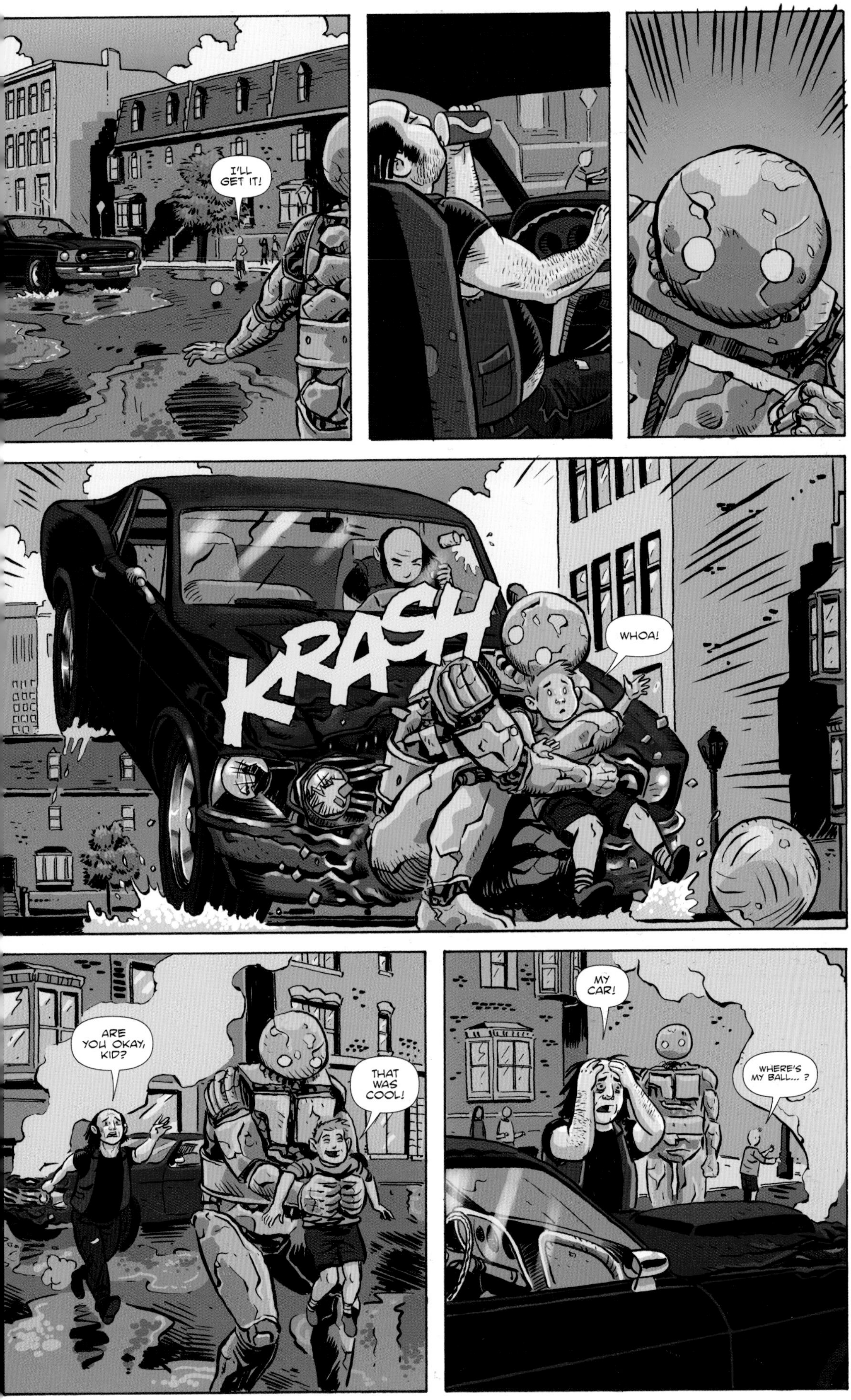

I'LL GET IT!
KRASH
WHOA!
ARE YOU OKAY, KID?
THAT WAS COOL!
MY CAR!
WHERE'S MY BALL... ?

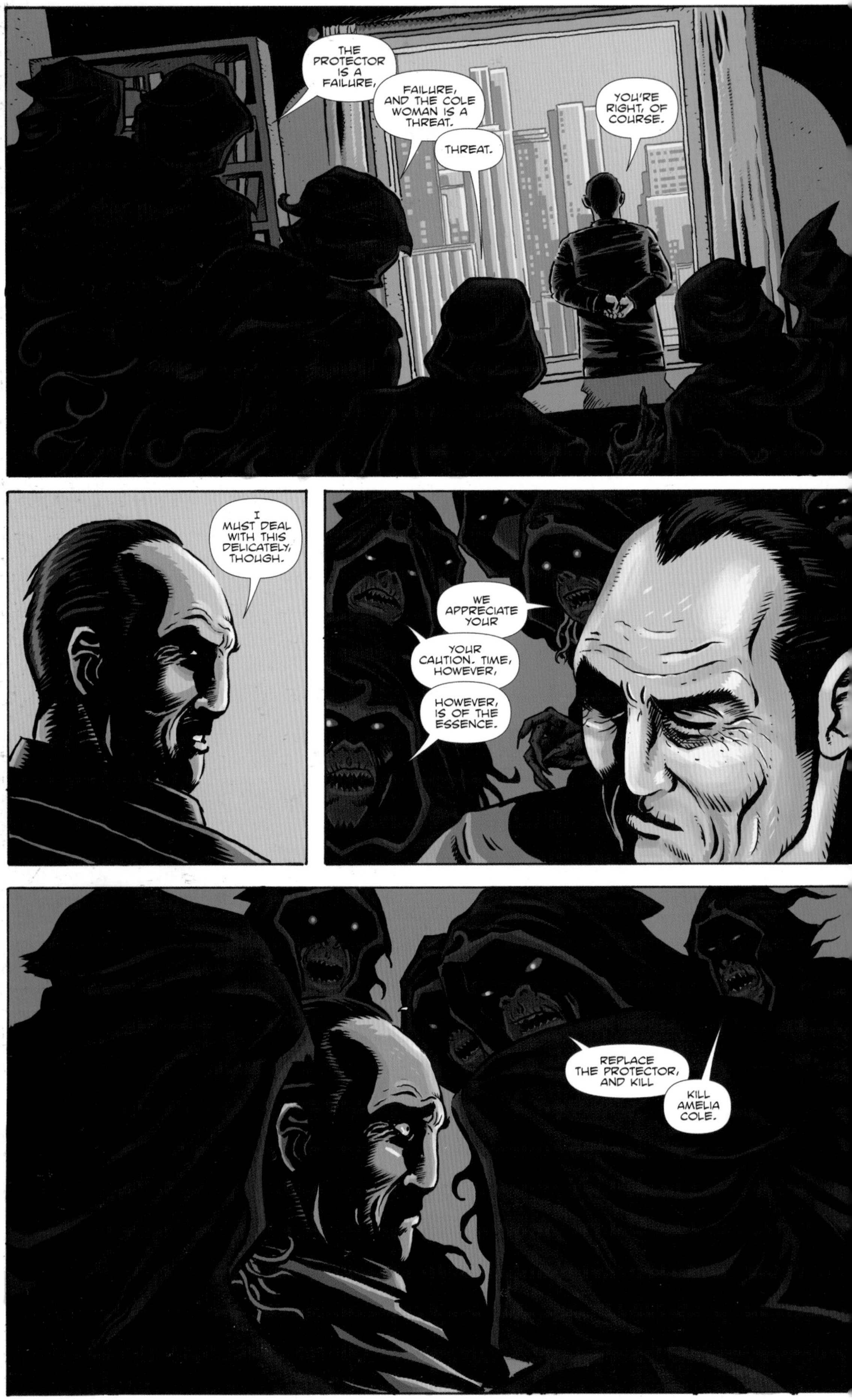
THE PROTECTOR IS A FAILURE,
FAILURE, AND THE COLE WOMAN IS A THREAT.
THREAT.
YOU'RE RIGHT, OF COURSE.
I MUST DEAL WITH THIS DELICATELY, THOUGH.
WE APPRECIATE YOUR
YOUR CAUTION. TIME, HOWEVER,
HOWEVER, IS OF THE ESSENCE.
REPLACE THE PROTECTOR, AND KILL
KILL AMELIA COLE.

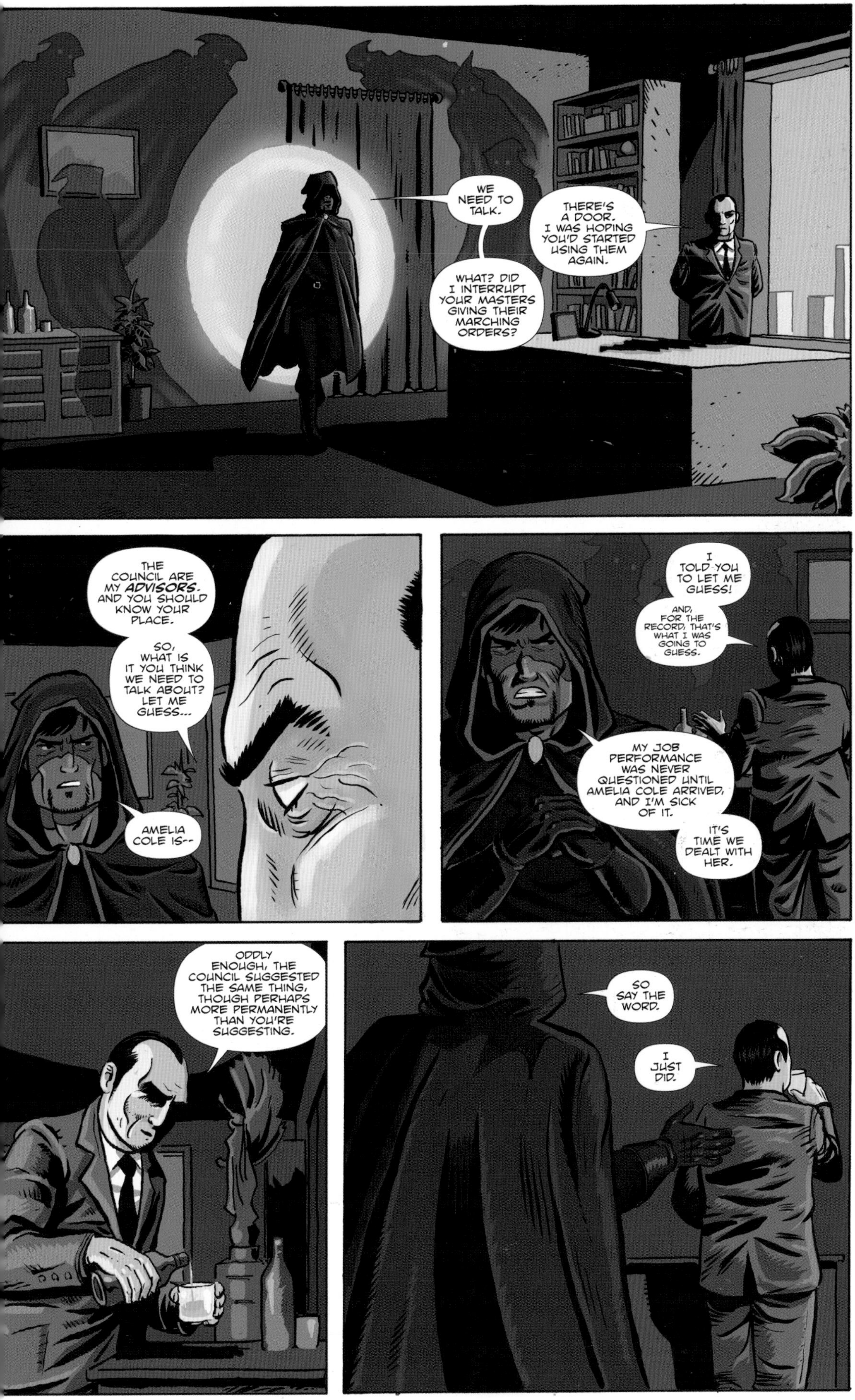
WE NEED TO TALK.
THERE'S A DOOR. I WAS HOPING YOU'D STARTED USING THEM AGAIN.
WHAT? DID I INTERRUPT YOUR MASTERS GIVING THEIR MARCHING ORDERS?
THE COUNCIL ARE MY ADVISORS. AND YOU SHOULD KNOW YOUR PLACE.
SO, WHAT IS IT YOU THINK WE NEED TO TALK ABOUT? LET ME GUESS...
AMELIA COLE IS--
I TOLD YOU TO LET ME GUESS!
AND, FOR THE RECORD, THAT'S WHAT I WAS GOING TO GUESS.
MY JOB PERFORMANCE WAS NEVER QUESTIONED UNTIL AMELIA COLE ARRIVED, AND I'M SICK OF IT.
IT'S TIME WE DEALT WITH HER.
ODDLY ENOUGH, THE COUNCIL SUGGESTED THE SAME THING, THOUGH PERHAPS MORE PERMANENTLY THAN YOU'RE SUGGESTING.
SO SAY THE WORD.
I JUST DID.

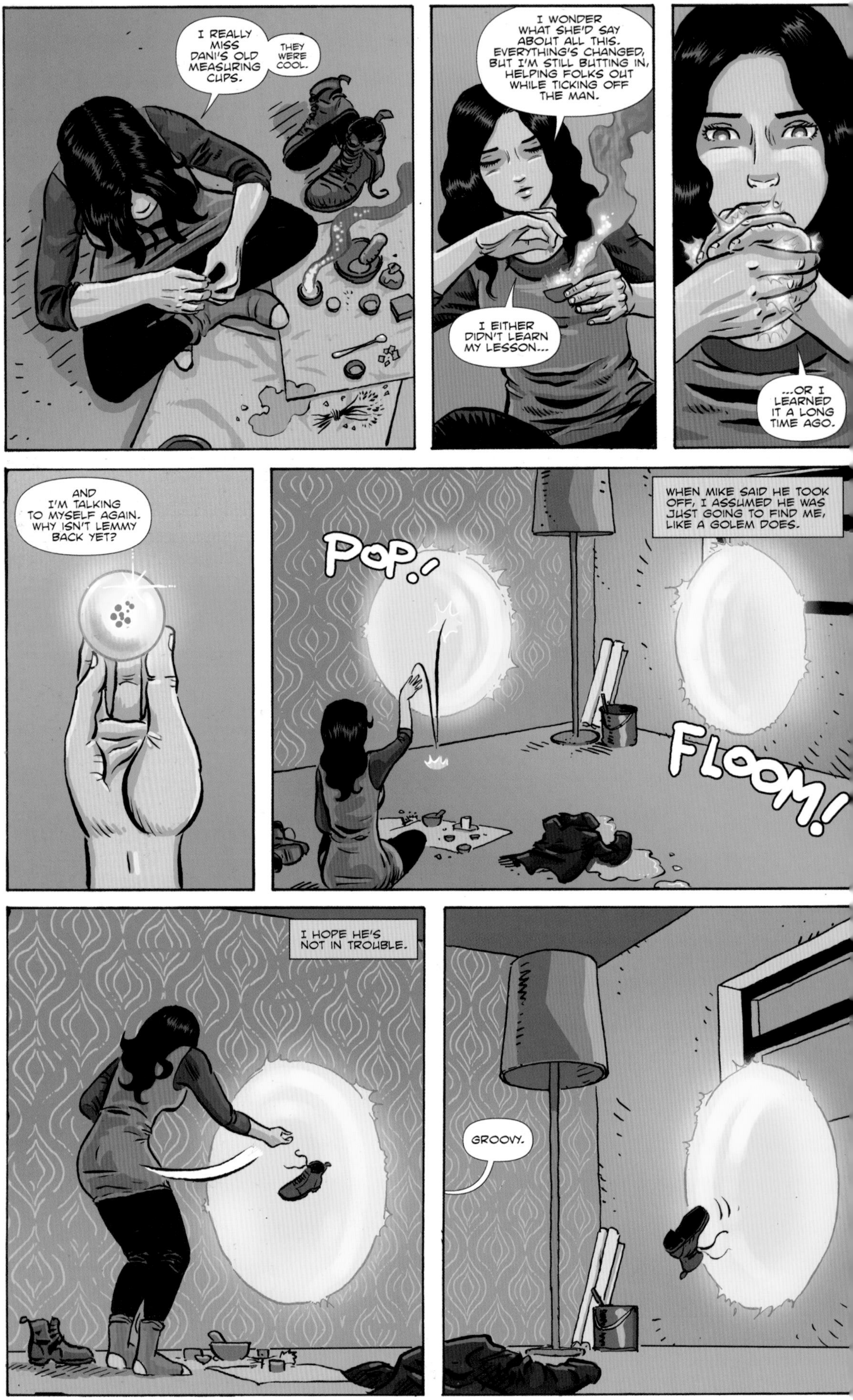
I REALLY MISS DANI'S OLD MEASURING CUPS.
THEY WERE COOL.
I WONDER WHAT SHE'D SAY ABOUT ALL THIS. EVERYTHING'S CHANGED, BUT I'M STILL BUTTING IN, HELPING FOLKS OUT WHILE TICKING OFF THE MAN.
I EITHER DIDN'T LEARN MY LESSON...
...OR I LEARNED IT A LONG TIME AGO.
AND I'M TALKING TO MYSELF AGAIN. WHY ISN'T LEMMY BACK YET?
POP.!
WHEN MIKE SAID HE TOOK OFF, I ASSUMED HE WAS JUST GOING TO FIND ME, LIKE A GOLEM DOES.
FLOOM!
I HOPE HE'S NOT IN TROUBLE.
GROOVY.

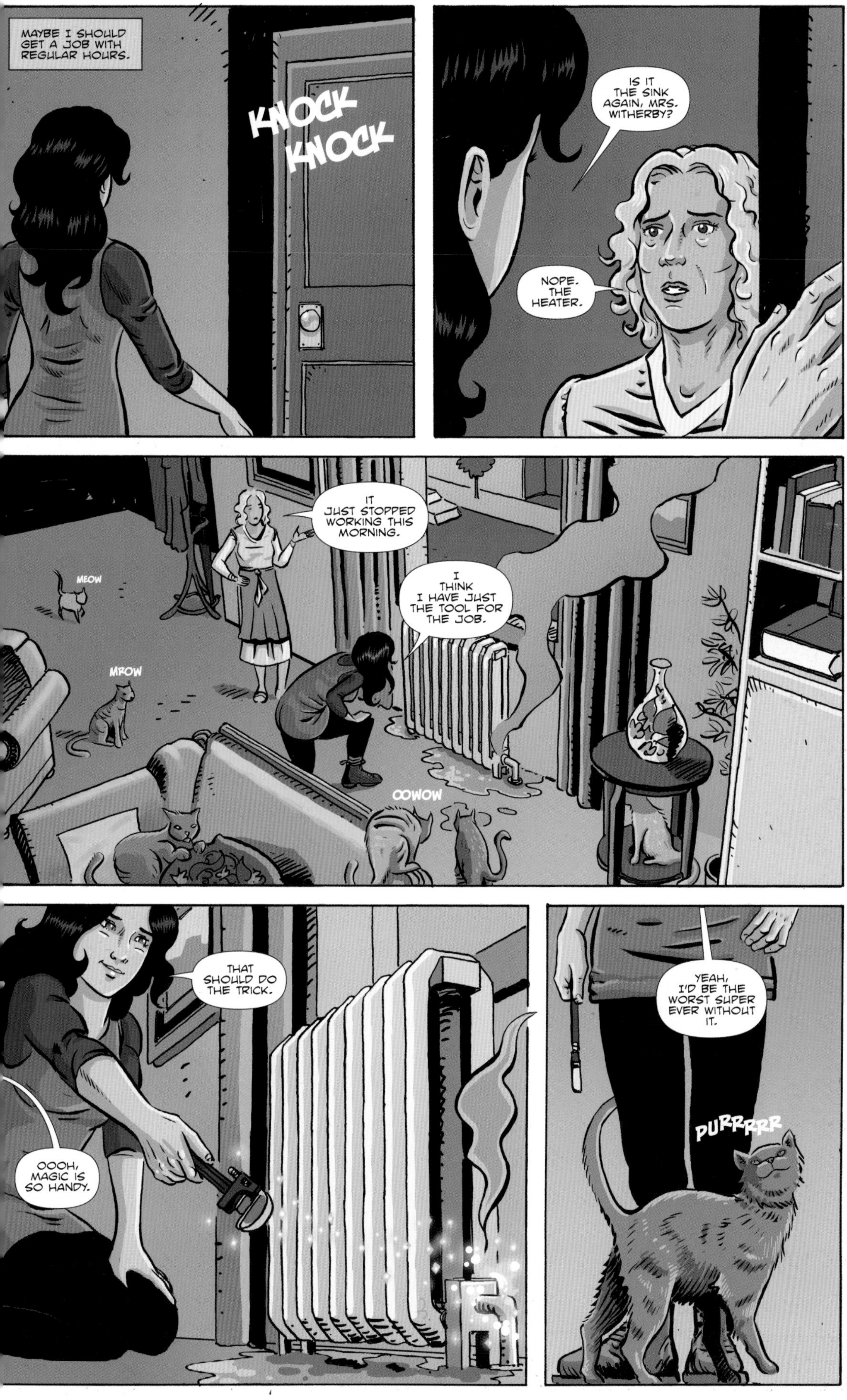
MAYBE I SHOULD GET A JOB WITH REGULAR HOURS.
KNOCK KNOCK
IS IT THE SINK AGAIN, MRS. WITHERBY?
NOPE. THE HEATER.
IT JUST STOPPED WORKING THIS MORNING.
MEOW
I THINK I HAVE JUST THE TOOL FOR THE JOB.
MROW
OOWOW
THAT SHOULD DO THE TRICK.
OOOH, MAGIC IS SO HANDY.
YEAH, I'D BE THE WORST SUPER EVER WITHOUT IT.
PURRRRR

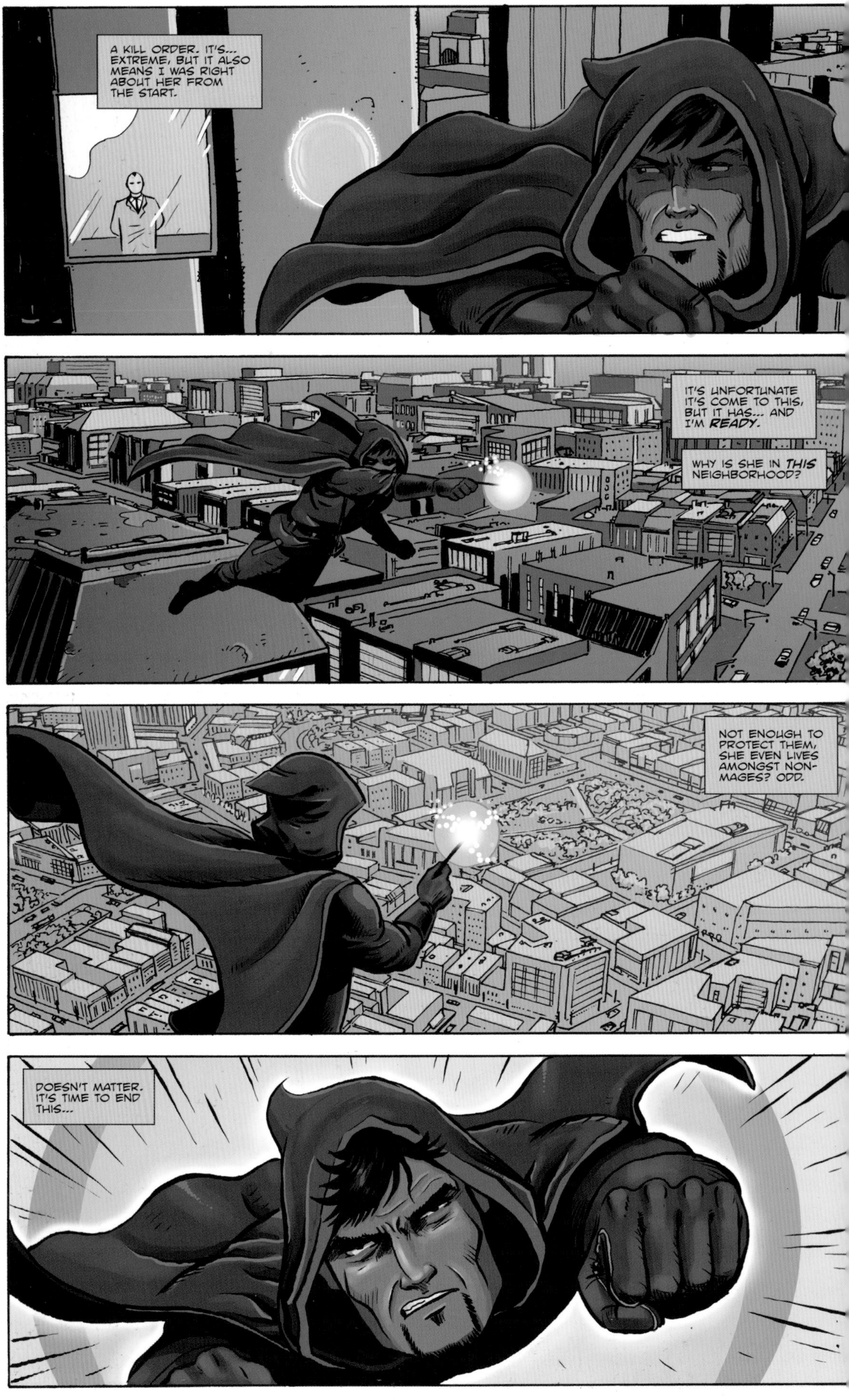
A KILL ORDER. IT'S... EXTREME, BUT IT ALSO MEANS I WAS RIGHT ABOUT HER FROM THE START.
IT'S UNFORTUNATE IT'S COME TO THIS, BUT IT HAS... AND I'M READY.
WHY IS SHE IN THIS NEIGHBORHOOD?
NOT ENOUGH TO PROTECT THEM, SHE EVEN LIVES AMONGST NON-MAGES? ODD.
DOESN'T MATTER. IT'S TIME TO END THIS...

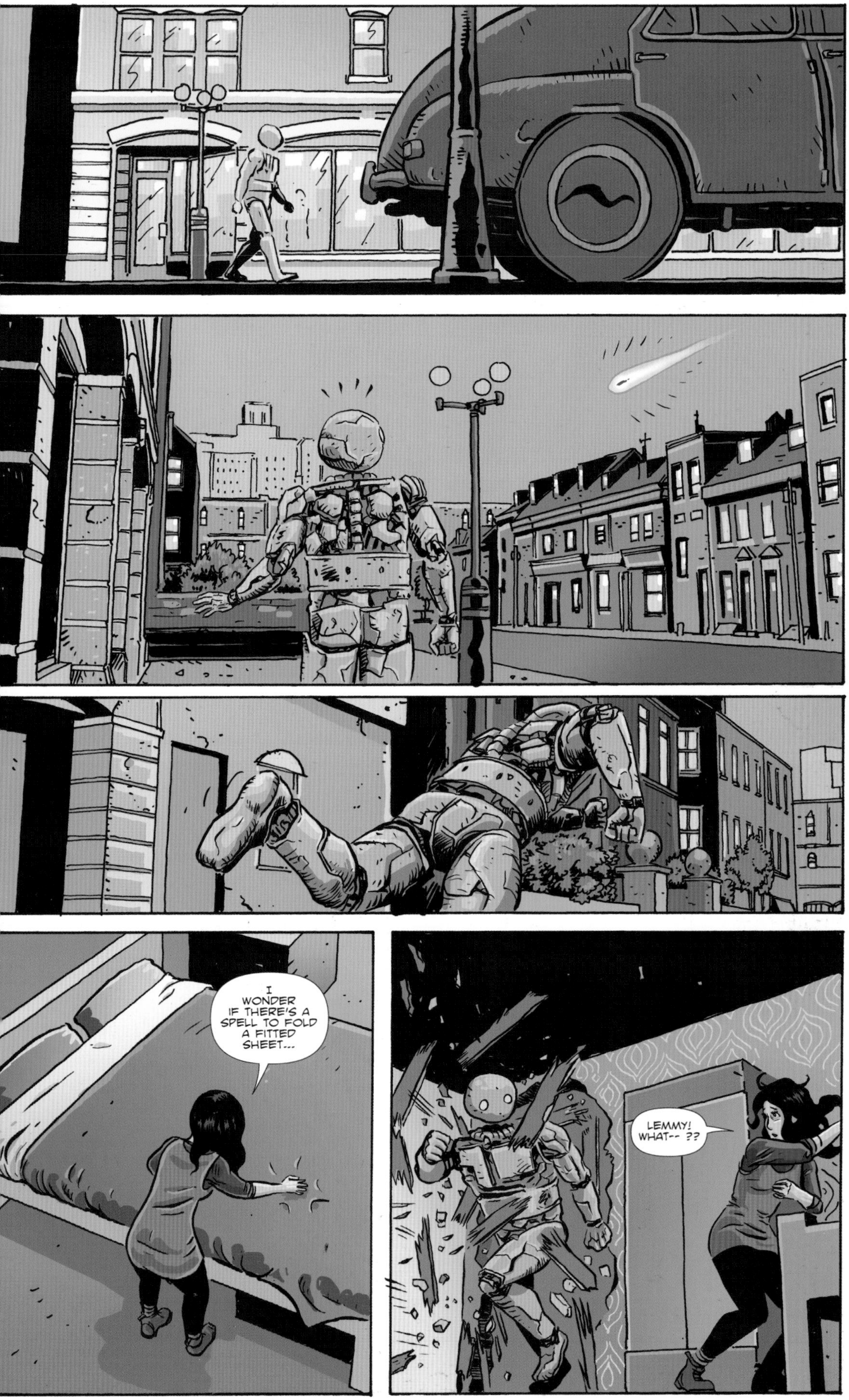
I WONDER IF THERE'S A SPELL TO FOLD A FITTED SHEET...
LEMMY! WHAT-- ??

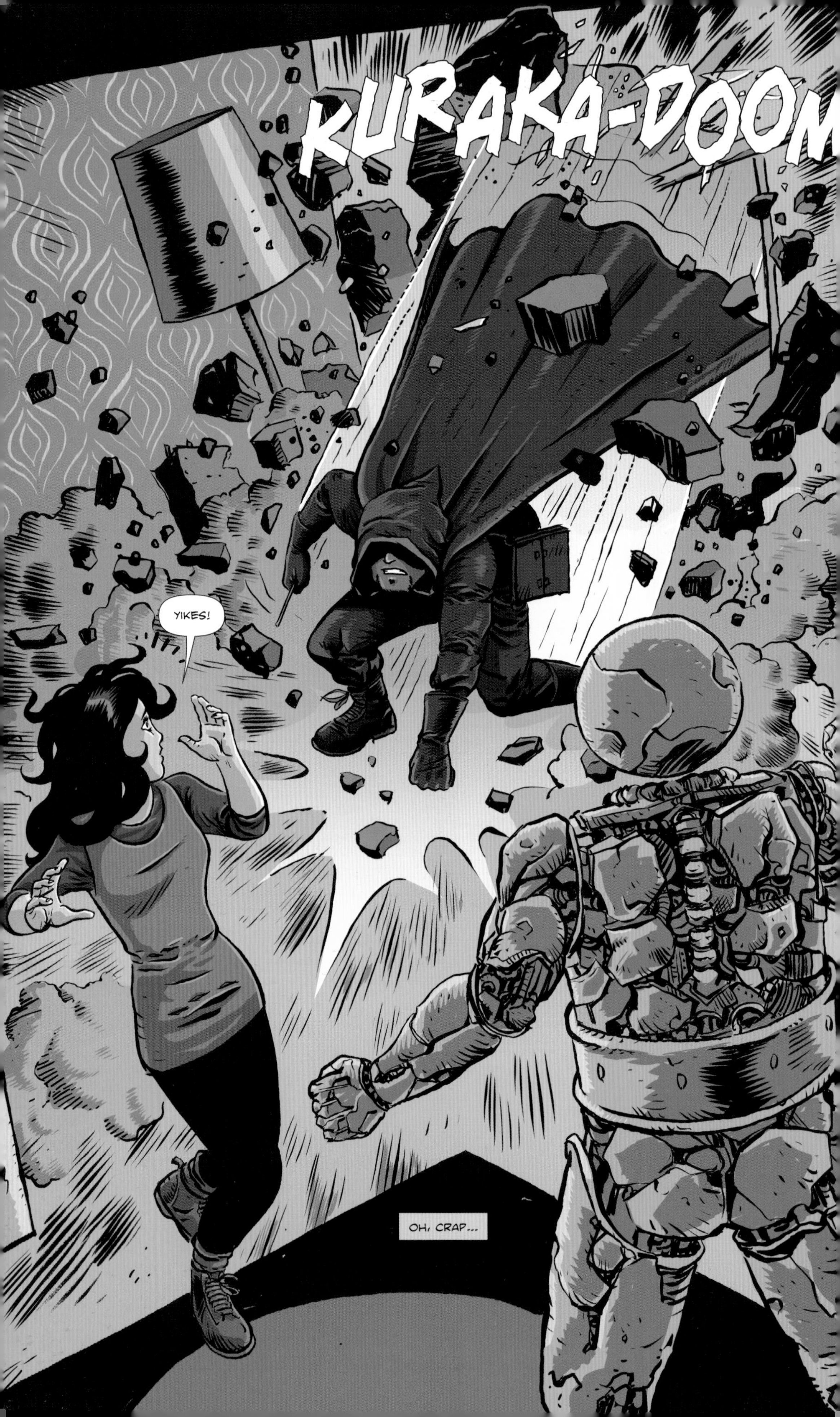
KURAKA-DOOM
YIKES!
OH, CRAP...

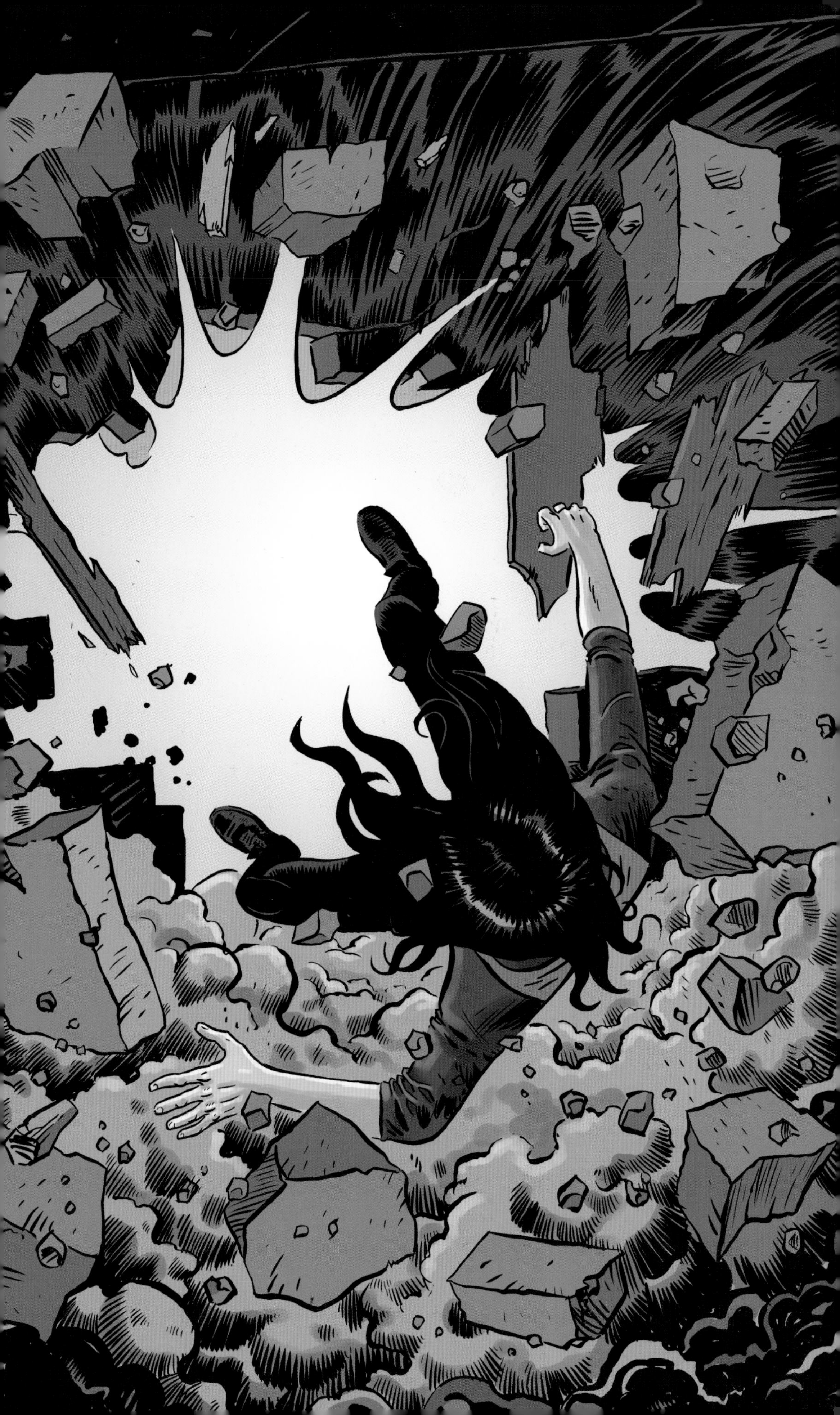

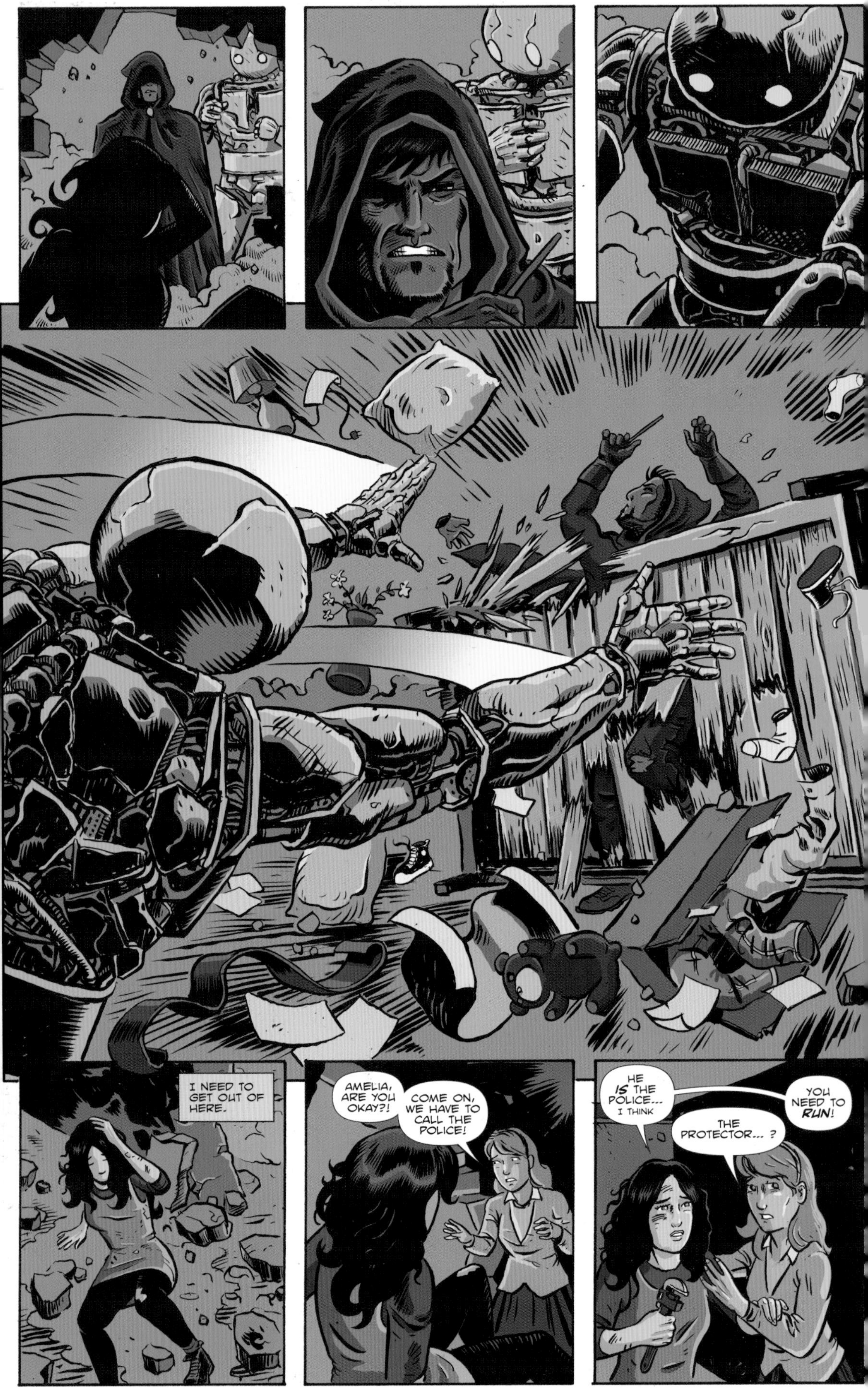
I NEED TO GET OUT OF HERE.
AMELIA, ARE YOU OKAY?!
COME ON, WE HAVE TO CALL THE POLICE!
HE IS THE POLICE... I THINK
YOU NEED TO RUN!
THE PROTECTOR... ?

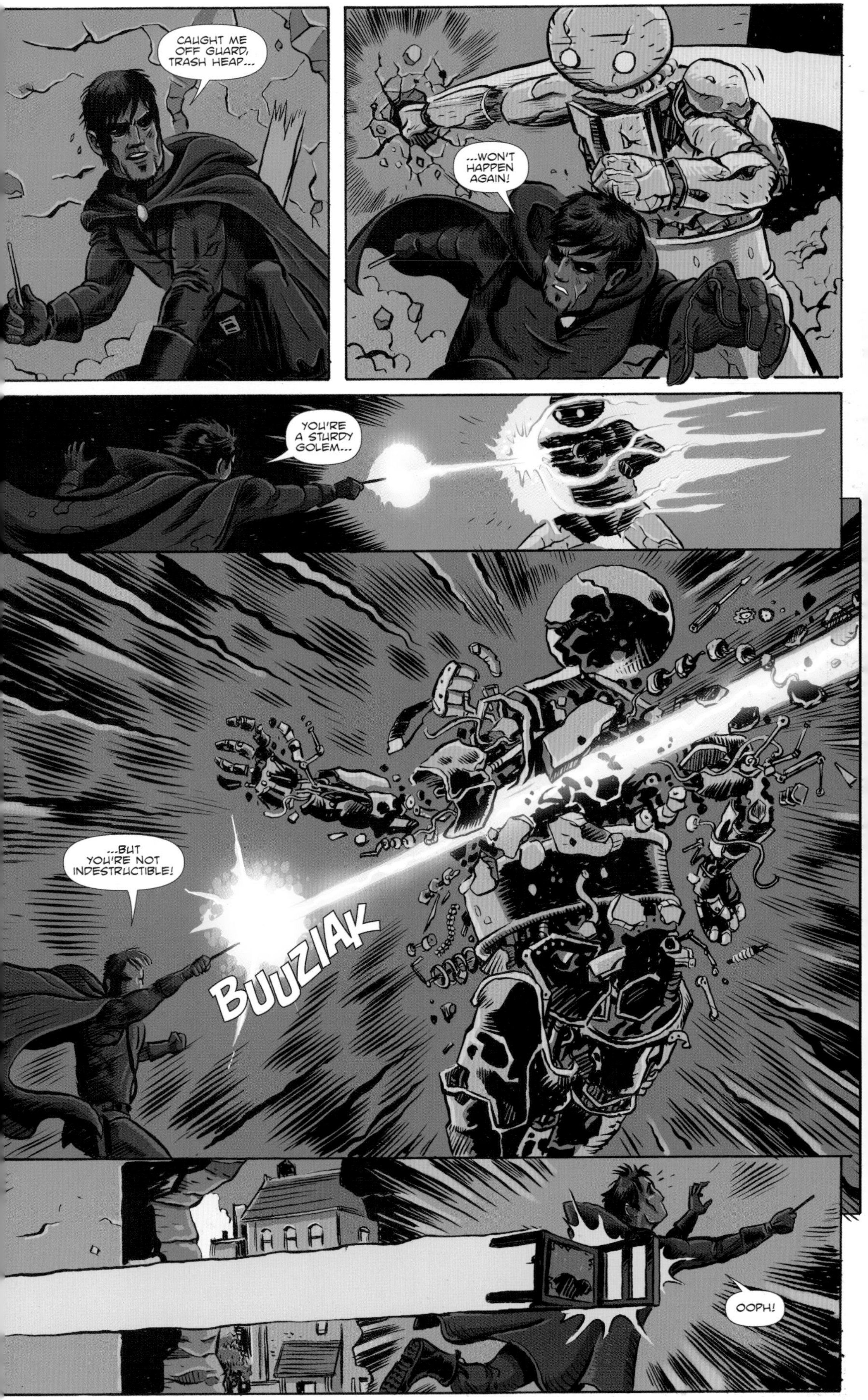
CAUGHT ME OFF GUARD, TRASH HEAP...
...WON'T HAPPEN AGAIN!
YOU'RE A STURDY GOLEM...
...BUT YOU'RE NOT INDESTRUCTIBLE!
BUUZIAK
OOPH!

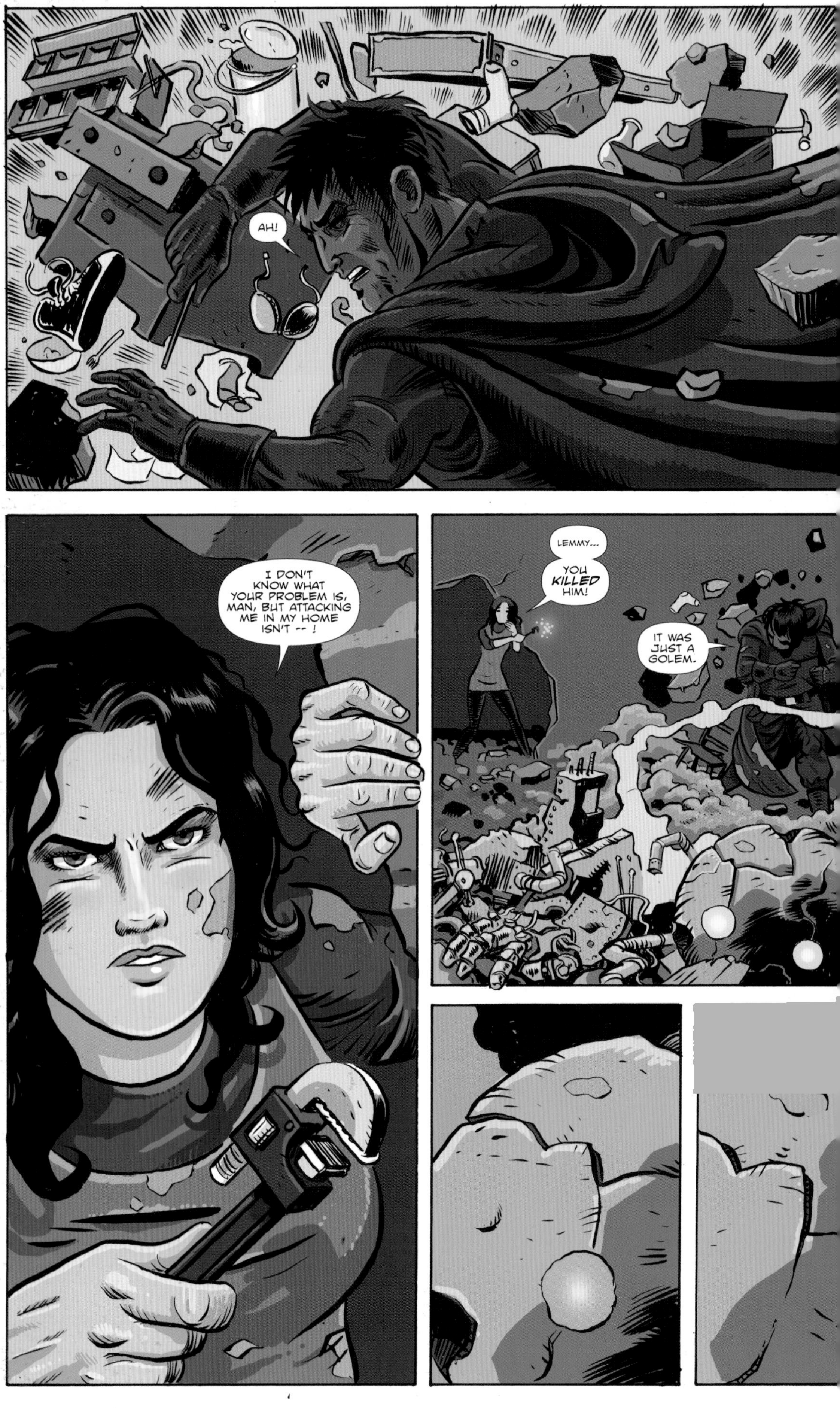
AH!
I DON'T KNOW WHAT YOUR PROBLEM IS, MAN, BUT ATTACKING ME IN MY HOME ISN'T -- !
LEMMY...
YOU KILLED HIM!
IT WAS JUST A GOLEM.

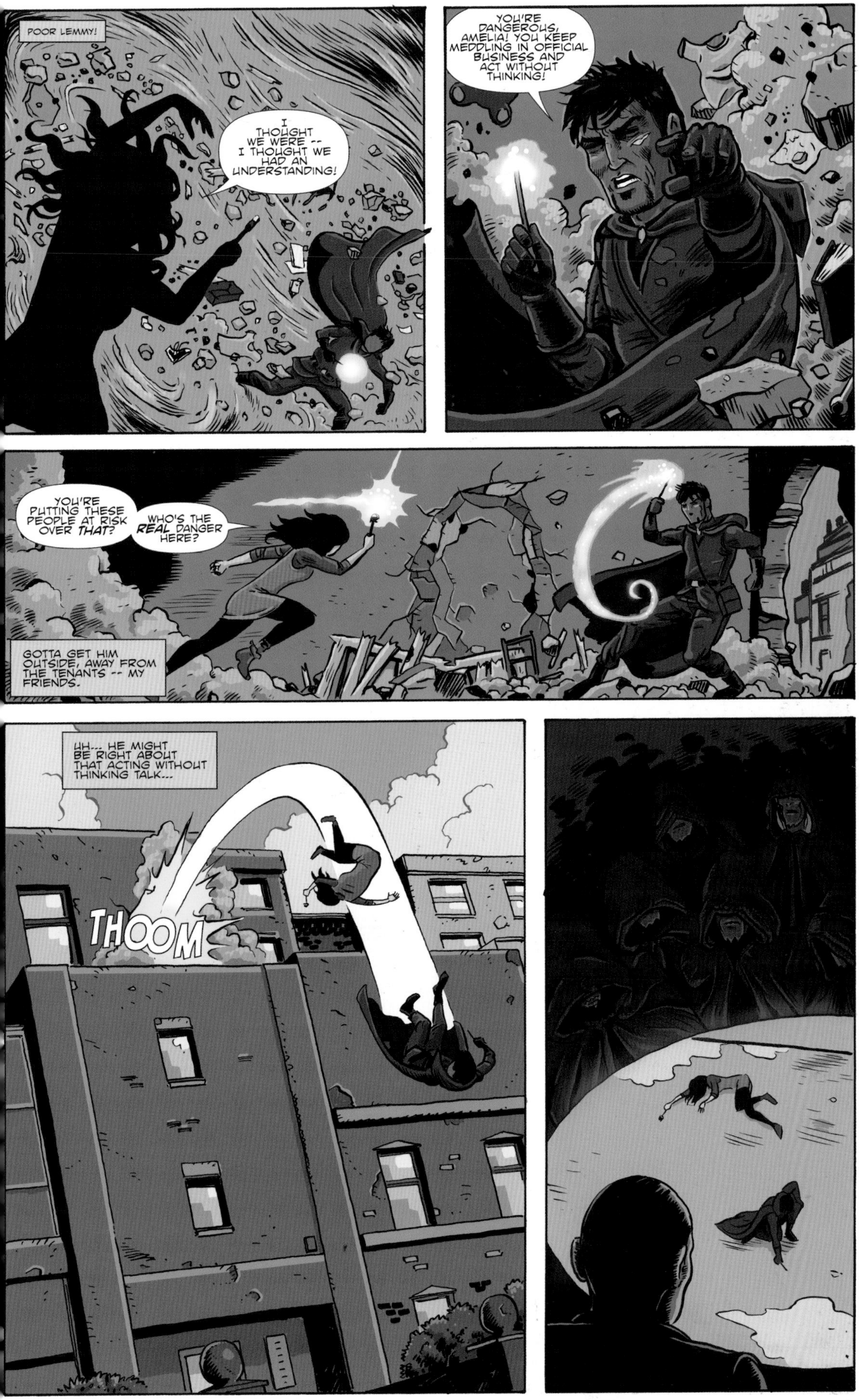
POOR LEMMY!
I THOUGHT WE WERE -- I THOUGHT WE HAD AN UNDERSTANDING!
YOU'RE DANGEROUS, AMELIA! YOU KEEP MEDDLING IN OFFICIAL BUSINESS AND ACT WITHOUT THINKING!
YOU'RE PUTTING THESE PEOPLE AT RISK OVER THAT?
WHO'S THE REAL DANGER HERE?
GOTTA GET HIM OUTSIDE, AWAY FROM THE TENANTS -- MY FRIENDS.
UH... HE MIGHT BE RIGHT ABOUT THAT ACTING WITHOUT THINKING TALK...
THOOM

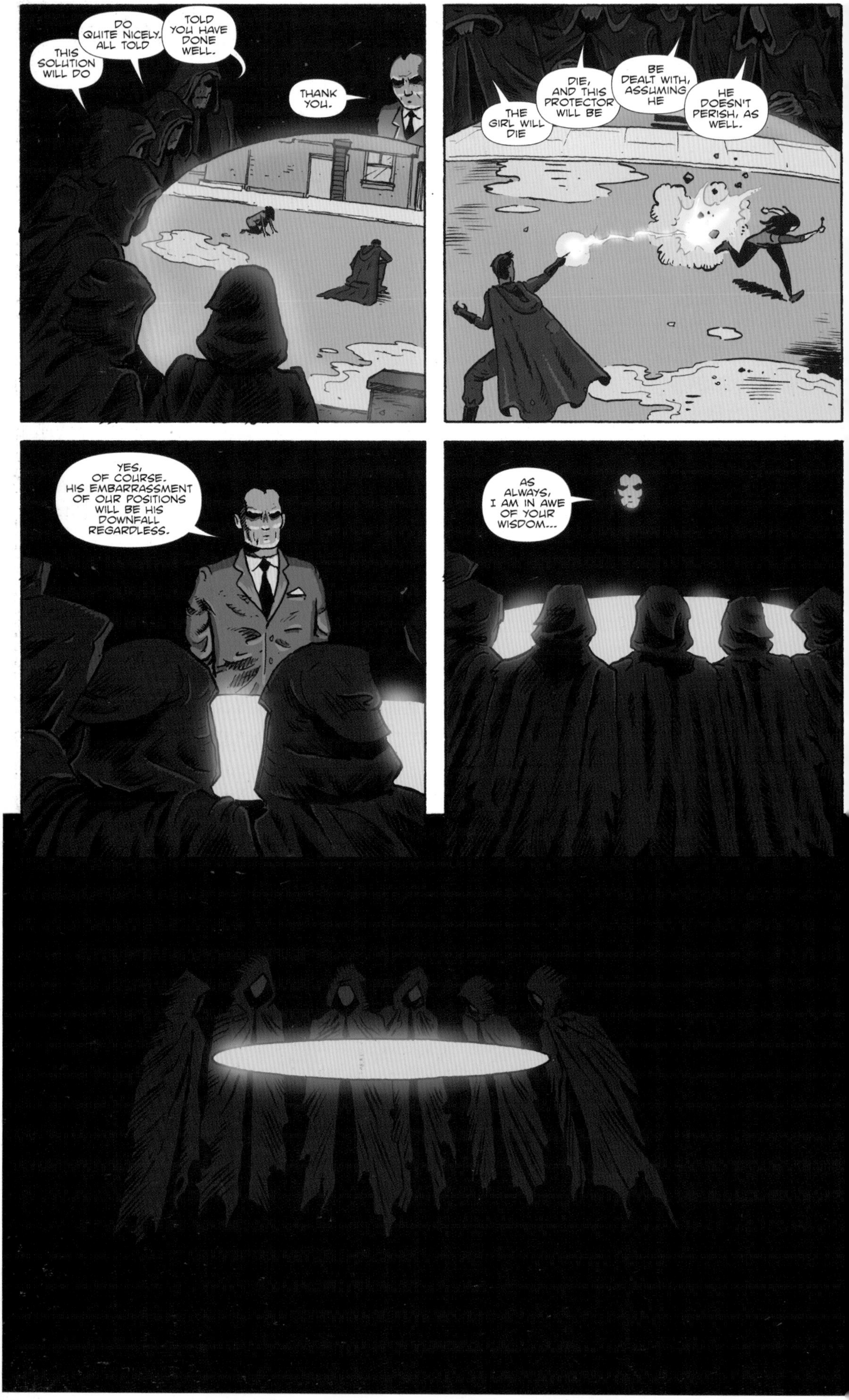
THIS SOLUTION WILL DO
DO QUITE NICELY. ALL TOLD
TOLD YOU HAVE DONE WELL.
THANK YOU.
THE GIRL WILL DIE
DIE, AND THIS PROTECTOR WILL BE
BE DEALT WITH, ASSUMING HE
HE DOESN'T PERISH, AS WELL.
YES, OF COURSE. HIS EMBARRASSMENT OF OUR POSITIONS WILL BE HIS DOWNFALL REGARDLESS.
AS ALWAYS, I AM IN AWE OF YOUR WISDOM...

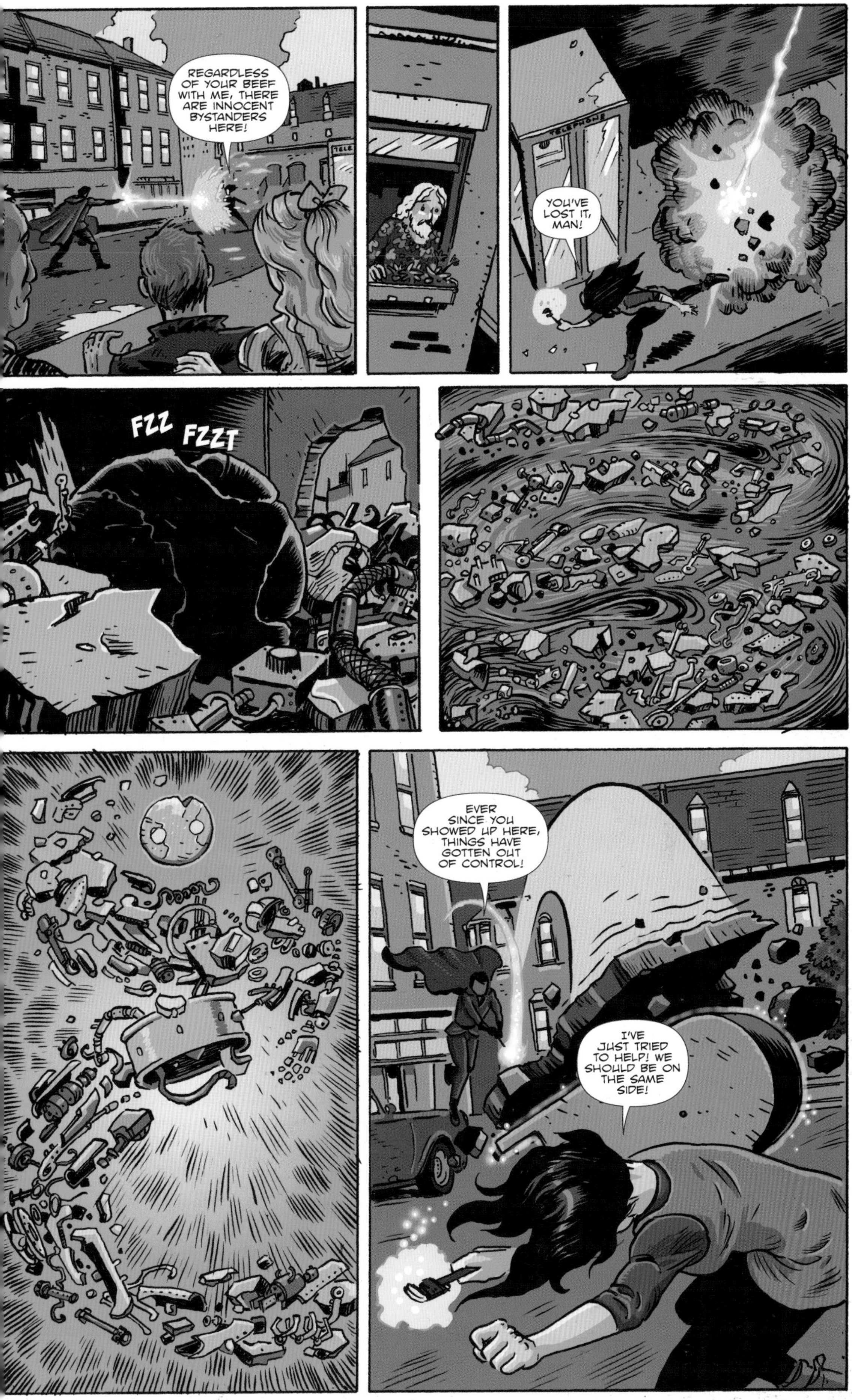
REGARDLESS OF YOUR BEEF WITH ME, THERE ARE INNOCENT BYSTANDERS HERE!
YOU'VE LOST IT, MAN!
FZZ FZZT
EVER SINCE YOU SHOWED UP HERE, THINGS HAVE GOTTEN OUT OF CONTROL!
I'VE JUST TRIED TO HELP! WE SHOULD BE ON THE SAME SIDE!

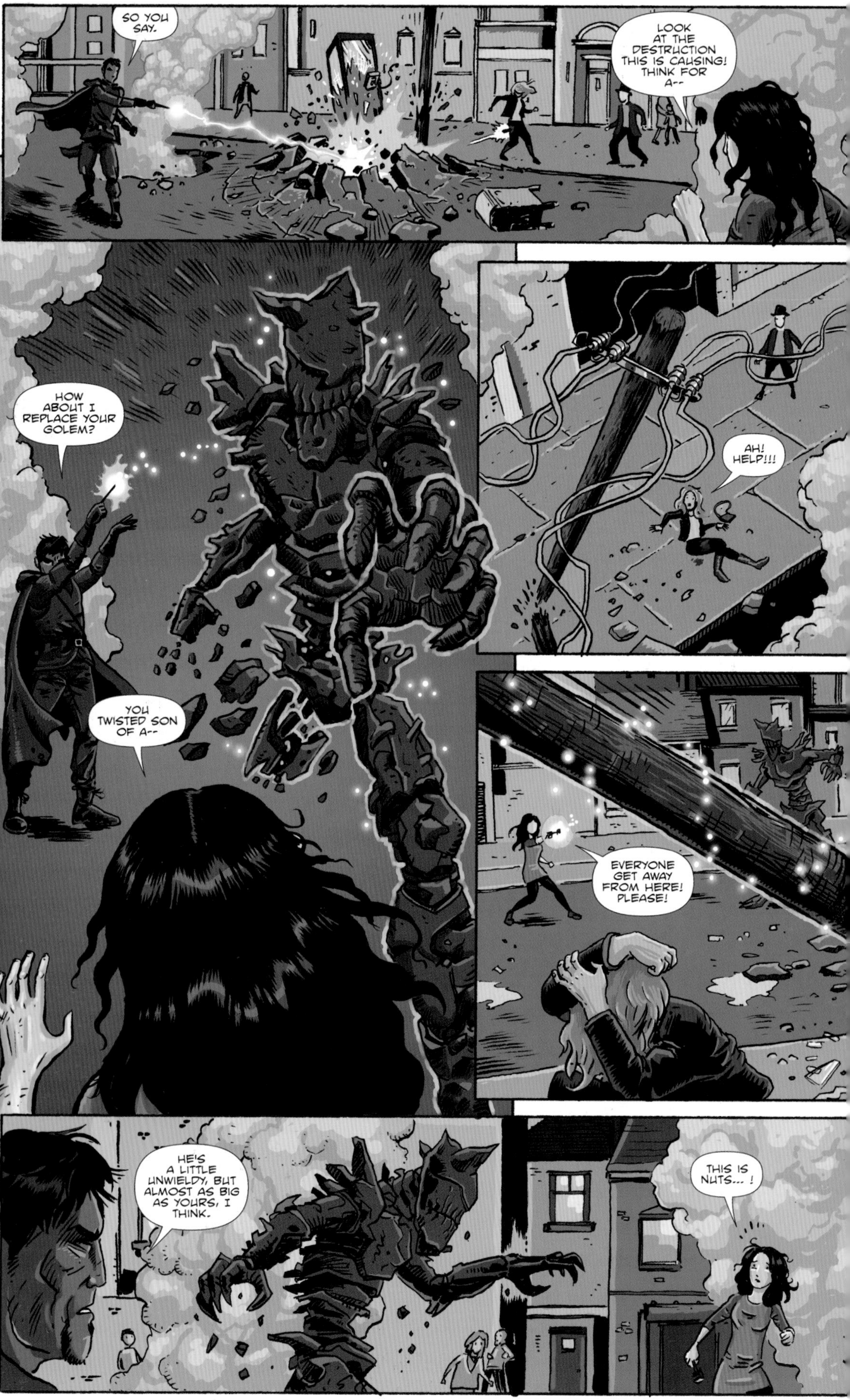
SO YOU SAY.
LOOK AT THE DESTRUCTION THIS IS CAUSING! THINK FOR A--
HOW ABOUT I REPLACE YOUR GOLEM?
YOU TWISTED SON OF A--
AH! HELP!!!
EVERYONE GET AWAY FROM HERE! PLEASE!
HE'S A LITTLE UNWIELDY, BUT ALMOST AS BIG AS YOURS, I THINK.
THIS IS NUTS... !

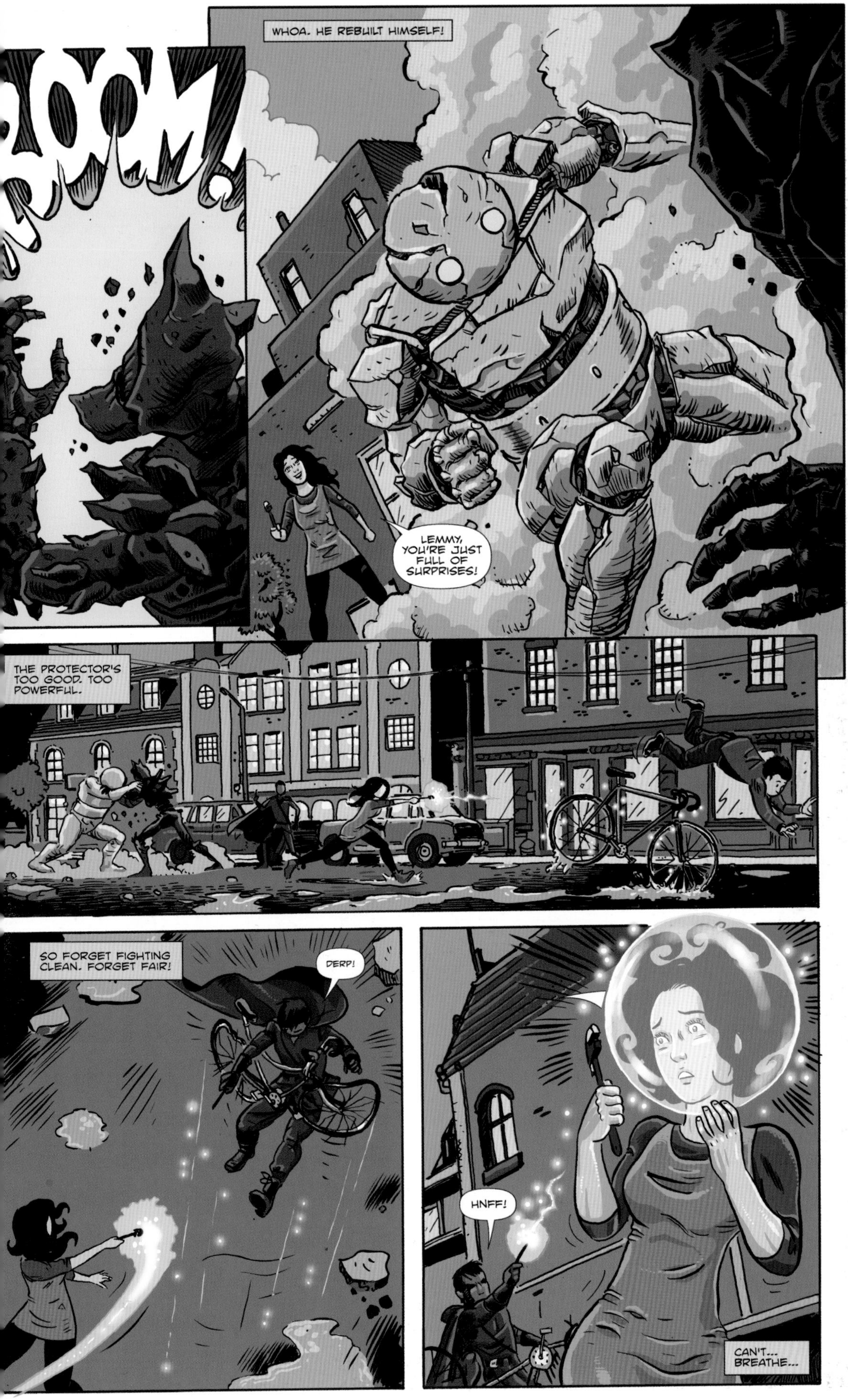
BOOM!
WHOA. HE REBUILT HIMSELF!
LEMMY, YOU'RE JUST FULL OF SURPRISES!
THE PROTECTOR'S TOO GOOD. TOO POWERFUL.
SO FORGET FIGHTING CLEAN. FORGET FAIR!
DERP!
HNFF!
CAN'T... BREATHE...

I'M SORRY IT HAD TO BE LIKE THIS.

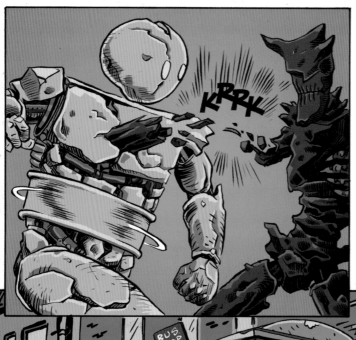

KRRK

SPELL... TOO STRONG...!

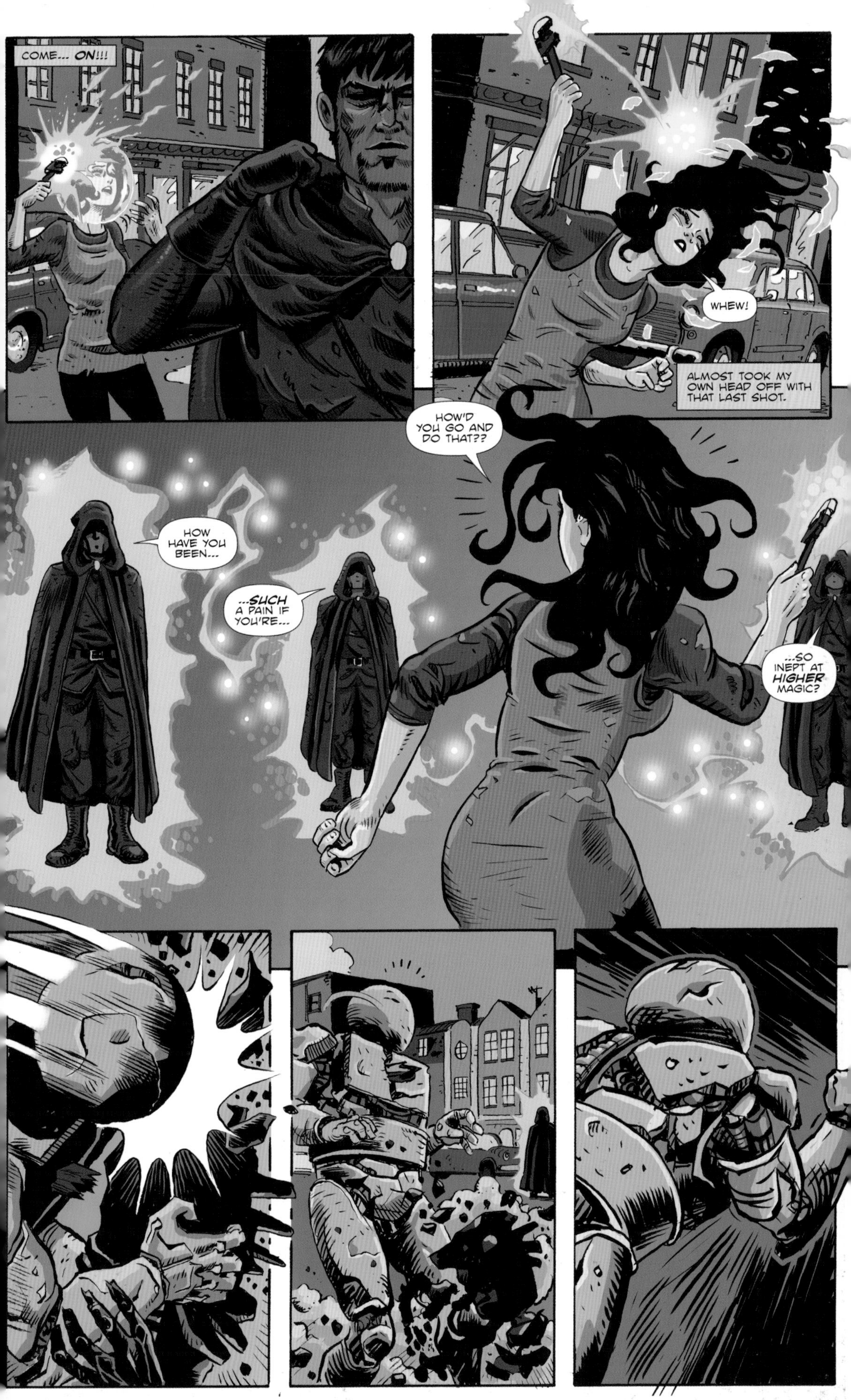
COME... ON!!!
WHEW!
ALMOST TOOK MY OWN HEAD OFF WITH THAT LAST SHOT.
HOW'D YOU GO AND DO THAT??
HOW HAVE YOU BEEN...
...SUCH A PAIN IF YOU'RE...
...SO INEPT AT HIGHER MAGIC?

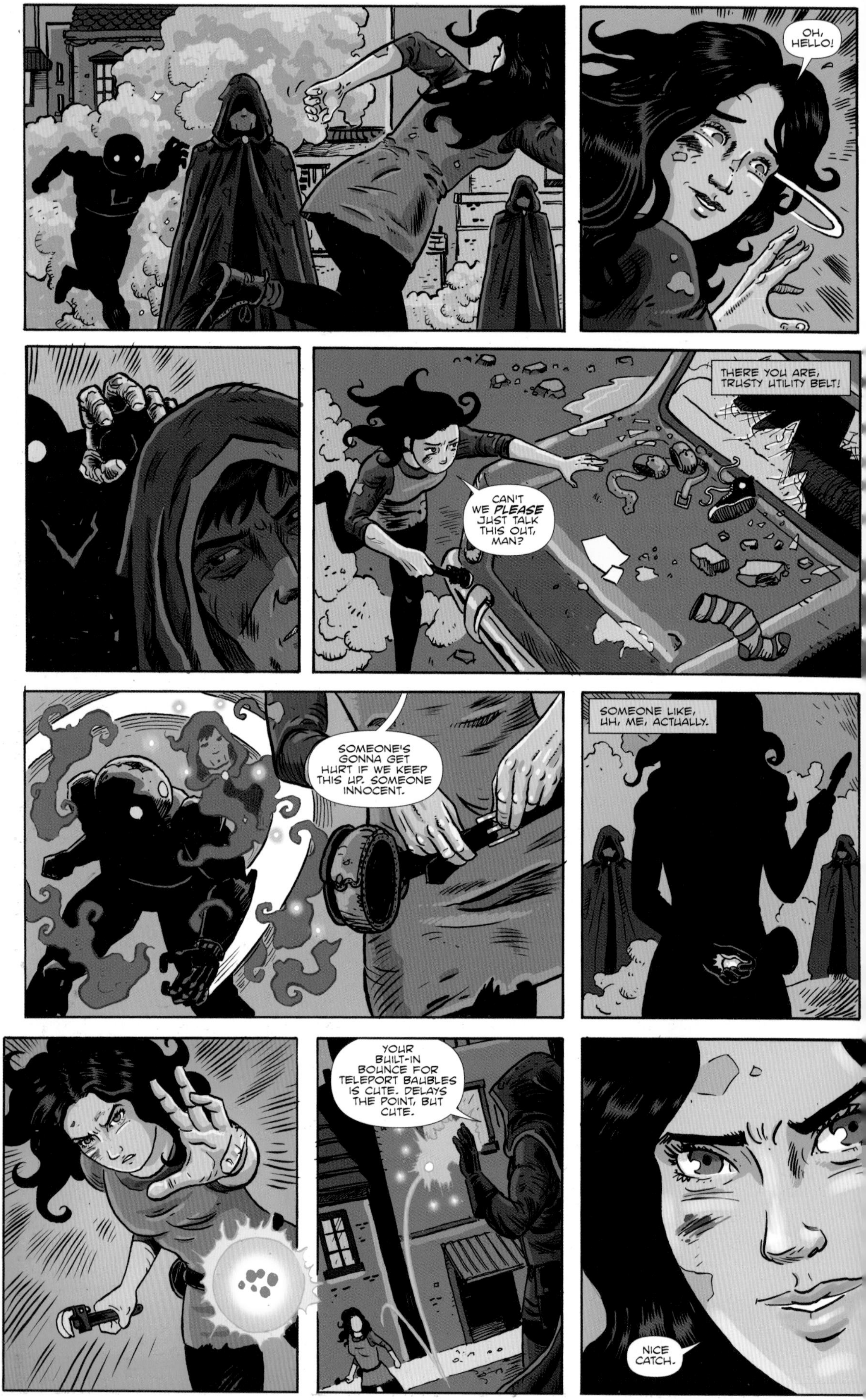

OH, HELLO!
THERE YOU ARE, TRUSTY UTILITY BELT!
CAN'T WE *PLEASE* JUST TALK THIS OUT, MAN?
SOMEONE'S GONNA GET HURT IF WE KEEP THIS UP. SOMEONE INNOCENT.
SOMEONE LIKE, UH, ME, ACTUALLY.
YOUR BUILT-IN BOUNCE FOR TELEPORT BAUBLES IS CUTE. DELAYS THE POINT, BUT CUTE.
NICE CATCH.

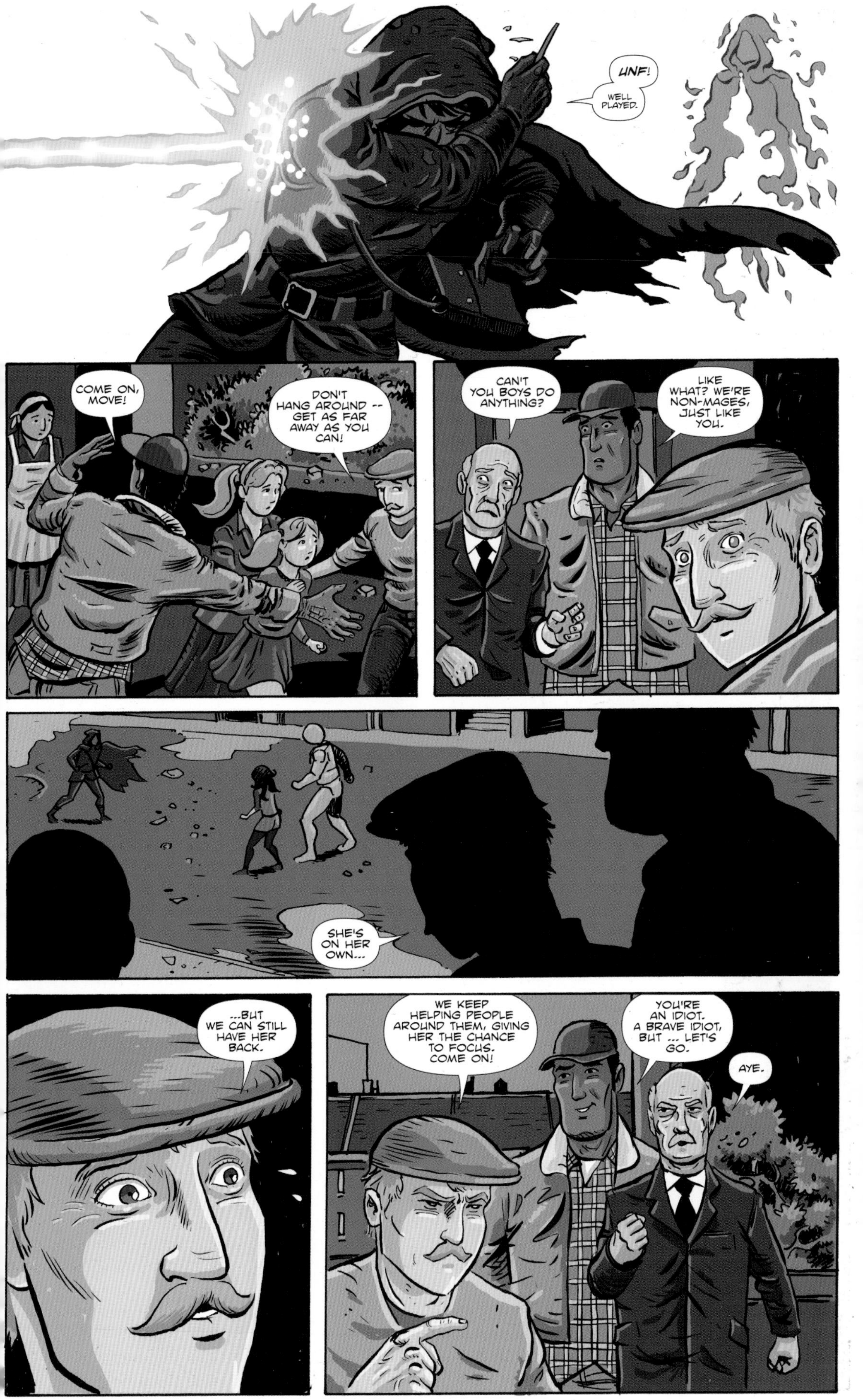
UNF!
WELL PLAYED.
COME ON, MOVE!
DON'T HANG AROUND -- GET AS FAR AWAY AS YOU CAN!
CAN'T YOU BOYS DO ANYTHING?
LIKE WHAT? WE'RE NON-MAGES, JUST LIKE YOU.
SHE'S ON HER OWN...
...BUT WE CAN STILL HAVE HER BACK.
WE KEEP HELPING PEOPLE AROUND THEM, GIVING HER THE CHANCE TO FOCUS. COME ON!
YOU'RE AN IDIOT. A BRAVE IDIOT, BUT ... LET'S GO.
AYE.

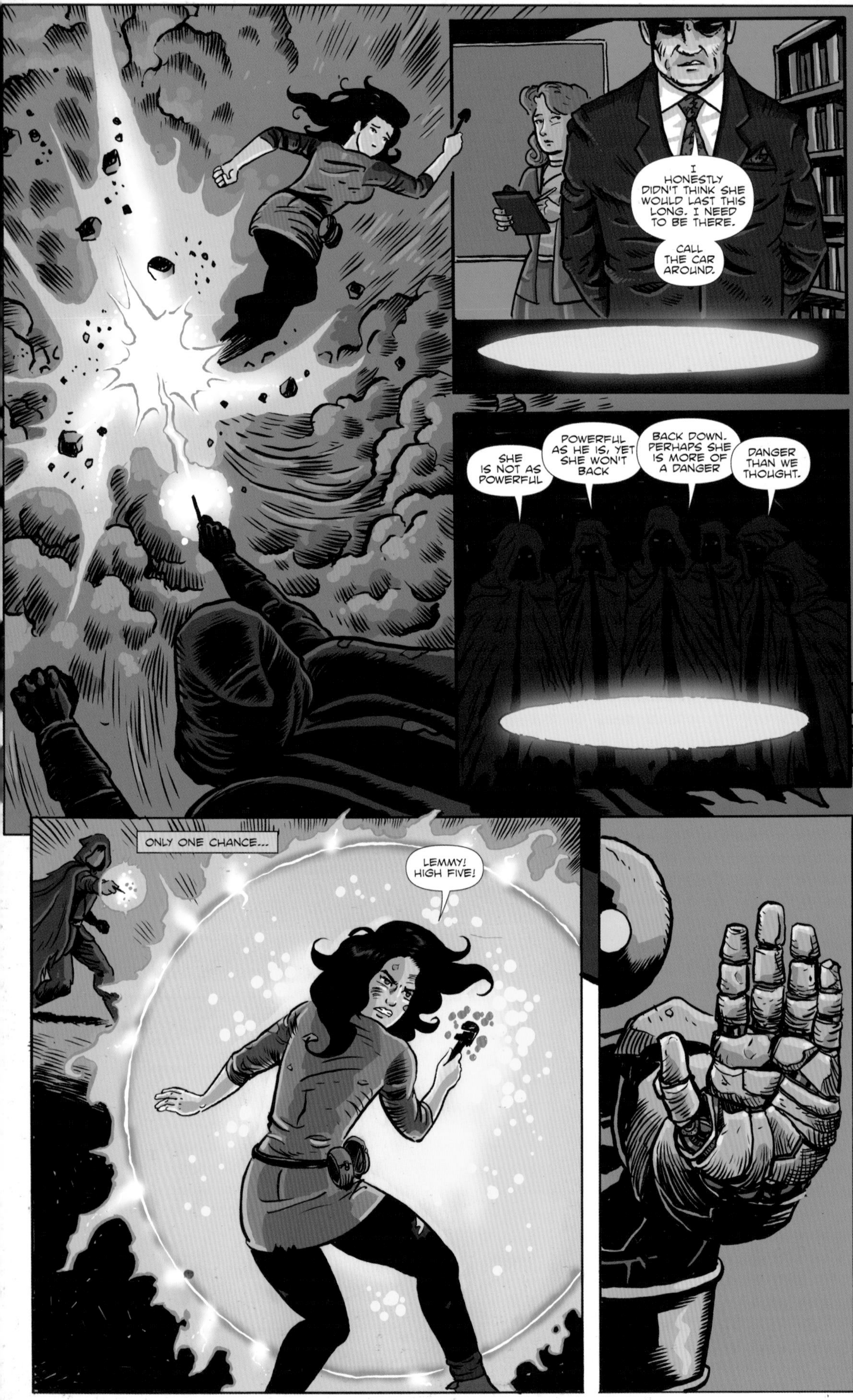
I HONESTLY DIDN'T THINK SHE WOULD LAST THIS LONG. I NEED TO BE THERE.
CALL THE CAR AROUND.
SHE IS NOT AS POWERFUL
POWERFUL AS HE IS, YET SHE WON'T BACK
BACK DOWN. PERHAPS SHE IS MORE OF A DANGER
DANGER THAN WE THOUGHT.
ONLY ONE CHANCE...
LEMMY! HIGH FIVE!

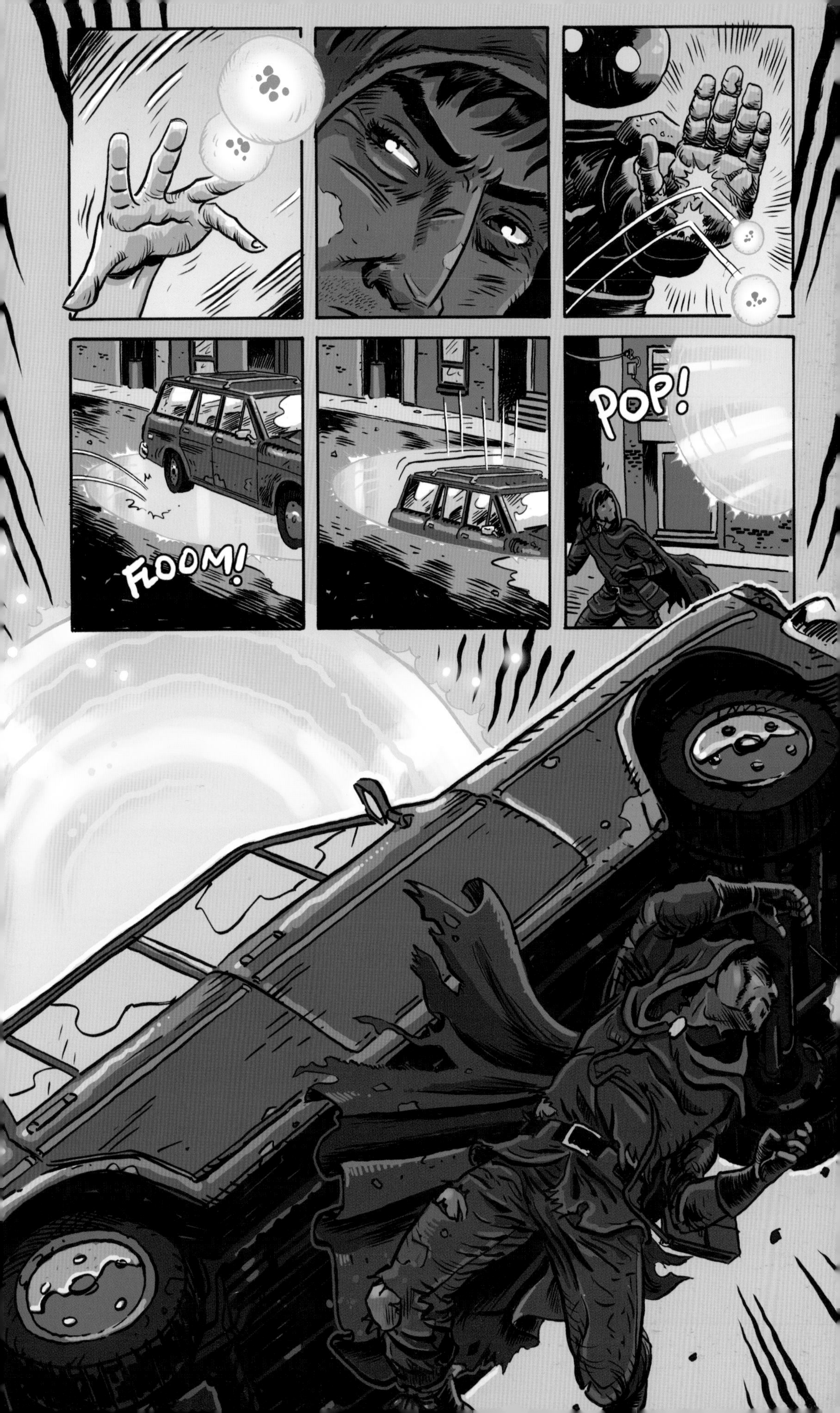
FLOOM!
POP!

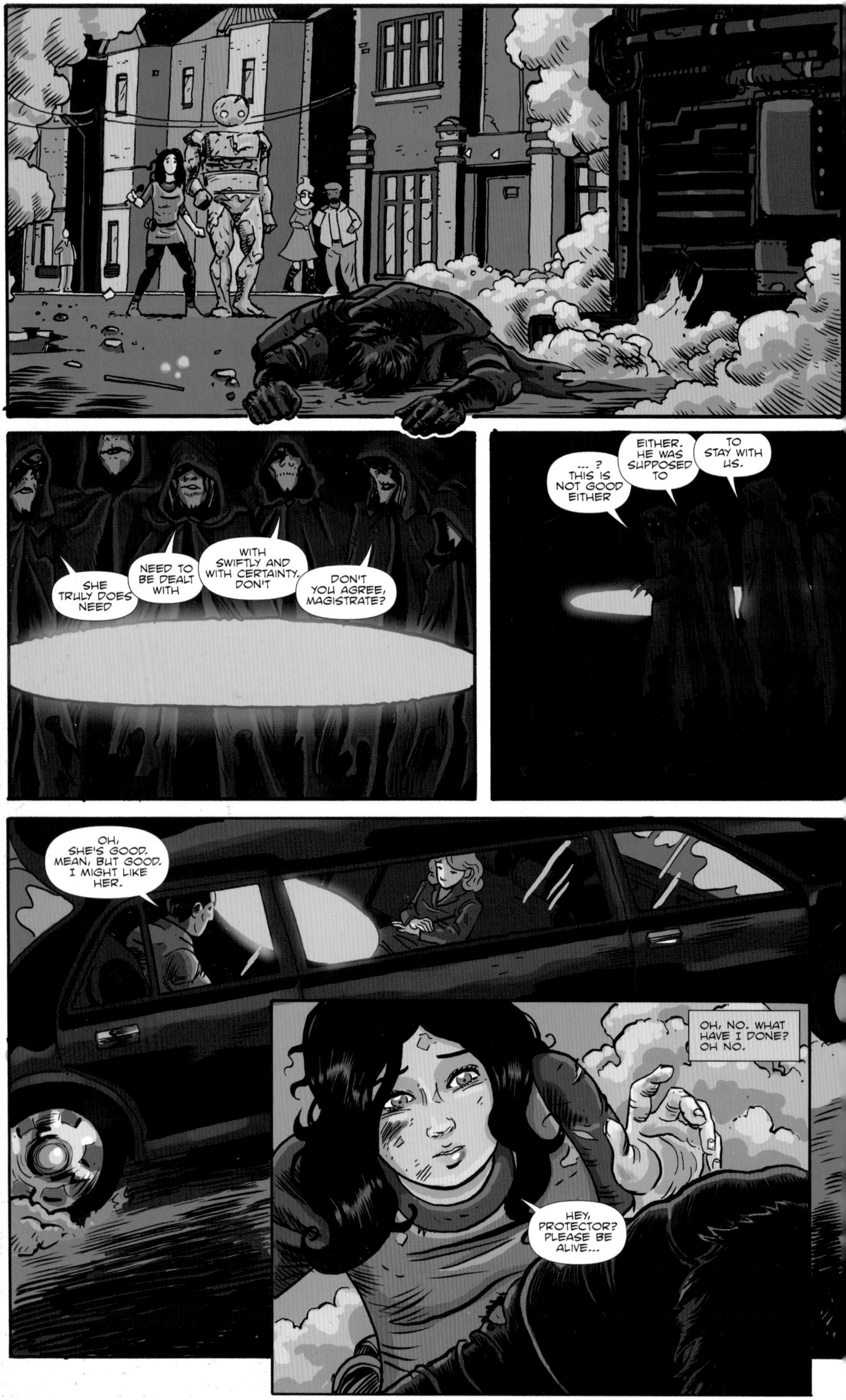
SHE TRULY DOES NEED
NEED TO BE DEALT WITH
WITH SWIFTLY AND WITH CERTAINTY. DON'T
DON'T YOU AGREE, MAGISTRATE?
... ? THIS IS NOT GOOD EITHER
EITHER. HE WAS SUPPOSED TO
TO STAY WITH US.
OH, SHE'S GOOD. MEAN, BUT GOOD. I MIGHT LIKE HER.
OH, NO. WHAT HAVE I DONE? OH NO.
HEY, PROTECTOR? PLEASE BE ALIVE...

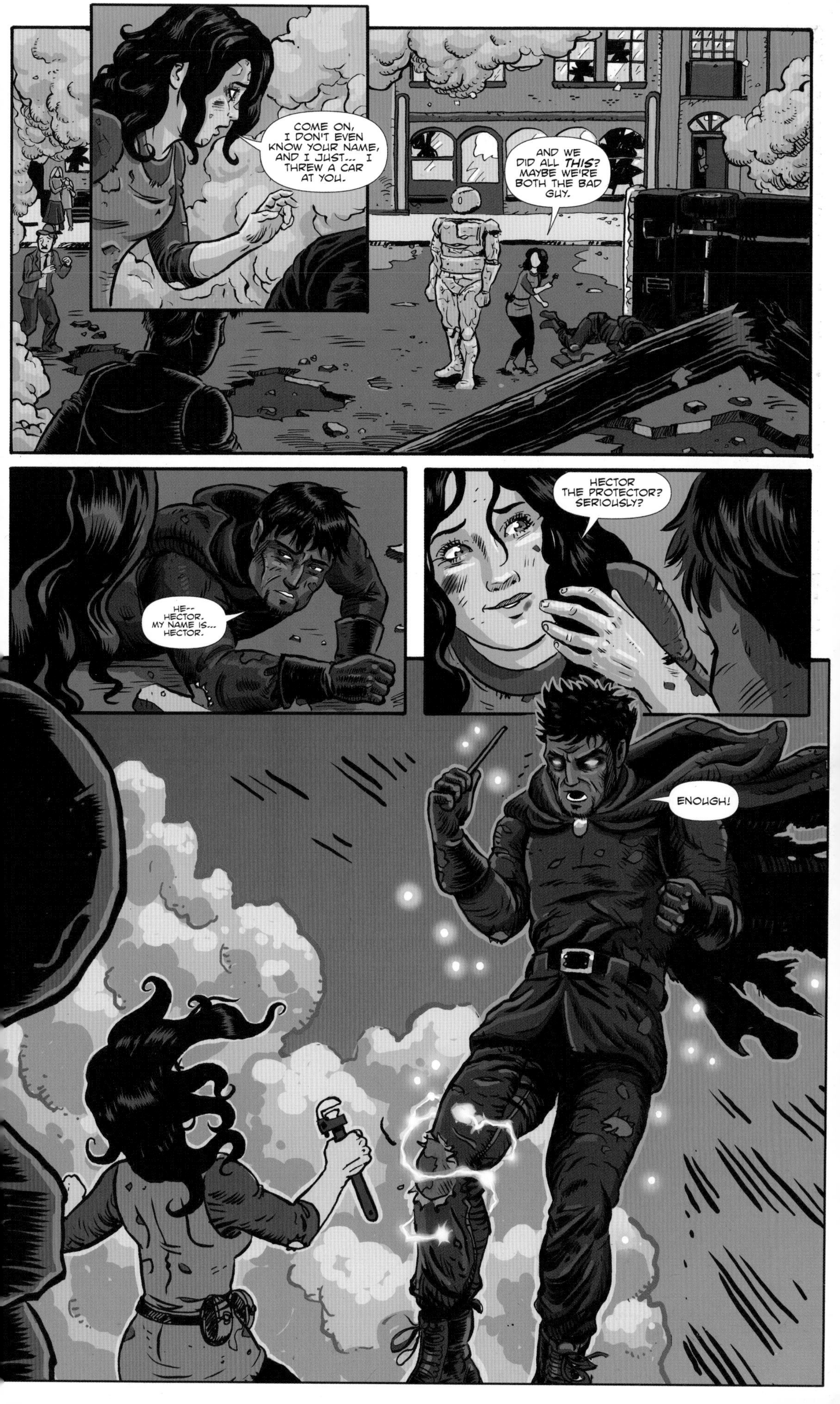
COME ON, I DON'T EVEN KNOW YOUR NAME, AND I JUST... I THREW A CAR AT YOU.
AND WE DID ALL THIS? MAYBE WE'RE BOTH THE BAD GUY.
HE-- HECTOR. MY NAME IS... HECTOR.
HECTOR THE PROTECTOR? SERIOUSLY?
ENOUGH!

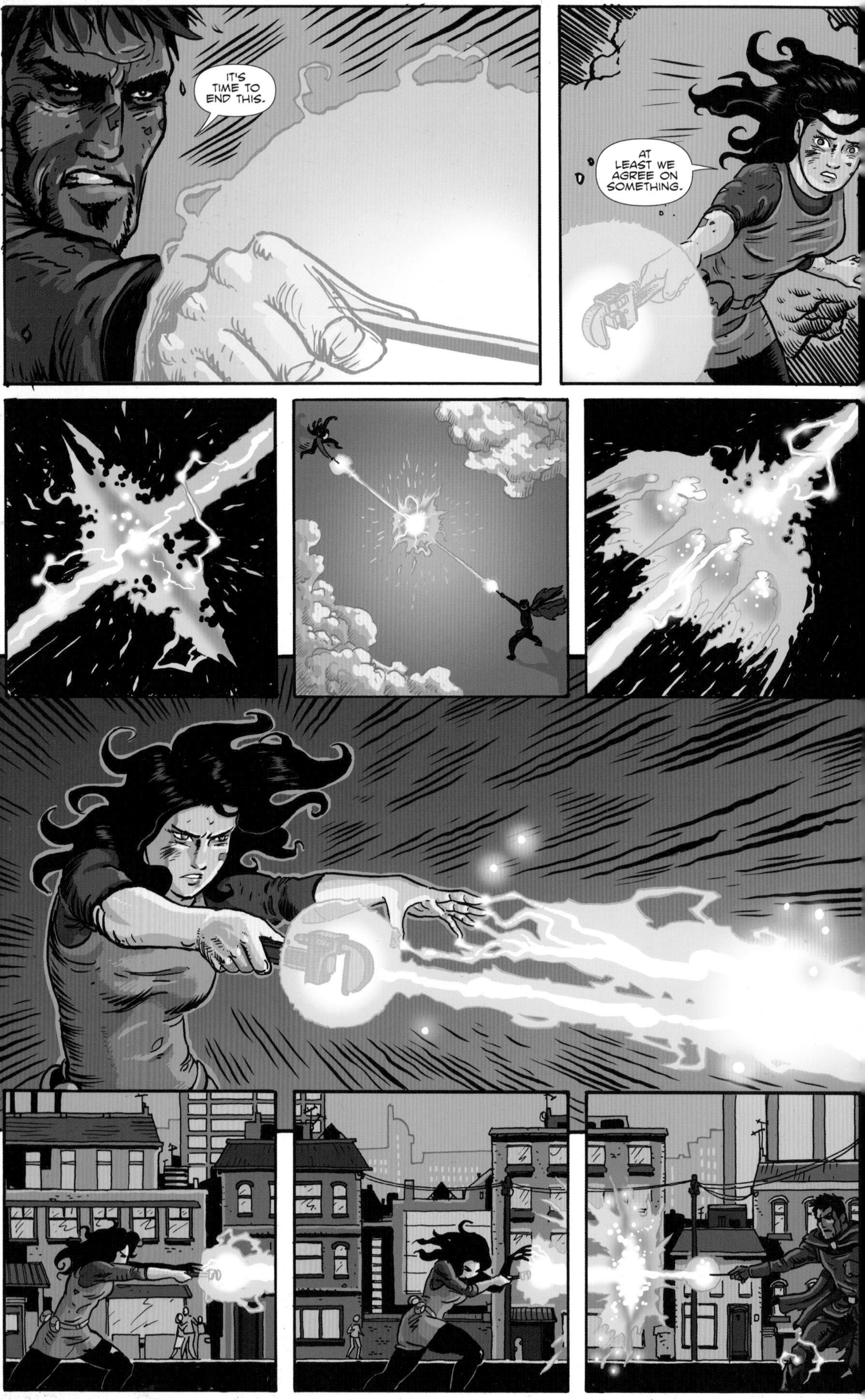
IT'S TIME TO END THIS.
AT LEAST WE AGREE ON SOMETHING.

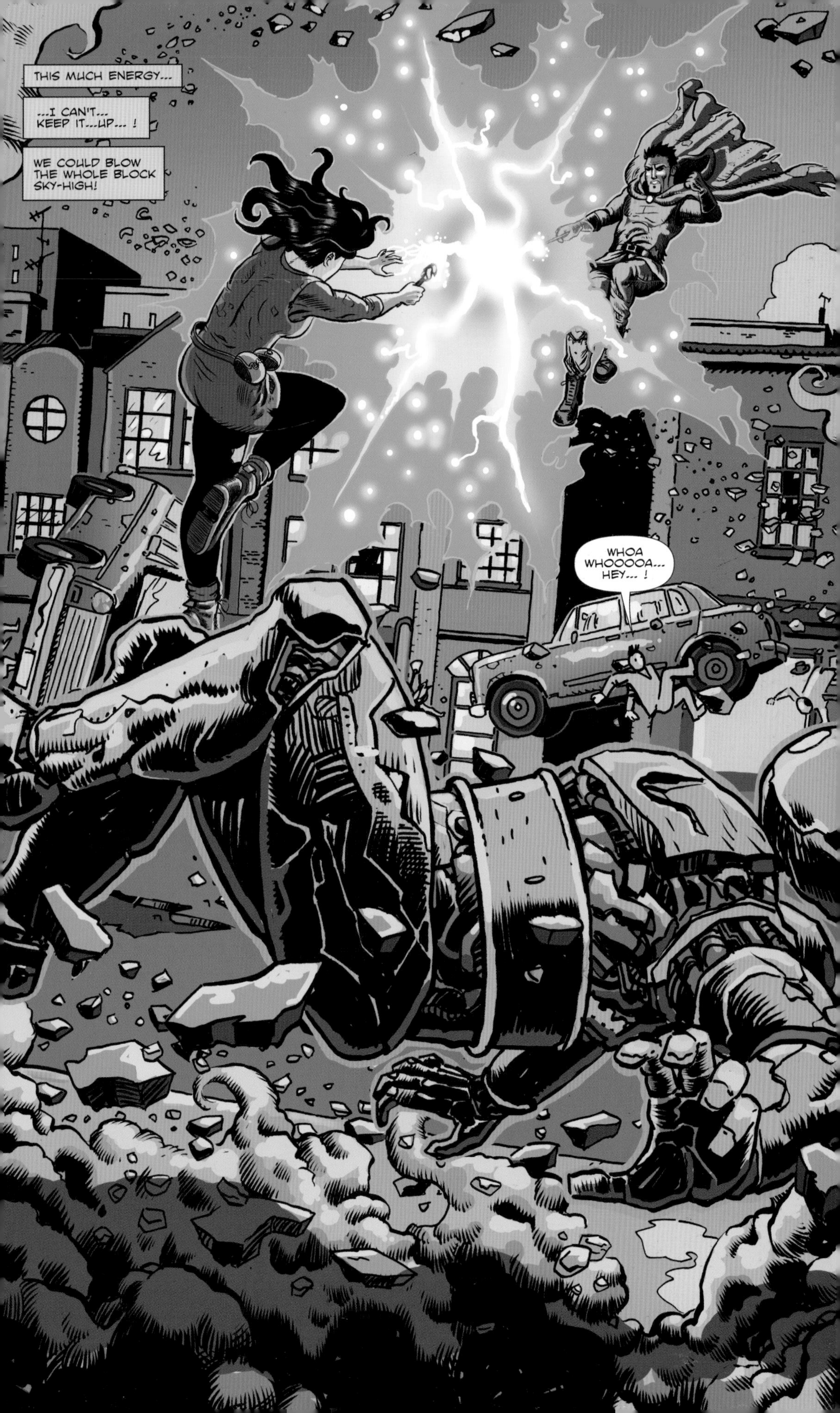
THIS MUCH ENERGY...
...I CAN'T... KEEP IT...UP... !
WE COULD BLOW THE WHOLE BLOCK SKY-HIGH!
WHOA WHOOOOA... HEY... !

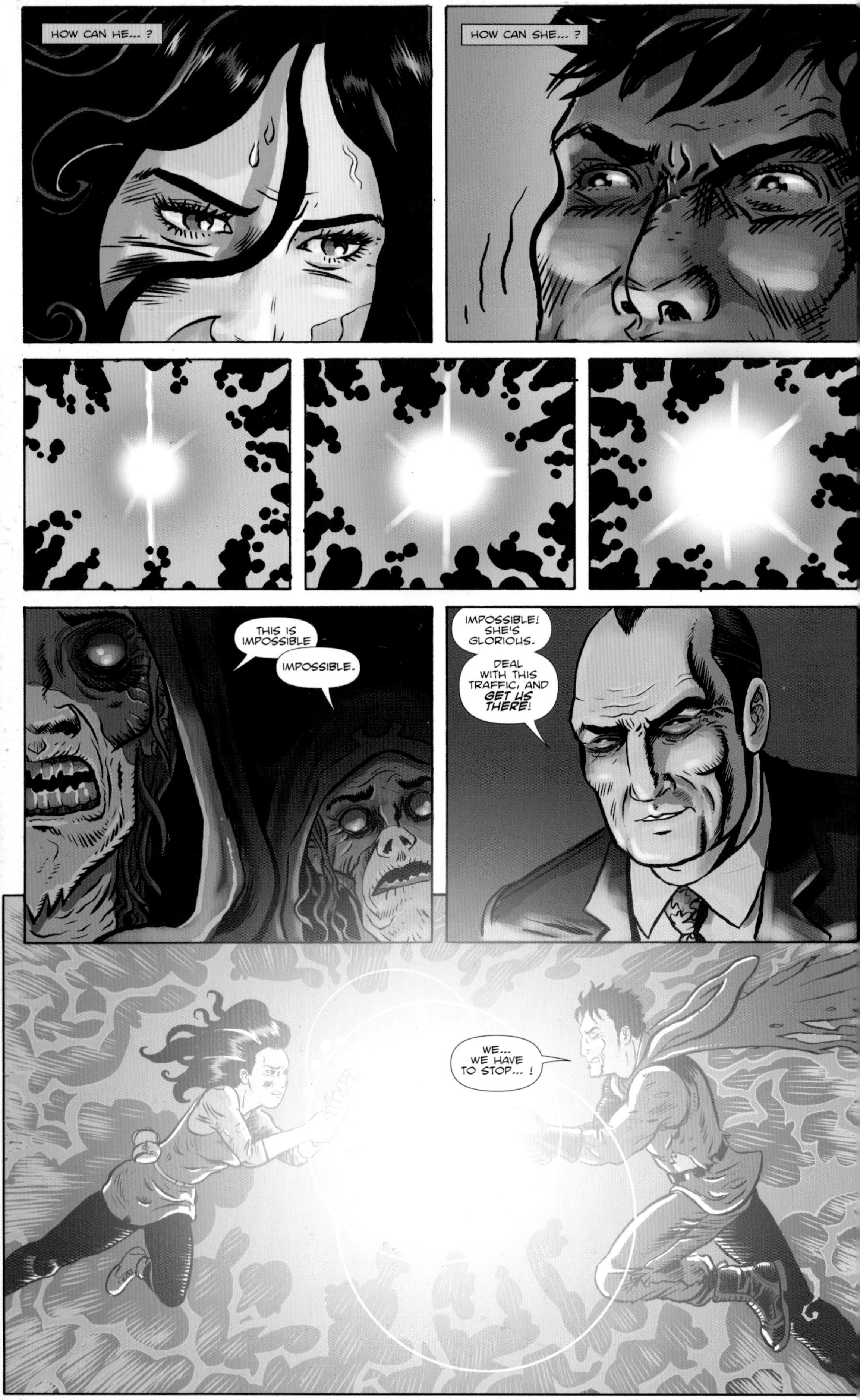
HOW CAN HE... ?
HOW CAN SHE... ?
THIS IS IMPOSSIBLE
IMPOSSIBLE.
IMPOSSIBLE! SHE'S GLORIOUS.
DEAL WITH THIS TRAFFIC, AND GET US THERE!
WE... WE HAVE TO STOP... !

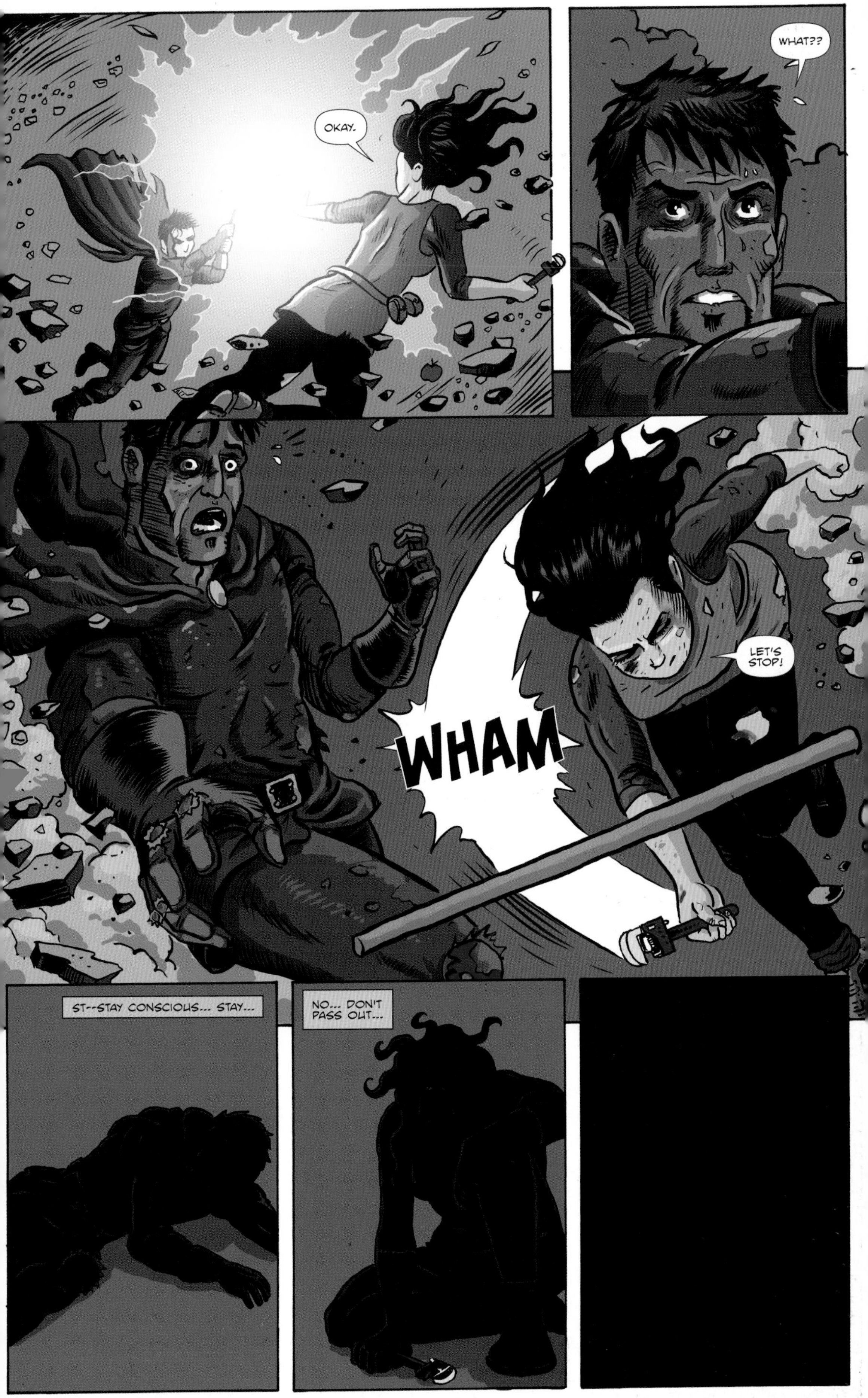
OKAY.
WHAT??
LET'S STOP!
WHAM
ST--STAY CONSCIOUS... STAY...
NO... DON'T PASS OUT...

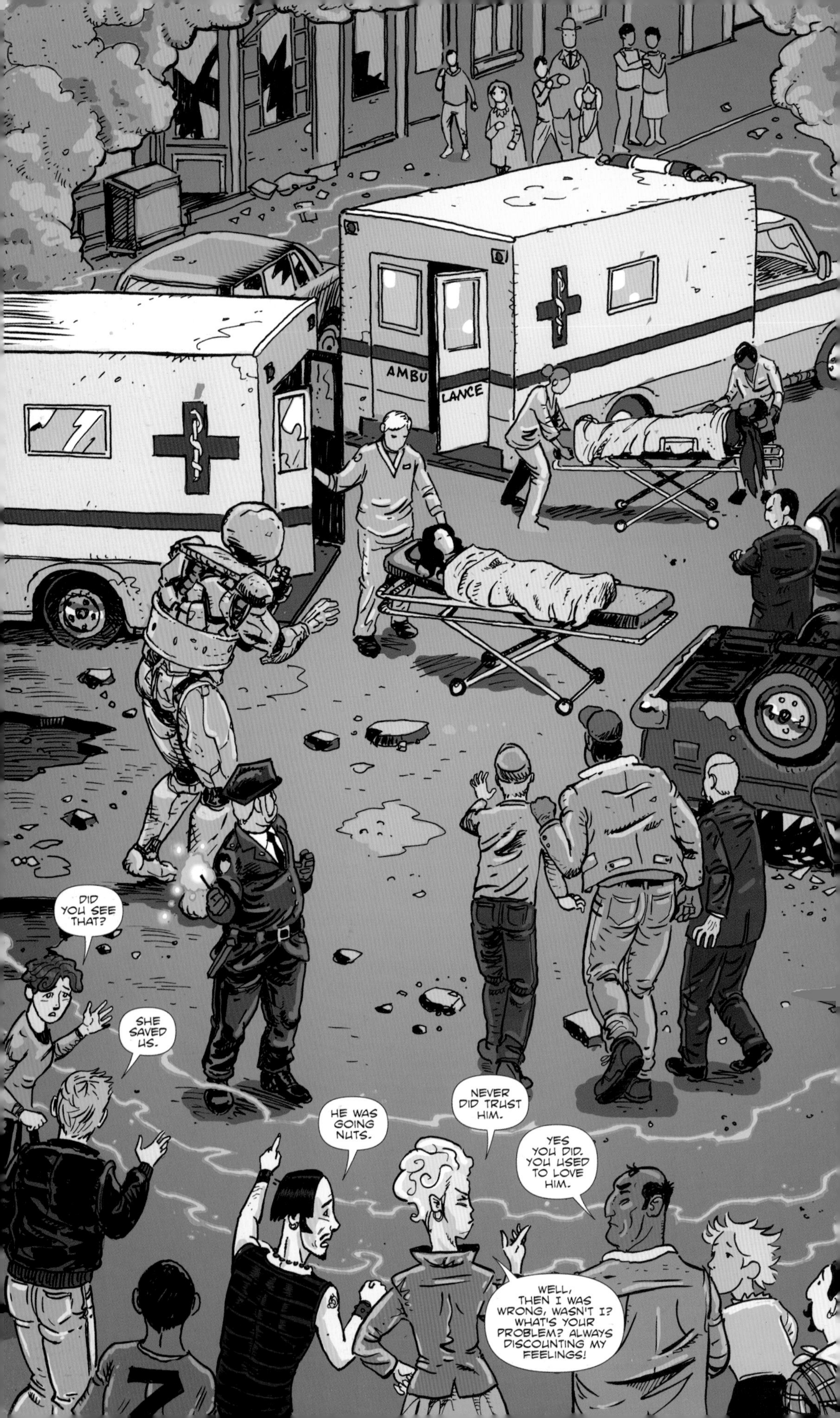
AMBU
LANCE
DID YOU SEE THAT?
SHE SAVED US.
HE WAS GOING NUTS.
NEVER DID TRUST HIM.
YES YOU DID. YOU USED TO LOVE HIM.
WELL, THEN I WAS WRONG, WASN'T I? WHAT'S YOUR PROBLEM? ALWAYS DISCOUNTING MY FEELINGS!

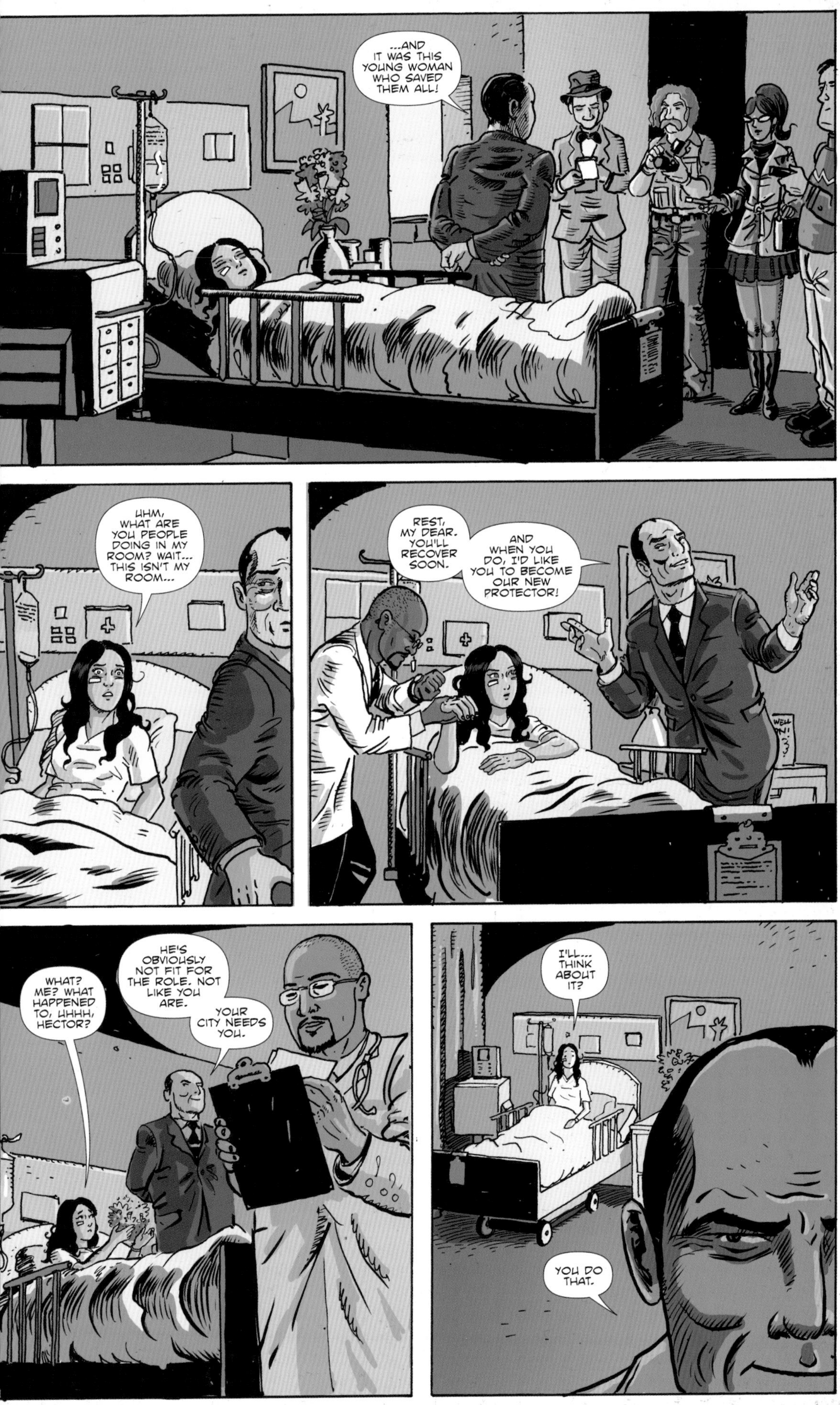
...AND IT WAS THIS YOUNG WOMAN WHO SAVED THEM ALL!
UHM, WHAT ARE YOU PEOPLE DOING IN MY ROOM? WAIT... THIS ISN'T MY ROOM...
REST, MY DEAR. YOU'LL RECOVER SOON.
AND WHEN YOU DO, I'D LIKE YOU TO BECOME OUR NEW PROTECTOR!
WHAT? ME? WHAT HAPPENED TO, UHHH, HECTOR?
HE'S OBVIOUSLY NOT FIT FOR THE ROLE. NOT LIKE YOU ARE.
YOUR CITY NEEDS YOU.
I'LL... THINK ABOUT IT?
YOU DO THAT.

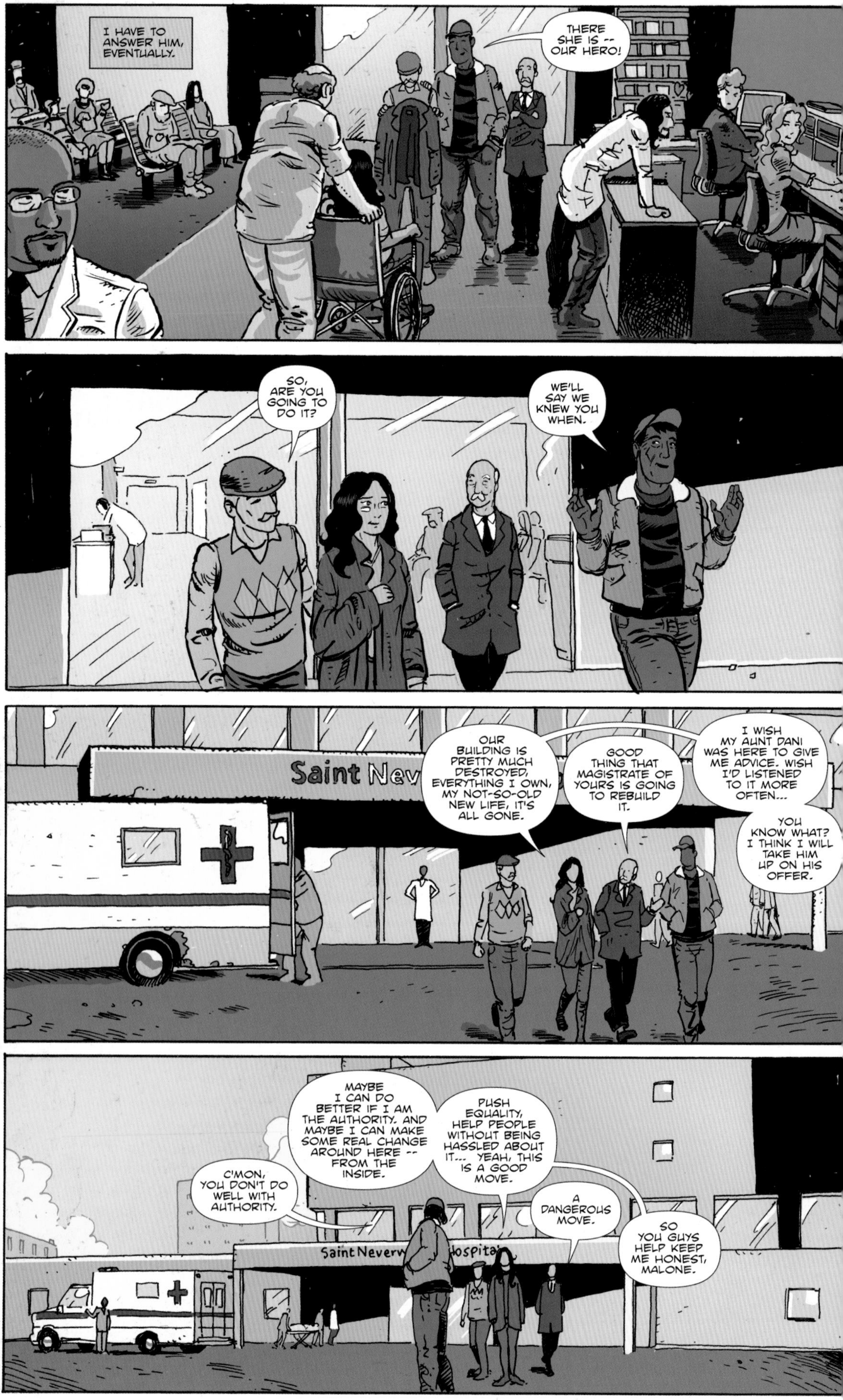
I HAVE TO ANSWER HIM, EVENTUALLY.
THERE SHE IS -- OUR HERO!
SO, ARE YOU GOING TO DO IT?
WE'LL SAY WE KNEW YOU WHEN.
Saint Nev
OUR BUILDING IS PRETTY MUCH DESTROYED, EVERYTHING I OWN, MY NOT-SO-OLD NEW LIFE, IT'S ALL GONE.
GOOD THING THAT MAGISTRATE OF YOURS IS GOING TO REBUILD IT.
I WISH MY AUNT DANI WAS HERE TO GIVE ME ADVICE. WISH I'D LISTENED TO IT MORE OFTEN...
YOU KNOW WHAT? I THINK I WILL TAKE HIM UP ON HIS OFFER.
C'MON, YOU DON'T DO WELL WITH AUTHORITY.
MAYBE I CAN DO BETTER IF I AM THE AUTHORITY. AND MAYBE I CAN MAKE SOME REAL CHANGE AROUND HERE -- FROM THE INSIDE.
PUSH EQUALITY, HELP PEOPLE WITHOUT BEING HASSLED ABOUT IT... YEAH, THIS IS A GOOD MOVE.
A DANGEROUS MOVE.
SO YOU GUYS HELP KEEP ME HONEST, MALONE.
Saint Neverw ospital

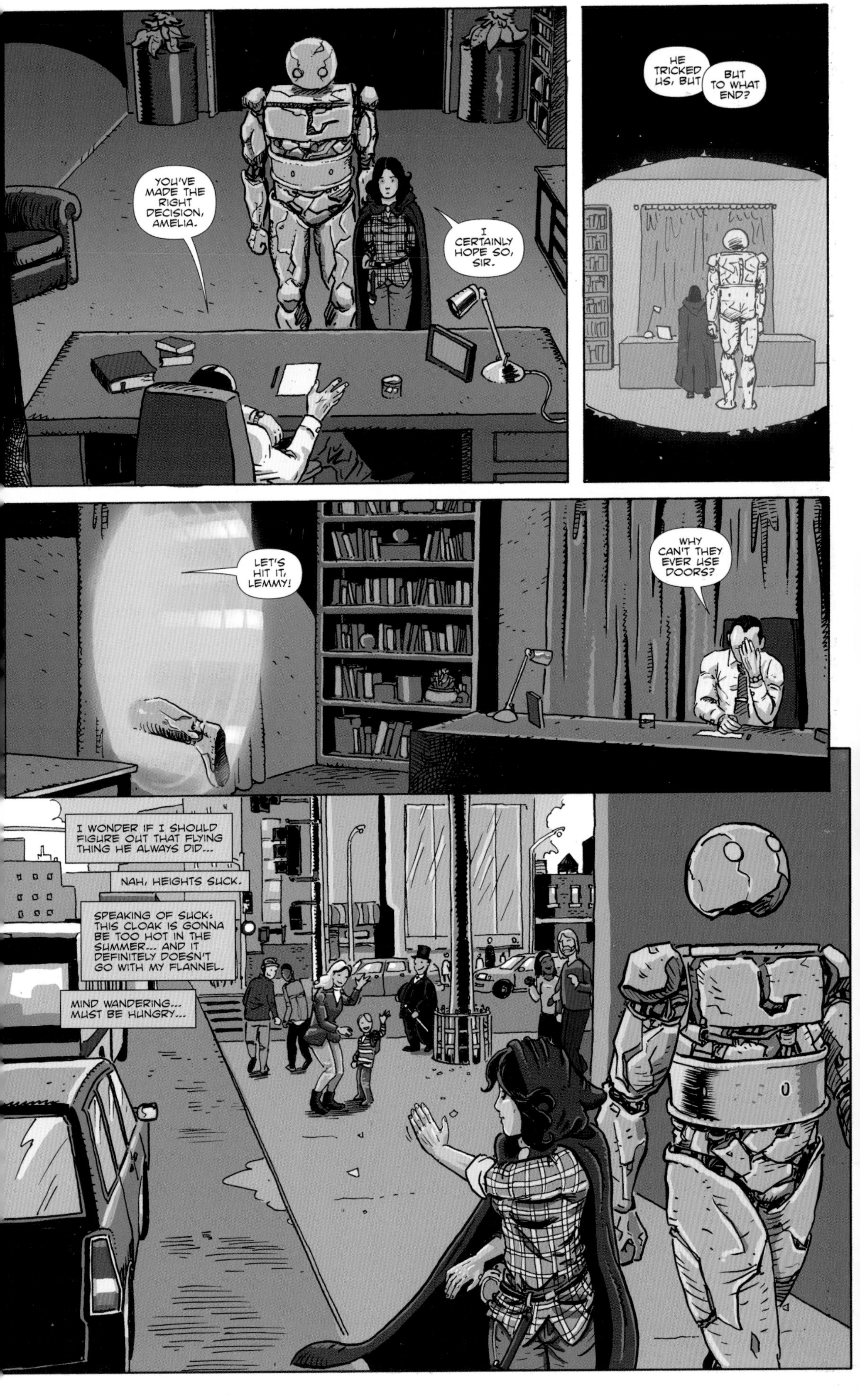
YOU'VE MADE THE RIGHT DECISION, AMELIA.
I CERTAINLY HOPE SO, SIR.
HE TRICKED US, BUT
BUT TO WHAT END?
LET'S HIT IT, LEMMY!
WHY CAN'T THEY EVER USE DOORS?
I WONDER IF I SHOULD FIGURE OUT THAT FLYING THING HE ALWAYS DID...
NAH, HEIGHTS SUCK.
SPEAKING OF SUCK: THIS CLOAK IS GONNA BE TOO HOT IN THE SUMMER... AND IT DEFINITELY DOESN'T GO WITH MY FLANNEL.
MIND WANDERING... MUST BE HUNGRY...

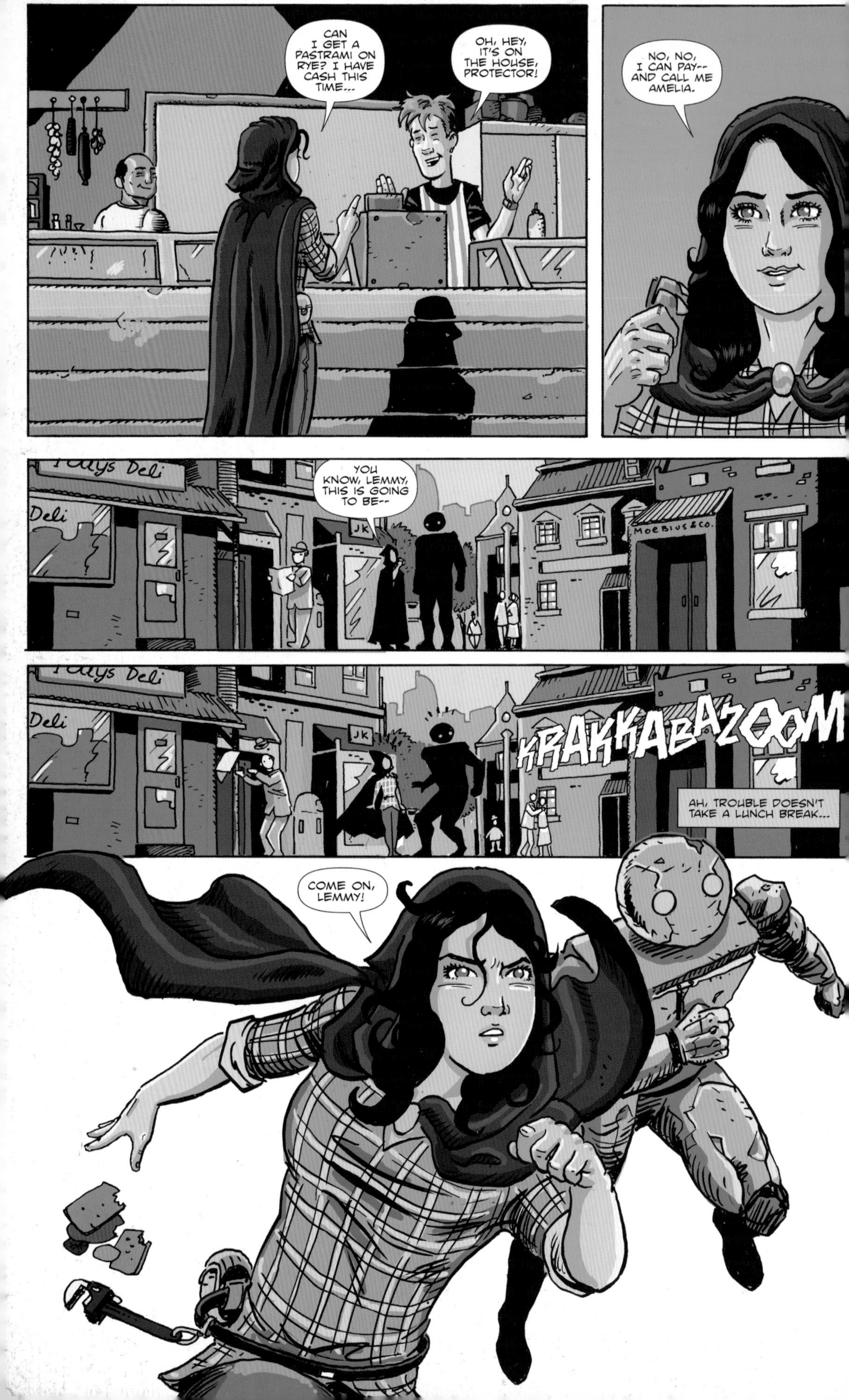
CAN I GET A PASTRAMI ON RYE? I HAVE CASH THIS TIME...
OH, HEY, IT'S ON THE HOUSE, PROTECTOR!
NO, NO, I CAN PAY-- AND CALL ME AMELIA.
YOU KNOW, LEMMY, THIS IS GOING TO BE--
KRAKKABAZOOM
AH, TROUBLE DOESN'T TAKE A LUNCH BREAK...
COME ON, LEMMY!

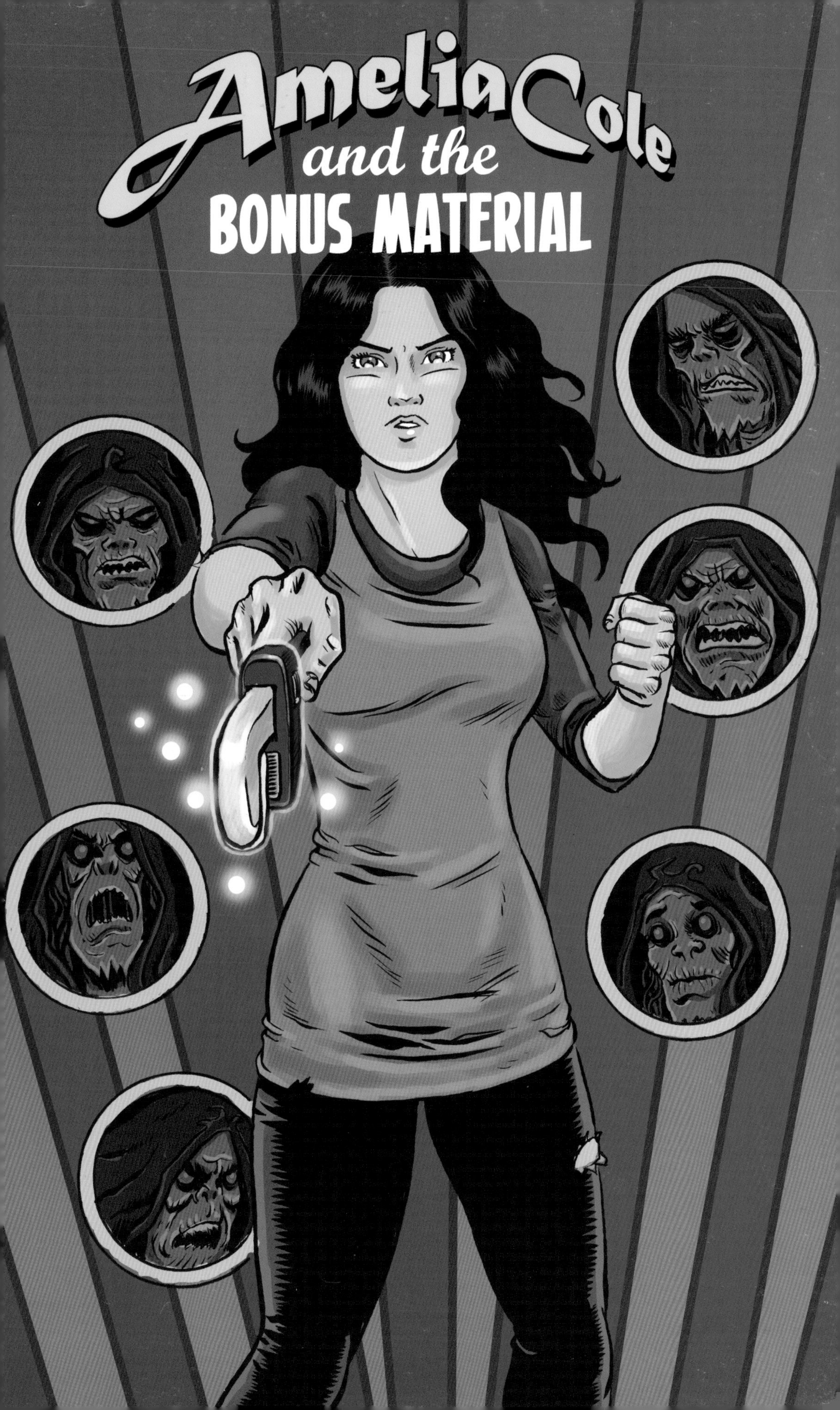
Amelia Cole
and the
BONUS MATERIAL

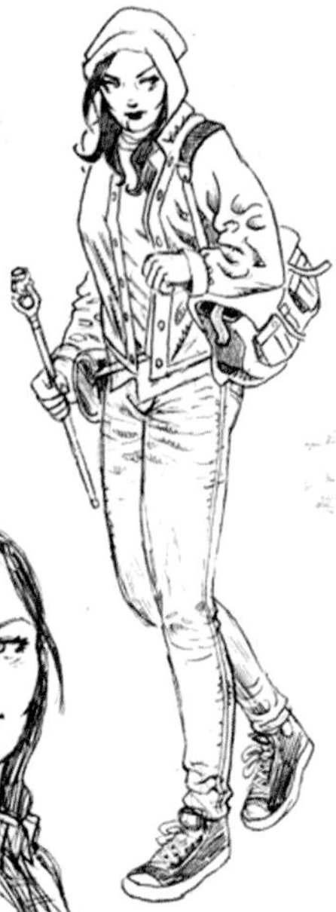

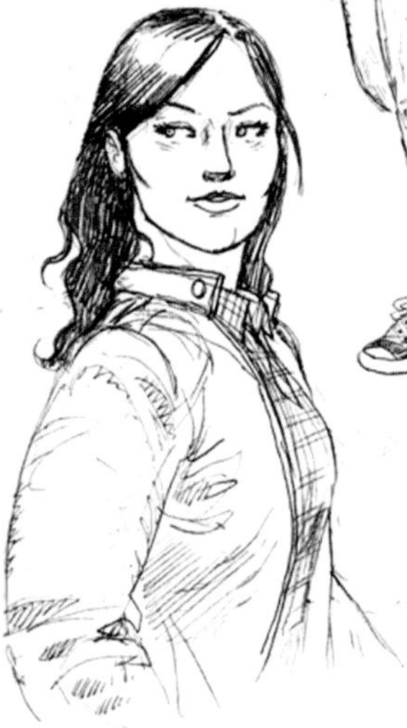

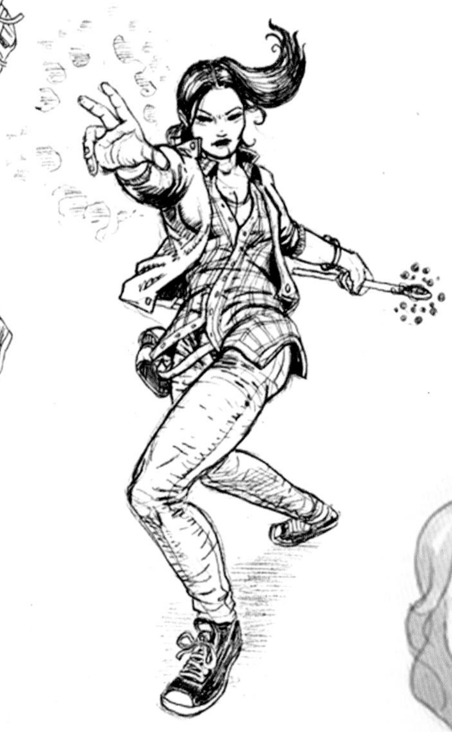

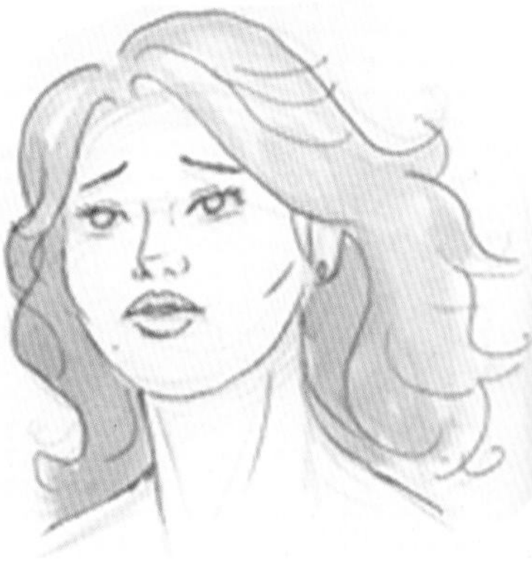

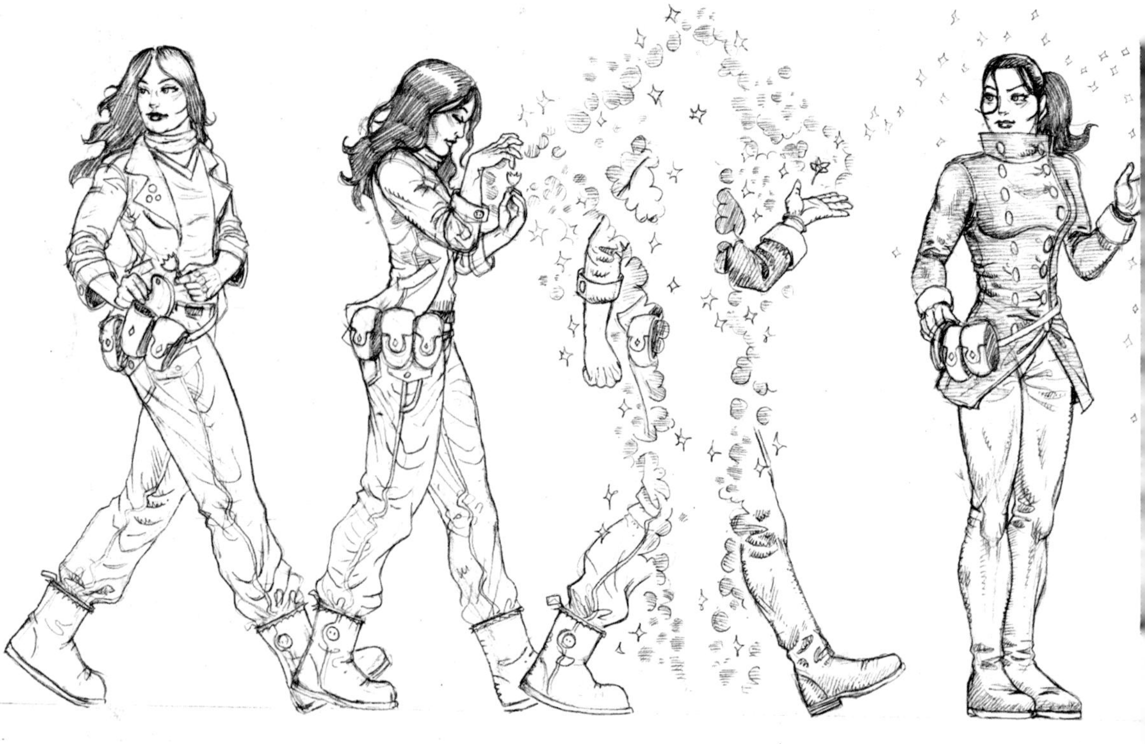